Xavier-Marie Bonnot has a PhD in History and Sociology, and two Masters degrees in History and French Literature. *The First Fingerprint* is the first of a quartet of de Palma novels and has won two literary awards in France.

Xavier-Marie Bonnot

THE FIRST FINGERPRINT

Translated from the French by
Ian Monk

MACLEHOSE PRESS
QUERCUS · LONDON

First published in 2008 by MacLehose Press
This paperback edition first published in Great Britain in 2009 by

MacLehose Press
an imprint of Quercus
21 Bloomsbury Square
London
WC1A 2NS

The First Fingerprint by Xavier-Marie Bonnot © Editions L'Ecailler du sud,
published with original French title: *La Premiere Empreinte*.
The First Fingerprint is published by arrangement with L'Ecailler du sud,
care of Agence litteraire Pierre Astier & Associes

A CIP catalogue reference for this book is available
from the British Library

ISBN 978 1 84724 593 9

10 9 8 7 6 5 4 3 2 1

Printed and bound in Great Britain by
Clays Ltd, St Ives plc

AUTHOR'S NOTE

The characters and situations
in this novel are part of my imagination,
and are not based on reality.

Some sections will probably bring a smile
to the lips of specialists in prehistory or members of
the Marseille murder squad. I have intentionally altered places,
transformed research laboratories, shifted around hospitals, upturned
hierarchies and metamorphosed the murder squad's offices. I have
also taken liberties with a number of official procedures.

Without asking a single word of permission . . .

TRANSLATOR'S NOTE

In the original French, a large amount of Marseille slang is used.
No attempt has been made to imitate its
probably inimitable presence.

To Patrick and Maurice…
Two eternal friends.

1.

For some time, there had been only a diffuse glow in the sky, a faint light whose source was presumably somewhere behind the jagged row of black rocks, high up there, far above the tiny form now hurrying along, guided by the narrow beam of a torch pointing at the ground.

The will-o'-the-wisp was dancing, a yellow and white elf skimming over the sloping surface in a jerky motion. A lonely and malicious light providing just enough visibility so as not to trip over any of the hundred and one stumbling blocks along its winding way. Just enough not to be seen.

But who could possibly have been watching a sleepwalker out in such a place?

No-one could have known she was there. No-one.

Now, the moon had risen over the huge cliff-face which plunged straight down into the sea, and a milky light slipped its way into the sea creek of Sugiton, making its enormous blocks of white limestone look like mighty diamonds standing out against the dark ink of the Mediterranean. Only the outlines of a few scrubby pine trees added life to this mineral chaos.

It was brighter, the walker turned off her torch, her shadow now could be clearly seen to her right: a strange, long, complex shape of sharp angles, a walking petroglyph which had nothing human about it, inching along the contours of the cliff and losing itself sometimes in a hole before surging back at once on to the pointed spine of a rock. The monstrous apparition of a mythical being risen from the depths of creation, an evil god, forgotten by mankind, come to commit some black deed against humanity in this half-night.

This moving shadow belonged to Christine Autran, leaping lightly from rock to rock, following a precise path, without making a single slip. If an imaginary onlooker had been there to observe the scene, he would have recognised that she knew this place like the back of her hand.

But no-one knew that Christine Autran was there. No-one.

The east wind had just got up and waves were beginning to slap hard against the jagged rocks. At each blow, the sea compressed the air trapped in the gaps of the coastline with its slow motion, before tumbling backwards into a furious swirl. The surges of water were rhythmic, the creek was being filled with a dull rumble like the gigantic resonance of a titan's drum.

The tide was coming in, foul weather was brewing out at sea; before long it would bite even further into the coastline.

Christine Autran stopped for a moment and breathed in the mood of the sea spray. She looked up at the moon, then turned towards the sea: that cold eye was making beautiful silvery glitters on the surface of the waves. She sat on a flat stone and took off her rucksack. The sea breeze bit into her sweat-soaked clothes and an icy chill gripped the small of her back. She got out a fleece pullover, slipped it on and then from one of the rucksack pockets took a cereal bar which she chewed while thinking over the events of the day. Far off, a bird was whistling.

No-one could know she was there. No-one.

She looked at her watch: 8.00 p.m. It was now exactly one hour since she had left the terminus of the number 21 bus in front of the university at Luminy. First, she had gone one kilometre along the broad pathway which leads towards Sugiton pass, while sticking to the signposting of the hiking path GR 98. Night was falling, a few finches were giving their final bursts of song. Christine had then passed through a scrub of Aleppo pines and stunted holm oaks before reaching the Sugiton pass. She had sat there for a moment to make the most of the last moments of daylight.

It had been warm for late November, so warm that a fine blue mist had risen from the sea to mingle with the last glimmers of the day. Slowly, the emerald and sapphire of the water had melted into a still-hot pewter brown amid the whiteness of the limestone, while the matt green of the bushes of mastic, sarsaparilla and *sabline de Provence* had become black blotches in the scars of the contours.

In the background, to the left of Sugiton creek, the familiar outline of Le Torpilleur had vanished into the grubby shadows, its limestone prow stuck into the shallows some thirty metres from the coast; this mineral vessel, as big as a frigate, had beached itself in the middle of the creek like a navy ship which, in the hollows of the cliffs, had lost its battle against an invisible submarine.

Christine had decided to pass to the right of the signpost indicating the hiking track and instead took the winding path that led straight into the valley of Sugiton. She let herself be drawn down by the slope, taking care not to trip over the roots of the pines which stuck up from the dusty ground like huge snakes. Twenty minutes later, she had reached a panoramic viewpoint which she knew well. It was there that the night had enveloped her.

No-one could have known she was there. No-one.

She had left her comfortable flat, at 125 boulevard Chave, at about eight that morning. Tuesday was the day she taught at the Aix-en-Provence faculty of Literature and Human Sciences: three hours in the morning from 9.00 to 12.00 with bachelor degree students, then one and a half hours starting at 2.00 p.m. with history research students. She preferred the morning lessons – *une unité de valeur* in the university jargon – which allowed her to dwell on her favourite subject, the Magdalenian era in Provence. She had devoted her entire academic career to its study, starting with a bulky thesis on the sharpened flints found in Upper Palaeolithic sites in south-east France and Liguria.

Once lessons were over, she had had to talk for some time with Sylvie Maurel, a researcher from the Centre National de la Recherche Scientifique who wanted some details about the site she was studying. Christine did not like Sylvie because of her self-assurance, her daredevil poise, her bourgeois manner and the way she hovered around Professor Palestro, Head of the Department of Prehistory. Christine had to admit to her herself that she was jealous, and that this jealousy was a point of weakness, which was probably what she disliked most of all. She hated hearing the Professor talking to her rival in a familiar way and using her first name. She had the impression that the only man she had ever respected was doing it on purpose, to mortify her.

3

Sylvie was the reflection of what she might have been, had she not sunk her life into the depths of academic literature.

Sylvie Maurel was radiant, with refined gestures, a body that was both firm and supple, a head of heavy, black hair, amber skin, ebony eyes that darted about, and fine features with slight traces of make-up as the one and only sign of any concession to age awareness. She was always discreetly dressed, generally in jeans and plain tops as though to disguise her bourgeois origins. There was only one nod towards the wealth of her class: a large diamond on her left hand.

Christine had always had a problem meeting Sylvie's classiness eye to eye. She shuddered when her hand brushed against her enemy's hand, or when she was taken in by her delicate voice and felt a luxurious sweetness dissolve into her stomach, like the essence of a rare opiate; her scalp tingled, she crossed her legs quickly, in a game of attraction and repulsion around this sensual beauty that dominated her.

So Christine Autran had been late and had had to speed along the northern motorway so as to reach Marseille before the evening rush hour.

In the stairwell of her building, she made as little noise as possible, so as not to let the old lady on the first floor know that her second-floor tenant had come home at the usual time. This old woman owned the building and was forever on the lookout, like an eel in its lair, watching the comings and goings of her tenants through her spyhole. On her way out Christine took the precaution of going downstairs in her stockinged feet. She had then leaped on to the first tram and travelled as far as Vieux-Port métro station. One anonymous person among all the other anonymous people on the move at the close of the afternoon.

In the town centre, beside the Bourse shopping mall, she took the number 21 bus and nobody had so much as glanced at her. Not even the driver, a fat, bald lump with an enormous moustache who, at each stop, started clicking his gold signet ring against the black plastic steering wheel in time to a Johnny Hallyday song, which played on a loop throughout the entire journey. At the back of the bus, some architecture students on their way back to their halls of residence in Luminy were chatting noisily about their final degree projects without paying any attention to this eccentric woman in a dusty, sweat-stained rain-hat.

And taking an excursion to the creeks at the end of November at 5.00 in the afternoon was indeed eccentric.

She had gone back thus far over her day, when the east wind got up. From where she stood, she could just make out the presence of the islands of Riou, Plane and Jarre; to her right, but out of sight, lay Maire island and, in front of Marseille, Frioul archipelago; to her left were the wildlife sanctuaries of Port Crau and Porquerolles. She pictured this fantastic landscape during the Magdalenian era, 20,000 B.C.E., when the sea level was twenty metres lower and a vast valley ran down to these islands.

She often told her students that the coastline at the time looked rather like Norway's does now. A fossil beach had been discovered there, at a depth of forty metres, with shellfish otherwise found only in northern Scandinavia. The universe of the Provençal Cro-Magnons was a steppe covered with vegetation and colonised by angel's hair, grasses and juniper bushes. A few Austrian pines, Scots pines and alders scraped an existence in the shelter of the limestone rock-faces, beside streams and little lakes where men and beasts came to drink. The sea temperature barely exceeded six or seven degrees. Pack ice probably covered a large part of the *mare nostrum*.

For thousands of years, the first men had lived there, hunting, fishing and gathering as described in children's books. It was a primitive life spent tracking bison, aurochs, Irish elk and Mediterranean monk seals. Everything they needed was there, at arm's reach: the sea, big and small game, as well as dozens of caves for shelter when night fell.

Christine liked to imagine Cro-Magnons in the evening, dressed in their clumsily stitched furs, with their long, filthy hair, going back to the dark caves which the sea had now submerged. Sheltered by the depths of the earth, around a fire which had been cunningly kept burning for days on end, they would grant themselves a moment's rest, away from the women who had gathered life's essentials during the day: fruit, roots and fungi. The men would think about the next day's hunt, one of them sharpening flints in staccato blows, turning the hard stone into pedunculate tips, scrapers, saw-edges and rudimentary knives – the equipment of the great hunters and fishers of the Palaeolithic era.

Like Professor Autran that evening, the first men must have looked up at the self-same monochromatic, pale light coming down from the sky. They must have questioned the moon, invented answers to the grand mysteries of existence and peered into the future. Beliefs were born in the world of spirits, which had then been painted, sculpted or engraved in the gloomy living spaces of their prehistoric caves. An art of shadows and rock was born: the first men had wanted it to be different from their crude daily existences and had conceived the fantastic bestiary of their wall paintings.

For a long time it had been known that Provençal prehistory had sunk beneath the waters. This hypothesis had been verified by a large number of finds, such as the underwater caves of Le Figuier and La Triperie near Morgiou creek. Then, in 1991, a diver from Marseille discovered a decorated cave, like a Provençal Lascaux sleeping beneath a roof of stone. Its entry lay at a depth of thirty-seven metres, at the foot of the colossal slopes of Sugiton creek. It had a narrow entrance that led to a tunnel measuring a hundred and fifty metres, at the end of which lay the now famous frescoes of silence: negative and positive hands, horses, bison, penguins ... The cave had been named after its discoverer, Charles Le Guen, and its entrance had been sealed by a heavy iron gate and blocks of stone. Beside the opening, there was a notice which looked strange at such a depth:

MINISTRY OF CULTURE. KEEP OUT.

A whistling noise woke Christine Autran from her meditations. She stood up, ran her fingers through her hair and looked at her watch: 9.00 p.m. She set off once more, going from rock to rock, silently reproaching herself for giving in to such reflections. It was something she rarely did, and never in these circumstances. She had no time to lose.

She reached the last rock, and from there she could just make out the tiny beach of smooth pebbles she was looking for. She leaped from her perch and at once found herself surrounded by the massive limestone rocks she had just crossed, with the threatening sea to her right and in front of her the huge cliff-face that rose up towards the infinity of the sky. Only a skilled climber could have gone any further than the mousetrap in which Professor Autran now stood.

She could scarcely see. The moonlight was feeble in this little creek. She advanced a few more paces, as far as the cliff, her feet sinking slightly into the damp stones. Blindly, she felt around for a dry place on which to put her bag.

The noise of the sea was ever more present, like the breathing of a savage beast on the move only a few metres from her. Further out, Christine could see the lights of a cargo ship which must have left Marseille at nightfall and was now going full steam ahead for Corsica or North Africa.

Without wasting any more time, she removed her torch and a notebook from the right-hand pocket of her bag. She laid them beside her, then plunged her hand into the main section of the rucksack to take out a small, folding spade. She picked up the torch and aimed its beam at the foot of the cliff, where the limestone met the pebble beach. She examined the rock inch by inch, then stopped when she located a barely perceptible bulge. The whistling noise could be heard once more. Christine shivered. It came from somewhere close by. Just a few metres away. Her whole body trembled. She played her torch across the rocks.

Nothing.

She tried to reassure herself by telling herself that her imagination must be working even faster than her concentrated senses. It was an illusion.

Several times, she swallowed back the saliva which was sticking in her throat, then she let the adrenaline dissolve into the most distant extremities of her body and started to dig. Methodically.

Her spade made a sharp, rhythmic sound. She scarcely heard the heavy footsteps on the gravel just behind her.

2.

"Già nella notte densa
s'estingue ogni clamor . . . "

Commandant Michel de Palma was humming out of sheer boredom: Verdi's "Otello" – *mezza voce* – the Moor's shades mingled with the discreet symphony of police headquarters.

"Gia il mio cor fremebondo
s'ammansa in quest'amplesso e si rinsensa."

De Palma was sitting at his desk, on the second floor, to the left out of the lift, last door on the right, beyond the photocopier and the coffee machine. The murder squad.

"Tuoni la Guerra e s'inabissi il mondo
se dopo l'ira immensa
vien quest'immenso amor!"

Slumped in his chair, his muscular legs stretched full length beneath his desk, he was killing his last hour on station duty by flicking again and again through his bumper school exercise book, in which he noted down everything, from the smallest to the most significant details of the investigations he was conducting.

One exercise book a year. An old-school policeman's habit which he had inherited from a grumpy old commissaire when he had started out on the force.

"Mio superbo guerrier! Quanti tormenti,
quanti mesti sospiri et quanta speme
ci condusse ai soavi abbracciamenti!
Oh! Come è dolce il mormorare insieme: te ne rammenti?"

Before the end of November, the book had been filled by a case which had been obsessing him for months. A murder: Samir, aged seven, raped, then his throat slit with an industrial cutter. In cold blood. And no-one had heard a thing, of course. He had been found at the end of August, in the rubbish chute of a ten-storey block of flats in the La Castellane housing estate, far off in the northern suburbs of Marseille.

De Palma had stood for a long time in silence in front of that child's body, wound in a bin-liner, its eyes half-closed, its throat agape. He had taken little Samir's cold hand, leaned over his puffy face, holding his breath to stop himself from vomiting, and had spoken to him tenderly, the way you speak to a child who cannot go to sleep in the dark: "I'll get whoever did it. Trust me, kid. I always get them. I'm the best. I'll make him eat his fucking mother."

Duriez, director of the regional police department, had told Commissaire Paulin, the head of the murder squad, to put de Palma on to the case because he was an ace. Since which time the affair had grown in importance: young Arabs were crying out for justice, the Maire wanted the police to be irreproachable, and Duriez had put him under immense pressure by declaring to the press, with his hand on his heart: "I have no doubt that this case will be solved in the very near future."

De Palma ran through the details of the Samir case for the umpteenth time. Occasionally he frowned as he examined a telephone number jotted in the margin, or a name followed by a question mark. His intense dark stare, as sharp as a facetted sapphire, darted out from his angular face, then faded again in an instant before returning to its journey through the tiny handwriting which went off in all directions, like rapacious weeds, across this great hunter's pages of memories.

> *"Quando narravi l'esule tua vita*
> *e i fieri eventi e i lunghi tuoi dolor,*
> *ed io t'udia coll'anima rapita*
> *in quei spaventi e coll'estasi nel cor."*

De Palma would soon celebrate twenty-five years on the force. Five had been spent at 36 quai des Orfèvres, the holy of holies of the national police; the next twenty at the regional police department in Marseille. That made twenty-five exercise books. His retirement day was approaching slowly but surely, and with it the great emptiness of his future life.

He would not be celebrating that.

He looked up from his exercise book and peered around. The desk opposite was immaculately spick and span. Its occupant for the past six months was Lieutenant Maxime Vidal, a tall, dark lad who was as dry and thin as a capital I, and who smiled innocently in all circumstances. He had left the office at about 6.00 p.m. just like any other young officer who still had some kind of life outside of his job.

De Palma's gaze strayed over the white walls, lingered for a moment on the empty chair in front of him, then went back up to the grey metal ring hanging from the wall. He tried to remember various faces, but none came to him.

> *"Venga la morte! E mi colga nell'estasi*
> *di quest'amplesso*
> *il momento supremo!"*

The décor was no longer quite what it had been since the false ceiling collapsed on to the heads of the officers in the Murder and Organised Crime Squads. It smelled of wet paint, enamel, fresh plaster and wallpaper paste. A heavy, heady, glycerophtalic smell still hung in the air.

De Palma sat up on his chair, stretching his arms to waken the network of muscles that covered his solid bones, then he cracked his resin-brown fingers. The night before, he had had bad dreams. A quarter of a century in the force had no doubt driven him somewhat crazy, maybe semi-paranoid, and definitely insomniac. But he had gone to bed early, with the firm intention of snoring like a sawn log so as to recover from all those long nights spent looking at night-birds dressed up to the nines in the flashy bars on Carré Thairs.

Around 2.00 in the morning, fatal crime scenes burst into his mind without any warning. Always the same images of lacerated bodies, faces with eyes rolled upwards, guts torn open, corpses blue under the striplights in the morgue. Women and men of all sizes, all colours, going in and out of the morgue's drawers, mechanically, like the staging of some modern play.

And then children. Many too many children. Like night-watchmen, the lifeless faces of the little dead invaded his sleep and kicked him awake pitilessly, asking again and again for impossible justice. The image of his brother, a close-up of his fine, soft eyes, had finally replaced all the others.

He had spent a couple of hours on the balcony, staring into the night, listening to the murmurs of his sleepy neighbourhood. His wife, Marie, had hated this quartier more than anything. It was the ugliest part of the eastern sprawl of Marseille, and one of the poorest too, despite its lovely name which filled your mouth like a zest: La Capelette. He had always lived there.

Marie had left a month ago.

His policeman's salary had allowed him to buy a spanking-new three-bedroom flat on boulevard Mireille Lauze, in a leafy, "classy" cluster of buildings, named Paul Verlaine Residence by its inspired promoters: three cubes of compressed concrete, each of four floors, built over a stretch of what were once gardens of the convent of the Holy Sisters of Saint Joseph of the Apparition. The rest of the park was now occupied by a psychiatric hospital and a nursing college. On summer nights, when the nice and normal slept with their windows open, lugubrious howls tore through the purring of the televisions, providing a strange ground bass of human suffering to this theatre of shadows.

> "Già nella notte densa
> s'estingue ogni clamor,

già il mio cor fremebondo
s'ammansa in quest'amplesso e si rinsensa."

Capitaine Anne Moracchini pushed open the office door and slipped her head of long brown hair through the gap. She flicked back her locks gracefully and gave de Palma a wicked look.

"You doing overtime, Michel? We're going for a drink at Le Zanzi. Want to come?"

"No thanks. I'm going to have a quiet evening at home. Tomorrow, if you want."

"Come on now. You're not going to play at being dark and mysterious again?"

"Oh yes I am," he answered, forcing himself to smile. "I'll take you to dinner tomorrow."

"I can't tomorrow."

"Some other time then?"

"You're not trying it on with me, are you? Watch yourself, Michel, I might end up taking you seriously."

De Palma liked Capitaine Moracchini. First of all, he respected her for what she was: a police officer of rare qualities. She was the only woman on the squad. All the boys had more or less had a go at her, including Duriez, the big boss, and Paulin, the squad's head. Every one of them, except de Palma, who had never betrayed the slightest sign of physical attraction, even though her supple, slim body, as gentle as it was dangerous, provoked waves of desire in him which he sometimes had trouble controlling. As far as he knew, she had not had a serious relationship with anyone since she had divorced a dentist in Vitrolles two years before on the grounds of their political incompatibility.

"Goodbye, Michel. See you tomorrow."

"Goodbye, my lovely," he answered, slipping his exercise book into the top drawer of his desk.

When he was alone again, de Palma repeated to himself the oath that he had sworn to Samir's body. He had now to go back to La Castellane. His plan was in place, he would just have to wait two more hours before putting it into action. Instinctively, he checked the cylinder of his Bodyguard and went out into the city, with no special destination in mind and just one desire: to get this case over and done with as soon as possible – along with that "Otello" air which he could not get out of his head.

> *"Venga la morte! E mi colga nell'estasi*
> *di quest'amplesso*
> *il momento supremo!"*

It was verging on hot for a December night. He drove along the old port, with his window open, the smell of fuel and dry seaweed in his nostrils, then cruised up La Canebière, which was crammed with headlamps coming towards him and Christmas decorations – the same for last twenty-five years – forming two lines of light, one yellow and one white, leading towards the Reformed church. At the far end, he turned right in front of the church and went back up rue Thiers. It was dark and deserted, except for a pair of tatty transvestites who swivelled their hips grotesquely every time a car drove past. They were two black whores who used to work for the Beau Jacques and were now looking out for a pimp. Their previous one had been dug out of a blockhouse in Les Goudes the previous month, with his cute features full of lead. An occupational accident, so to speak. Case closed.

At the top of rue Thiers, he turned into the empty outskirts of La Plaine. Driving steadily in second gear, his arm leaning heavily on the car door, he surveyed the bars that were still open, now spewing out their clientele of students and dole boys. He almost pulled in to attract the attention of the small groups forming around the crouched figures of dealers. No reaction. Snatches of a blues song drifted out from a weary-looking club. The quavering notes rose up among the red lights of the belvedere only to rest in the branches of the nettle trees which the mischievous mistral had decked with plastic bags. As he passed in front of Les Nuits Bleues, he spotted Serge Pugliesi, or "Petit Serge" – the bent policeman's godfather – sounding off, crotch forward, arms outstretched, waving his hands with their five fingers and six rings in the stinking atmosphere of his local bar.

He drove swiftly down to the town centre again, taking boulevard Salvator, then the bus lane along rue de Rome towards place La

Castellane. His instinct told him that Samir's killer was still right there, in the heart of the estate, and maybe in the very same block. Several clues backed up this hypothesis. He had been cruising round the neighbourhood for days, each time in a different car so as not to be spotted in such a vertical microcosm.

Samir had been murdered at 6.00 p.m. At that time of day, no-one could wander around the estate without being noticed by the kids, who acted as lookouts at its entry points. Samir had probably been a lookout too. Not one of the few witness statements he had so far managed to gather made mention of seeing a stranger in La Castellane. This was his only chance: he had to make the witnesses talk.

"At any price," he said aloud.

One way or another, he had to break through the law of silence which governed the small world of drug pushers. He had to rid himself of that feeling of impotence and guilt which rose from his guts.

He accelerated. His life had a meaning once more. A quarter of an hour later, he was on boulevard Barnier. He parked in traverse des Transhumants and then walked over to the huge La Castellane housing estate.

A red light was glowing from the tops of the tower-blocks, refracted by the dampness of the cold air. At the entry to the estate, he spotted the group of kids who kept their eyes on any comings and goings. As de Palma walked by the group, he picked out the youngest of them, then went around the block to return to his car without drawing attention to himself. He started up and drove off into the night.

This kid's name was Karim. He had heard it during the questioning after Samir's murder. Karim lived in the same block as the victim, and had been his best friend. "Like a brother," he had said. De Palma had sensed that the boy was hiding something, that he had been silenced by a terror which was indefinable, invisible, but definitely there. He had seen it from the way he squirmed in his chair during questioning, from the way he filled up all the silences which the police imposed on him, and from his disturbed gaze when he had been shown photographs so as to identify the deceased.

Ten minutes later, de Palma had reached the Commissariat of the third arrondissement: a concrete fortress, stuck there like a bad joke at the gloomy entrance of the Parc Bellevue housing estate. Everyone called it "Félix-Pyat". Half of the population was Comorian and the other half Slavic. It was dangerous. With a sea view for those on the top floors.

Every time de Palma went there, he reminded himself that the Third World was not necessarily several hours' flight away from Marignane airport. Félix-Pyat, with its smell of ozone, its façades eaten away by poverty, its walls towering over car parks full of decaying motors and gutted washing machines, exactly conveyed all of the failings of society. It was a pitiless zone amongst the blind zones of a great city.

Outside the Commissariat, a plain-clothes team was waiting for it to be 9.00 p.m., their arses parked on their Safrane's bonnet. The Brigadier arrived and tossed that night's equipment on to the back seat: truncheons, rifles and rubber bullets, walkie-talkies, Maglites. The men exchanged a few inaudible jokes. Then the Brigadier spotted de Palma.

"So you've come to see how the job's really done."

"Where are you going with that Safrane?" de Palma retorted. "Do you reckon you're going to catch any hoodies in that thing? Wake up, use a Solex. That way, they won't spot you so fast."

De Palma went inside the Commissariat, gave a friendly wave to the officer who was fighting off sleep behind the switchboard, and walked round to the other side of reception, through the debriefing room, shaking a few hands on the way and glancing at the filthy plexiglass cages which seved as cells. Pell-mell, they contained everyone who had been picked up by that day's patrols. Drunks who were already snoring, two young dealers looking like beaten dogs, a huge tramp in a once-white, blood-stained shirt, who was pacing up and down, slapping his forehead and mumbling: "fuck, cunt, fuck, cunt, fuck . . . " as if it were a mantra. There was an acrid smell: sweat, bad breath and anxiety, mingled with the smoke of Gitanes and Marlboros.

In the staff room, separated from the debriefing room by a row of grey metal cupboards, an old boy was doing his crossword while waiting for the change of shift. On a wobbly shelf, a portable TV was spilling out the late-evening programme on the most popular channel. To general indifference.

De Palma went up the stairs at the far end that led to the first floor, taking them two at a time, then pushed open the door of the North Sector. For the first time that evening, a friendly hand was laid on his shoulder.

"Good day, Baron. Are you here on a visit? Is your old lady in the family way? Or are you just here to see how the real fucking police do the business?"

De Palma leaned his cheek towards his old friend, Commandant Jean-Louis Maistre, or "Le Gros", as he was called.

"What about you? Have you told those arseholes that they can forget about all those nights when you used to be a Parisian?"

"Forget it, Baron, they'd never forgive me."

Maistre was short, direct, as furry as a demon, with hair like a raven's wing, sparkling eyes, frowning brows and a dimpled chin. His pronounced nipples, heavy thighs and fighter's hands made him look like a ox. And yet, he was a man whose great sensitivity made him suffer terribly for not looking as he really was. His physique meant that he could never carry off the uniform of a mild commandant of public safety.

He dragged his friend into his office, closed the door and sat down with a sigh. De Palma watched as he carefully removed from a top left-hand drawer a bottle of Four Roses and two mustard glasses decorated with Achille Talon cartoons.

"Have a drink, Baron, then tell me why you're here."

"I've come to ask you a favour."

"Again!"

Maistre poured two large shots of bourbon, clacked glasses with the Baron, then knocked down his dose in one, with a grimace.

"I'm still on the Samir case," de Palma said. "I think I've now got the right idea about La Castellane. But I'll need you."

"When, this evening?"

"What do you think? In six months' time?"

"Take it easy. I'm on duty till 4.00 a.m."

"I know. But then you're free!"

"Yeah . . . free to go and sleep."

"No, free to come with me on a little trip to La Castellane."

"Baron, I'm your friend, you know that, but this time you're definitely out of your tree. What the hell do you want to do in La Castellane at 4.00 a.m? With the cold coming on as well. They'll all be home with their mothers."

"Do you want to be in on the arrest of the century, or don't you?"

"Calm down, Baron. Don't get carried away."

Maistre and de Palma met when working together at quai des Orfèvres, at the end of the '70s. After five years, de Palma asked to be transferred to Marseille, and Maistre then followed so as not to lose his friend. He had not immediately liked the city. He had even hated it for quite a long time. This pure-bred Parisian had not at all appreciated the shabby quartiers in the centre, their grandiloquent inhabitants, or the haughty and secretive bourgeois heights overlooking the town. Marseille had given him the impression of being like an over-made-up slapper, with her skin wrinkled from the midday sun, a tart of an Artemis offering her heavy dugs to the highest bidder.

Surreptitiously, like a rare opium, the city had taken Maistre over. When he would go back up to the capital to see what was left of his family, he felt bored out of his skull. He missed Marseille. He could not have explained why. Yet it was a fact. The city would not now let go of him, it was forever on his heels, like a jealous mistress.

The first surprise awaiting the two officers was that they were transferred, without a word of discussion, to the drug squad with the unwritten agreement that they would return to the murder squad within two years.

At the time, Marseille was still a grim town, rusted over by the economic crisis. It was a time of disillusion, the end of the glory days. Forget the flesh trade on the routes from Indochina, or the speakeasies in the back rooms of dives around the Opera, just then it was all about drugs. In discreet villas, the chemists of Marseille cooked up the world's finest heroin, and business was damn good: mobsters in gold-stitched suits were blowing one another away on every street corner.

The French Connection. A planetary fuck-up.

Both France and the U.S.A. had their eyes fixed on the dozen officers in the Marseille drug squad. And the opposition were no amateurs either, far from it: Jo Cesari, the king of 98% pure juice;

Gaëtan Zampa, a.k.a. "Le Grand Tany", and Francis Vanverberghe, "Le Belge", his enemy, along with their squadrons of soldiers. They were the crème de la crème of the scene, at the top of this can of worms, along with quite a few policemen from headquarters who were well in with the gang. So you had to be good. Very good. And de Palma and Maistre were very good.

They were the best.

Their friendship was bonded in life and in death when they raided their first lab: a villa, trying to pass itself off as a snug cottage, tucked up on the heights of Gémenos.

April 30, 1980. Judge André has set up one hell of an operation, Alouette III, with kepis everywhere waiting for the signal: the Baron is playing at being a wounded hunter, his eyes glazed over, slung like a lump of meat over Maistre's solid shoulders. They ring the doorbell, with its lucky charm cicada over the button and a jingle: "Do Mi Si La Do Re". Once inside, they stick the barrel of a Browning 12-gauge automatic full of buckshot – big hunt, big game – up the noses of their "saviours". HUSH! De Palma and Maistre then tiptoe upstairs to the first floor and noiselessly open the door. The chemist is there, bent over his boilers. "This is the police, Monsieur," de Palma says, courteously. The horse trainer stands up quickly, short of breath, eyes red, a look of terror on his acid-ravaged face.

That day, Maistre had been so impressed by his colleague's cold, calm intelligence that he had nicknamed him "The Baron". He thought it went well with the 'de' in his surname, his aquiline profile, his look of a long-distance runner, his height of one metre eighty-five and his tragic nobleman manner.

The American ambassador had expressed his satisfaction, the Ministre de l'Intérieur had applauded, and the Maire, Gaston Defferre, had too. Maistre and de Palma went on with the hunt, spending long, sleepless nights in beaten-up cars, having farting competitions and pissing into plastic bottles. Without winning a single medal. Just celebrity. After twenty months on the drug squad, they went back to murders.

October 21, 1981. 12.45. Boulevard Michelet. Judge André is whacked. Francis "Le Blond", the archangel of smack, a mafia beast, gets off his motorbike, tense, in slow motion, holding an 11.43. Three bullets. One year before, Defferre had said: "You don't kill judges in Marseille!"

After ten years in the squad, a marriage and two children, Jean-Louis Maistre sensed the approach of divorce and decay. He had opted for simple pleasures rather than big-game hunting and asked to be transferred to the public safety department. A different police force, uniformed, with more regular hours and less work. But he missed the squad terribly.

"So, are you coming along or what?"

"No, not at 4.00 in the morning."

"O.K., right away, then . . ."

"Now you're talking, you gobshite. I could see you coming. I hope you've got a plan at least."

"For the past ten days, I've been going backwards and forwards outside La Castellane. I just can't get it out of my mind . . ."

De Palma stared at the floor, as though concentrating his thoughts.

"This isn't a sadist. That simply isn't possible. If it was, then the kids would have turned him in at once. Or else killed him. No, it isn't a sadist, it's the fucker who's lording it over La Castellane. Or else someone else who's powerful enough to make everyone keep their mouths shut. But it's a local boy. See what I mean, Le Gros?"

"You're probably right, Baron. But what can we do about it? As soon as we show up, the birds will fly. It's like a village in the back end of the country. Everyone knows you're there before you've arrived."

"I've been watching the kids in front of the building where they found Samir. One of them is always there, all day, sometimes until late at night. He's a lookout. And a more regular one than the others. Driving by just now, I recognized him. I've already questioned him. He lives in the same block as Samir. They were mates. He's standing there right now, in the doorway of the tower-block. I want him, Jean-Louis."

"And how do you intend to go about it?"

"When someone shows up for a fix, he's the kid who goes to fetch the stuff. From under the wing of an old Mercedes parked on avenue Yves Giroud. For that moment, he's out of sight of the others. We'll stake him out there, at the corner, wait for him to have something on him and then collar him quietly. From what I've seen, he goes there roughly every fifteen minutes."

"Baron, they run faster than bats out of hell. I don't want to hurt your feelings, but you're no spring chicken."

"Don't worry, Le Gros. When you see the place, you'll understand. All I ask is that you have a squad of plain-clothes boys on hand. But tell them not to drive up and down outside the estate. Have them patrol around it. Because they'll have to be with us in twenty seconds flat. Go and change. You look like a policeman from four hundred metres."

They drove through the deserted northern districts: a complex web of dual carriageways and dead-end streets as broad as boulevards, lit by the yellow sentinels of the municipality; a maze of asphalt which now looked more like a shopping centre, then an estate, with the occasional tiny cluster of swanky pads in winding alleys.

As ever in this kind of situation, the Baron did not say a word. His friend glanced across at him, as usual unable to resist admiring his tenacity and insight. He knew that the Baron would get what he was after because he knew that he had prepared everything down to the last detail. Leaving nothing to chance.

As they drove back up avenue Henri Barnier, they saw the group of youngsters at the top of the slope, at the foot of the immense tower-block. The kid was there, in a blue and white tracksuit, the collar of his fleece jumper turned up, his woolly hat down over his ears. He was stamping the ground in his brand new Nikes to warm himself up.

Without slowing down, the two officers drove past the estate and took the first right into chemin de la Barre, then turned right again towards the Grand Littoral shopping centre.

The place was deserted. A burned-out Ford Fiesta had been dumped on the pavement. Red blotches of light from the streetlamps reflected in the windows of Collège Elsa Triolet. After taking the two grass roundabouts at the bottom of the shopping centre, Maistre and de Palma turned back into avenue Henri Barnier. They drove up its two hundred metres, then, just before the estate, turned into avenue Yves Giroud. De Palma spoke at last.

"Le Gros, see that doorway there, just by the Mercedes? I'm going to wait there. You stay in the car. As soon as the kid bends down and slips his hand under the wing, I'll be on top of him. If he manages to make a run for it, too bad. But really I shouldn't miss him."

"Then what do we do?"

"We sing him a Johnny Hallyday song."

De Palma got out of the car and walked to the end of the street. Maistre saw him peer round up the avenue then withdraw quickly. He walked back towards the Mercedes, felt under the wing and removed a small packet – a bar of shit – which he slipped into his pocket before vanishing into the doorway.

A good half-hour went by. Jean-Louis, who was no longer used to stake-outs, began to find the wait a little tedious. He had to keep rubbing his eyes to stop himself from falling asleep. His mind was starting to wander among some vague memories when he saw the figure of a young boy appear at the end of the street.

The kid bent down without even looking around. Casually, he felt under the wing of the Mercedes. When he found nothing, he bent down even further and ended up on his knees to look under the belly of the car. It was then that the Baron jumped him like a big cat. He picked him up off the ground, put one hand over his mouth and carried him, struggling like a captured beast, as far as the car.

"Listen to me, son. I've got just one question for you. If you tell me who killed Samir, then I'll let you go at once. And no-one will be any the wiser. Otherwise, we're taking you with us and putting your name around. O.K.?"

The kid did not cry. He stared into the Baron's eyes and saw in them a tiny glimmer of cruelty. He looked for a little comfort from Maistre, who just stared at the end of the street. The boy's entire body started to shake and he tried to stammer something, but the words stuck in his throat. De Palma gave him a terrific, violent slap.

"Karim," he said. "Look at me. Do you remember me?"

The kid did not dare look into the Baron's eyes. He nodded his head vigorously. He was no longer trembling.

"Who was it?"

"It was Givre, monsieur."

"Who?"

"Nordine . . . or 'Givre' . . . We call him that because he's completely crazy."

"Le Gros, call the boys. Tell them to drive straight to where we are, with sirens flashing and the whole works."

"No, for fuck's sake, not them!"

"Don't worry, son. It's for your protection. Your dickhead friends will just think you're being chased, that's all. Oh, and I'll give you your stuff back. I'll just keep a little bit for later on. But first you've got to tell me something. This bastard, 'Givre' as you call him . . . where does he live?"

"Block C, third floor, door on the left."

The squad's sirens were rising up in the night. When de Palma heard the tyres of the Safrane screech at the roundabout at the bottom of avenue Henri Barnier, in front of the swimming pool, he took Karim by the arm and pulled him out of the car.

"Listen up, kid. Run like hell, as fast as you can to warn your pals. I'll run after you. Don't worry, I won't catch you. Go on, kid, beat it."

De Palma waited until Karim had turned at the end of the street before setting off after him. The Safrane boomed into the street, flashing ultramarine on to the walls of the rabbit hutches. When it stopped beside the Baron and Maistre, who was labouring in his wake, Karim had already vanished into his universe.

Untraceable.

Two days later, at 6.00 a.m., Givre was sleeping like a cretin. His little old mum heard a knock at the door. Through the spyhole, she saw the friendly face of her neighbour, old Madame Oumziane. She opened it. Trustingly.

De Palma surged in, stuck his hand over her mouth and forced her outside. She made no protest, tired of protecting her shit of a son.

The Baron walked down the corridor, its wallpaper covered with huge round flowers dotted with red and golden medallions. A pleasant aroma of harissa, mild honey and halva came from the dining room. It smelled of a sweet, simple life. He walked on, gun outstretched, as far as the bedroom at the end, then gently pushed open the door and saw Samir's murderer curled up under his duvet in the foetal position. On the wall was a poster of Zinedine Zidane, the infant king of La Castellane. A crumpled Olympique de Marseille shirt trailed out of the rickety wardrobe. De Palma tugged on it and uncovered the dark form of a Scorpio, the preferred weapon of the Palestinians.

Nordine was still asleep, his fine profile resting on his pillow like an icon of piety. He looked fragile, barely out of adolescence. Sleep had returned the innocence which society's buffetings had stolen from him.

De Palma raised his Bodyguard and aimed it carefully, straight at the centre of the left temple.

A heavy hand appeared on the revolver's short barrel.

"Don't kill him," Maistre whispered.

The Baron's bottom lip trembled. He lowered his gun.

He looked round at the bedroom's dirty walls once more. He spotted some brownish stains and traces of fingernails on the discoloured wallpaper. It was a colour he seemed to have known for a very long time.

Dried blood.

His instinct told him that it was Samir's blood.

The forensics department proved him right.

3.

He strolled up cours Mirabeau passing the fashionable cafés, savouring the rare mildness of this late December day. He went slowly, as though inspecting the rows of wicker chairs with their flowery cushions, and the low tables placed like cornucopias between the leafless plane trees.

The afternoon brightness lingered. The unseasonable temperature had undressed the women: miniskirts, black, tan or sheer stockings – his favourite.

In a few days it would be Christmas. The shortest days of the year. It had been months since the last time.

Freakish weather like this put him in strange moods. For the past couple of days he had not been able to make up his mind how to dress, and this really annoyed him. The pullover he was wearing was too hot, and he felt drops of sweat collecting in the small of his back after their slow descent down his spinal cord.

He took a seat on the terrace of Les Deux Garçons, a respectable, somewhat snobbish bar at the top of cours Mirabeau, a few paces away from the burbling fountain with its haughty statue of King René.

It was 3.00 p.m. All he had to do was wait. He ordered a beer and stared at the passers-by.

As he often did.

It would soon be the agreed time. If all went to plan, she would quite simply sit down at a table and show him his next prey.

At 3.30, the goddess appeared. She walked in front of him without even a glance in his direction and sat down at the next table. Five minutes later, a woman of about forty arrived. They kissed each other in the most ordinary way possible.

Once again, he appreciated how the goddess could quite naturally seduce all kinds of different people.

He listened.

The new arrival was apparently one of those idle, upper-middle-class women who spend their time in the chic boutiques of Aix's old quartier. She was blonde, of average height, with a sporty physique, jutting breasts and perfectly tapered legs. Most of all he noticed her protruding chin, which hardened her long face despite her small brown eyes and soft, almost naïve smile. She spoke like all Aix women of her type, without an accent, looking skywards every time she uttered a sonorous superlative about some meaningless piece of nonsense.

He learned that they had met the previous evening, at an "utterly stunning" show in a "super bijou" gallery in the town centre. He failed to understand why his goddess was interested in all these bourgeois clichés. But there was no disputing her desires.

She got the other woman talking, to the point that they exchanged addresses and telephone numbers.

That is how he found out her name: Hélène Weill. He registered it mentally, like a snapshot.

Beside the picture of her name, he placed her phone number and then, a little further on, her address. Methodically.

He then learned that Hélène Weill had for the past few years been consulting an "utterly brilliant" psychiatrist, an "extra-ordinary" man on place d'Aix called François Caillol, whose "absolutely dazzling" mansion was on route de Puyricard.

He swallowed the rest of his beer and went for a stroll through the streets of Aix. The sun was beginning to set, cold shadows flittered into the narrow streets of the historic centre. He looked at his watch: 4.00 p.m. He decided to go back to Marseille. He had to make plans while he waited for the moon.

He followed Hélène Weill for two days.

She would leave her home in the centre of Aix at about 11.00 a.m. to do a little food shopping, then go back home around 3.00 p.m. Then she re-emerged to spend the rest of the afternoon going in and out of boutiques.

In those two days, all she bought was a few feminine items: fine silk lingerie, some costume jewellery, two pairs of shoes, a few fashion accessories . . . And none of it was ever gift-wrapped.

He phoned the number of Dr Caillol's practice. He was told that the psychiatrist was taking no new appointments until January 3, and that he was fully booked until December 24, but could still be contacted in an emergency. He surmised that Caillot would be staying in Aix over the festive period.

He made a decision. It was now or never. On December 23, he went to Puyricard, parked his motorbike in the village and walked to the doctor's house.

It consisted of a farmhouse, a mansion with a swimming pool and tennis court, as well as a few outhouses. The mansion stood about fifty metres from the farm; the buildings were surrounded by a dozen hectares of vines, which must have produced an unpretentious little Côteaux d'Aix-en-Provence.

After a few days' surveillance, he knew that the doctor never came home before 9.00 p.m.; that his tenant farmer invariably went to the vineyard at about 4.00 p.m. and stayed there until at least 7.00 p.m.; and that the farmer's wife, who ran the Puyricard playschool, never came home before 6.00 p.m.

Which meant that between 4.00 and 6.00 p.m., he had plenty of time.

He decided that this would be the best time to break into François Caillol's house. If he could, he would take the Mercedes, which was always parked in the garage, and bring it back before 9.00. If the worst came to the worst, the farmer would just see his landlord's car drive by.

On December 23, at exactly 4.30 p.m., he observed the premises from the clump of pines and brambles beside the tennis court, and waited for the farmer to vanish, followed by his mongrel, into the vines. He slipped on a pair of latex gloves, leaped up the twelve steps, opened the heavy door without any difficulty and closed it quickly behind him.

Inside, it was dark; only a glimmer of daylight filtered through the shutters. He did not turn on the light and stood for some time in the corridor, until his eyes had become used to the gloom.

The house oozed comfort and smelled of dust, wax and wood-smoke. Beams on the ceiling gave it that old fragrance of rustic charm.

Walking up the corridor to the salon door, he filled his lungs with this scent which reminded him of his childhood.

The mistral rising in the mighty branches of the plane trees carries the children's cries far away. All day, the sun beats down. The night is heavy and dense.

In the salon, Papa reads his paper, as he does every evening; he goes to sit next to him on the leather sofa and gently lays his cheek on his lap. In front of him is the small leather easy chair, reserved for his mother, and the Persian rug with its geometric patterns and complex arabesques – he imagines high-speed circuits for his toy cars. But he is not allowed to play in the salon.

He looks up, glances at the knick-knacks on the sideboard before lingering over the painting he likes best: a landscape of the port of Marseille in the '30s. He imagines being a naval officer like his grandfather and his great-grandfather, like most of the men in his father's family.

A naval officer with a spotless uniform and beautiful, gold-stitched stripes.

Sometimes, his grandfather takes him on cargo ships. Shyly he looks at the old sailors and shakes their gnarled hands, scared by their little laughing eyes, by the huge wrinkles surrounding them – indelible marks of long watches spent on the decks of ships, with only the dazzling gleam of the sea for scenery.

He would have liked to have known the port of Marseille in the '30s. To have seen the steam from the ships on their way to Indochina, the Sainte-Marie strait with its massive, black, fat-bellied tugs, strenuously pulling along the mail ships from Asia, the Far East or America; the dark coal-smoke which swathed La Major cathedral; the sailors' sons coming to wave home a father who had been away all these long months. Marseille back then must have smelled of camphor, cinnamon and precious wood, of coke and the heavy fruits of Black Africa.

He screamed, closed his eyes and let his thoughts drift back into place. Methodically. As always. A few minutes later, he opened his eyes: his childhood had disappeared. He was calm, but his body was now completely drained of energy.

It was time for the hunt. After the long hours, the bird was coming. It was there, a few metres away, behind the tall grasses. It had come to drink from the only pool on the entire, vast plain. The lance with its flint tip had been placed in its stick of hooks. The bird approached. He looked up.

A good hunter must not miss his first shot.

The bird was a few paces away, dipping its beak in the water, then stretching its neck. Once, twice.

In a flash, he launched the lance. The bird took wing . . .

A great hunter must not miss his first shot.

Beside the front door, the answering machine was flashing in the half-light. It showed the number eleven, in red batons. Eleven messages. All from patients cancelling their appointments between Christmas and the New Year. The eleventh was a woman's voice:

"Excuse me, Doctor, this is Hélène Weill speaking. I'm sorry to disturb you at home, but you never answer your mobile. Anyway, I'd like to cancel my appointment on Thursday 28. And I was wondering if you were available today."

The night augured well.

He picked up the telephone and dialled. Hélène told him that she really needed him. Christmas was making her feel terribly anxious. She could come now, or any time he wanted, even late that evening. But she simply had to see him, at any price. He suggested taking her to a restaurant, a lovely little place which he knew well. It would be nicer than the psychiatrist's couch.

"I'll pick you up from your house before 8.00. We'll go to Cadenet. I have a friend there who's just opened a little bistro. You'll see, it's a bit of a drive, but it's just perfect."

It was 6.00 p.m. He glanced at the cast-iron hooks above the telephone: the keys to the doctor's Mercedes were there.

But first of all he had to perform the ritual.

He went up to the first floor, to the psychiatrist's vast study, placed his rucksack on a Chippendale chair, and took out a small bottle of mineral water and a plastic box containing some red powder.

He pulled on a pair of surgical gloves, opened the box, poured a little of the powder into the palm of his right hand, lifted it to his mouth and started to chew carefully before taking a mouthful of water. He placed his hand on a sheet of white paper, bending his little and ring fingers. He then spat out the liquid over his hand, again and again, until it was covered in red. When he lifted it up, a negative image of his hand had been left on the white paper.

He waited for it to dry, looked at the result of his labours and said aloud:

"Spirit of the hunt
Goddess of life
Here is the hunter's sign
Take her life to fortify mine
May her death be swift
May I not make her suffer
May your spirit guide me in the shadows
May the force of her blood enter into my blood
May her flesh fortify the first man."

Carefully he slipped the sheet of paper into a green plastic folder and left the mansion.

Hélène Weill lived alone in a flat on rue Boulegon, right in the centre of Aix. At 7.30 p.m., he called her from a phone box to say that he was late, and that it was impossible to park in her narrow street, so could she wait on the ringroad, just by the Ford garage.

"Hélène, I'm a bit late," he said. "I'll send along a friend of mine. Another patient . . . He'll pick you up in my car. You'll see, he's a wonderful guy. Just won-der-ful! He'll recognise you, don't worry, he's already seen you around in my consulting room. Then you can come and have a drink at my house. How about that?"

Hélène had chosen a rather strict suit. When she got into the Mercedes, he noticed that she had raised her skirt high enough so that he could see between her thighs. He paid no apparent attention and pulled away.

It took them fifteen minutes to get out of Aix. The streets were jammed in a late rush-hour of people who had being doing last-minute Christmas shopping. He managed to win her trust by inventing a few problems for himself and an imaginary therapy. Hélène told him of her hallucinations, dwelling on an image that had recurred constantly in her nightmares since her last visit to the psychiatrist: being raped by three scouts. And the nights she spent smoking joints and masturbating. He listened to her without a word, drumming his fingers on the steering wheel.

They left Aix. Hélène talked about herself non-stop, into a vacuum. He was not listening any more.

When they had passed the village of Puyricard, he slowed and turned down a forest track. He drove on for a good hundred metres, then stopped the car.

"Get out," he ordered firmly.

Hélène smiled limply, her chest rose, her thighs drew apart.

"Get out," he ordered even more forcefully. "And wait for me there, in front of the car. I won't be long."

She obeyed at once, got out of the car and took a few steps in the white light of the headlamps. He opened the boot of the Mercedes without listening to the romantic chat the woman was serving him up. He put on his latex gloves and picked up a strange object shaped like a tomahawk: a rudimentary axe, with a wooden handle measuring about fifty centimetres and, at the tip, a huge piece of biface flint, perfectly sharpened and held in place with dried gut.

Slowly, he approached Hélène, his eyes on fire. She heard him recite out loud, in a calm voice:

"I am the hunter

Give me your blood

May the spirits of the dead guide you through the night

May your flesh fortify the first man . . . "

Hélène gasped.

"But, what do you . . . ?"

She stepped back, falling over a tree trunk on the ground, her legs spread.

He grabbed her arm, yanking her upwards while repeating through gritted teeth:

"May your flesh fortify the first man."

The flint axe lodged itself deep in the skull of his prey. He hit her again coolly, like a butcher. Small shards of bone and scraps of grey brain flew into the air. Then there was silence.

He examined the prostrate body: Hélène, her face crushed, looked like a crazed puppet. Her muscles were still twitching. He dipped his finger in the blood which was foaming out of her mouth and tasted it.

"May your flesh fortify the first man."

He pulled up her skirt and tore off her stockings. The nylon soughed, and an acrid smell rose up. He stood back to get a good look at the slaughtered flesh still quivering at his feet.

It was at that moment that he started to howl like a beast, and bit into the still-warm flesh of her thigh.

Once. Twice.

Then he went back to the car to fetch a long, narrow piece of flint, as sharp as a kitchen knife, kneeled down between Hélène's thighs and began to slice her up. When he reached the femur, he struck it with the axe with one swift movement, as precise as a horse butcher.

Five minutes later, he was holding Hélène's left leg at arm's length, swinging it to and fro in a broad arc to empty it of what was left of its blood. He then paused for breath before wrapping the mass of wobbly flesh in several bin-liners and putting it in the boot of the Mercedes.

He returned to the body, placed the sheet of paper with its negative hand under Hélène's right arm, then disappeared into the night.

He was in no hurry.

4.

At around noon on January 4, de Palma and Jean-Louis Maistre walked into Le Zanzi, the squad's local bar on rue de l'Evêché. Dédé the landlord yelled thunderously as he served up the rounds of pastis and J&B:

"Watch out, here come the real men!"

Dédé was the only person who found this funny. De Palma and Maistre let him get on with it. Two Ricards arrived almost at once, along with the landlord's big, fat, sweaty hand, which they had to shake.

Dédé had been running Le Zanzi for the past four years. He served on average fifty meals a day and hundreds of drinks, and could get the parking tickets of his friends and family written off in return.

"O.K., boys?"

"As ever."

"You're looking off-colour, Baron. Like you're miles away."

"No, I'm fine . . . I just had a bad night's sleep. And I don't like pastis."

"So why do you drink it?"

"To be like everyone else . . . "

Dédé had not yet cleaned the Christmas decorations off the window of Le Zanzi, even though the illustrations were no better than last year's. With "genuine snow" spray, he had tried to sketch out a tree, then squirted out a Santa and added stars here and there, like jewels. Large, back to front, joined-up writing read:

"Saturday December 20, Grand Lottery at Le Zanzi, big prizes, Xmas hampers, a DVD player to be won . . . "

De Palma spotted Maxime Vidal staring absently at his glass of mint syrup at the corner of the bar. He walked over to him.

"Did you hear about that business at Cadenet, Michel?"

"What, the woman they found?"

"Yes."

Maistre stuck his nose between the two of them, spinning the ice in his empty glass.

"Baron, a drought is setting in!"

"We're talking about that Cadenet business."

"He must have been a complete maniac. They haven't found all the bits!"

The previous day, de Palma had received a call from the Cadenet gendarmerie, who were looking for possible information about a murder in the countryside around Aix. They were still trying to come to terms with the case; they had never seen anything like it before.

"A hunter found her," he was told. "It's atrocious, absolutely fucking atrocious. How could a human being do something like that?"

The state prosecutor had allocated this investigation to the gendarmerie. So de Palma could do nothing. Yet, he sensed that this murder was just the beginning of a series of murders, or else a repetition of a similar case which had happened in Aubagne a year ago. They hadn't found all the pieces then either, but what interested him most was the gendarmerie's mention of an image of a negative hand. It showed that the killer was a maniac, a cold, precise individual who liked signing and staging his murders. Then there was the lack of material evidence: the gendarmes had not found a single, usable clue on the scene of the crime apart from the traces of tyres belonging to a large car, probably a Mercedes. It was something they still had to check out.

Capitaine Anne Moracchini burst into Le Zanzi. She was rubbing her hands to warm them up.

"Michel, did you hear about what happened at Cadenet?" she asked with a tremor.

"Don't talk to me about it! It's been given to the gendarmerie."

"I've never seen anything like it! They're talking about cannibalism . . . I thought things like that only happened in America, or in darkest Africa!"

"What have you got against Africans? The world never changes, my lovely, there have always been loonies like that, and there always will be. The only problem is that there seem to be more and more of them! We've put two of them up for trial in the last year. Not counting the ones we never catch!"

"What's all this about a picture of a hand found beside the body?"

"I've got an idea or two about that. I'll tell you later."

The hand was a signature. The beginnings of a lead, but what sort of lead? Eventually it would get its author caught. But when?

No-one could answer that question. They would have to wait. De Palma shuddered at the very idea of waiting for the next death, and the next hand. The next autopsy. Then comparing, analysing and theorising. The steamroller of the police force: entire days spent cogitating for nothing, waiting for a third corpse, starting all over . . . Until the killer slipped up. If he did.

It bugged de Palma – it was a matter of pride – the gendarmes had already solved the two finest serial-killer cases so far. They had checkmated the police force, no doubt about it. When he had gone to bed late the previous night, completely exhausted, he had cursed the prosecutor for handing the investigation over to the gendarmerie.

He emerged from his thoughts. Moracchini was talking with Vidal about a case of legal identity. Maistre walked over to him looking mysterious.

"Do you know what happened to me last night, Baron?"

De Palma shook his head and grunted, his mouth working on a particularly resistant olive.

"We got a message . . . "

Still struggling with his olive, de Palma grunted again.

"A message from the M.L.A., do you know what that stands for, M . . . L . . . A . . . ?"

"No."

"The Marseille Liberation Army . . . "

"Are you feeling O.K., Jean-Louis? You're with friends here, having a nice quiet drink . . . So calm down and quit raving!"

"I swear to you, it's true! The message read: 'We are the M.L.A., the Marseille Liberation Army. We demand the release of Eric Laugier, the Marseille patriot. The people of Marseille are behind us.'"

"After the Corsicans, the Bretons and the Basques, now we have the

M.L.A. . . . Really, Le Gros, you're so funny. When you've had one too many, you wax amphigorical!"

"What?"

"Amphigorical. It means an intentionally obscure spoken or written style. Gibberish, in another words. It's in the police force handbook. So who is this Laugier?"

"He's the guy from La Plaine who planted some bombs at the National Front's premises two years ago. Remember? You're getting past it too! There was a death. We were on the scene together."

"So what's the connection between a spotty militant and the Marseille Liberation Army?"

"They're a group of agitators. They want to liberate Marseille from French colonialism, from the domination of Paris, that kind of thing . . . They want to return to the days when Marseille was a republic. It all goes back to the year dot."

Laugier had set a large amount of explosives in the premises of the National Front on rue Sainte like a real pro. At the time, they had thought that the Corsicans were behind it. A man had been killed during the explosion, a former paratrooper who was also a member of regional counsellor Francis Codaccioni's entourage.

A few months ago, Laugier had been tried and sentenced to ten years. Ever since, a group of militants had been campaigning for his liberation, covering the walls of La Plaine and surrounding areas with posters demanding justice, and writing regularly to the President and Prime Minister, either to ask for a pardon, or to insult them, depending on the mood of the writer. Laugier was a new-look terrorist, a shadowy fighter for an unexpected cause, and had become the off-beat martyr of Marseille's independent fighters. The Che Guevara of La Plaine, minus the beard and the cigar.

"I thought Laugier was a good guy," de Palma said, swallowing a final olive, which turned out just as stubborn as the others; its flesh stuck firmly on to its stone, like a limpet resisting the knife of a starving fisherman. He turned to Dédé.

"Where do you buy your olives?"

"My mother-in-law makes them. It's a time-honoured recipe. Just like olives of old!"

"Your mother-in-law isn't a member of the M.L.A. by any chance?"

"The what?"

"Never mind, I'll explain one of these days."

In the early afternoon, de Palma was alone in his office. He had nothing to do and intended to spend a few hours trying to discover the meaning of the negative hand found beside Hélène Weill's body. It was the basic curiosity of a passionate investigator. A vague idea had occurred to him: he wanted to contact a specialist, someone at the university who would be able to explain the meaning of this drawing. He picked up the phone book and started to flick through it while whistling the opening of the overture of "Aida".

Commissaire Paulin walked in without knocking. He did that with everyone, to see if his squad was working conscientiously. He found de Palma going through the phone book.

"You know that we have the Internet now. You should try using it," Paulin remarked reproachfully.

"You never find anything on the Internet, Commissaire. It takes hours just to find the right name, but only two minutes with the phone book. And no-one else knows what you've been up to."

Paulin was a shabby fifty-something who wore lousy suits and had a pot belly. A pair of small, twitching eyes were framed by specs placed at an acute angle over a hooked nose too big for his narrow skull. It all made him look as insincere as hell. But essentially de Palma did not like him because of his shoes: dated grey moccasins. He could not stand moccasins.

The big boss did not dare ask him what he was up to, as he generally did with his younger officers. He was treating his best soldier well, because this man would help to push through his own future promotion. He just smiled, showing his horsy teeth in the gap between his puffy lips.

"I've got a good customer for you, de Palma. A walker found her body some place – I can't remember where exactly – in the creeks. A preliminary investigation says it was a murder. The prosecutor has appointed us, and I'm giving you the case. Go along to the morgue. Forensics are slicing her up now."

"I'm on my way," de Palma said. He stood up slowly, hoping that this would annoy Commissaire Paulin even more. "But there's something I have to point out to you."

"What?" said Paulin, irritated.

"Normally, the presence of two police officers at an autopsy is obligatory."

"I know that, de Palma. It's not my fault. There's been a mix up with the municipality . . . We're in Marseille, and that's the way it goes! Everyone does whatever they want. Anyway, an officer is there to identify her, and the judge has already called by. You know Mattei. He starts work at 8.00 a.m., whether the police are there or not. Take Vidal with you!"

"He's not available."

Paulin squinted a little, turned on his heel and left with a shrug.

Whenever he had to pay a visit to forensics at Timone, de Palma always felt decidedly off. He did not like this kind of appointment, especially on a Wednesday after Dédé's cooking.

At 3.00 p.m., he walked into the vast Timone teaching hospital complex. In the changing room of the forensics department, as he put on his white coat, gloves, mask and over-shoes, he smelled the awful odour that hung all around.

Despite all his years in the force, de Palma had never got used to the smell of dead flesh mixed with a bouquet of chemicals: phenol, ether, formalin, chloral hydrate . . . To make themselves understood by police officers, the forensic scientists often translated these strangely named fragrances into everyday terms such as pear, orange, rotten egg or caramel. To the specialists, each odour had its meaning.

"You start out by sniffing a stiff, like a vintage wine. You appreciate its bouquet, then you look at its colour, finally you test it . . . " Dr Mattei had explained gravely.

De Palma pushed open the door between the changing room and the dissection room. The smell of the rotting corpse grabbed him by the throat. He stopped to swallow back his saliva several times, then gave a friendly wave to the two officers charged with identification and stood beside Mattei. The doctor was not wearing a mask, and was flanked by two assistants wearing huge goggles, like skiers', except for the colour. The trio of specialists was bending over the naked body.

When he saw de Palma's face, Mattei winked at him, and chuckled.

"So, the boys have dropped by. And not just anybody, if you don't mind. The prestigious Commandant de Palma. Sorry, Monsieur, but this isn't a pretty picture. Especially not after Le Zanzi. So step forward. You're going to get your money's worth."

"Mattei, once again you've started the job before I arrived . . ."

"No choice, Baron," he said with a shake of his head. "There are too many corpses in my drawers. Too many scores being settled! I called you three times this morning. No answer. It's your job to sort the situation out. Here, we start work at 8.00 a.m. sharp."

The doctor was sewing up the woman's thoracic cage. Her flesh was puffy and covered with a fatty translucent liquid, like grease. De Palma saw the chrome-plated steel of the curved needle as it entered and then re-emerged from the epidermis which had been bleached by the sea. To save face, he picked up his notebook to write down the doctor's conclusions.

"Christine Autran. Caucasian, female – as you can see for yourself. I'll skip her personal details, you'll find them in the file. We've put her papers in a bag, just as it says in the rulebook."

De Palma was about to remind this doctor of the dead that it was the job of the police to take care of all that, but he held himself back. This forensic surgeon was as stubborn as a mule, but also the best in the region.

The corpse's face was covered with a blue cloth.

"We hid her face because we were beginning to get fed up with her watching us work. But for you, Michel, we'll make a little effort. Take a look."

Mattei lifted the cloth. Two empty eye sockets stared dumbly at some point on the grey ceiling. The face had been devoured. All that remained were scraps of flesh, entirely bloodless now. The dead woman had no lips, her mouth was slightly open and her teeth jutted from greenish gums which were disintegrating. Her half-eaten cheeks revealed the depths of her throat. De Palma noticed that her tongue and a large part of her scalp had disappeared, gobbled up by some carnivorous sea creature. The surgeon showed the police officer the signs of strangulation, two distinct black marks around her neck like a tattooed necklace.

"Apart from the bruising on the body, I don't have much else to tell you. She was strangled, then thrown into the sea. Her abdomen was full of gas, which is why she was floating on the surface . . . The salt then absorbed the water in her blood, which has a high chlorine content. There's a very weak presence of diatomeae. This tells us that she was thrown in post-mortem. The nape of her neck was snapped; cervical vertebrae four and five are broken. She must have been hanged, or something similar. But one thing's certain: someone broke her neck."

With a well-practised movement, Mattei turned Christine Autran's head to one side and pointed to the position of the fracture. A brown blotch indicated the fatal wound. The kind of trace the murder squad sees all the time.

The doctor pressed down on the flabby flesh with his index finger, protected by a double layer of surgical gloves, and moved it in small circles. The movement made the half-empty skull emit a slight glugging sound, like a siphon being opened.

"The marine fauna has done its work. I even found some tiny worms from the mediolittoral zone in her thoracic cage. Look at her hands – they were eaten by congers, morays or some other creatures, without big jaws . . . I can't date the death accurately. But it was at least a month ago, and more likely a good forty days ago! In other words, around the end of November or the beginning of December. Not before."

De Palma jotted down the scientist's conclusions. The date of death did not ring any bells. He would have to check the missing persons file.

"There's something that bothers me," Mattei went on.

"What's that?"

"She'd buttoned her anorak up wrongly. She'd put the first button in the second hole, and so on. I'll show you later, in the photographs we took. And she had some pebbles in her right pocket. I put them in the jar over there. Go and have a look."

Mattei pointed towards a stainless steel table mounted on wheels. It was covered with small jars containing a variety of objects: sea worms, scraps of cloth, hair ... In one of them, the Baron could see some small stones which were almost round and about two centimetres in diameter.

"Do you know what she did for a living?"

"No. How should I?"

"She was a lecturer in prehistory, no less."

De Palma picked up the coastguard's report and went through the pages one by one. Christine Autran had been found in almost the same place as the corpse of Franck Luccioni, a small-time thug. Below Le Torpilleur.

"That's odd," he said.

"What is?" Mattei asked.

"She was found in the same place as Franck Luccioni. Do you remember that little crook?"

"Perfectly. But his was an accidental death. There were no traces of any violence. Nothing at all. Drowning preceded by a serious decompression accident. I think he must have stayed on the seabed for too long. His cylinders were empty and he had to come back up too fast, without being able to respect the decompression stops. A classic accident that bad divers have. A good diver would never do that. Never."

5.

"I'm from the police, Madame," the Baron called out. "It's about your upstairs neighbour. Can I talk to you for a few minutes?"

Yvonne Barbier had just come home from the market when de Palma rang on her doorbell. It took her an excessively long time to answer. He could sense her presence behind the door, peering through the spyhole. Then the door was opened on its nickel chain. De Palma saw the made-up face of an eighty-year-old woman, one of those grannies with real character who spend hours preening their seniority in chic boutiques in the city centre. He produced his tricolour card and raised it to her eye-level.

"Come in, come in . . ."

In the huge, sumptuous flat dating from the late nineteenth century there hung a slight fragrance of ilang-ilang mingled with bergamot, marzipan and vetiver. It was the smell of dated opulence, with an acidic tinge of sweat and vegetable soup. Yvonne had been beautiful once and she still maintained that presence, those graceful gestures and the natural charm of an attractive person. Her faded, turquoise eyes gave her sharp stare an infinite depth, and there was something astonishingly young about them. With a broad smile, she showed the officer into the salon. He sat down on a pink velvet sofa, in front of the piano, a Pleyel mini grand, on which, in a silver frame, stood a photograph of a severe-looking man. The half-closed shutters let in two shafts of golden light which cut their way obliquely through the air. Several canvases by minor masters decorated the walls, which had the sheen of age. One of them, in strong red and black blocks, with no half-tones, depicted a corrida: a signature and a grandiloquent dedication, presumably from the artist, showed prominently in the bottom right-hand corner of the painting.

Yvonne peered at her guest as discreetly as possible. It must have been the first time in her life that she had received such a person in the comfort of her home. The situation intrigued her just as much as it brought out her congenital nosiness.

De Palma spoke first:

"When did you last see your neighbour?"

"The last Wednesday of November. I can't remember the exact date . . . "

Yvonne thought it over, puckering her brow and adopting a mysterious air as if she were the possessor of great secrets.

"Usually, on Tuesdays, she goes to teach in Aix, then comes back at about 8.00 in the evening. She hardly ever goes out. I didn't hear her that evening. I thought she must have stayed late with her students or something. Then, when I didn't see her the next morning, I thought that something must be wrong. I went to see your colleagues at the Commissariat on boulevard Chave. They told me to wait. A couple of days later, I went back to tell them that she still hadn't come home. That time they listened to me. They told me that they'd put her in the missing persons file."

"Where do you think she could be?"

"I have absolutely no idea, Officer. All I know is that she didn't pay me rent for November or December. In my opinion, she must be dead by now, or else kidnapped by some sadist."

De Palma did not tell her that Christine Autran had been hanged and thrown into the sea like a piece of dead meat. He wanted to get as much information as possible from this witness, so for the moment he had to avoid any psychological shocks.

"What did she like doing? Did she have any hobbies or anything?"

"Her job. She loved her job. Apart from that, I don't know of anything . . . "

The elderly woman thought it over. She stared at her shiny shoes, tapping them on the thick Chinese rug.

"Oh yes!" she suddenly exclaimed, as though re-emerging from a long meditation. "She liked walking in the creeks. I used to tell her that it was no place for a woman, but she wouldn't listen to me. She went there all the time. Alone. She was always alone, the poor thing. She was a beautiful woman, she could have got married. But she preferred her freedom. You know what young people are like these days ... I got married in 1940 to the gentleman you see there, on the piano. He was a conductor. I was twenty and he was thirty. It was a different era ... Christine's mother died about twenty years ago. She had no other family, and as far as I know she had no friends."

"I suppose you have spare keys to her flat?"

Yvonne Barbier suddenly lit up. She got to her feet and vanished into what was presumably her lumber room.

"Of course I have a spare. Do you want us to go up and have a look?" she said, heading towards the front door.

"We'll see about that later."

"From what I can understand, you think that she really has disappeared, or that she's dead, is that right?"

"It is a possibility we are bearing in mind," de Palma replied vaguely. "But as you know, we police officers see so many strange things ... "

"She's dead. I'm sure of it. Just like two and two makes four. She's been living her for twenty years, coming home every evening. Sometimes she doesn't go out all day. I can hear her walking from one room to another."

"And you haven't noticed anything unusual of late?" de Palma asked. "No-one has been here to ask after her, no sales reps or workmen, nothing?"

"No, nobody. There's just the old folk like me who live here. You can question them, if you want. But they'll only tell you the same thing."

He was not going to learn much that day. It was 12.30. De Palma asked Yvonne Barbier to show him Autran's flat.

"Shouldn't you have a search warrant?"

"No, Madame Barbier. That's just in American cop shows ... Under French law there's no such thing as a search warrant. All I need is one or two witnesses, such as you. Normally the person living at the address should be present, but I have to admit that I lied to you earlier. Christine Autran was in fact found yesterday."

"She's dead, isn't she?"

De Palma lowered his head.

"I just knew it. My God. The poor little thing."

Professor Autran's flat was identical to Yvonne Barbier's. It measured about 150 square metres and was laid out around a large, central corridor, which led into vast rooms with high ceilings decorated with fine plaster mouldings. The prehistorian had painted the walls white and, here and there, placed a few bits of cheap, chipboard furniture.

All the shutters were closed. The sun filtered in, weak and discreet between the slats and through the net curtains. The policeman looked for the nearest light switch. Pulling on a pair of gloves, he told Yvonne not to touch anything and to stay in the hall. He was hoping to find the beginnings of an explanation for this affair.

Two of the rooms were crowded with books and files stacked up on red, metal shelves. It was almost impossible to cross the floor. In the salon, a plain showcase contained some pieces of cut flint. Christine Autran had hung a few black-and-white photographs on the walls. In one picture, taken in one of the creeks, she was smiling at the photographer, her hair dishevelled by the wind. In another she was grimacing as she kissed the mouth of a human skull with no lower jaw, presumably a find from a dig. Above the black marble mantelpiece was a photograph of her posing in front of a cave painting of a gentle-eyed bison.

The salon, like the rest of the flat, was furnished without taste. In the kitchen, a pile of dirty washing-up had dried out in the sink; tomato sauce had crystallised on a plate.

The dark blue bathroom did not tell the Baron much either, except that Christine Autran was not some flirt who spent hours making herself up before going to work. A few hardened lipsticks lay in a pile above the basin beside a three-quarters-full bottle of Chanel Number 19, a shabby make-up bag and a hard brush full of brown hairs. The lecturer had not left on a long journey.

In her study, the answering machine showed that there were no messages. He picked up the receiver to listen to the dialling tone. The phone still worked. He jotted down all these details in large letters in his exercise book.

He opened the desk drawers slowly, one by one: there was little of interest in them either, apart from piles of notes which meant nothing to him for the moment. He would have to go through all this mess over the next week. It would take quite some time. He looked through the rest of the study without any apparent results. A few files had been placed on the floor. One of them had been labelled with a large, red felt-pen: "Le Guen, various photos". He opened it and discovered a stack of snapshots; positive and negative hands, paintings of animals and carvings. One of the hands looked like the picture the gendarmes had found beside Hélène Weill's body. De Palma had been sent a series of photographs of it.

He picked up a second file entitled 'Le Guen, topology', containing a series of topological studies which were totally incomprehensible to him. Blue blotches, some light, others darker, were spread out over a brown background which also showed darker zones. Some captions had been added in a fine, energetic hand. He glanced quickly at a few of them: 'horse section', 'boulevard of sea spiders', 'the three penguins', 'mural of black hands' . . .

A third file was marked 'Le Guen, September 2000'. Inside it were two almost identical photographs, of poor quality compared with those in the other files, showing a painting of an animal which looked rather like a bird. He held them under the desk lamp. There were several fingerprints on them. He slipped them into a plastic folder and put them in his pocket.

He went back into the salon, sat down for a moment on the sofa-bed, and tried to imagine Christine Autran's last day. Had she come home before going to the creeks?

"Madame Barbier," he said. "Could you tell me where Christine Autran parks her car?"

"In a hired garage at the beginning of rue du Progrès. It's not far, just on the corner by the bank across the road."

"Thank you, Madame."

De Palma wrote down his name, work and mobile numbers on his notepad. He delicately tore off the page and handed it to her.

"Madame, if you notice anything strange, please contact me at once. It's very important, do you understand? Do you know Christine Autran's phone number?"

The old lady looked at the ceiling, pretending to search her memory.

"Of course. It's 04 91 47 02 13."

Then she repeated each number as clearly as possible, her eyes fixed on the policeman's notepad to check that he was noting down what she was telling him correctly.

De Palma took out his mobile and dialled Christine's number. After three rings, the answering machine cut in, and the voice of the woman discovered in Sugiton creek filled the empty flat. It was a soft, somewhat hoarse voice. A sensual voice.

"Hello, I'm not at home right now, but you can leave me a message . . . "

Yvonne Barbier burst into tears.

In the Garage de l'Alliance on rue du Progrès, a fine layer of dust covered Christine Autran's flame-red Peugeot 306. Jean-Marc Menu, a nervy little character who owned the garage, walked several times round the car, waving his arms.

"She hasn't used it for over a month. The lady owes me two months' rent. Soon it'll be three."

"The lady's dead," de Palma told him.

"She can't be!"

"Oh yes, she can!"

Menu wiped his oily hands on his overalls. He did not know what to do with himself. Only one thing really interested him: how to get rid of the car as quickly as possible.

"Do you have a spare set of keys, Monsieur Menu?"

"No, never! We never have spares. I never ask for them, it's not done . . . "

De Palma glanced inside, using his hand as a shade against the glare of the striplights in the garage.

"Could you open this car?"

Menu looked embarrassed.

"That's always possible. But I don't like doing it."

"Monsieur Menu, I am a police officer! The sooner we search the car, the sooner you'll be rid of it."

The owner vanished into his workshop and returned a few moments later with a metal rod.

"We use it when we put cars in the pen," he said, to explain why he had such an implement.

Menu slid the rod between the window and the rubber of the left door of the 306, pulled hard and opened it.

De Palma inspected the interior carefully, but found nothing except for a maintenance handbook and an unopened box of tissues. The counter read 26,584 km, hardly anything for a car which must have been about four years old. De Palma also noticed a few traces of sand and dried mud on the mat below the driver's seat, around the wheels and in the boot. It had rained hard in December. Christine must have driven down a track saturated with water. The mud was ochre, with some red pigments.

On the handle of the glove compartment and on the dashboard, he found some fingerprints which were larger than those on the steering wheel. They clearly belonged to a man.

He closed the door again carefully, by pushing on the window with the tip of his index finger.

"We'll be round to collect it as soon as possible. Probably tomorrow. There shouldn't be any problems. Will you be here?"

Menu nodded.

"Meanwhile, don't touch a thing."

"O.K."

"The technicians might take your fingerprints . . . Don't worry, it's just to compare them in case . . . "

The owner asked no more questions, delighted to know that Christine Autran's car would soon be leaving his garage.

6.

The waitress at the Why Not! was nibbling at a ham sandwich and browsing through *La Provence* when he arrived in the bar. A little melted butter dripped from the bread, and she discreetly licked her thumb and index finger with their blood-red nails.

"Good morning," she said without even looking up, her mouth full of fingers.

At that time of day, the Why Not! was empty. He would have preferred there to be a few customers. They would have been something to look at while he was waiting for his appointment.

He dragged the waitress away from her newspaper by ordering a large glass of lemonade and strawberry cordial, with a straw, and went to sit at the table nearest to the window, looking out over the street. From there he would be able to watch the pupils and teachers coming out of Lycée Longchamp.

He waited.

When the waitress brought him his drink, her hips swaying to the rhythm of some cerebral soul, he asked if he could borrow her paper.

"Of course, it's for the customers, I was just reading the small ads ... I'm looking for a flat in the neighbourhood. You wouldn't know of one, by any chance?"

He did not like chatty people, especially when he was about to enjoy a lemonade and strawberry cordial, just as in the very happy days of his childhood, in memory of his father, who always bought him one after their long walks together. Chatty people disturbed his nostalgia, making him feel twitchy.

"No, I don't think so," he said as curtly as he could, to cut short the intrusion.

"It's not easy to find anything around here, it's getting more and more expensive."

"Prices are going up in Marseille at the moment."

She put the paper down on the table.

"It's yesterday's. I haven't had time to go and get today's yet."

"It doesn't matter."

The waitress walked away, waggling her arse to the same rhythm as she had on the way over.

He went straight to the local news page, at the top of which was a large headline:

Brutal Murder In The Countryside Around Aix

AIX-EN-PROVENCE. Last Sunday, the body of a woman was found by a hunter, not far from Puyricard, on the road to Cadenet. The victim – Hélène Weill, aged 43, living in Aix – was presumably taken there to be brutally murdered with a knife. The exact circumstances of the murder are still unknown but police sources have confirmed that it must have taken place about ten days ago, just before Christmas.

The public prosecutor has entrusted the investigation to the gendarmerie . . .

He read the article avidly to the end, then threw the paper on to the table in fury. They had not published a photo of Hélène, and there was no mention of the hand that had been left by the body. Maybe the gendarmes had hushed up that point. Never mind. The article had obviously been copied from an Agence France-Presse dispatch.

The clock said 11.30. The pupils of Lycée Longchamp were starting to come out: from their look and the way they were pushing each other around, he assumed they must be sixteen-year-olds. He paid and went out into the street.

The goddess was demanding another sacrifice: Julia Chevallier, an English teacher at Lycée Longchamp. He stood outside the gates, among some parents who still checked up on the comings and goings of their kids. He felt his entire body tingle. He closed his eyes for an instant to stop his memories from haunting him at a time like this.

All of a sudden he saw Julia at the top of the steps. She was tall, slim, and she looked as fragile as ever. She had hardly changed at all.

She spoke for a while with a chubby fellow with a pointed beard – presumably a French or history teacher – then left him and started walking down rue Jean-De-Bernardy. He let her turn the corner into boulevard National, then almost at a run he covered the hundred metres that separated them.

When he reached the boulevard, he spotted her inside her Mercedes A-Class, working away at her steering wheel in an attempt to turn out of a tight parking space between two plane trees. He quickly went back to his motorbike and followed her.

She drove up boulevard de la Libération, which was heavily congested because it was lunchtime. He had to ride around several blocks to avoid remaining stationary among the cars – a motorcyclist who does not zigzag through a traffic jam looks decidedly conspicuous.

In avenue de Saint-Barnabé, the congestion eased. He noticed that Julia was a fast and nervy driver. She even ran a red light outside the engineering school. After that, he followed her from a distance of two hundred metres.

He watched as, to his amazement, she turned into chemin du Vallon, just by Saint-Julien church. Driving past her front door, he noted it was number 36. He quickly drove round the block again and went home.

His plan had to be ready within a fortnight: if not, the new moon would be imminent and he might run out of time. The goddess could not wait any longer.

First task: reconnaissance of the area. Julia's house was surrounded by high walls topped with shards of broken glass. It would be difficult to break in without being spotted, especially as her street was so narrow. It would be a stupid risk and should be avoided.

He laid out a map of the neighbourhood on his metal bed and studied it closely. Behind Julia's house there was an old canal which wound past several gardens. He followed its course with his finger, and stopped when it turned into a dotted line: the canal ran through a tunnel before re-emerging on the far side of the cemetery.

In a sudden, feverish state he was filled with joy; the base of his neck tingled and sweat pearled his forehead. The hunt, his sole purpose in life, was about to begin again.

His plan was taking shape: he would go along the canal as far as Julia's house and break in from the back. But first he had to find out more.

And so he watched Julia for a few days, but without risking going back to the lycée.

She lived alone, the goddess had made no mistake about that. He never saw her go home with a man or another woman. She did not have a guard dog, and she never went out in the evening. The canal could be reached easily over a low wall at the far end of the cemetery.

7.

The girl waiting on the second floor of headquarters, in the corridor outside the offices of the murder squad, did not even look twenty-five years old. A few rebellious curls of blonde hair tumbled over her pretty face and half hid her emerald stare. From time to time she blew aside her locks out of the corner of her mouth, the movement of her lower jaw making her fleshy lips twist like a real Lolita.

She had told the officer in reception that she wanted to see Commandant de Palma in person. She claimed that she had some important revelations for him. So she had been escorted to the offices of the murder squad and left there to wait. The wait could well be a long one.

As she stood in the harsh brightness of the "guaranteed daylight" striplights she watched the comings and goings of members of the squad as they emerged from one office to go into another for no apparent reason.

At about 10.00, de Palma burst into the corridor and saw this platinum doll twisting her feet at every angle to get a better look at her monumental platform heels. She was obviously losing her patience.

"Are you waiting for someone, young lady?"

He sensed that she knew him.

"Yes, I want to speak to Monsieur de Palma."

"You're speaking to him. Come with me."

This unexpected meeting did not suit de Palma at all. He had been planning to use the last morning of the week to go over initial findings in the murder of Christine Autran.

Capitaine Anne Moracchini opened the office door, put her head inside and gestured at him.

"Hi, Michel."

"Good morning, Anne. You haven't seen Maxime, by any chance?"

"He's at criminal records."

"Tell him there's no hurry. I've got someone else to deal with."

Anne Moracchini glared at the blonde, who was staring at the floor, then looked quizzically at De Palma.

"It's nothing."

"See you later, Michel."

Anne Moracchini slammed the door, leaving behind a strong scent of musk perfume and apple shampoo.

De Palma gave a huge yawn. No amount of black coffee would ever drive away that biting fatigue which no longer left him. The young blonde was getting impatient. De Palma pretended to tidy up the paperwork piled up on his desk and gave her a long blank look.

"And you are Madame . . . ?"

"Bérengère Luccioni."

The name Luccioni chimed in Michel's weary memory.

"So you're Franck's sister, Jo Luccioni's daughter?"

"Yes," she said shyly, pouting her fleshy lips which were faintly coloured with brown lipstick.

Jo Luccioni had been a serious hood. He ran a smack factory at the back of a bakery, and used the shop to launder his earnings. De Palma had not known his son Franck; only that he had been found dead in Sugiton creek.

"So what do you do for a living, Bérengère Luccioni?"

"I work for my father, at the bakery on boulevard Piot, in Pointe-Rouge. I sell the bread and the cakes."

Bérengère was pretty, but vulgar: too made-up, too blonde, her skirt was too short and her accent too pronounced. Too everything! She kept fiddling with her caramel fingers, sliding a silver ring up and down the middle finger of her left hand. This kid looked every inch the wife, sister and daughter of a gangland boss; her particular physique was shaped by a life with the mob, which de Palma knew only too well. She was a real doll.

"Do you still make cream buns?"

"Only on Sunday mornings . . . why?"

"I love cream buns, that's why. Especially your father's ones. I'll come and buy some one of these days. How old are you?"

"I'll be thirty in ten days."

"So, you're twenty-nine . . . " he said, attempting a gallant smile.

"That's right."

De Palma pretended to flick through a bulky file, lingered over some unimportant reports, went back a few pages, then opened another folder. Bérengère watched him, chewing her gum, making small, wet sucking noises and clicking her teeth together. He let the silence drag on. Bérengère slowly uncrossed her legs. The gentle rustle of Lycra woke him from his torpor.

"Why have you come to see me? I thought my colleague, Lieutenant Vidal, had already interviewed you. Do you have anything new?"

"Yes. It's just that . . . well, in July, before my brother was killed, I kept seeing this motorbike outside of the shop. Then I went on holiday to my grandparents' place in Corsica, and that's where I heard about my brother . . . When your colleague questioned me, I'd forgotten about it, but then the other day I remembered that a man came into the shop once to buy bread and croissants. He parked his motorbike on the pavement. Then he asked me about my brother . . . where he was, what he was doing. That's all."

"Mademoiselle Luccioni, there are thousands of men around here who could go and buy croissants on their motorbikes."

"Sure, but this one wasn't like the others."

"Why not?"

"Because his motorbike looked like one in this picture in the papers . . . "

"A Kawasaki Zephyr 1100! Do you know how many Kawasaki Zephyr 1100s there are in Marseille?"

"O.K. . . . But it was the first time one stopped at the bakery at 6.00 in the morning, just when we were opening. If he was a friend of my brother's, he'd have known that he was hardly ever at the bakery. Especially not at 6.00 in the morning! And his motorbike was red, just like in the papers. Plus he kept his helmet on, like he didn't want to be recognised. He just had the visor up. He had little blue eyes and bushy eyebrows."

What was Bérengère Luccioni doing there, telling him about a red motorbike she'd seen in the papers? Gangland members never came to the police just by chance. It might cost them too much.

A Zephyr 1100. Of the most recent gangland killings – a record eleven in the past year – most had been carried out by hitmen on motorbikes. As usual, the local police had investigated nothing, and so found nothing. Apart from a burned-out motorbike, a photo of which had been published in *La Provence*. Bérengère was right; it had been a Zephyr, and according to the boys in the lab it had been red.

"Do you remember which day this happened?"

"That's hard to say. I think it was sometime the week before I went to Corsica, but the exact day . . . Maybe it will come back to me. I went to buy my tickets on the 24th, and I took the boat on the 26th . . . And it was before then, maybe July 20 or 21."

"A week before you left!"

"Yes, around then, I'm sure of it."

De Palma took a long look at the young woman. She was more relaxed now, and becoming prettier and prettier. There was another rustle of Lycra.

"Mademoiselle Luccioni, thank you for this information. I think it's of the highest importance. Now, if you don't mind, we'll go over the whole thing again from the beginning, O.K.?"

He jotted down her story in his exercise book. When he came to the date of the event, he wrote the 20th because she remembered then that it had been her father's birthday. He asked her for a detailed description of her mysterious customer.

"He was wearing jeans and a leather jacket. He must have been about one metre eighty tall. With broad shoulders. And blue eyes. He seemed very calm . . . I dunno! He spoke with a strong accent."

"I'll be straight with you, Bérengère. There's no official investigation into your brother's death. The state prosecutor refused to take up the case. Franck was no angel – you saw him in prison often enough to know that! And you know too that he drowned in a diving accident. The forensic surgeon was sure of this. I realise that this is very hard for you, but that's the way it is. You have to trust us on that score."

Bérengère looked down. She probably knew far more about her

brother than she was letting on, but she was not going to give anything away. Not there, in any case. Maybe later. Time would tell . . .

She was a gangland girl, and hard too, despite her appearances. She was the sort of person whose character has been forged in prison visiting rooms. De Palma knew her father well. He had arrested him twenty years earlier, when he was with the drug squad. It had taken them a very long time to nail him in his laboratory just outside a tiny village in the Alps. It had been a painstaking investigation, with years of effort and plenty of patience following Luccioni in his little white Renault 4 along the twisting roads of the Alpine valleys, against the backdrop of a Bavarian picture postcard.

Jo Luccioni came and went with no apparent purpose. He drove at a pensioner's speed, half in a dream, but with his eyes darting in all directions, while his two hounds (the only weapons he ever possessed) sat dribbling on the back seat of his old banger. If all was well, he would be off to stock up on chemicals, the carbonate and various acids required for the transformation of morphine. Those who needed the white powder had made a special trip from Marseille to deposit the goods in some hotel on a hill which no-one now remembers.

Little Bérengère had been taking skiing lessons on the day the big man was arrested. When she came back to the chalet, walking awkwardly in her ski boots, she came across a brigade of gendarmes armed to the teeth. The Brigadier had looked at her rather sadly. There stood her father, in his scruffy clothes with his hands behind his back, his acid-marked face turned to the ground. In a grave voice, he had asked the young Inspecteur de Palma to release him for a moment, so that he could embrace his little girl for the last time. De Palma had accepted. The Brigadier had written it up in his report.

Luccioni got off lightly in the end: twelve years behind bars for having concocted the best heroin in the world. Meanwhile, his little girl grew up as best she could, waiting for visiting times, trying to understand the value of secrecy and the burden of a such a marginal life, and inventing a presentable father for the sake of her friends at school.

Her brother Franck had taken a rockier road, full of shady deals. Instead of working as a baker, he wanted to be like his absent father.

But he was a pale imitation. A series of burglaries of the middle-class houses on rue de Paradis had earned him enough dosh to set himself up as a small-time drug wholesaler. A few trips to the police station and inevitably to prison had calmed the young hood's ardour for a while. But when he got out, he started all over again. Now Big Jo's son had died a miserable death among rainbow wrasses and voracious conger eels, the victim of his one passion: diving. Police frogmen had found him under a rock several metres down, gently rolling in an invisible current, as underwater scavengers feasted on his corpse.

That was on July 30. At the time, they had presumed it was a diving accident, and they hadn't investigated any further. As far as the police were concerned, that was one less crook. Case closed. Old Luccioni had never got over it, and on bad days the quality of his cream buns suffered.

The old hood must have sent along his daughter to act as an intermediary with the only policeman he had ever respected. The Baron sensed that he should be on his guard. If he did identify Franck's killer, then Luccioni Snr. would take it upon himself to extract justice.

"Thank you, Bérengère," said de Palma as amicably as possible. "I'll come by and see you. We'll have a chat with your father."

"Thanks, Monsieur le Divisionnaire."

"No, not Divisionnaire. We say Commandant now. It's stupid, but that's the way it is. I'll show you out."

In the headquarters' courtyard, the mistral was spinning furiously, like a typhoon in the Roaring Forties. An anemometer would no doubt have been able to measure its vertiginous speeds. No-one, not even the building's architects and certainly not the police, had been able to explain this phenomenon.

Outside the criminal records office, a group of thugs, one of about fifty and two younger men, were waiting to sign in. They loitered there with dripping noses, pretending not to recognise one another as they stoically put up with the fury of the Provençal wind.

Perched on her platforms, Bérengère Luccioni almost fell over under the force of the gusts, just managing to right herself by grabbing hold of the wing mirror of a heap of rust belonging to the city police. She shrieked, and de Palma gripped her by the shoulder to help her.

At that moment, he had a clear memory of the five-year-old girl he had seen in that chalet hidden in the Alps. She had stared at him with eyes as green as mint leaves, without really understanding why this young policeman, this Prince Charming, had put stainless-steel handcuffs on her papa. In her infant mind, those cuffs had looked like silver.

He watched her leave, this woman with her life of baguettes and pastries, her skimpy skirt, her audible Lycra, and make-up which was too excessive to seduce the old commandant he had become.

Tomorrow, or another day, he would go and see her father.

8.

From his height of one metre seventy, Tête watched his stream of urine land in rapid spurts in the toilet bowl of Le Bar des Sportifs in Endoume. He looked up at filthy, yellow, badly joined tiles which covered the urinal's walls. It was then that he heard a conversation start up on the other side of the partition.

"Gopher will be in La Madrague around noon. You take the two parcels he gives you, then come and drop them off here, like I told you. Don't drive too fast. Especially not on the Corniche – there are police speed controls there all the time. O.K.?"

"No problem."

Tête went on pissing. With all the beers he had got through that evening, there was no end to it. But now the stream was beginning to peter out.

"And you, Richard, you leave the bar around 2.00. You know where to go?"

"You've told me at least four times."

Tête recognised the voice of Laurent, a.k.a. "Lolo", the owner of Le Bar des Sportifs. He knew the other voice too, but couldn't put a name to it. His brain was in a spin, as though the mistral had just blown up and was now whistling through the empty corridors of his poor little neurons. It sounded like Féli, but it couldn't be him – he should have been in his pizzeria, filling his red-brick oven with oak logs.

Lolo was a great guy, a big man in the mob. After twenty years behind bars for various crimes, he had finally seen the error of his ways and taken over a small café in Endoume, right by Anse de la Fausse-Monnaie. Recently he had been calling up his childhood friend, Gérard

Mourain, a.k.a. "Tête", to offer him odd jobs. Sometimes Tête had to be on the lookout for police, at other times he had to tail someone. Lolo never explained to Tête what was going on, he just gave him a precise task and then paid him handsomely, cash up front. Mourain could not have asked for more.

"Is Tête in this evening?"

"Yeah, I called him up and he arrived about 8.00. Since then he's been knocking back beer after beer. If he goes on like that, he's gonna be completely pissed. You want to see him?"

"No, just see if he can do the job. As usual . . . Just get it sorted!"

"Shit, now I've pissed myself," Tête said out loud. All this thinking meant that he had lost control of his stream of urine and had now wet his trousers; a dark line stretched from his crotch to his left knee.

"Fuck it . . . shit and fuck it!" he yelled.

The conversation on the other side of the wall came to a halt.

When Tête emerged, Lolo was back behind the bar as though nothing had happened. He walked sideways to get to his seat, pretending to look at the pétanque championship trophies lined up along the far wall so that no-one would see the piss mark on his leg.

"Hey, Gérard, come here."

Tête stood up awkwardly and walked over to the bar as quickly as he could. Lolo didn't notice a thing. And there was no-one else in the bar.

"Tell me, Gérard, are you free next Wednesday, around midday?"

"Um, sure . . . "

"O.K., good. You know that restaurant in La Madrague overlooking the harbour? I can never remember its name. Anyway, it's the only one."

"Yeah, I know it. What about it?"

"Drive up there for lunch at about 11.30. Order whatever you want, but take a seat near the window, where you've got a good view. If you notice anyone dodgy, call this number from your mobile and let it ring three times. If the guy then leaves, call back and let it ring twice. Got that? Fine. Take a good look around, even below the rocks to the left of the port. You can stop at around one o'clock."

"And then?"

"And then you quietly finish your lunch and go home. I'll call you. Want a drink?"

"Sure, a beer."

Tête and Lolo raked over a few childhood memories. They talked about the Endoume football club, in which Lolo had been goalkeeper and Mourain the left winger.

"You know, they're having a really good year. If things go on like this, they'll end up replacing l'Olympique!"

"Be serious, Lolo, people have been saying that for the past thirty years. With O.M. it's different. Can you imagine the Endoume players with their broken legs on the pitch at the Vélodrome? You know damn well they wouldn't last ten minutes."

"Don't talk shit, Gérard. This year, they're playing really well. I reckon they'll get promoted to the second division. You'll see."

"You can always hope. But if the Endoume players are that good, why don't they go and play for O.M.? It's because a whole bunch of them are called but only a few are chosen. And O.M. are professionals, not a load of shitty amateurs like we've got here."

"Come on, Gérard, we're not going to fight about it, are we? Do you want to make a bet?"

"No, I never bet."

"'Cos you're shitting yourself?"

"Nope, it's just a principle."

The last time Tête had betted on anything, he had ended the evening at police headquarters before spending two years in Les Baumettes. The bet was as follows:

"I'll bet you're too much of a chicken to get your piece out and make some music."

"You wanna bet?" Tête had replied.

He had got out of the car, crossed the road, opened the door of a jeweller's, drawn his gun and pointed it at the manager. Unfortunately, a hysterical customer had started screaming. As the jeweller's was only ten metres from the local station, the police had shown up within a minute. That was the bet: to hold up a jewellery store ten metres away from a commissariat. Only Tête had been daft enough to do anything like that. Age had taught him that he was no genius and now he had settled for being a lookout for the big boys. Sometimes he did a bit of grassing too, to keep himself out of Les Baumettes for as long as possible.

He ordered a final beer and picked up *La Provence* to see what had been going on. On the local news page, he saw a photograph of a woman.

PROFESSOR CHRISTINE AUTRAN FOUND MURDERED IN A CREEK

... according to police sources, Christine Autran was hanged then thrown into the water. The investigation has been entrusted to the murder squad under the direction of Commissaire Paulin ...

Tête peered more closely at the black-and-white photograph.

"Jesus Christ!" he said. He looked up at Lolo, whose wife was yelling at him down the phone. The landlord was not looking in his direction.

"Jesus fucking Christ!" he repeated, then closed the paper.

He had just recognised the woman he had tailed for days on boulevard Chave.

9.

De Palma passed the night of Saturday to Sunday in the murky depths of Le Valparaiso, a nightclub by the port – thongs and salsa guaranteed – which had been opened recently by an old friend from the drug squad. He'd been thrown out of the squad after some dodgy business about broken seals on the doors of a heroin lab in Martigues.

At 6.00 a.m., his head full of moritos, congas and the loud laughter of lewd women, he'd had enough of ogling the young waitress. He went out into the emerging dawn and drove home slowly, trying to get his head together. Soon he was driving along the smarter side of boulevard Michelet.

De Palma recognised her from a distance. For a good twenty years she had been delighting night owls at the foot of La Maison du Fada, Le Corbusier's dazzling construction – now a desirable residence for snobs. All the old guard of the city's police knew this exotic bird of the streets of Marseille. De Palma slowed down to get a look at Solange's face, for that's what she called herself. She had not changed; she seemed immune to time, this woman who was as hard as the pavement she pricked with her shiny high heels. He stopped alongside her and wound down his window.

Solange welcomed him with a false smile.

"A hundred francs for a blow job, and two hundred for love. With a condom."

"Don't you recognise me, Solange?"

"My God, is it you Inspecteur?"

"Commandant, Solange."

"Same difference. With all these new words for the ranks, I'm completely lost."

She looked at the weary officer greedily.

"Do you fancy something?"

"No, I was just passing and I spotted you. Not a soul out this morning."

"You're telling me! It's a disaster area. There's only the Holy Ghost left. I haven't had a single customer. I'm always the last one here, you know that. In the morning there's always someone who stops. So I stay here. That's all I know how to do."

Solange looked up. A dark grey BMW had turned back along the boulevard. The first customer that night. And maybe the only one. De Palma put his car into gear, said goodbye to his old acquaintance and drove off. In the rear-view mirror, he saw Solange getting into the BMW.

Never mind, he would have had trouble getting it up.

He thought about Marie, and about his good-time girls. Their faces mingled together, their soft smiles, the subtle scents of their skin and the fragrance of their sexes. He closed his eyes to block up these thoughts, and when he opened them, they were brimming with tears.

At the top of boulevard Michelet, at the square with its obelisk, he turned right into Mazargues, to get a sense of the neighbourhood where Christine Autran had grown up.

He drove a good hundred metres between the small houses bordering boulevard de la Concorde and turned left into rue Emile Zola, trying to get slightly lost so as to put off the time when he would have to go home to his flat.

At the end of the road, the modest Mazargues church blocked out the skyline. The neighbourhood still looked like a Provençal village, far from the tumult of the city centre. On place de l'Eglise, a pensioner was letting his incontinent dog piss along the parked cars. A few strings of multicoloured fairy lights were still glimmering above the streets, even though Christmas was now over, even though the day was now dawning. A vertical banner hung down from the clock tower reaching the ochre façade of God's house: "A saviour has been born to us".

De Palma looked at the clock on his dashboard: 7.00 a.m. It occurred to him that Jo Luccioni must be sweating by his ovens this Sunday morning and could be paid a little visit.

Fifteen minutes later, he pushed open the door of Joseph Luccioni's bakery in Pointe-Rouge. He was welcomed by the aroma of warm bread and butter cream. Little Bérengère was presumably still asleep, because it was her mother who emerged from the bakehouse to serve one of the first customers of the day.

She stared at him frostily before forcing herself to speak.

"Can I help you?"

"Good morning, Madame. I'd like to speak to Jo."

"I knew I recognised you," Ma Luccioni said, glaring. "I'll go and see if he's free. As you know, a baker's work is never done."

She disappeared for some time. De Palma looked at the cream buns, lined up neatly in two rows between the chocolate and strawberry tarts. They looked excellent down to the last detail, with a sprinkling of icing sugar and a generous dollop of praline cream between the two layers of choux pastry.

Madame Luccioni reappeared.

"O.K., you can see him. Come behind the counter."

In his lab, Luccioni was leaning over his kneading machine, monitoring the mechanical production of his brioches. He looked up at de Palma.

"Good morning, Inspecteur. How are you?"

"Fine, and you?"

"About as good as someone whose son's been murdered."

De Palma did not answer and instead shook the floury hand of the former chemist of the French Connection.

Jo had aged terribly. He was white-haired and hunched, broken by life, prison and baking. But his expression had not changed; behind his fine, round glasses he still looked like a priest who could be taken straight up to God without confession. He stared down into his kneading machine as his dough rolled beneath its blades, sticking long, yellow strands on to the shiny metal sides. Before long, the brioche dough would stop sticking and be ready for the oven.

What could Jo be thinking about? The young policeman who had nicked him? The son he would never bail out again? The daughter he had sent to police headquarters to lure the Baron to the bakery?

De Palma wanted the old boy to start off the conversation but

Luccioni, who had been expecting this visit, was taking his time, deciding what he wanted to say. All of a sudden he stopped the kneading machine and left his lab without a word. De Palma automatically put his hand to his right hip. He had forgotten his gun. But he shouldn't have worried. The old crook wasn't going to blow him away in his lab.

Luccioni came back a minute later with something in his hand. He looked aside as he gave it to the police officer. It was a large diving watch equipped with a depth display, a highly sophisticated article that only experienced divers would have. Luccioni spoke first:

"I gave my son that watch for his eighteenth birthday, more than twenty-five years ago – at the time I was going straight . . . He never forgot it when he went diving. Never. Understand? A diver never forgets his watch. If you do, you can't dive . . . "

Luccioni was on the verge of tears, and his lower lip trembled. His son's murder had been disguised as a diving accident and neither the police nor the forensic surgeon had realised it. "That idiot Vidal slipped up," thought the Baron. His young colleague should have noticed this crucial detail. But as no investigation had been instigated, the case had been closed. As though the murder of Franck Luccioni didn't need to be solved like all the others.

The Baron asked Luccioni gently if he knew who had been behind it. The old man shook his head.

"Jo, you didn't get me here just to show me Franck's watch, did you? If you know something, then tell me. I need to know. Otherwise there'll be no investigation. You understand, don't you?"

Luccioni did not react, but stared at De Palma for a long time.

"There is one thing I do know, Inspecteur. If I find the fucker who did it . . . follow me?"

Jo wanted his revenge and was ready to do anything to get it. But one thing was sure: his son's murderer was not a mobster; if he had been, gangland justice would have been done by now. He had sent his daughter as a scout, to see if an official investigation could be opened. De Palma knew that he had to tread carefully. Police headquarters was full of leaks, and Jo must have a few close acquaintances among his more dodgy colleagues.

"Don't even think about it, Jo. Don't forget your daughter. And don't try to tail me to get to him."

"I was too strict with Franck. His poor mother did the best she could. But boys aren't like girls. They want to have honour and be strong, they want to be like their father . . . "

Luccioni remained silent for some time, as though all his life's failures were passing before his eyes.

"Do you know who he hung around with?"

"No idea. He never told me his business, if you see what I mean. He was too scared of me . . . and then there was that motorbike, the one my daughter told you about, and a so-called diving accident. A drowning. But my son had been diving ever since he could swim. Your dickhead of a forensic surgeon didn't know that! And as he was old Jo's son, no-one gives a damn if he snuffs it."

Luccioni leaned over his kneading machine, picked up the heavy dough, put it on the marble worktop and separated it into small, regular spheres.

"Why did you seek me out? Why me, and not someone else?"

"Because I know you're straight and a very good policeman. Those are two things I respect. Plus I reckon you're the only person who'd agree to looking into my son's death."

"Why would I do that?"

"Because I know you like this kind of case."

Jo picked up a ball of dough, shaped it in the palm of his hand and placed it on a tray. Then he took another one.

"Inspecteur, I'd rather you left that way," he said pointing a floury finger at a door at the far end of the lab.

Luccioni turned his back, and de Palma walked out without a word.

Outside, the town was beginning to shift about like a reptile. He felt fatigue overwhelm him like a shock wave. He got into his car and drove home, his head vacant. He would see about all of this on Monday.

*

The answering machine showed that he had two messages: the first was from his mother, who was expecting him for their usual Sunday lunch; the second was from Maistre, who had called and not said much; for the past few years he had been convinced that his phone was bugged.

It was 9.00 a.m., time to have a shower and call Maistre. He placed his latest acquisition in the CD player: "Aida", with Renata Tebaldi, Carlo Bergonzi and Giulietta Simionato. There was nothing new about it, it was simply a classic.

> "Ritorna vincitor! . . . E dal mio labbro
> Uscì l'empia parola! Vincitor
> Del padre mio . . . di lui che impugna l'armi
> Per me . . . "

The divine Tebaldi filled his four-room flat while he smothered his cheeks with shaving foam.

He thought about the negative hand. It did not mean much to him, but it brought back some vague memories from primary school: a lesson about prehistory learned by heart, which said that men at that time dressed in animal skins and lived by hunting and fishing. He remembered an image in a history book: a cave feebly lit with Cro-Magnon torches showing paintings of animals on its walls – like in Lascaux – and the prints of hands.

He went over to his coffee machine, put two measures of coffee into it and lined up two cups to collect the black liquid. As he watched the foam form, he realised that he had put two cups, just as he had every Sunday morning. But Marie was gone. It had been two months now. He had asked to see her at her parents' place in the Alps, but she had refused. It was not yet the right time.

> "Vincitor
> De' miei fratelli . . . ond'io lo vegga, tinto
> Del sangue amato, trionfar nel plauso
> Dell'Egizie coorti . . . E dietro il carro,
> Un re . . . mio padre . . . di catene avvinto! . . . "

As he drank his coffee, he tried to make a connection between Luccioni and Christine Autran, but found nothing that could give him the slightest clue, or the beginnings of a lead.

> *"L'insana parola*
> *O Numi, sperdete!"*

Hunger tickled at his stomach. He opened the fridge and took out a slice of apple tart, which must have been three days old. As he bit into the soft pastry and the wrinkled apples, he racked his brains. Nothing. In fact, the only time he had had anything to do with prehistory was when Le Guen's Cave was discovered. At the time, he had been put in charge of an investigation into the deaths of three divers found in the entry passage, a few metres away from the opening. This accident, which took place just two days before the official declaration of the discovery, had alerted journalists. Some sinister rumours had been doing the rounds.

Le Guen had been suspected of declaring his discovery only as a result of the deaths of the three men. De Palma had questioned him for a long time, and Le Guen had described the terrible dangers in the cave; he had made his discovery public so as to avoid any more such accidents.

Le Guen then told him that he had shared his discovery with a few friends, and had asked them to keep it secret. But the news had spread through the small world of diving like a trail of gunpowder, sparking fits of jealousy among the divers. Le Guen's version checked out, so de Palma had not proceeded any further, but he had kept copies of statements from this unusual case in his personal records.

De Palma mentally traced an initial line: Le Guen's Cave – diving – Luccioni – Autran – prehistory – negative hand. Luccioni's name alone did not fit into the scenario.

The telephone rang. It was Maistre.

"Baron, I have to see you . . . "

De Palma did not have time to respond before Jean-Louis hung up, which left him only a few minutes to get dressed and make more coffee.

"Al seno d'un padre
La figlia rendete
Struggete le squadre
Dei nostri oppressor!"

Ten minutes later, Maistre was ringing his doorbell like crazy.

"What's up with you, Le Gros? Have you come to tell me more about the M.L.A.?"

"It's no laughing matter . . . yesterday I got another message from that bunch of loonies."

"What did they want this time?"

"The same thing."

"And that's why you've woken me up on a Sunday morning? Listen to what I bought yesterday."

"Is it 'Aida'?"

"With Tebaldi and Bergonzi."

"The older you get, the newer the recordings!"

"Piss off, Le Gros."

"Marie phoned me up yesterday."

"And?"

"We spoke for two hours. You should go and see her. She misses you."

"Not yet. And anyway, I've got one hell of a case on my plate. I tell you, I'm in for some sleepless nights."

The Baron cut through the air with his right hand, then sat down and poured out some more coffee.

"I sacri nomi di padre . . . d'amante
Né profferir poss'io, né ricordar . . .
Per l'un . . . Per l'altro . . . confusa . . . tremante . . . "

"Tell me, Le Gros, do you remember Le Guen's Cave?"

"What, that prehistoric site they found in the creeks? It's at Sugiton, isn't it? There were three deaths. Weren't you on the case?"

"Yes, I was. I kept copies of the statements."

"Why are you telling me about all this?"

De Palma told him about the death of Christine Autran, the search of her flat, and his meeting with old Luccioni. He then mentioned the strange death of Hélène Weill and the negative hand found by the gendarmes. A hand drawn using a stencil, as they did in prehistoric times, in Le Guen's Cave for example.

Maistre looked at his old friend. He seemed tired, but the flame was still burning.

"I don't trust these kinds of connections," he said. "Beware, Baron, many mistakes have been made by working like that. You think it all fits together, then you end up in a terrible mess . . . Just because two corpses are found in the same place five months apart, it doesn't mean there's any criminal link between them. As for the woman in Cadenet, that might just be a coincidence. The *modus operandi* wasn't the same. Not even similar. Neither Autran nor Luccioni were sliced up by a lunatic. You know how serial killers work: always the same method!"

De Palma disappeared into his bedroom without a word. Maistre heard him pull open a cupboard and rummage though his papers. Some time later, his friend returned holding a wad of documents as fine as cigarette papers. He passed half of them to Maistre, who cast an expert eye over the witness statements. They were carbon copies of the originals.

```
DEATH BY DROWNING
QUESTIONING OF MR AUDISIO Francis, aged 38,
French, residing 34000 MONTPELLIER
```

The report was dated September 1, 1991, and signed by Inspector Claude Duluc:

```
Statement by Monsieur Audisio Francis, born
14/11/53 in Montpellier, commercial engineer,
residing Montpellier, tel: 76.35.25.78.12,
who declared:

I am a member of the Grande Bleue Club, Port
des Goudes, 13008 Marseille, and as such I
```

led a group of divers from Montpellier.
The course was to last for ten days,
beginning on 31/08/91.

There were fifteen people in the group. Today
we organised a dive for eight people. They
left the port at about 9.45 in two groups,
with two boats of four people, me included.

They went to Sugiton creek. At 11.00, the
dive began, with four people going down 25
metres to reach the cave. Of these four
people, one was inexperienced. I was one of
this group. We went into the cave, a kind of
underwater cavity, which we explored with our
torches. We stayed for about eight or ten
minutes before starting to go back up. I was
leading, and when I looked down I could see
the group of three people. I emerged from the
hole. I waited for the others, in vain.

I resurfaced to call for the security group
to help those three people.

We tried to go back into the cave. But there
was a cloud of silt and opaque matter making
this impossible. We tried everything, I did
all I could to find them, and I ran out of
air. A companion took me back up by sharing
his air with me.

I can't explain what happened because it was
behind me. Did they panic? Couldn't they find
the way out?

In terms of equipment, everyone had a

```
cylinder of compressed air with capacity for
40 minutes, a diving suit, flippers, a mask, a
snorkel, a ballast belt and a torch. In the
group were Patrick Granville, Gérard Sylvain
and Christophe Pietri.

I declare the above to be true.

The witness signed the original document,
which is appended.

Inspecteur de Police.
```

Maistre looked up at de Palma and waved the paper at him.

"There isn't much of interest here. But I do remember that, at the time, they said on television that the entrance was thirty-eight metres down, and he says twenty-five."

"At times like that, people often can't remember the details."

"If you say so . . ."

Maistre, doubtful as ever, continued to leaf through the pages. He came across a report by the Baron:

```
Observations on the body of PIETRI
Christophe, born 11/10/60 in Montpellier. 6
rue Ampère, 34000 Montpellier.

The body of the third victim was brought up
and taken in charge by the boat "La Bonne
Mère", from the Marseille coastguards.

It was transported to the port of Pointe-
Rouge for examination.

On board "La Bonne Mère" with coastguards, we
registered the presence of a man's corpse in
a bodybag.
```

He was already dead. Caucasian type. Dark
brown hair. Dressed in a blue diving suit.
The coastguards gave us the objects found on
the victim: diving cylinders, almost empty.
The first one registered 0302685, the second
0304726. The coastguards indicated that when
he was found, the tanks' valves were set
in the parachute position. Two flippers, a
snorkel, a mask, a knife and an ascension
parachute.

All of these objects were taken in charge by
the team of the 8th Arrondissement, before
being deposited at the headquarters of the 9th
Arrondissement of Marseille.

A requisition was made and the body
transferred to Saint Pierre morgue at 19.40.

Inspecteur Divisionnaire.

Further on, Maistre found another report drawn up by the Baron.
It was briefer than the others:

DE PALMA Michel
Inspecteur Divisionnaire.

I declare that Doctor Claude MARCELLIN, of the
coastguards, examined the three bodies, and
for each delivered a descriptive certificate
in which he indicated that death occurred by
drowning during a scuba-diving expedition,
and that examination of the bodies revealed
nothing to contradict this fact.

Examination of the faces of Gérard SYLVAIN

```
and Christophe PIETRI showed that each of
them was covered with saliva, mucus coming
from their orifices, their eyes and mucous
membranes swollen.
```

"Hey, Michel, do we have to read all this stuff? It happened ten years ago."

De Palma rapidly flicked through the pages.

"You never know, Le Gros. I do remember that at the time there was something which surprised me. That's why I kept copies. Here, this is it. Listen, this is one of the coastguards talking:

```
The cave's entrance is approximately 1 metre
wide by 1.50 metres high.

We found one of the bodies about 13 metres
down the tunnel of the cave. I must point
out that inside the cave there is zero
visibility.

The body was floating about 50 cm above the
bottom, its head turned towards the far end
of the cave, its feet towards the entrance,
facing the ground.

The diver no longer had the mouthpiece of his
regulator in his mouth. His lead belt had
slipped down and was around his knees.
He had no BC vest.

I confirm that when I found the diver's body,
visibility was about 5 to 10 cm and there
were no jutting rocks on which he might have
become stuck.

I found no torch on the body.
```

"What do you find surprising in all that?" Maistre asked.

"I don't know. But it did make me wonder. Why didn't he have a torch? Why was his lead belt around his knees?"

"You're right, it is a bit odd. But still, nothing to get into a fix about. Maybe his belt was around his knees because one of his companions tried to pull him backwards . . . And maybe he lost his torch earlier. The coastguard says you couldn't see further than 10 cm. How could he find his torch in such a soup? So what are you trying to prove, Baron? That these diving accidents are linked to today's murders. You're losing the plot. It was all ten years ago."

"You never know!"

"There's one thing I do know. You need some rest and relaxation. Go and see your wife. Tell her you love her, and that's all there is to it."

"A serial killer, Jean-Louis . . . "

"In that case, it's a job for the gendarmerie. I know how you feel. You're a hunter. A big-game hunter! An obsessive investigator. It's all you have in your life. But Jesus, just for once, slow down a bit! You're forty-seven, for crying out loud! In ten years' time you'll retire and it will all be over. So concentrate on your prehistory lecturer and tell the rest to fuck off."

Maistre leaped up like a wild cat and went over to his friend.

"As a matter of fact, I know why you want to join up all these cases!"

"Why's that?" de Palma mumbled.

"Because you want to nobble some psychopath. You've often talked to me about good and evil and all that claptrap. I know your theory: the bad side of human nature; we're all monsters deep down, and the only difference between the nutters and us is a padlock in our heads, locking the door on our impulses. I know you want to nail the loony, like you nailed Ferracci. And I know why! It's personal business, let's put it that way . . . What you're thinking is: 'At last, someone worthy of my abilities!' But you're barking up the wrong tree. I repeat, the *modus operandi* isn't the same! He can't have drowned those divers ten years back, killed your lady and massacred the other two, whose names now escape me. There are no recurring behavioural patterns. But you reckon that at last you're on to the master of murder! You're proud as hell and all you're thinking about is finding someone who's up to your own megalomania. Even if you have to bend the evidence!"

Maistre fell silent for a while.

"Just you watch it, Baron. I might not be around to cover for you! In fact, I won't be! I know you blew away that faggot Ferracci, like the piece of shit that he was! I'm not as thick as I look."

De Palma looked up. His friend was staring at him harshly, as his father had when he had behaved particularly badly. Maistre was right. To achieve serenity and harmony, he would have to abandon a part of himself. But that was impossible. Either you were born a big-game hunter, or you weren't.

"*In notte cupa la mente è perduta . . .*
E nell'ansia crudel vorrei morir"

"Come on, Jean-Louis. Let's go for lunch at my mother's. She'll be pleased to see you."

10.

At 2.00 a.m. on the morning of January 10, he slipped between the graves in Saint-Julien cemetery and reached the far wall. No-one could have seen him.

In one leap he was over the wall and beside the canal. The night was dark. He waited a while until his eyes became used to the darkness. The light from the lamp posts on place de l'Eglise glittered on the surface of the water, just enough to guide him and stop him from falling in. In the distance, he could hear the roar of a powerful car on its way up avenue Saint-Julien.

He set off without a sound, like a cat. After fifty metres he stopped and shrank into the high grasses. He could hear snatches of conversation coming from a house nearby. A man and a woman were arguing about their son's behaviour. Amused, he listened to them for a few seconds before moving on.

Ten minutes later he was standing outside what he took to be Julia's house – if his calculations were correct. He produced a tiny torch, shone it for a moment at the wall, then turned it off. It was higher than expected, but by standing on the trunk of an old bay tree, he managed to take a look over the other side.

Then he pulled himself up to the top.

A tall, bay window looked out over the garden, giving off a bright light. Despite the late hour, Julia was sitting on the sofa in her salon, reading a large, leather-bound book.

He climbed down from his observation post and sat in the moist grass. Julia was a night bird. She might hear him jump over the wall or see him in the light as he approached. He would not take that risk.

A hunter should never fail at the first attempt.

He switched on his torch and noticed a door in the wall, just a few metres away. He examined the lock for a moment and saw that it would open without too much difficulty.

The next day he came back with his tools: a flat screwdriver, two pairs of pliers and some thick wire. Ten minutes later, the lock gave way. He opened the door and found himself in a shed. A smell of old earth, dry grass and dust invaded his nostrils. He breathed deeply. This smell reminded him of hiding in the lean-to in his grandfather's garden when he was a boy.

He noticed a shaft of yellow light coming from what he took to be Julia's kitchen. It was past midnight, and Julia was still up. He came out of the shed, took a few steps into the garden and suddenly found himself surrounded by light. Julia had just turned on a lamp in the salon and was now sitting on the sofa, in the same place as the day before. He hid behind a box shrub and got his breath back. Despite the chill air, droplets of sweat were running down his cheeks. Violent shivers ran through his body. He pushed aside some branches and watched Julia. She had let her hair down and was wearing a dressing gown which revealed her white thighs.

A pain invaded his belly and crept down his legs. His eyes were hurting, as though they wanted to burst out of their sockets. The goddess spoke to him in her smooth voice: "The moment is not favourable, the spirits command you to wait."

In the distance, the cries of children. He wants to see, but the sun dazzles him. He squints, but can see only indistinct forms. He is alone at the bottom of the garden. He is always alone. Aloof from the others.

Suddenly, a firm hand pulls his shirt collar back. A first slap bites into his face, then a second even more violent one. He raises his arms to protect himself. Another slap. His nose starts to bleed.

A strident voice: "YOU LITTLE BASTARD . . . "

He closed his eyes to chase away the bad dream. The rhythm of his breathing accelerated.

The shaman holds at arm's length a hollow stone filled with reindeer fat. A straight, red flame rises up from the wick, ending in a thick line of black smoke.

The shaman stops for a moment, raises the lamp above his head, then lowers it. Once. Twice. The stone animals begin to dance at each movement of the weak light. A bison flees into the darkness, another emerges from the gaping hole.

Everywhere, hands are at work. The ghosts of the great hunters surround the shaman. He falls to the ground.

From the shadows rises the mysterious chant of the spirits. They come from the beyond the rock. From dream time.

All he had to do now was wait for the moon.

11.

"Do you know this woman?"

For the past two hours, Vidal had been going round Mazargues with a photo of Christine Autran. No-one recognised her. All the Baron had said to him was: "I'm going to Sugiton. You pick over Mazargues for me."

"What's her name?"

"Christine Autran."

The landlord of the Bar de l'Avenir, a fat moustachioed Italian, shook his head as he gave one last wipe to his chrome espresso machine.

"Never seen her before. There aren't that many women who come to my bar, and I know them all."

Vidal was nervy for a Monday morning. He had not slept much. That weekend's conquest, picked up on Le Prado beach, had taken him to a ragga party at a warehouse in the docks. This young police recruit, fresh from his native Aveyron, had found himself among hoodie-wearers rolling joints and writhing to the synthesised noise of a Massilia Sound System.

"*Le commando fada est avec toi . . .* "

He'd kept his leather jacket on all night to conceal his service Manurhin.

"*Commando fada, c'est terrible!*"

Two spliffs later, Vidal was singing the praises of Olympique de Marseille and Provençal food – the city was beginning to take him in its embrace.

"*Le commando fada est avec toi . . .* "

He and the girl had parted at about 6.00 a.m. As they said goodbye, she touched the cold barrel of his 357. He'd had to come clean, but she just whispered: "Not now, phone me this evening."

"Commando fada, c'est terrible!"

That week he had found out a great deal about the victim: she was born on April 4, 1957, in Versailles, to Pierre Autran – a civil engineer, deceased 1970 – and Martine Combes – a housewife, deceased 1982. Her father had been transferred, and the family moved to Marseille – from where the couple originally came – and set up home at 36 rue de la Bruyère in Mazargues. Christine had left school in 1975, lived at 23 rue Falque in the town centre, before finding lodgings in Aix – address as yet unknown – and then rented a flat on boulevard Chave, her last known address.

Vidal had been into all the shops on rue Emile Zola and boulevard de la Concorde. Nothing. It was nearly 12.00, and all he had left was the Autran family's former address. As he turned into rue de la Bruyère, he saw two old boys sunning themselves like lizards, sitting back to front on wicker chairs with their weary arms supported by the backrests.

"Good morning, gentlemen," Vidal began, trying to sound as pleasant as possible. "Sorry to disturb you, but I'm trying to find out about some people who lived in this street over twenty years ago, the Autran family. Does the name mean anything to you?"

One of the old men looked at him with suspicion, his face etched with wrinkles.

"Are you from the police?"

"Murder squad, I'm investigating a homicide."

"Really?"

"Christine Autran has been murdered."

The old boy stood up hurriedly and stared at the policeman.

"Murdered, you say?"

"Yes, it was all in the papers."

"I haven't read a paper in years . . . I can't believe it! Such a lovely little girl!"

"I'm sorry."

"The Autrans lived there, at number 36, next door to me. We were neighbours. But that's going back a bit."

"And you are Monsieur . . . "

"Allegrini, Dominique."

"And you, Sir?"

"Robert Libri, but why do you need to know?"

"Don't worry, it's just for the report."

Maxime took a long look at number 36. It was a two-storey '30s house, flanked by a couple of crooked pines and a Judas tree. The shutters were closed.

"The Autrans had a lovely house!"

"Oh yes, they were a good family," Allegrini replied. "The father was a civil servant, but high up. He was a big cheese."

"Did you have much contact with him?"

"Not really. He wasn't much of a talker. We knew his wife better. She's dead now too, but a long time after him. I can't really remember any more. It was all so long ago."

"What about you, Monsieur Libri?"

"I didn't know them. I don't live here. I'm in rue Enjouvin. I must have seen them from time to time, but I can't remember."

"They weren't like us. They spoke very little, except to say good morning and good evening. But I do remember that the father died falling off a table. He was trying to change a light bulb and he fell."

"That was in 1970?"

"Yes, at the latest. At the time, I was still working in shipbuilding, and that was a long time ago. We hardly saw them after that. The girl moved away, and then her brother died. He'd been ill for some time . . . No, we never used to see him."

"So only the mother was left?"

"That's right. She died later on, in a car accident. There was hardly anyone at the funeral, except for the daughter. I remember my wife went."

"Can I see your wife?"

"If you want, but she's as deaf as a post."

The old boy slowly turned round.

"Lucienne! Hey, Lucienne!"

An old Corsican woman, dressed in black, appeared on the threshold.

"Do you remember the Autrans?"

"Of course I do, we were neighbours."

"There's a police officer here asking questions. Apparently the daughter's dead, murdered."

"Good heavens!"

Lucienne raised her hand to her forehead. She tried to say something, but was overcome with sadness. She took a handkerchief from the pocket of her apron and dried her eyes.

Vidal approached her and introduced himself. Lucienne stared at the ground.

"Christine was a sweet girl . . . for her to die like that . . . Lord, I can picture her standing there . . . "

Huge tears rolled down her cheeks.

"Monsieur Autran was a good man, he really was! He took good care of his children. Every weekend he took them camping in the creeks. My God, the poor little things. I can just see them there with their rucksacks and big boots."

"What about his wife?"

"She wasn't a good woman. She didn't look after her children properly. How can I put it? She was very strict with her son – all that mattered to her was her daughter. She disciplined her boy as though he were in the army. Even though they were twins."

"Really, they were twins?"

"Yes, but what does that matter?" Lucienne said, waving her arms. "As far as I'm concerned, she ignored the fact that she had two. All she wanted was a daughter, so she mistreated her son. God save her soul, she wasn't a good woman."

"All the same, you went to her funeral."

"Yes, of course!"

"My wife goes to all the funerals in the neighbourhood!" observed Dominique Allegrini.

"Do you remember that day?"

"Her funeral? There weren't many others, apart from her daughter Christine and me."

"What about her son?"

"That was the day Christine told me he was dead."

"Do you know what he died of?"

"An illness, I think, but I don't know what was wrong exactly. He became ill after his father died, then things went from bad to worse."

"While Madame Autran was living here alone, did she have any visitors?"

"Not as far as I know."

"Did her children come to see her?"

"Hardly ever. Christine came from time to time, but never the son. I remember, when his father died, he was sent to boarding school. I don't think he ever forgave her. You know, twins shouldn't be separated like that."

"Is there anyone living at number 36 now?"

"Yes, the Alessandri family. An old couple like us. But they're not here at the moment."

"Do you know when they'll be back?"

"After the winter, as always, sometime in May. They always spend the winter at their house in Corsica, on Ile Rousse. When the tourists arrive, they come back to Marseille. Do you want their phone number?"

"Why not? You never know."

Lucienne disappeared into her house for a moment, then re-emerged with a piece of paper, on which she had carefully noted down the Alessandris' address and phone number in old-fashioned handwriting.

"It's come back to me. The boy's name was Thomas."

"Thank you."

"I can't believe she's dead just like that. Do you know how . . . "

"No, for the moment we don't know anything."

"What a shame. Oh lord, what a shame!"

Thirty minutes later, Vidal arrived at 23 rue Falque, in the centre of Marseille. This time, he was not so lucky. No-one there remembered a young woman called Christine Autran.

Standing motionless on a beak of limestone which jutted out from the Sugiton pass, de Palma could not believe his ears. For a quarter of an hour he had been listening to Sugiton creek echoing with a strident cry. Someone with less keen hearing would have heard nothing above the vulgar screeching of yellow-legged seagulls in the air above the rocks.

It was a fine Monday morning; there was scarcely a breath of wind and the sun beat down on the white rocks, bringing out subtle fragrances from the small celadon leaves of the sandwort which mingled with hints of pine, the scent of thyme and a number of other unidentifiable elements. Below, between the promontories of grey and white rock-faces, the sea stretched out like a vast oil slick as far as the opposite shore of the Mediterranean.

De Palma had decided to go to the site of the murder alone, one hour ahead of the team from forensics. He turned towards the surrounding walls of Sugiton creek and once again heard that strident cry. It was a Bonelli's eagle. His father had taught him to recognise it during the days they had spent walking among the creeks.

He took the downward path and, a few minutes later, stood facing Le Torpilleur, just opposite where the coastguards had found Christine Autran. He sat down to think. A diver friend had told him that there was no current at this point, which led him to conclude that Christine had been thrown into the water from the shore. He had an inexplicable feeling that she had not come by boat. She couldn't have.

"Why would she have come here by sea?" he repeated out loud. "It would take longer, for one thing. And then landing here . . . "

The forensic surgeon had found some round pebbles in Christine's jacket pocket. De Palma had an idea about that. He made his way around the creek, from rock to rock, then leaped down to the spot where the murder was supposed to have been committed: the beach was indeed covered with the same pebbles rounded slowly by the sea into perfect shapes. The fact that some had been found in Christine's pockets could have meant that she had been dragged along head first.

He sat for a while on the edge of a rock. Nothing occurred to him. Not the slightest trace of anything at all, apart from the certainty of seeing the same scene as the victim. He was sure that Autran's killer had placed her body here on purpose. Like a sort of rendezvous. He wanted her to be found.

But the body had been found a month later. Why not before? There were plenty of walkers, especially at weekends. She had been half devoured, so she must have spent a long time in the water.

Something did not fit.

Down below, thirty metres above the seabed, was Le Guen's Cave. There was a connection between the cave and the murder. The victim and the killer knew each other. Maybe even very well. They knew the creeks like the backs of their hands. But why?

These were the beginnings of a logical hypothesis. But still he felt powerless. And he didn't like it. The creek had taught him next to nothing. He knew that he had to find the answer to just one question: why had Christine Autran come here?

The entrance to the cave was underwater. Otherwise, just rocks, cliffs, fallen stones, this beach of gravel . . . Nothing of interest to a prehistorian out for a stroll.

Nothing.

The gulls were still haranguing each other. Some of them had landed a few metres behind him and strutted about with petulant, distrustful expressions. Their white, impeccable outfits made them look like a gang of Mafiosi at a conference for organised crime. What ill deeds were these seaboard mobsters plotting?

Christine Autran came here. With an objective. A clear plan. That had to be the case. She did not come here by chance. Her killer knew she was coming here. Either she had told him, or he followed her.

So why didn't he kill her before? Among the rocks? Or elsewhere, at her home, in the street . . . But a different location would have been impossible because he could not have transported her. Apart from that, he had wanted to take something to its logical conclusion, or check something else. For example, what Christine had come here to do. Yes . . . that's it.

A Bonelli's eagle glided above a ridge in supple, fluid flight, then corrected its direction with a twitch of its wings to find one of the few thermals on this windless day. It was carrying something in its claws, presumably a mouse which had not had time to hide under the scree. After a broad sweep, the eagle headed for its eyrie, where its ravenous nestlings were waiting.

And what about Franck Luccioni? The forensic surgeon had declared that it was a diving accident – it appears it was a fake, a grotesque piece of subterfuge. But why in the same place?

Is it the cave? Had Luccioni intended to go into it? De Palma had checked with a marine archaeologist at the D.R.A.S.M., la Direction des recherches archéologiques sous-marines, and had been told that it was impossible to enter Le Guen's Cave. Ab-so-lute-ly, the specialist had said.

That afternoon, Vidal was going to pay Charles Le Guen a visit. Maybe the diver would be able to supply some additional information about all of this.

It had been eight years now. Eight years since anyone had gone into the cave . . .

He thought about the divers who had been found dead, about the rumours in the press and the libellous campaign against Le Guen and the scientists in Marseille. All those haughty opinions and scornful declarations. A spectrum of contempt. Le Guen had suffered terribly.

At the time the newspapers, and especially *Paris Match*, had told the story using numerous photos of hands, horses and bison and illustrations which showed how the sea had submerged that prehistoric Provençal world. De Palma thought to himself that he would have preferred to do Christine Autran's job instead of hunting down human game all year round.

The sea rolled over its secrets. It mocked the prehistory it had swallowed as it tickled the rocks covered with red and violet seaweed, the paradise of gobi, dartfish, cowardly dwarf crabs and razor-sharp mussels.

The gulls had come to rest on the superstructure of Le Torpilleur, like stiff-necked sailors on parade. They seemed to have calmed down for now, but anything would be enough to set them off again.

De Palma's gaze lost itself in the horizon. He did not understand a thing. He felt small and alone in this mineral world, which sent back a hazy reflection. There were only two things he could be sure of: that the victim knew her killer, and that Le Guen's Cave was at the centre of this affair. In other words, practically nothing.

He could hear the forensic technicians in the distance as they began their slow progression towards the far end of the creek. Glancing down at this far-off scene, he had the impression that there were three long tracks running from the foot of the cliff-face down to the sea. He clambered up on to another rock to get a better view. He was right: three barely visible lines crossed the centre of the beach from one side to the other. The gravel, which was finer at this point, had been turned over, and he could now see that it was not as level as elsewhere.

He was going to have to ask the technicians to inspect the limestone of the cliffs, especially the nooks where rain and violent winds had bitten into the soft rock, leaving tiny protrusions as sharp as needles. He was hoping that a hair or something else from the victim or killer, might have been trapped there.

"Autran was without doubt murdered here, and not by hanging, but leave that aside for the moment. Her body was dragged down to the beach and thrown into the sea. It then drifted over to Le Torpilleur. Luccioni was murdered here too, but in the water. The crime was then made to look like a diving accident. But why? If there is any connection between the crook and the scientist, it must be extremely tenuous. We were stupid not to look into Luccioni's case. But then we're always being stupid."

The boys from forensics arrived. De Palma got out his exercise book and sketched the scene as accurately as he could. He drew the cliff, the long tracks on the beach and finally the sea. In the imaginary blue he wrote: "Le Guen's Cave, 35 metres down."

The village of Les Goudes looked distinctly Sicilian: hostile and deserted, and hunched up in the harsh sunlight. At 3.00 p.m. Vidal went down towards the port, passing modest buildings crowded in beside the sea: two ancient bars, fish restaurants with signs which read "Authentic Bouillabaisse", and Charles Le Guen's diving club, which was closed.

He zigzagged between upturned boats and worn ropes. The sun glared off slabs of concrete, and Vidal thought of de Palma who must still be trudging around Sugiton creek. From behind a heap of nets, he heard the nasal sound of a radio; the air resonated with a hit from the

'60s. Two fishermen, presumably father and son, were pulling in their net and talking in low voices. They fell silent as Vidal approached.

"Good afternoon, Messieurs. I'm looking for Charles Le Guen."

"He's on his boat over there, at the end of the first jetty," said the older man, glancing at him with hostility.

Between two decrepit yawls, Vidal identified the boat belonging to the Grande Bleue Club, an old trawler converted for diving. A man of about fifty was giving a lick of paint to the fore rail. Vidal climbed on to the jetty and went over to Charles Le Guen.

"Good afternoon . . . Monsieur Le Guen?"

The diver turned round.

"That's me. Can I help you?"

"My name is Maxime Vidal, from the murder squad. I'd like to ask you a few questions."

Le Guen laid his brush on the pot of blue paint and looked at the policeman warily.

"Is it about the woman they found in Sugiton?"

"Exactly, did you know her?"

Le Guen slowly wiped his hands, put down his cloth and stood up. He was a short, stocky man, with a face weathered by the sea and the sun. A few grey hairs highlighted the blackness of his crew cut.

"I met Christine Autran when I first discovered the cave. She was just one specialist among many. And not particularly likeable."

He jumped on to the jetty.

"Did you see her again?"

"Off and on. She barely spoke to me. You know what these scientists are like . . . "

"What do you mean?"

"They're a shabby bunch. When they needed me, they made use of me, then after that, nothing. Apart from Professor Palestro, the other lot . . . "

"You seem angry with them. Did something happen?"

"No, nothing. They just froze me out. It was hard to swallow . . . "

"Especially when you'd made such a discovery!"

"Yeah, but they couldn't give a damn about me. All that mattered to them was their careers. Autran was no different."

Vidal glanced at the quay. The two fishermen had gone. The port looked more deserted than ever. The yachts rolled in the slight breeze.

"East wind," Le Guen remarked. "It'll blow up tomorrow morning. I don't know if we'll be able to go out this week."

Vidal took from his jacket a police photo of Franck Luccioni and handed it to Le Guen.

"What are you showing me now, some crook?"

"Do you know him?"

"I don't hang around with people like that."

"That's not what I meant. He was also a diver, so I thought you might have seen him. Am I mistaken?"

Le Guen took a long look at the photo and frowned.

"I think I may have seen him, but where? I couldn't tell you."

"His name was Franck Luccioni."

"Wasn't he the one they found by Le Torpilleur last summer?"

"That's right. How did you know that?"

"Word gets round in the diving world, especially when there's been an accident."

Le Guen took a few steps along the jetty towards the quay, where a man in blue overalls was waving at him.

"Afternoon, Loule. O.K.?" said Le Guen.

"I'm going to start on the crane . . . strip it down . . ."

"When?"

"Right away."

"About time!"

Le Guen placed a foot on the edge of his boat. He seemed more relaxed.

"At the time, I was bringing a group of divers back from Riou. We'd been diving beneath the cliffs . . . When we passed by Jarre, I spotted *La Bonne Mère* heading towards Cape Morgiou. I radioed them to ask if they needed a hand. They told me they didn't. That was it."

"But had you ever met Luccioni?"

"I think so. But I can't remember where."

Beneath his appearance of a placid sailor, Le Guen was a nervy type, and he was starting to get impatient. He went aboard his boat, picked up his brush and added a few drops of solvent to the paint. He looked up at Vidal with even more distrust.

"Do you ever get clients who ask you to show them the entrance to the cave?"

"Loads of them, every weekend. One of your colleagues phoned me up the other day, and I had another request only last weekend."

"Did you go?"

"No."

"Why, because it's dangerous?"

"No, it isn't dangerous, there's just nothing to see. People from the ministry put a grating and huge blocks of concrete over the entrance. There's no point going to look at that. What's more, you have to be a very good diver to get to the bottom at this time of year. You wouldn't imagine it, but the water is really cold at ten metres and deeper."

"So it's impossible to get into the cave?"

"Absolutely. After the final research session in 1993, they put up the blocks of concrete. You'd have to be pretty smart to get inside. They've put up a 'Keep out' sign!"

"Have you been to Sugiton recently?"

"I often go there."

"Were you there in early December?"

"Yes, for sure. When I take people to Les Pierres Tombées or L'Oule, I go that way."

"You didn't notice anything?"

"That's a strange question. There's just the sea!"

"Apparently Autran's body was in the water for a long time. It's strange no-one saw her."

"I went to Sugiton at the beginning of December, and I can assure you that there were no drowned bodies near Le Torpilleur then."

"You're sure?"

"Definitely. We dived all around it. We'd have seen her."

"Do you remember the date?"

"It was the first weekend in December. I can't remember the exact date."

"Did you return there later on in December?"

"No, I didn't. I go on holiday at that time of year. But I should be going back there next weekend, as long as there's no east wind."

Vidal handed him his card. Le Guen examined it, then put it in the pocket of his overalls.

"We're in the fog right now. If you hear anything, or notice anything, call me.'

"Yeah, O.K."

Le Guen crouched down, put a few more drops of solvent into his paint and watched Vidal walk back along the creaky jetty. As he stirred the royal blue liquid, he observed the police officer standing for a long while in front of an old rigger, a fifteen-metre-long wooden ketch, the only beautiful boat in the port of Les Goudes.

12.

The sea was relatively calm in the port of Marseille. During the night, clouds had moved across the sky. It was gloomy. Early that morning, a fine drizzle, whipped up by the sea breeze, had dampened the red roofs of the city.

Passing by Maire point, the east wind slapped *La Bonne Mère*, and a wave lifted the coastguards' ship starboard. The chief petty officer waited for a second wave, slid the bar between his hands and changed tack. *La Bonne Mère* picked up speed again to the rhythm of the current.

A larger wave flooded the bridge. De Palma raised the collar of his jacket and took shelter in the steer-house. Whenever he was on water he fell silent, in communion with this liquid element. Vidal was leaning against the partition of the cabin and looking at the frothing sea with half-dead eyes. He was as white as a sheet, and trying not to bring up the coffee and croissant he had had at Le Zanzi.

As they passed the islands of Plane and Jarre to starboard, the waves grew less insistent. Further off they could see Cape Morgiou. Vidal was about to go out for a breath of fresh air, but the chief petty officer stopped him.

"You could get swept overboard. If you're feeling sick, there are some plastic bags in the cupboard behind you."

Once beyond Jarre, *La Bonne Mère* began to dance furiously in the waves. Leaving the cliffs of Riou to starboard it headed towards Cape Morgiou, and twenty minutes later it was sailing into Sugiton creek in the shelter of Le Torpilleur. Vidal managed to hold out until then.

De Palma went to the bow of the boat. Two coastguards had just put on their wetsuits and were spitting in their masks to prevent mist forming when they were underwater.

"First of all," de Palma said, "check that the entrance hasn't been forced open in some way. Then, try to find any trace of attempted break-ins – torn seaweed, any other signs – and collect any unusual objects you find on the bottom. And don't forget to photograph everything."

The divers strapped their tanks on to their backs, adjusted their lead belts and checked their regulators by letting a little air escape. De Palma was about to add something, but the two men, equipped with powerful lamps, had dropped backwards into the sea.

The two forms went slowly down before they vanished into the grey water. A few moments later, only their air bubbles agitated the surface. They would be down for at least half an hour.

Another group of divers was preparing to explore the depths where Autran and Luccioni had been found.

"The slightest object could be vital," Vidal told them. "Pick up everything within a radius of ten metres. Even if it looks insignificant."

"That won't be easy . . . there are loads of rocks where Autran was found, and it's impossible to get between them."

"I know, I know . . . " said de Palma, resigned.

The chief petty officer pointed out the place where Autran's body had been fished out.

"She was there, under that darkish spike."

"What about Luccioni?"

"He was much farther out, at the end of Le Torpilleur, by that cavity over there."

"O.K., I see . . . " said de Palma as he turned to the divers: "Concentrate more on where Luccioni was found. That's where we stand the best chance of finding something."

"Why?"

"Because there must have been a struggle, a fight underwater . . . you can't drown a good diver like Luccioni just like that."

*

The first group of divers reached the entrance to Le Guen's Cave. In the beams of their lamps, they could see the huge blocks that marked the start of the tunnel. A solitary grouper had taken up residence between two concrete cubes, in a hole no bigger than thirty centimetres across.

Visibility was now down to a few metres. They saw hardly any fish. The storm had shaken everything up and there was still a lot of silt suspended in the water. The frogmen swam around the blocks several times, but nothing attracted their attention.

The entrance didn't appear to have been forced open. None of the seaweed had been torn away, and there were no marks of a pick or any other metal tool which might have been used on the gate or concrete. They each took a photograph of the site, then went down until their masks were almost touching the seabed.

Suddenly, the diver on the right signalled to his colleague and kicked his flippers: he had noticed that one of the blocks was coloured differently. It seemed less dark. Close up, he observed that the layer of marine deposits was finer than on the other blocks. He moved a little way off, took a photograph, then swam back up to it.

This concrete cube was right in front of the gate. Unlike the others, it was marked with several scratches, one corner had been broken off and it was clear that someone had tried to use a crowbar to move it.

The two divers took a few photographs, then enlarged the circumference of their investigations. But half an hour later they had found nothing else.

They began to come up, one decompression stop at a time.

Vidal sat on the bridge of *La Bonne Mère* in a sorry state. De Palma allowed himself to be rocked by the motion of the sea as he gazed at the little beach in Sugiton creek. From time to time, he looked up at the huge cliff that overhung it. He thought of the wall paintings that slept in that fortress of stone, of the truths it concealed and refused to divulge.

At the place where Franck Luccioni had been found, there was not much in the way of a seabed. The rock formed a shelf of about twelve metres by six, then fell away into the dark depths. The coastguards rapidly covered the surface of the shelf. Amid the dartfish and rainbow wrasse, they found nothing of any interest.

After about a quarter of an hour, they began to go down the rock-face side by side, separated by a distance of two metres. Five minutes later, the diver to the left spotted a metallic glint between two anemones. He swam over to it and saw the tip of a small torch poking out of a red actiniaria. Having taken several photographs from different angles, he delicately picked up the torch and stowed it in a net on his belt before joining his companion.

The dive lasted another half an hour. The deeper they went, the colder the water became and now it looked almost blue. When they reached the bottom, at a depth of forty metres, they searched the base of the cliff with a fine-tooth comb. Nothing. They swam a little further away from the undersea cliff and stayed two metres from the bottom aiming their lamps at the grey floor. Just then one of the divers spotted an underwater hunter's knife lying on a rocky mound. He took a photograph before placing it in his net. He then made a note of the exact position and looked at his watch: they had been down for almost three quarters of an hour. He signalled their return to the surface.

Aboard *La Bonne Mère*, the first two had already dressed in fleeces and given their report. Vidal noted down their conclusions before going back to the steer-house, his face reddened by the chill air.

Fifteen minutes later, two moving patches of colour could be made out in the grey water, before their shapes became distinct and the second group resurfaced.

Once on board, the divers put down their cylinders, took off their flippers and handed their nets to de Palma.

"We found them just below the location of the body. The torch was twenty metres down, and the knife right on the bottom, in other words just under forty metres. They hadn't been there for very long . . . there wasn't much deposit on them."

Vidal noted down these details at once. De Palma examined the torch and the knife for a few seconds, then handed them to his colleague, who placed them in two plastic bags.

"Not a bad find, Michel!"

"I hope so, son, I hope so."

"He might have lost them while fighting with Luccioni."

"Maybe . . . But it might be the other way round . . . "

The east wind softened abruptly. A few gulls let themselves be carried as far as the rock which overhung *La Bonne Mère*. They squinted at the crew, on the lookout for something to eat.

De Palma and Vidal debated whether to continue looking or go back. They would not have another chance like this for a long time. The investigating magistrate had already made a great deal of fuss about this diving trip, and it had taken a lot of persuasion to convince him. They decided to take the photos, torch and knife to forensics to see if they could be made "to talk".

As *La Bonne Mère* left Sugiton creek, the Baron leaned on the rail and gazed once more at the sea. All it sent back to him was a reflection of his own uncertainties. He looked up at the rocks and told himself that this creek would not teach him a thing. The truth lay elsewhere.

"The torch is a small model. A 'mini G 50', made by Triton, serial number 13269 6235 KL 349. Its beam is extremely concentrated and it is switched on by a simple twist of the top. It's powered by four AA, 1.5 volt alkaline batteries."

Lieutenant Richard from forensics rested his elbow on a large microscope, wrinkled his nose, and looked at de Palma and Vidal over the top of his half-moon glasses.

"It's the kind of lamp that you can hang off the strap of a diving mask," he said. "I've got one, and I use it for hunting. It means you can get a good view while keeping your hands free. Some divers wear two, one on each side . . . They work for about an hour, no more . . . as long as they have new batteries."

"Is that all?" de Palma asked.

"Hang on, Michel. This all takes time!"

Richard picked up the knife and examined it.

"This is a Lagoon Legend, by Seafirst. Serial number: K6-2216. A fine weapon and an expensive one . . . very expensive! They cost about 800 euros. The blade is fourteen centimetres long, the longest on the market . . . It has a double blade, with a notch for cutting lines . . . And a flexible handle, which is very comfortable to use . . . Stainless steel type 431 AISI, which never rusts."

"What about . . . "

Richard placed the knife on his work table next to some jars containing scalp samples.

"Not a single fingerprint or pubic hair, if that's what you mean. Nothing, my poor Michel . . . nothing at all. It's spent too long at the bottom of the sea."

"Can you give me a rough idea of how long it was down there?"

"According to what the coastguards have said, and the micro-organisms found on the knife's handle, it would seem logical to deduce that these objects were both lost in the depths four or five months ago, no more."

"No traces of blood? Zero?"

"Zero, boss . . . stop dreaming!"

The technician picked up the knife again and turned it in front of his eyes. Its top edge was slightly serrated.

"It's brand new. Not a scratch on it, nothing at all. The blade is perfect. This knife has never been used. Never. What's more, it's a recent model. It came out in May last year. The real innovation is the stainless-steel reinforcement at the end of the handle."

Vidal jotted down Richard's conclusions, then drew de Palma to one side.

"Do you want me to check out suppliers of diving equipment?"

"You're going to have to, son. You never know. We'll see about that tomorrow."

Richard held out the envelope containing the photographs taken during the dive.

"The quality isn't great, but you can still see the scratches on the large cube. It's obvious . . . "

De Palma looked at them for some time. With the tip of his pen, he showed Vidal the marks in the concrete.

"He must have tried to lever it with a crowbar," Richard said.

"Is that possible thirty-eight metres down?"

"Perfectly, Michel. Underwater, objects are in fact lighter."

Vidal fanned the air with the photos.

"But you'd have to be a really good diver to do things like that, wouldn't you?"

"Yes indeed, Maxime," the technician replied, sitting at his desk. "You'd have to be extremely good! I've been diving for ten years, but I wouldn't play at being a miner at that depth."

"Why not?"

"Too dangerous, Maxime . . . that kind of underwater work is for the experts. If you make the slightest mistake with the length of the dive, the decompression stops and what have you, you end up as fish food."

"All of which might explain Luccioni's death," mused de Palma.

13.

Christine Autran's flat on Boulevard Chave smelled musty. At 10.00 a.m., de Palma, Vidal and three technicians from forensics arrived for a thorough search.

The Baron headed straight for the prehistorian's study; he had decided to look at that first. He recognised the multicoloured folders. There were no messages on the answering machine, which raised his worst fears.

These were confirmed when he opened the first drawer. Empty. Nervously he opened two others. They were empty as well. The documents he had seen during his initial visit were no longer there. He tried to remember them: sketches, photos, topographical surveys, the sorts of things that would be important. Important enough for someone to break in despite the risk of being spotted by Yvonne Barbier. And yet the old dear had just told him that she had seen no-one and heard nothing. He assumed that the thief must have been familiar with both the flat and the old lady's nosiness. He had not even bothered to make his visit look like a classic burglary. He must have had the keys.

De Palma cursed himself in fury, but it was too late. The documents he had come to get, which were certainly vital evidence, had gone. Before leaving, he glanced around the study, then went into the small bedroom which served as a library. Hundreds of books were lined up before him. *Le Geste et la Parole* by Leroi-Gourhan, the same author's dictionary of prehistory, a collective work entitled *Art et Civilisations des Chasseurs de la Préhistoire*, Taïeb's *Sur la Terre des Premiers Hommes* . . . The books contained pink, green or red markers: A4 pages folded in half or in three on which Christine Autran had noted down observations and criticisms in her agitated handwriting. He came across *La Grotte Le Guen* by Palestro and Autran, a handsome, coffee-table book with a beautiful jacket and sumptuous colour prints. He sat down on a sky-blue Formica stool and began to leaf through it.

An overview of the creeks took up a double page. Cape Sugiton was a huge arc of cliffs jutting into the sea, then there were the white and rusty-red faces of La Triperie, the summits overlooking Morgiou and, in the distance, lines of limestone that stretched to the horizon.

On the next page, a drawing showed the same landscape thousands of years before. Men were hunting a monk seal on the seashore, a large deer was cocking a cautious ear, and there were horses and bison. The caption read: "The landscape of the Le Guen Cave in the era of Upper Palaeolithic man. The red circle marks the entrance to the cave. At the time, it lay seven kilometres away from the coast."

Two pages later, Palestro and Autran could be seen deep in conversation on the bridge of *L'Archéonaute*, the D.R.A.S.M. boat. Palestro appeared to be asking Christine about something which lay out of frame. A little further on, there was Palestro in a wetsuit, his hair dripping, posing beside Le Guen inside the cave. Intrigued and enthusiastic, de Palma skimmed through the text, cursing his lack of time. He also cursed his profession, which excluded him from all this.

He came across a chapter entitled "Nature, Man and Animals in the Era of the Le Guen Cave". On the left-hand page, there was a large image of horses with their hoofs in the water, as though crossing a motionless stream. The caption read: "The great horse mural. Samples of carbon pigment taken directly from the paintings indicate a date of approximately 18,000 years ago."

As he flicked through the pages, he saw bison, aurochs and a large black horse painted on the ceiling. Palestro and Autran had included drawings to explain how prehistoric men went about painting the walls and ceilings of their decorated caves.

Vidal interrupted his reading.

"Do you want us to take anything with us, Michel?"

"I've no idea. Let's see if there's anything, maybe a piece of paper slipped into one of these books."

"That'll take hours! There are papers everywhere."

"What do you expect me to say? What about you, have you found anything?"

"Nothing of real interest. Various fingerprints. Some are comparable. Others not. But we think they may belong to just two people. It's merely a theory at this stage. It's as though only two people ever came here."

"That's far from nothing!"

"You think so?"

"It tells us a lot about our lady's character, and the fact that she invariably entertained the same person. Where did you find the second prints?"

"More or less everywhere. In the kitchen, the salon, the loo . . . Everywhere."

"An intimate friend, then. We'll have to take this further. Anything else?"

"No, apart from the answering machine . . . No messages, which is odd."

"What do you conclude from that?"

"It bugs me. I have the impression that someone came here before us."

"Exactly, my boy. On my first visit, I thought exactly the same thing."

"Really?"

"The worst of it is that since then I've phoned five times leaving messages saying that I was a friend or a student . . . at various times, which I noted down."

"When was the last time?"

"The day before yesterday, at midnight . . . "

"So we can conclude that our man, or woman, has been here in the past twenty-four hours."

"Brilliant, Vidal! You're starting to turn into an ace!"

"O.K., Michel, leave it out. I haven't got your experience."

"It will come, kid. Just try and surprise me."

"We'll have to check out all the people who have called this number. And then see if anyone has phoned from here."

"Now you're talking . . . What else? In your opinion, why did our visitor erase the messages?"

"Because they pointed to him. Because the person who broke in here obviously killed Christine Autran. Otherwise he wouldn't have bothered."

"You're right. Feelings of guilt pushed him into making a mistake. Because a mistake it certainly is. There was no reason for him to erase the messages again, after I'd dropped by, because he couldn't have called his victim. It was a stupid, reflex action – the sort of error that people make when they are so methodical that they lose their common sense. They forget that a crafty old sod like me can lay this kind of trap. So now he's condemned himself. Except that . . . "

"What? Aren't you sure?"

"Yes I am, but, you know, I always distrust things that seem too simple. Apparently we're up against someone who's incredibly intelligent. I wouldn't be surprised if all this wasn't meant to frame someone else. We'll check out the phone numbers."

De Palma went down to Yvonne Barbier's flat and asked her a few questions. She had of course heard the phone ring several times, but no other sounds of footsteps or doors closing. Nothing.

"When someone comes in, I inevitably hear them because the main door slams as it closes. Only regular visitors close it gently because they know it disturbs me. But I still hear it. I've lived here for more than sixty years, so I know all the sounds in this place."

"Think carefully, Madame Barbier. Can you remember a man or a woman who came here frequently? A friend or acquaintance of Christine's?"

"Of course. Last time I told you that she never saw anyone. But, in fact, that's not quite true. He hasn't been around much for about a year now, but he used to come regularly enough."

"Who do you mean?"

"Professor Palestro. He never spent the night here, but I think that he and Christine . . . There are some noises you can't mistake. Or else silences. As you like."

"Really?"

Yvonne looked as inquisitorial as Louella Parsons.

"Oh yes. Don't you know what I mean? Anyway, I believe he really was in love with her, but she didn't give a damn. All that interested her was her career. Period. Palestro was just part of her game plan."

"Thank you, Madame Barbier."

De Palma went down to the entrance of the building, then opened and closed the heavy oak door several times. Sure enough, it slammed loudly if not prevented from doing so. However, it was also possible to close it without Madame Cerberus upstairs hearing a thing.

14.

The Vieux Scaphandre was as much a symbol of Marseille as its boats and wood-fired pizzas. It was the town's oldest, best-known, and best-stocked diving store. Vidal pushed open the door and immediately felt as though he was walking into a cartoon. To his right, he was welcomed by a mannequin dressed in an ancient deep-sea diving outfit, its orange colour partially bleached by years in the sea. Vidal was intrigued and stared at its face through the meshed window of its bronze helmet, then looked down at its lead-soled shoes.

"Can I help you, sir?"

"Good morning, Maxime Vidal, murder squad . . . "

Gilbert Simian, the shop's owner, propped his glasses up on his bald pate and looked at Vidal with eyes as round as marbles.

"You're from the police?"

"That's right. I'm investigating a disappearance."

"Really?"

With a wave of his hand, Simian beckoned him into the back of the shop.

As they passed a display case, Vidal noticed the same type of knife as had been found in Sugiton. A collection of flippers of every conceivable colour were piled up any old how on some shelves. Below them, two fluorescent yellow and blue wetsuits dangled from hangers, with large labels pinned to them: "Special Offer".

The office was in the same apparent mess.

"So, how can I be of help?" Simian asked.

"Well, I want to know if you sold a diving knife and torch with the following serial numbers."

Vidal handed him a piece of paper.

"What makes you think they were bought here?"

"You're the best-known shop, that's all."

Simian grimaced, pursing his lips.

"For the 'Lagoon Legend', it won't be difficult because I don't sell that many. But for the torch . . . "

"So start with the knife."

"I don't have a computer. I don't know how to use them. Otherwise, it would be quicker! And as I don't keep customer records . . . "

Simian stood to open a decrepit cupboard. On top of it stood a huge, scale model of a clipper in full sail, measuring about a metre long.

"Here, I still have all the bills since last May. I say 'May' because that's when the knife came out."

The owner of the Vieux Scaphandre looked about sixty and spoke with a heavy Marseille accent. The skin of his hands and face had been weathered by the sea. Two deep lines furrowed his forehead.

"There . . . I sold two 'Lagoon Legends' . . . one on May 20 and the other on August 30 . . . and you say the serial number was K6-2216?"

"That's right."

"Here's a copy of the guarantee . . . you're lucky, it was a customer who has an account here! His name's Franck Luccioni."

Simian pushed his glasses on to his forehead and sat up in his chair. His eyes searched Vidal's.

"Wasn't Luccioni found dead at Le Torpilleur?"

"Exactly . . . "

"Goodness me! But just now you told me you were investigating a disappearance."

"We can't reveal everything . . . "

Simian's hand flopped heavily on to a stack of bills. Vidal remained impassive.

"You also asked me about the torch . . . "

"Indeed."

"That could take some time. It's a very popular model . . . "

"Look at the same period. You never know . . . "

"I'll try a different way . . . I'll take a look at the stock book."

He went back to his cupboard and removed a file covered with stickers of various brands of diving equipment. After a few minutes, Vidal stood up and paced around the store. On a noticeboard, several small ads offered trips out to sea. Beside them was a poster for the Le Guen Cave exhibition, going back to the time when it was first discovered. Vidal read the large letters printed on a negative hand: "The Frescoes of Silence. The Treasures of Le Guen's Cave".

Then Simian's voice called out from his office:

"O.K., I've found it!"

Vidal returned to the room.

"It was Luccioni as well. It's lucky he had a customer account, otherwise we'd never have found the name! There you are, he bought it on March 15."

Vidal wanted to ask him a few questions about lifting blocks of concrete under water, but he restrained himself. He produced a photo of Luccioni.

"Did you know him?"

"No, he was a customer, that's all."

"Did he come here often?"

"Quite often, yes. He bought a lot of things here: crossbows, masks, a knife . . . He was a good customer!"

"Nothing else?"

"No, nothing . . . "

Simian looked sorry as he shook his head.

"He was a good diver, was he?"

"To judge from the equipment he bought, he must have been very good. He must have done underwater pot-holing too. When I looked through my bills just now, I noticed that at the beginning of last year he bought a 20-watt lamp and a T 25, a superb lamp with two Xenon bulbs and a revolver grip. It can last for up to four hours . . . a marvellous piece of kit!"

"What would equipment like that be used for?"

"For anything, just to see underwater . . . "

15.

De Palma emerged from the Prado-Carénage tunnel at 9.30 a.m. A dull light had settled on the dome of La Major and was creeping down its salt-eroded Byzantine walls. On the horizon, the sky had lined up small mouse-grey clouds; winter rain, fine and steady, was on its way. Stuck in a traffic jam just a few metres from headquarters, the Baron waited patiently. He lit a Gitane and watched as the lights on the upper decks of the *Danièle-Casanova* gave in, one by one, to the new day.

A quarter of an hour later, he pushed open the door of Le Zanzi, shook a few hands and sat down beside Vidal who was reading *La Provence*, his nose between the crumpled pages. The Baron roused his team mate from his usual morning lethargy by tapping his finger on the front-page headline:

JEAN-JACQUES SARLIN GUNNED DOWN
OUTSIDE HIS HOME

"So, kid, aren't you interested in gangland bastards when they get whacked?"

"Hi, Michel. He's the second one this year . . . "

"They have to die of something, don't they? A work accident!"

"Did you know Sarlin?"

"Of course I did. People say that he gunned down half of Marseille at the beginning of the '90s. He'd just come out of prison. Eight years for a burglary in the north of France."

"Lulu and Jean-Pierre have gone from headquarters to pay homage."

"Those two just love executions. They know they won't be up all night trying to find out who killed who and why. They just have to say that they're working on it but the going is tough. That's all. Then Paulin's happy, Duriez doesn't give a damn, and the press count the bodies. Anyway, the gangland has gone. It's all gambling syndicates now . . ."

"Who knows . . ."

"Two out of twenty-three executions solved in the last two years. Pretty good statistics! And even then, when they come up for trial, the defence attorney will pull the case apart like a set of Lego. No proof, only tapped phones and plenty of explanations. I can just picture them yammering away in the witness box."

De Palma took quick sips of his coffee under Dédé's weary gaze.

"Why are you looking at me like that, Dédé?"

"Because you drink your coffee with a stiff little finger, like a real baron."

"I *am* a real baron, never forget it."

De Palma turned towards Vidal.

"Right, kid, stop reading all that crap about Sarlin. Time to go."

A few minutes later the two men were in their office.

"How about a little sitrep?"

"About time."

Since his first visit to Autran's apartment, de Palma had been wondering about the total absence of family souvenirs: not one object, not a single photo, nothing. No trace of her past at all. It was as if the prehistorian had systematically destroyed any vestiges of her childhood and adolescence. He had never before encountered such a void. He was finding it impossible to think his way into the victim's personal life, and this made him feel uneasy. He did not like being in the dark about the past histories of the corpses he dealt with. There could be only one explanation: Christine must have suffered in her youth and she had drawn a line beneath the entire period.

"So, Maxime, have you found out anything about her?"

"I've had problems discovering what she did when she was young. Her father died in 1970 and her mother in 1982. She left school in 1975 and went to university. She moved from Marseille to Aix. I have all her addresses except those in Aix. Apart from that, not much."

"Obviously, twenty-five years on . . . It's almost the year dot!"

"As I said, the old couple I met didn't tell me much, except that her father died an accidental death, while changing a light bulb . . . he fell straight on to his head. That's pretty original! Then her mother died in a car crash."

"And does that all sound odd to you?"

"I dunno. The couple told me that the father was an engineer and adored his children. But, according to Madame Allegrini, she didn't really have the ideal mother."

"Well, nothing exceptional there . . . not a thing to go on. Didn't she have any other family?"

"No, except for a twin brother. But he's dead, too. Madame Allegrini couldn't remember when. Just that it was before the mother died."

"Her neighbour on boulevard Chauve told me that she never had any visitors."

"So for the neighbourhood investigation it's not a great start," sighed Vidal. "Do you want me to keep at it?"

"No, not for now. I don't think it's that important. We'll probably find out more at the university. I'm going to call on a few people, her close colleagues first of all."

"Maybe they'll know something about her past."

"I doubt it. I reckon Autran had completely broken with her youth. There's nothing in her flat, not a single photo of her parents or of school. Nothing. I've never seen anything like it. A real blast of cold wind!"

"Yeah, I know."

"Get in touch with everyone in her address book. Check their phone numbers. Have you got the report from the creek? You know, the investigation they did on dry land which they should have given us ten days go . . . "

Vidal handed a file to the Baron, who opened it and flicked through it for a few seconds.

"As usual, the buggers didn't find anything more than I did. Not a single pube."

"I know, I read it last night."

"Did you get me everything on the stiff at Aubagne?"

"I put it on your desk, it's right there in front of you."

De Palma laid his hand on the file and stood up.

"I think the first thing to do is to look into her adult life. Who she hung around with when she was a student. Who she worked with. Her life and works! And her sex life, too. That's vital."

"What about the torch and the knife?"

"You did a good job there, but that's Luccioni. We're not on that case, and don't you forget it! Our darling Commissaire is going to ask us to report on Autran, not Luccioni."

"But can't we say that there's a connection?"

"In my opinion, there's more than just a connection. But keep that to yourself. We'll have to convince the public prosecutor to open an investigation. Then we'll have room to manoeuvre."

Anne Moracchini came into the office, her face still damp from the rain. A dark lock of hair stuck to her cheek which was glowing from the chill air.

"What time do you call this, my little Capitaine?" de Palma remarked, glancing at the stainless-steel clock.

"I was at Sarlin's place. You should have seen his wife!"

"She told you she didn't know why her husband had been whacked and then burst into tears."

"Of course. They're always innocent. You know that as well as I do! But it's a shame for the kids."

"Tell me, Anne, do you recall that woman at Aubagne?"

"Yes, I was the first person at the scene."

"Good, do you remember anything in particular?"

"No, nothing, except the missing bits. One leg was never found. Do you think it was the same person?"

"Why not! He cut off Weill's leg."

"But he didn't leave the same signature. In fact there wasn't one at all. No hand, remember? Generally they sign their murders in the same way."

"That depends. Sometimes things develop."

"Anyway, for the past year we've made no progress on Aubagne. All we've found out is the woman's identity."

"Agnès Féraud?"

"That's right. She was forty-three and lived alone. No family, nothing. Quite a sad existence!"

"Did you manage to find out anything about her past?"

"No, nothing at all, except what was in the report."

"I was just checking. I'll read it this afternoon."

"You want a coffee, Michel?"

"Oh yes, my lovely. I never say no to you. NEVER, understand?"

"Cool it, Michel."

That afternoon, Vidal and de Palma put together the few pieces of information they had gleaned. The fingerprints found in Christine's car probably belonged to a man. They did not match those in her flat. Computer records had shown up nothing.

Of the information gathered by Vidal in Mazargues and Les Goudes, only one thing really interested them: according to Le Guen's statement, Christine's body had not been in Sugiton prior to December 6. Apart from that, nothing.

Then there was the information about Luccioni. De Palma said they should be patient. He did not want to proceed any further until the state prosecutor had been convinced of the value of their investigation. They would have to wait for the right moment, when the two cases would converge of their own accord.

They spent the rest of the day going through Christine Autran's finances. They did not find out very much. No suspicious movements of money had taken place. Her lifestyle had not changed all of a sudden.

From France Telecom, Vidal had obtained a record of every call that had been made in the past two months. The most frequent were from de Palma himself, who had rung five times, and Palestro, with eight calls in late November and early December. Apart from that, there were very few. But what puzzled the young officer were the calls from phone booths scattered across most of Marseille.

De Palma and Vidal took this extremely seriously. They tried to pinpoint the booths on a map. The result showed that they really were spread out all over the place. With no apparent coherence.

"Tell me, Vidal, do you notice anything?"

"Come on, beat me up again, Michel."

"Don't be daft. Are we working together or aren't we?"

"Sometimes I feel a bit out on a limb . . . "

"O.K., what about the calls from Palestro?"

"They stop at the presumed moment of Autran's death."

"Spot on."

"But that doesn't make him guilty. We won't get very far with that in court."

"If he stopped phoning, it's because he knew something. I'm sure of it. And it does make him a suspect because theoretically he couldn't have known she was dead until he read about it in the papers."

"Yes, but we're not sure about the date she died. There's a possible span of almost ten days. He might have stopped phoning when he realised that she'd disappeared, after a couple of days. And in fact that was about the time she was declared missing."

"I know, I know. I'm just trying to build up a scenario. Otherwise, we'll get nowhere."

"O.K., but we might end up in a dead-end, and zilch!"

"I'm going to see the famous Professor Palestro tomorrow. I'll try and discreetly take his prints. Who knows?"

16.

De Palma left La Capelette at 8.00 a.m. To get to Aix-en-Provence, he had to negotiate the huge four-lane boulevards linking the south of Marseille to the north motorway. He plunged into heavy traffic between the grey blocks built at the end of the '60s, then proceeded, bumper to bumper, along the metal flyover which snaked above the shabby neighbourhoods of Plombières and La Belle-de-Mai.

He opted to go widescreen: a plunging, panoramic view over the bay of Marseille. At the spaghetti junction at the end of avenue de la Capelette he headed directly into the flow of cars, and took the Prado-Carénage tunnel to avoid the morning congestion. Ten minutes later he was at La Major cathedral, just by headquarters. From there, the tentacles of the flyovers above the docks looked down on to the immense port to the left, and further out over the seawall to the Frioul archipelago. It was his favourite view.

Despite the sun, the temperature had plummeted. Official forecasts were even predicting snow. This was unusual for March. De Palma drove slowly, making the most of the splendid view. In Mourepiane harbour he noticed a huge crane dipping into the guts of a cargo ship to deposit a heavy, navy blue container. In the distance, the rising sun gilded the hills of L'Estaque, still covered by a light layer of mist from the night. He had time for one last glance at the landscape before diving into the half-light of the tunnel which ran beneath the heights of Marseille, and eventually reached the Provençal hinterland. The city's microclimate had no hold beyond the circle of rocks which surrounded it. The plain was covered with a fine frost, as though silvered over on the cheap.

The Baron had a noon appointment with Professor Palestro, Head of the Prehistory Department at the Université de Provence. The great man had asked him to be as brief as possible because he had to go to Italy that evening; he had been invited to a congress of prehistorians. Out of courtesy the Baron had requested permission to attend his lecture. The old fellow had replied in a jovial voice:

"Room 105 at 10.00 a.m. I warn you, it lasts two hours. But it's quite a general undergraduate course for students from other disciplines. It might even interest you!"

De Palma arrived early, to soak up the atmosphere and to penetrate Christine Autran's universe. He wanted to get to grips with that last Wednesday in November, the last day she had been seen alive. Professor Palestro had told him: "The prehistory department is at the end of the corridor facing the top of the main staircase."

A long, unheated corridor led away into the shadows, crowded with students silhouetted against a rectangle of grey light, the sole vanishing point in this closed-in universe. He made his way between the groups chatting outside the classrooms. At the end, he turned right, went through a fire-door and found himself in the prehistory department.

Some sections of wall had been repainted with dubious colours, with no apparent attempt to make them match, as though someone had wanted to finish off some pots of old paint. The university was still a decidedly stingy place: on some walls there was straw yellow beside bright orange and lime green; on others he could still see the original cream paint flecked with grey, even though it went back to the '70s. Noticeboards indicated the dates of the future exams. On one sheet printed with the university crest, de Palma read:

It is with great sorrow that the Chairman of the Université de Provence, the Director of the Faculty of History, the Head of the Department of Prehistory and its teaching staff inform you of the death of their friend and colleague, Christine Autran, aged forty-three. Her funeral will take place on Friday January 28 at 10 a.m. at Saint Pierre cemetery.

In this strict universe devoted entirely to the sweating of grey matter, de Palma suddenly smelled the notes of a sweet perfume. He turned his head a little and saw a woman aged about forty standing beside him. She was staring at the announcement.

"Did you know her?" de Palma asked.

"She was a colleague. I really admired her."

"Could you tell me about her?"

"Why, are you from the police, or are you a journalist?"

"Take your pick."

"If you're a journalist I'm not telling you anyhing."

"In that case, I'm from the police and I'll buy you a coffee. If you agree, of course. Just for a quarter of an hour. After that I have an appointment with Professor Palestro."

"Let's go then. I know a quiet little café just behind the university. And you are . . . ?"

"Michel de Palma, from the Marseille murder squad."

He reached for his card, but she stopped him.

"I believe you, officer. My name's Sylvie Maurel."

He followed her to a shabby bar, next to the railway which ran alongside the literature department. The place was owned by a beatnik who had seen better days.

"It's funny," she said, sitting down. "You don't look like one of them. More like an intellectual."

"How flattering. But I am one of 'them' really."

"Don't be offended. I've got nothing against the police. In fact, my grandfather was in the force. He was even a Commissaire. So, in a way, we're all part of the same family. Inspecteur de Palma has a good ring to it."

"We say Commandant now."

"Like in the American movies?"

"Exactly."

Sylvie Maurel was a tall, slim brunette with strong Mediterranean features which betrayed her Italian origins, despite her Provençal surname. Her face was narrow, with a small, pointed nose, high cheekbones and strikingly beautiful, large, dark eyes. As she sipped at her coffee with her full lips, she peered in amusement at de Palma, her eyes lingering for a moment on his mouth. To keep his cool, he took a slurp of coffee. Beneath her Irish sweater, he could make out her firm, unfettered breasts and the smooth skin of her stomach. Without really knowing why, he found himself thinking about Bérengère Luccioni, so fragile beneath her mobster's doll appearance. He looked at this self-confident intellectual who spoke so casually without a southern accent. He could so easily have loved these two women if his life had not set an enormous gulf between him and each of them. If there was no Marie . . .

"Could you tell me about Christine Autran?" he asked dumbly, to break the silence.

"She was an excellent researcher. She was passionate about what she did. I don't understand how this could have happened to her. I read in the newspaper that she'd been murdered. It's been a terrible loss for me, for our department and for prehistory studies in general."

Sylvie Maurel spoke without emotion, without the slightest hint of sorrow or grief in her voice. De Palma supposed she might be the kind of woman who can control herself perfectly, or else an egocentric monster who saw in her colleague's death a position which was now open to her. He decided to rattle her cage a little.

"It's funny, you speak about Christine as though you don't feel a thing. But just now you told me she was a friend."

"Yes, but you don't have to wear your heart on your sleeve all the time. Especially in front of a policeman."

The researcher was not as cold as she seemed. There must have been a reason for her sudden aggressiveness.

"Did you see her on Tuesday November 30?"

"Yes," she answered curtly.

"Do you remember anything in particular?"

"No, not really. We spoke for a while about the hearth found in Le Guen's Cave."

"The hearth?"

"Yes, Monsieur Policier, the place where they made fires," she said with a sneer.

"They made fires at that time?"

Sylvie Maurel smiled at his question.

"Yes, indeed. They weren't as thick as they look."

She smiled at him derisively, but she didn't appear to be mocking him. In fact she seemed to be smiling at herself, at her obscure studies which were of interest to hardly anyone. She wasn't mocking this policeman's ignorance.

"What was Christine Autran like as a teacher?"

"I don't know. I never attended her lessons. But I do know that she spoke without notes during seminars and they were extremely entertaining. She was certainly no bore. When she talked of her favourite subject, Le Guen's Cave, you felt like you were inside it. She was really impressive! Especially when you know that she never set foot in it."

Sylvie Maurel stared at the table and sipped her coffee. Her face was extremely beautiful, even without a trace of make-up.

"Do you often go diving, Sylvie?"

"Yes, why, is it written all over my face?"

"No . . . well, yes, a little. Your nose is slightly red. I bet you've got chronic sinusitis."

"That's right."

"What's right?"

"That I'm a diver and have chronic sinusitis, like everyone who goes diving regularly," she replied with a nod.

"And you often go diving with Palestro, I suppose?"

"Yes, generally in the summer. Last year he showed me two under-sea caves where he'd found flints."

"And Christine stayed in the boat," de Palma went on confidently.

"That's right. But so what? She always stayed in the boat. Sunbathing. She hated the water. Why are you asking all these silly questions?"

Sylvie Maurel's face flushed slightly.

"I just wanted to understand her psychology a little better," de Palma replied, as though apologising. "I saw some photos of her. She was very beautiful."

Sylvie seemed somewhat embarrassed. Her expression had changed. He had just touched a nerve.

"What does it matter to you if she got her bum wet or not?"

"It's far more important than you imagine . . . "

"Don't play mister know-all with me . . . "

"I'm not . . . Just don't take me for a fool. I'm not as thick as I look either. Here, take my card. Call me this afternoon. Without fail. I've got lots more questions for you."

De Palma tossed two coins on to the table and stood up, without listening to what Sylvie was saying.

"Last week, I spoke to you about Upper Palaeolithic man, or *Homo sapiens sapiens*, who is essentially represented by Cro-Magnon man. This species which, do not forget, cohabited with Neanderthal man, was in fact the first human! And this first human was surprisingly tall: between one metre seventy and one seventy-seven. Sometimes more. He could be as tall as one metre ninety or more."

Professor Palestro stood up and paced sonorously over to the edge of the podium, standing straight as a poker in front of his students. He looked amazingly young for his sixty-three years. Deep-sea diving had preserved him so well that he could easily have passed for forty: with his sportsman's physique, his easy smile and huge cultural knowledge, he was a man who must appeal to the ladies a great deal.

"He's as tall as I am, do you see? And he presents a mixture of modern and archaic characteristics – unlike me on that point – as you'll see later on the slide . . . But there's something else I'd like to add, and as my late lamented colleague, Christine Autran, and I have always emphasised, in western Europe there was also another type of human, the Combe Capelle man, who was shorter, standing at about a metre sixty-five. He was more widespread in central Europe, where he is often called Brno man. In my opinion, he could well have been the origin of the Mediterranean peoples. He would have been the first of us Provençals . . . Which perhaps, I repeat perhaps, explains a certain particularity in the Mediterranean art of the time. It features animals which look stiff, as though stuck on to their stone backing, with legs that end in sticks and no further detail. There was a real school here in Provence . . . This was also the opinion of Christine Autran. Poor Christine."

Palestro looked visibly moved. He tried to hide his grief by leaning on the back of his chair.

"During the course of the technological evolutions in the Upper Palaeolithic, around 18,000 years ago, a new industry appeared in western and central France, and more precisely to the west of the rivers Saone and Rhône. It was distinct from the Aurignacian and Upper Perigordian. And I can tell you that it sparked off a great deal of discussion about its origins. I am talking about the Solutreans, who were remarkable for their highly specific tools such as bifacial points, willow leaves and, to a lesser degree, bay leaves ... These tools had particularly elegant decorations, generally covering one or both of the faces. There have been various studies to find the origins of this beautiful industry, and it is now thought – and I share this view – that it was autochthonous in France. The Solutrean then suddenly disappeared, to be replaced by the Magdalenian. This was the zenith of Palaeolithic civilisation, a particularly brilliant period which developed during the course of the last phase of Wurmian glaciation. Or, to be more precise, Dyras I and II between the interglacial periods of Lascaux and Allerod, in other words between 15,000 and 9,000 years B.C.E. Of course, as you all know, here in Provence we have one of the finest examples of this stunning civilisation, Le Guen's Cave, in the creeks by the city of Marseille."

Palestro lectured for an hour. De Palma listened to him, gripped by this teacher's generous voice and attentive as a kid suspended on every word of a beautiful yarn. When he heard: "Now, shall we have a short break?" he emerged from his reverie. Palestro looked at him and motioned him over. The policeman walked down the steps.

"Good morning, sir. You're here earlier than expected."

De Palma shook the hand which the prehistorian was warmly offering him. It was firm, muscular and a little rough. A real sportsman's handshake.

"And I've learned a lot," said de Palma.

"The second part is far more interesting. I'm going to show them some slides. Many of them were taken by Christine, you know," he said sadly. "After that, we can have a quiet chat in my office."

Palestro disappeared down the corridor. Five minutes later he was back, his arms weighed down by boxes of slides. They closed the curtains in Room 105.

"We shall now devote the second part of the lecture to a study of Marseille's coast and, to conclude, Le Guen's Cave."

Palestro's face was lit up from below by the projector, making him look like a devil. He pressed the remote control, and a metallic click cast light on to the screen. The slide brought together flints of assorted sizes.

"Here, then, are some typical characteristics of the industries of the Upper Palaeolithic. At the top, the flints numbered from 1 to 8 are Aurignacian; from 9 to 13 Gravettian; from 14 to 17 you will notice a slight evolution, they are from the Solutrean, while 18 to 22 are Magdalenian."

Palestro leaped to his feet and approached the screen. He passed his finger over the Solutrean and Magdalenian flints.

"Look at how finely they are cut. If you compare them with the ones in the top left-hand corner, which date to the Aurignacian, you will see what incredible progress had been made since the first man. But don't forget that everything is relative. Prehistoric time is not like our time. The Aurignacian pieces date to about 36,000 years ago, and the Magdalenian to 18,000. So the first men needed some 18,000 years to make this progress, which seems so slight to us. As for the Aurignacian, in Provence we have Baume-Périgaud – there we have found lots of scrapers, but very few burins. This is far from the case with the Gravettian and even less so with the Solutrean – named after Solutré in the department of Saône-et-Loire – where we have found many more articles and, of course, the Magdalenian, named after La Madeleine rock shelter in Dordogne. There, we have found assegais, harpoons with one or two rows of teeth . . . Plenty of flint tools . . . "

Palestro changed slides. They showed tools of far more elaborate shapes. De Palma listened. He had forgotten all about his investigation, the police, the public prosecutor who would soon ask him for a report, and Commissaire Paulin who wanted results.

Another slide.

"Here we have a perforated baton, a harpoon tip and an eyed needle. It was in fact during the Upper Palaeolithic that such tools first appeared. They allowed early man to practise new activities such as fishing and sewing, presumably for clothes made of animal skins, like for example the squirrel-skin tunics of the children in Grimaldi, Italy. The harpoon tip is the major invention of the Magdalenian, but we shall come back to it another time. On the left, there is a perforated baton whose use is not really understood: to hold an assegai perhaps, or the handle of a sling . . . it's a mystery. In any case, this one is made of bone, but others are made from the antlers of deer, generally of reindeer. Musical instruments were also made from bones, especially of birds, and whistles were carved from the phalanges of herbivores. As you can see, the first men took a leap forward, so to speak, during the Magdalenian. It has been said again and again that the Magdalenian is the apogee of prehistoric art. Just think of Altamira in Spain, Lascaux in Dordogne, Niaux in Ariège and, of course, Le Guen in Provence."

The next slide showed a cross section of Sugiton creek and the sea. The policeman in de Palma stirred and he observed the drawing. It was an ordinary vertical section of a cave.

"Here is the entrance through which the diver Charles Le Guen went into the cave. You might not be able to see it from this drawing, but the entrance is only one metre in diameter. Having been there myself, I can assure you that it's extremely scary. You have the impression of entering Purgatory. The tunnel is more than a hundred and fifty metres long, as you can see. And believe me, underwater that's a long way! Here is the sunken chamber, and here is where Le Guen found those famous paintings."

There followed images of positive and negative hands as he lectured on. He lingered for some time over a bison and some penguins. De Palma recognised the photo he had seen in Christine Autran's flat, but this one was of far better quality. He realised that Autran's photo must have been taken by an amateur. But why?

Then Palestro launched into a long presentation of the engravings in Le Guen's Cave. He showed the students a series of photographs taken using frontal lighting, and then with low-angle or oblique light sources. Each method revealed new shapes. The engravings, which initially looked uninteresting, slowly revealed the range of what they depicted. The professor had to admit that science had not yet been able to explain this type of engraving. He asked someone to open the curtains.

"See you next Thursday. We'll talk about all those famous hands in Le Guen's Cave."

Palestro took de Palma by the arm.

"Let's slip away, otherwise the students will corner me and we'll be stuck here for an hour."

The prehistorian's office lay on the far side of the faculty of literature, on the first floor, at the end of a corridor lit by windows as narrow as loopholes.

From his briefcase, Palestro removed an extraordinarily large bunch of keys, which he twisted around before picking out a bronze-coloured one. De Palma glanced at the various types of key. None corresponded to the lock on the door to Christine Autran's flat.

The office was spacious but terribly cluttered, with two grey metal tables facing each other. As he put down his case and files, Palestro indicated Autran's former desk with a wave of his hand.

"You know, it's rather untidy because we don't come here very often," remarked Palestro, to break the silence. "Christine was here only two or three times a week, on Tuesdays when she lectured, on Thursdays to see her postgraduate students. And sometimes on Monday afternoons."

"What did she do the rest of the time?"

"She often went to the marine archaeology laboratory in Marseille. It's in Fort Saint-Jean."

"What about the creeks?"

"She didn't go there to work. I know she particularly liked walking there. In fact, she knew them like the back of her hand. She preferred going on foot rather than by boat."

"And yet, you often took her with you, by boat."

Professor Palestro blushed. He stared at the floor, as though conjuring up the moments he had spent in his colleague's company, then he looked back up at the policeman. There was an expression of infinite sadness in his grey eyes.

Palestro clearly knew a number of things, but he was not going to talk that easily. He was psychologically smart, despite his apparently jovial behaviour and winning ways. He had had an affair with

Autran. It was obvious, despite all his attempts to conceal it. De Palma saw that this relationship must have been one-way. Autran had been an ambitious woman who did not burden herself with unnecessary emotions. The sort of person who only kissed those people she could not tread on.

"Did you notice anything odd before her death? The slightest detail might be important."

"No . . . I don't think so."

"Try to remember. It's vital. You didn't bump into anyone you didn't know?"

"That's hard to say. There are so many people around here!"

"In your immediate circle?"

Palestro racked his brains.

"No, nobody," he said, shaking his head.

De Palma walked over to the shelves. They held a few books, files of various colours left there any old how, as well as a stack of communications and publications.

"None of your papers has been disturbed? Nothing was missing? I don't know . . . some detail that surprised you?"

"I'd have to check, but I don't think so."

"We're in the dark, Professor. Any small detail could be important."

"There's nothing particularly important here. Or nothing that's likely to be stolen."

Palestro slipped a few pieces of paper into a folder, then placed it in a drawer of his desk.

"But last winter," he said wrinkling his brow, "we were burgled . . . but I don't think it could have had anything to do with Christine's death."

"What was stolen?"

"Some collector's items, so to speak."

"Art work?"

"No, not really. They were pieces of flint. Beautiful pieces, all dating back to the Magdalenian. In particular, a rather rare axe blade."

"Why didn't you report it?"

"I wanted to inform the police, but Christine talked me out of it. She said that if we did, then word would get out because the police don't know how to hold their tongues. Then there'd be the press, and so on . . . "

"Where did these pieces come from?"

"Le Guen's Cave . . . They weren't very valuable. There was also a blade of white chalcedony, about fifteen centimetres long . . . You must understand, in our little world, such thefts go down extremely badly. We would have been the laughing stock of the profession. I suppose you remember all the media attention about Le Guen's Cave, about how much the big-wigs at Le Musée de l'Homme hated us . . . The people in the prehistory world are at war with one another, you know, just like the first men were. It's a real battle . . . Before the discovery of Le Guen's Cave, we were nothing in this little universe. There were the Parisians and the researchers in the south-west. Then suddenly we had our own Lascaux, and I was the only specialist qualified to study the site. So people got jealous . . . Just imagine what would happen if they discovered we were now losing the pieces we found during the fieldwork!"

"Did you suspect anyone at the time?"

"No, no-one."

"Come on, Professor, you must surely have had your suspicions! There aren't that many people who have access to such a collection . . . "

Palestro hunched his shoulders and looked apologetic.

"That's exactly what I said to myself. But I don't have any answers to your question. I really don't."

De Palma took a photograph of Christine Autran from a shelf.

"Did you take this photo?"

"Yes, I did. Why?"

"No reason . . . I have one last question, Professor. Can you explain this to me?"

De Palma handed him a transparent plastic bag. Inside was a colour photocopy of the negative hand found beside Hélène Weill. The Professor held it up between his fingers.

"As you can see, it's a negative hand. Of the same type as those we find in many of the decorated caves. Except this is a reproduction, or even a reconstitution. Two of the fingers are bent over."

"What does that mean?"

Palestro looked up at the policeman.

"We don't know. Truly, we don't. Everyone has their favourite explanation, but no-one really knows. I agree with my old teacher, Leroi-Gourhan, who thought it was linked to hunting, a sort of sign language, hence the bent fingers. Others think it was ritual amputation. But these are mere hypotheses, and I'm afraid we'll probably never be sure. There are limits . . . How can I put it? Some think that these hands had simply been amputated. This idea is backed up by the fact that it is physically impossible to bend some of the third phalanges. So it is thought that they were wounded fingers, frozen phalanges which had been cut off . . . that kind of thing. Anyway, the debate is still wide open."

Palestro fell silent, and his expression betrayed his unease.

"Why are you showing me this picture?"

"If I told you, you probably wouldn't believe me. I'll tell you one day, but right now I can't. One more question . . . "

"Yes?"

"Do we know if the first men, as you call them, were anthropophagous?"

"Yes, but here too there are different theories. Not so long ago, there were still some cannibal tribes, notably in New Guinea. In fact, I think they still exist. I studied such groups in the field, thirty years ago now . . . You see, these tribes live a little like the first men did. We were able to observe them in detail, and that was how we learned so much about prehistory. We noticed that some people ate one or more of their fellows. The men consumed the muscles, and the women and children the innards, and the brains. To come back to the first men, I believe that during severe periods of starvation, and especially during ceremonies and certain rituals, they ate people, presumably to fortify themselves . . . We don't really know. But we can be sure that the Celts were cannibals. My British friend Jim Lippleton is currently directing a dig to study this aspect, and they've found a femur which had been split in two, with its marrow removed. This was at the beginning of the Christian era. Imagine that! What's more, it was probably the remains of a huge sacrifice, of about fifty people. One of the skulls had been smashed open with an axe . . . As for prehistoric times, we can be sure that Neanderthal man devoured his fellows. We know this because remains have been discovered in the Moula-Guercy Cave in Ardèche, on the west bank of the Rhône. The discovery was made by a colleague at the Université de la Méditerranée in Marseille. The victims were adults, adolescents and even children. They had been skinned like big game. Their remains had then been thrown away without distinction among the bones of reindeer and other animals – there had been no ceremony this time. That goes back about 120,000 years, so there's no reason why Cro-Magnon man wouldn't have eaten his fellows too. It seems to have been all the rage . . . "

"And there's no connection with the painted hands?"

"Maybe, maybe. Who knows? This was the dawn of time. And we haven't got a very clear vision of it at all!"

"Still, try to think who could have stolen those pieces . . . You never know."

17.

The church of Saint-Julien stood in the heights of Marseille, towards the east, in the middle of what had once been a small village. This had since been swallowed up by the conglomeration, as had most of the outlying quartiers, but there remained a few shadowy lanes that led towards a square with two small bars and a corner store. All around, desirable residences were hidden behind high, dry-stone walls topped with broken glass.

The façade of the little church had been completely restored the previous autumn. Masons had stripped the entrance arch until it was pristine. As a result, this house of God had recovered its Provençal look, which made Saint-Julien all the more attractive. But the parishioners still had not come back. Like many others, the priest had to divide his time between this and two other parishes, Trois-Lucs and Les Caillols.

It was dull and rainy. The inside of the church was barely visible in the gloomy light from the stained-glass windows. Father Paul looked at his watch. It was 4 p.m. His few parishioners were presumably expecting him.

He kissed his purple stole, put it round his neck and came out of the presbytery. He passed the altar, put one knee to the floor, crossed himself and meditated for some time.

He saw that no-one was waiting for him outside the confessional, so he walked slowly along the ambulatory and stopped for a while beside the crib. Shortly before Christmas, the primary school children had repainted the mill and cave. They had also carefully placed green and red fairy lights in the tiny cardboard houses. The priest looked long and hard at the children's work. The crib seemed to him to be even more naïve and lively than it had a year ago. But Christmas was over, and now he would have to put away the cottages, the pieces of cork, the backdrop of the sky and the figurines, and store them in the presbytery until next year.

In a few days, the little church would become calm once more. Father Paul knew that he could count on only a handful of the faithful, while the Christmas crowd would not be seen again until Easter or else for a wedding, baptism or funeral. He would enjoy a quiet life. Apart from catechism on Wednesday mornings, he would have the opportunity to devote himself to other concerns.

He glanced again towards the confessional, a cage of glass and wood which, according to the diocese's recommendations, had been placed to the right of the entrance in the chapel of Sainte Marie Madeleine. Personally, he preferred the old confessional just beside it, which was more impressive thanks to its shadowy Gothic appearance and the anonymity it provided.

A woman was waiting there. From this distance, she looked young. The priest crossed the nave towards her.

"Good morning, Father. I want to make a confession."

She must have been about forty, maybe a little older. The fine lines on her face showed that she had been through a lot.

"You've come to the right place," the priest replied.

He smiled broadly at her and pointed at the two confessionals.

"Do you prefer this one, or that one? Here we have the new model, face to face or side by side, in the open. And there we have the traditional one: kneeling in the dark, seeing nothing of the other person except their conscience. For serious sins, it's better. So which would you prefer?"

The woman nodded towards the old confessional. The priest showed her inside, and almost at once she started speaking.

"Bless me, Father, for I have sinned," she murmured in the silence of the confessional. "It has been years since my last confession . . . "

Behind the lattice-work of wood, the priest coughed. She felt like running away, but stayed there, glued to the floor by a mysterious force.

"How long? How many years? I suppose you mean a very long time . . . "

"For ever, in fact . . . "

"Ah . . . " Father Paul's voice grew softer. "So you've never really made a confession, is that right?"

"Yes, it is. My parents used to force me to go, so I made things up to tell the priest. I said I'd stolen sweets, or lied. That kind of thing."

The priest sighed. She heard him shift about on his chair. It made little creaking sounds which echoed around the church.

"I know," he said. "It's the sort of thing I hear every day. People make up all kinds of things to try to mislead the Almighty. But I'm afraid he isn't so easily fooled. So what do you want . . . ?"

"Father . . . "

"Call me Paul. 'Father' is so old-fashioned. What's your name?"

"Julia."

"What a beautiful name."

The priest's voice was even gentler. Julia felt uncomfortable; an indefinable sensation made her shiver. At each word, the sound of his voice entered her more deeply. Her neck prickled.

"Do you live in the parish?"

"At 36, chemin du Vallon."

"Yes, I see," he said. "A lovely street. Splendid houses. So, the Lord has spoiled you! In material terms, at least."

"Oh, Father, you know . . . "

"No, Paul."

"Father Paul, then!"

"If you insist . . . but you know that the disciples called the Lord by his first name."

"Yes, I know," she answered timidly.

"Tell me, Julia, why do you so want to confess?"

"I don't know, I . . . I have sinned. That's why."

"I have no doubt about that, but how? Have you cheated on your husband?"

"No, I'm single."

"Forgive me for such a personal question. I'm just trying to help you."

"You wouldn't understand. As a priest . . . "

"Stop right there. I've not always been a priest. I had another existence before. I know just as much about life as you do. And I sinned a lot. I have done things that might make you blush or run straight out of this confessional if I told you. And then, you know, what with all the things people have told me . . . Some even accuse themselves of murder."

"I know, but it's hard for me to admit to."

"Maybe you'd prefer to come back later? On another day? I remain at your disposal at any moment of the day and night," he paused, then started to laugh. "But the night's only for really serious sins. The sort that can't wait."

"What if I came back tomorrow, at the same time, would that be alright?"

"Absolutely. But be punctual, because I have to go and preside over a funeral at Les Caillols."

"I'm never late."

"Go in peace, Julia."

"See you tomorrow, Paul."

The bells in the clock tower were chiming nine o'clock. All that could be heard in chemin du Vallon was the purring of televisions. A gentle breeze was blowing through the pine trees. Paul rang at number 36. Julia was alone, as she was every evening.

She had phoned him an hour earlier, completely distraught. She wanted to deliver herself of a burden which was weighing down on her. He had agreed to come and talk to her after a certain amount of hesitation. To avoid gossip, he never went to see his parishioners at such a late hour.

Father Paul felt ill at ease in the huge salon. It reminded him of the life of luxury he had had as a child. Julia sat on a coral-pink sofa and stared at him. The man of God shifted in his armchair, his little knapsack lying between his feet.

She offered him a drink, which he refused. She poured herself a whisky and began to talk about this and that. Gradually, the conversation centred on her, her lonely life and her despair.

The priest listened to Julia in silence, tapping his fingers on the arms of his chair. She told him that she never saw anyone, like most of the young women who came to him for confession. This was the sad reality he had observed since starting to spend most of his time taking care of people's souls.

They spoke for an hour before Julia began to feel at ease. At the age of forty-two, she was finding it more and more difficult to bear her homosexuality and loneliness. In her youth, after a strict Catholic upbringing, she had turned to spiritualism and the Occult, and had then taken an interest in early religion. Shamanism had fascinated her as a return to genuine practices, untainted by the moral weight she had experienced in her childhood. After such a progression, she had had her doubts, and considered becoming a nun to escape a world which seemed to her full of turpitude. The priest replied that you did not take holy orders like that, without first having received the call from God, a sort of illumination in the mists of life. She admitted that she had never received such a call.

At about 11.00, visibly tired, the priest went home. She watched him walk through the trees in the garden, like a disturbing yet familiar shadow.

Fast asleep, Julia had a nightmare. Black on black. Inside the confessional, she was admitting her sins to Father Paul, who was laughing at every word she said. Long, sonorous, mocking laughter. The sarcasm of sanctimonious moralists from her tender childhood.

She woke with a start, her forehead covered with sweat, her hands and feet as cold as ice.

She looked towards the window and noticed that she had forgotten to close the shutters. There was a full moon, a bluish light enfolded the garden, and only the top of the tall pine tree reflected the yellow glow from the lamp post, as it was swayed in the slight breeze.

She decided to get up and shut out this hollow vision of the night. As her feet touched the floor, she heard a strange, barely perceptible sound, like a breath. She turned towards the door, but saw nothing except the familiar shadows of the corridor that led to the salon. And yet, she was not dreaming. The sound of breathing was definitely there, now even more distinct.

She sat on her bed and nervously felt for the switch of her bedside lamp. In her haste, she knocked over some books and a pile of fifth-year homework which was lying on the table. There was a crash. Then silence.

The breathing was coming from right in front of her.

She suppressed her fear so as to overcome the darkness and saw a moonbeam's pale reflection glint in the glassy whiteness of a savage eye. A monstrous shape was approaching in the cold light. A tall, thickset figure from the dawn of time.

And then, this strange prayer:

"I am the hunter

Give me your blood

May the spirits of the dead guide you through the night

May your flesh fortify the first man . . . "

18.

"Jean-Louis, do you have any mussels left?"

"Yes, a dozen."

"Little ones?"

"No, they only had big ones!"

"That's why they're not biting. Just look at the mussels we're giving them. They've never seen anything like it!"

"It's not a question of mussels, it's a question of time. Sea bream generally feed at night."

"But how do you think they can spot mussels at night, dimwit! My grandfather used to fish at any time of the day."

"Yes, but in those days, there were still fish!"

The waves broke against the seawall of Pointe-Rouge, flopping against the blocks of concrete. Since 7.00 that morning, Maistre and de Palma had been enjoying a day off and were attempting to fish using sugared mussel as bait. The technique was as complicated as it was mysterious, and it required a certain skill. First, the hook was placed in the mussel, which was then held shut with elastic wrapped round a sugar cube . . . Once in the salt water, the sugar would dissolve allowing the mussel to open gradually. It looked more real than real! It was an infallible method which Maistre had learned from a fisherman in L'Estaque, but he still hadn't mastered it.

It was nearly noon.

"Have you got any worms, Le Gros?"

"I bought two."

"Is that all?"

"We said we were going to try with mussels."

"Give me a worm. They work better than your carry-on."

De Palma picked up the long worm and slipped it on to a hook with the help of a piece of metal wire as thin as a needle. He was about to cast out when his mobile rang.

"Michel, it's Maxime. I didn't want to disturb you, but you're going to have to come to Saint-Julien, 36 chemin du Vallon. It's absolute carnage . . . Jesus . . . I think it's the same one as at Cadenet. I'm even sure of it."

"I'll be there in an hour."

In exasperation, de Palma cast out. The lead and the worm whistled in the air, before falling into the water twenty metres away.

"What's up, Baron?"

"He's struck again."

"Who?"

"Our Cadenet customer."

"The fucker!"

"Quite."

At 12.30, there were not that many people outside 36 chemin du Vallon: a few pensioners and neighbours who had been passing by. Maxime Vidal had parked the police Mégane right in the middle of the street, with its light still flashing on the roof and the windows wide open.

A young officer standing on the threshold with his arms crossed hailed de Palma with a vague gesture and looked at him glumly. In the salon, Vidal was talking to a young woman from forensics. He was wearing latex gloves and gesticulating as he spoke, trying to appear composed.

"Ah, there you are Michel! Unfortunately, Judge Barbieri has just gone . . . Come and have a look. But I warn you, it's not a pretty sight at all."

They went down a long corridor cluttered with forensic equipment. De Palma kept his eyes down, noticing traces of vomit on the floorboards and on the blue, Oriental wallpaper. When he entered the bedroom, he could smell recent death, the tenacious odour of blood and the stench of spilt intestines. He swallowed back his bile several times, trying to leave his disgust deep down in his guts. Lieutenant Agnès Bernal from forensics came over to him. "Hi, Michel. We're done here."

"Hi Agnès."

"No joke at all . . . she was hit in the face and then gutted. Her left leg is missing."

De Palma slowly approached. Intestines were hanging down to the floor, wobbling slightly every time the photographer bumped into the bed. The skull had been completely smashed in, a mush of shards of bone mixed with brains. There was only one eye left in the middle, where the nose should have been. The other had disappeared.

Her left leg had been severed at the knee. The amputation looked almost perfect, but de Palma noticed that the skin tissue was torn. He mentally compared it with the body of Hélène Weill, and saw that the amputation had been carried out using the same kind of knife, with rather a blunt blade.

He examined the hands: the nails were curiously clean, but that of the middle left finger had been reversed. This was not immediately visible, because the nail had been put back into place, then carefully cleaned with a cotton swab: fibre from it remained stuck to a piece of dead skin.

"The work of a madman. Classic. Cold. No traces. No proof. Not the slightest clue . . . And yet, he must have left something behind . . . They all do. But what?"

He stayed for a while in the bedroom, trying to understand this killer who had found his way in, presumably while his victim was asleep. He thought hard.

"He knew his victim. There's no other possibility. He'd known her for at least a few days. Maybe he met her yesterday. But he definitely knew her. He didn't break in. She was asleep and woke up when he was already on top of her. The body hasn't been moved. There are very few signs of a struggle. And no bite marks. It's the same man for sure."

Vidal broke his train of thought:

"Michel, there are two or three things I have to tell you."

"I'm coming."

He stared at the scene once more. He would have liked to have said something to the dead woman, but nothing came to mind. He looked at what was left of her belly and pubis and thought to himself that she had been an attractive women, with a soft belly, just as he liked. Then he went into the salon, where Vidal was pacing back and forth.

"Jesus Christ, Michel. I've never seen anything like it. How can you possibly stay so long in a room with a thing like that?"

"It's now or never if you want a chance to understand him. Try to imagine: he arrives in the middle of the night, she hears a noise and wakes up, he grabs her, she scratches him. Look at her nail . . . Then he hits her, once or twice . . . No more. That's enough. Then he cuts her up. He takes his time. After that, he guts her for good measure. He takes away one of her legs . . . Because he only eats the muscle. Finally, he cleans up anything that might give him away."

Agnès Bernal intervened:

"She doesn't seem to have been raped. He didn't torture her or tie her up. Death occurred last night, at about 1.00 a.m. We've been through the place with a fine-tooth comb, but we haven't found much: a few fibres, footprints on the carpet. The most significant item is a shard of stone in the skull. I think it's flint."

"Did you use your lamp?"

"The Polilight? Of course I did."

"And?"

"And there are traces of footprints all over the place. We've probably identified his. I'll tell you tomorrow once we've analysed everything."

Vidal glanced at de Palma, who said:

"Well, son, what have you found out since you got here?"

"The victim's name is Julia Chevallier. She was born on October 20, 1957, in Marseille. She was an English teacher at Lycée Longchamp. That's all. Apart from that, the door has not been forced, there's no sign of a break-in, and there aren't any fingerprints in the bedroom or salon. According to the neighbours, she lived alone and hardly ever went out. The body was discovered at 10.00 this morning by the cleaning lady. She was murdered during the night. Presumably around 1.00. Nobody saw or heard a thing."

"Which is only normal in this kind of house."

"And this was found next to the body."

Vidal handed the Baron a plastic bag containing a sheet of white paper: it was an image of a negative hand, just like the one found beside the body of Hélène Weill. The little and ring fingers had been cut almost in half. Professor Palestro had spoken of a hunting code. "A sign language," de Palma said to himself. "But why these two fingers? There must be a reason! From the depths of his madness, he's trying to tell us something."

De Palma considered that if one of the victim's hands were missing a finger or two, then that would have provided a rationale for all of this. He was disappointed to see that this was not the case.

"And you've been all over the room, Agnès? Including the armrests of the chairs?"

"Why?"

She sensed immediately that her question had not gone down too well. The Baron's expression became hard and cruel. He raised his voice:

"Because the killer knew his victim. Either he hated her, or he lusted after her, thinking her inaccessible. You see, Agnès – and this applies to you as well, Vidal – he came here and sat down, without his gloves of course, because at that moment he was a friend. He might even have had a drink. So you're going to collect all the fingerprints from every smooth surface in this entire sodding room. Is that clear? And, Agnès, check out the dishwasher."

"No problem, Michel."

"You know, Vidal, the worst thing is that even if we do find a print, it won't be on our records. But still, during questioning a print is invaluable; it means you don't have to stay up all night being nice to the fucker so as to make him talk."

De Palma went out into the garden. It was practically a park, measuring two thousand square metres and surrounded by walls barely higher than he was. It hadn't been looked after, and tall weeds were beginning to swamp the rose bushes. On the paths, a few flowerpots had been blown over by the mistral. De Palma saw a fifty-year-old woman on the patio and approached her. Her eyes were still red, and her expression still reflected the image left behind by this barbaric murder.

"Who are you, Madame?"

"Inès Santamaria, I'm the cleaning lady. I found the body this morning."

"At what time?"

"A little after 10.00. I'm always here at 10.00 sharp. I'm never late. My God, how horrible! How . . . "

She started to cry.

"Did you notice anything strange?"

"No, nothing."

"Was the street door locked?"

"All the doors were locked. As usual. She always locks up before going to bed. Imagine, living all alone in a huge house like that!"

"I see . . . And what's that shed over there?"

"It's a kind of workshop, full of tools. It goes back to the days when her father was still alive."

The grass in front of the shed was trodden down. Inside, some of the gardening tools had been disturbed. De Palma spotted a door at the back. He opened it and noticed that its lock had been forced. It led out on to a path that ran alongside an irrigation canal, just like many others dating from the time when this part of town had been full of market gardens. He went through the door, stared into the canal and tried to put his thoughts into some kind of order.

Vidal interrupted him.

"You were right, Michel, we've found something on the left armrest of one of the chairs: a fingerprint which has been half rubbed out, but it might be usable. The ones on the right have been wiped off. It's obvious. You can still see the trace of a cloth. There are several glasses in the dishwasher. We're taking them with us. Have you looked at her book shelves? They're groaning with books about prehistory!"

"We might well be on to something, my friend! Sooner or later, we'll get him . . . Compare the fingerprints with those found in Autran's flat. Have you asked the neighbours if they heard a car, or anything else in the street?"

"I've asked the nearest ones. Nothing. Even the next-door neighbour there, I can't remember his name, he's a professor of medicine, anyway he told me that he was up all night working on a project and he didn't hear a thing."

"Jesus, our customer's no fool, far from it! He came here on foot, nice and quiet. He came along the canal, then through that door. Then he disappeared the same way. Leaving nothing behind him. Except a fingerprint on a chair, and maybe on a glass, if we're lucky."

"He must have made at least one mistake!"

"They all do. They all forget something. It's not always easy to see, but there's always something. Their weak point is their arrogance."

"Why do you say that?"

"Because they think they're smarter than us. I'll bet he's had a higher education – you can sense that from the victims he chooses – and it might well have been a degree in prehistory. To gain access and suss out the place, he has to get all matey with his target, chat her up, impress her. Seeing how cultivated the victim was, he would have had to be on a level above her. Bourgeois English teachers don't invite just anybody into their house. You really have to be someone!"

De Palma began to walk towards the house, then stopped, his eyes fixed on the ground.

"Maxime, can you find out where she went to university? I'll bet it was Aix."

He stuffed his hands in the pockets of his jeans and arched his shoulders.

"You see, kid? We've already got a profile. You might not think so, but we have. He's a man in good health, a loner, but quite capable of being attractive and seductive. He's even-natured, incredibly cool-headed, he never panics. He's a top-level intellectual with some terrible event in his past, something unbelievable."

"A rape?"

"No, I know what you're thinking . . . a rape which is then repeated in later life. It's quite often true. That's what comes to mind. It's like at the police academy when they tell you all murders have a sexual motive. But this time, my boy, it's something different, even though I haven't got the faintest idea what it is. Perhaps frustration, which makes him be murderously covetous and jealous. We do know that he uses rudimentary weapons, like prehistoric man."

"So what do we do now?"

"The paperwork, as usual. But first of all, could you do me a favour?"

"What?"

"Try to see where this canal leads to. I'm going to take another look indoors."

The sun was beginning to set. A golden light was glittering on the pine needles. Vidal felt a slight breeze work its way beneath his jacket. He gathered his thoughts, went through the shed door and followed the canal.

He did not observe anything unusual, except that some of the tall grasses had been trodden down. He found no footprints or traces of blood. After a while, the canal disappeared into a tunnel, which was far too low for an adult man to enter, whatever his build. Vidal looked around and soon spotted the path taken by the killer. The grass had been flattened leading up to a wall which was about one metre fifty high. He followed the tracks, gripped the top of the wall with both hands, and with one leap was on top of it.

To his astonishment, he saw that he was overlooking the little cemetery that surrounded the church of Saint-Julien.

"So, what are your conclusions, de Palma?"

His lower lip damp and pendulous, Commissaire Paulin had adopted his dark and terrible look. His expressionless, beady eyes were staring at his paperweight, a kind of upward-pointing doornail which his wife, who owed a gallery in Le Panier, had found in a Paris junk shop. This genuine piece of abstract art, cast in bronze, was the only hint of the unusual in the otherwise frigid room. Ever since he had first come into his superior's office to discuss ongoing cases, de Palma had been trying to decide what this strange object might represent. In vain.

The Baron glanced at Vidal, who was trying to look confident as he sat in his chair.

"I don't have much to tell you, apart from the fact that it was a particularly violent murder. Skull crushed, intestines removed, amputation of one of the lower limbs with a knife or similar implement. For the moment, we don't have the slightest clue, except for the painted hand we found near the body."

"You're not telling me that you don't even have an inkling."

"This time I am. Nothing at all. Except for a piece of flint, half a fingerprint on the armrest of a chair, and the hand . . . which means that he either knew the victim or had conducted detailed observations of the scene. Anyway, we'll have to wait for the lab report."

Paulin turned towards Vidal. "What about you? Nothing?"

"The same as de Palma," Vidal answered. "It's obviously the work of a sadist. Apart from that . . . "

"You're going to have to find him for me, and fast. I won't conceal the fact that the press is already sniffing around, asking for explanations. You will accept that the results of the murder squad have not been that good of late. It's not your fault de Palma, nor yours Vidal, but since little Samir's death, we haven't solved a single crime. Not to mention the gangland killings. What about the Autran case?"

"We're making progress, Commissaire, we're making progress. Things will no doubt be clearer in a few days."

"I hope these cases aren't connected. That really would be the icing on the cake."

Paulin picked up his paperweight and twisted it around.

"They aren't, Commissaire, rest assured about that."

"And why do you say that?"

"Not the same *modus operandi.*"

"My instinct is to trust you, de Palma. You're going to work with Vidal on both cases. And I'd like you to take Anne Moracchini along with you. She's the only person on the squad with any time to spare. The others are all up to their eyes in gangland vendettas. In Paris they want results, so down here we're having to put all our men on investigations into hoods blowing each other away. So, let's be clear about this. Try to get something for me in the next ten days."

"Whatever happens, Commissaire, you shouldn't tell the press anything for the moment. This kind of killer is always out for publicity. It gives them wings."

"You think he'll strike again?"

"I'm sure of it."

"Why?"

"Because of the way he mutilates and guts his victims . . . and the hand, of course. We've had cases like this in the past. He's a killer who has a system. When I first joined the murder squad, we had the Ruggero affair, which was pretty similar. Do you remember?"

"I was still in Paris at the time. But you're right. We're faced with someone who's sick."

"And I hope he'll get going again as soon as possible. Ruggero waited years before starting once more. It all depends on their relative mental stability."

"You obviously think it's linked to the Cadenet murder?"

"Of course I do," de Palma replied. "But I don't know much about the Cadenet murder. And the gendarmerie are running that investigation. In other words, the whole situation's a mess!"

"You're not going to resurrect the war between the forces again. The gendarmes do very good work, especially their Institut de Recherches Criminelles . . . Let's try to proceed amicably. Have you contacted the gendarmerie?"

"Yes, or rather, I was contacted by them."

"So you know, then."

"Know what?"

"It's the main reason I called you in. Because, of course, the two cases *are* linked. Never mind. I just wanted to tell you that the gendarmerie are making progress, despite everything . . . They've found a witness: a man aged about fifty who was passing that night and saw a woman getting into a grey Mercedes. Unfortunately, he didn't see the driver's face. So, I hear you ask, how did he recognise the woman? Well, he also lives in rue Boulegon, like her, and he'd had his eye on her for some time, if you see what I mean."

"Extremely interesting!" said de Palma, pretending to find the news a real scoop.

"Most interesting of all is that she was being treated by a psychiatrist, who owns, no prizes for guessing . . . "

"A grey Mercedes," Vidal answered, for the sake of saying something.

Paulin slumped back in his chair looking pleased with himself.

"A 500 SL," de Palma added, after a few moments' silence.

Paulin went extremely red, put down his upturned doornail and stared at him furiously.

"How do you know that, de Palma?"

"A good friend of mine's a gendarme in Cadenet. I called him just now on the way over here. He filled me in. You know, Commissaire, police infighting isn't my cup of tea."

Paulin was lost for words. Vidal laughed silently, keeping his head down so as not to show any disrespect to his superior.

"So, pleased with your little routine, de Palma?"

"Not at all, boss. It's just professional curiosity. I wanted to compare your version with the one I'd been given. And they're the same. I'm wary about the gendarmerie. They haven't always been straight with us, as you know only too well."

The Baron was furious. The gendarmes had just won the first set. Now he had just annoyed his Commissaire for no reason and he was going to have to make good with a large piece of soft soap.

"And I think you're absolutely right. We should work in collaboration. But with the gendarmes, that's not going to be so easy."

Paulin picked up his doornail again.

"I called Barbieri earlier. He wants us to work together, in tandem with the gendarmes. He too thinks that the cases are connected. I asked him to get the investigation transferred, but he refused, saying that they had already made more progress than we have, and should be arresting someone soon. He doesn't want to screw it all up."

"Arrest who? A psychiatrist who picks up his victims in his car in the middle of the street? Don't make me laugh! I can smell a red herring from a mile off, or else my name's not de Palma!"

"You never know, de Palma. You never know. Sometimes things aren't as complicated as we like to believe. Murderers make mistakes too . . . "

"Not murderers like this one. Or at least, not that sort of mistake."

Vidal nodded vigorously and looked out of the window. Paulin's office had a view of the quays. The *Danièle-Casanova* was just setting off for Corsica, her bridge and fo'c'sle glimmering with a thousand black and turquoise reflections. It was like a fairy-tale vision moving across a sheet of glittering water. In the distance, the lighthouse on the Sainte-Marie strait was emitting its bright red flashes.

"I didn't hear you, Vidal. What do you think about all this?"

"I think Michel's right. Things are never easy with the gendarmerie."

"What else would you suggest?"

"That we should get on with our work independently until the two investigations link up. Let's wait and see what comes of their arrest. Not much, I should think."

"I think that's the wisest course of action."

De Palma lowered his head and said nothing. It was becoming more and more complicated to be a good policeman.

It was 7.00 p.m. when he pushed open the door of Le Zanzi, followed by Vidal. The bar was almost empty.

"Hi Dédé, a bit dead tonight?"

"As a doornail."

"What's going on?"

"There's a match on."

Dédé waved his bulky hand over the counter, his palm turned towards the ceiling.

"And what's up with you two?" he went on. "You look terrible."

"It's nothing. Work."

Two Ricards immediately arrived on the zinc. De Palma swilled his down in one, without any water.

"You haven't seen Maistre by any chance . . . "

"No, he hasn't been in today. Maybe he'll be along in a minute. This is the time he usually comes."

"Come off it, he's got a wife and kids."

"But the kids are big now!"

"True."

The Baron's mobile rang. It was Sylvie Maurel.

"I've been trying to get hold of you all day. Can I see you this evening?"

"Of course, where are you?"

"In Marseille, by Fort Saint-Jean, at the marine archaeology laboratory. I'd like to show it to you. What do you think?"

"I'll be there in fifteen minutes. O.K.?"

"I'll be waiting for you outside the main door, at the foot of the tower. Do you know where I mean?"

"Absolutely. See you there."

De Palma had completely forgotten about Sylvie Maurel. He had another Ricard, knocked it back in one and turned towards Vidal, who was still staring at the yellow contents of his glass. Dédé had vanished into his kitchen.

"You never told me where that canal leads to."

"It ends in a tunnel, but you can't get down it."

"So?"

"So, I followed his tracks and realised that he must have climbed over a wall . . . and guess where I ended up?"

"Tell me."

"In Saint-Julien cemetery."

"So what do you conclude?"

"I'm too knackered to conclude anything at all. Sorry, Michel."

"There's one thing we can be sure of."

"What's that?"

"He knows the area intimately."

"You reckon?"

"Obviously! How else would he know that there's a canal behind the cemetery which leads to Julia's house? He must be a local, or something! I tell you, we're starting to move in on him."

Vidal grimaced. Dédé returned from his kitchen.

"O.K., kid," de Palma said, "I'm off now. We'll talk about it tomorrow. Try to get some sleep. I know it isn't easy, but do your best."

"Don't worry, Michel. I'm starting to get used to it."

"That's what they all say. See you around, Dédé."

He turned on his heel and left Le Zanzi.

"Are you going out later?"

"I have a date with a friend around nine . . . "

Sylvie Maurel was radiant in a straight, cream-coloured shantung skirt, a silk top and a cashmere scarf thrown over her shoulder.

"So you just have time to show me your laboratory and its marvels," said de Palma.

"Oh, it's not that impressive. Come and see for yourself. But we'll have to be quick. The caretaker locks up in an hour."

He followed Sylvie into the courtyard of Fort Saint-Jean. It was the first time he had been inside the place, and he felt a twitch of emotion. When he was a kid, it had seemed to him that the fort contained profound secrets behind its high wall, buffeted by the sea. Going inside at nightfall only heightened his curiosity.

But he was disappointed. The inner courtyard looked abandoned. He had the impression of crossing a narrow stretch of wasteland surrounded by ageless fortifications. Against the black sky, he could make out the shape of a pine tree growing in the wall, between what looked like battlements. It had improvised a place for itself in this hostile universe and, indifferent to its ill fortune, was now rising up towards the sky above the old port.

De Palma stopped for a moment.

"Sylvie, do you know that it's the first time I've been in here? It's an odd feeling. I was expecting something better. In fact, it smells horrible and it's ugly."

"I know, I know . . . I found it strange the first time too. The local council has been trying to renovate the place for the past twenty years, but I don't think it's ever going to happen. There are other priorities in Marseille. The heritage commission we have here is . . . "

"I quite agree. But this is something else! It reminds me of La Vieille Charité when my father took me there. I must have been seven or eight at the time . . . it was like a shanty town, right in the middle of Le Panier. There were weeds everywhere, and tramps . . . But they did renovate it in the end. You just have to be patient."

De Palma and Sylvie walked up a short slope leading to the terrace which overlooked the courtyard, offering a view of the Palais du Pharo and, further to the right, Château d'If floating in the yellow glow of the floodlights which illuminated it. Sylvie led him towards a row of small, stone buildings with large windows fortified by cast-iron bars. They stopped outside a reinforced door, where she entered her code into the alarm panel.

A long corridor cluttered with amphorae and numbered boxes led to a large room crammed with old, civil-service-style oak cupboards. On a table in the middle, three brand-new computers, on standby, were the sole touch of modernity in this dated universe.

"Here's where I work," Sylvie said, gazing around.

"How charming," de Palma admitted.

"You think so? In winter we freeze to death, and in summer we boil. Anyway . . . at least we've got *L'Archéonaute* to go out to sea in from time to time."

"Do you often work here?"

"Practically every day, when I'm not in Aix. Look, this was Christine's computer."

"Really?"

"I know what you're thinking, Monsieur Policeman. But it's practically empty. It's new. We only got them in mid-November, and she never used hers."

De Palma eyed the cupboards.

"Is this where you keep your treasures?"

"Yes. I'll show you."

Sylvie opened the double doors of the first cupboard to the left. It contained ten shelves holding small, black plastic boxes. She took down one of them and put it on the table.

"Here's what we collect . . . old stones."

De Palma looked at a collection of flints laid out on yellow ticking.

"They're small flints found in the La Triperie Cave, at Cape Morgiou. Palestro led the explorations at the time, in the mid '6os."

"The La Triperie Cave?"

"It's not far from Le Guen's Cave, at the tip of Cape Morgiou, in the middle of the hook . . . you know, it forms a sort of hook, and there's a huge, greyish vault beneath the cliff-face."

"Yes, I know it. But I didn't know there were caves down there containing prehistoric artefacts."

"The sites lie about twenty-five metres underwater," Sylvie explained. "Out of sight of daytrippers."

She carefully put the box back on the shelf, opened a second cupboard and removed an identical-looking one.

"These come from the Trémies Cave on Cape Cacaù, in the Bay of Cassis. They're cut flints . . . "

She took down two more boxes.

"Here we have bones and coals. These remains were preserved in deposits compacted by concretion. They're from human habitations dating back to Palaeolithic times."

Each item was marked with a number, finely traced in Rotring, and with its place of origin.

"How strange," he said, to break the silence.

"What?"

"I don't know . . . all these little pieces of the past! At the bottom of the sea . . . "

"Oh, you know, there are quite a few sites in this region, from the Italian border as far as Marseille, and probably further on if we looked . . . the Coral Cave, the Agaraté Cave, Mérou, Deffend, Pointe Fauconnière . . . they're all near Nice. Closer to us we have Trémies Cave, Devenson, Figuier, Sormiou . . . and, of course, the famous Le Guen Cave."

"Famous? I don't think many people in Marseille even remember when it was discovered. The local authorities ought to build a little museum or something."

"We have to finish excavating it first, and that takes time. But there's a permanent exhibition at the Musée de l'Histoire."

Sylvie put her boxes away and opened the third cupboard.

"These are more impressive," she said, pulling out a box which was wider and deeper than the others. "But don't tell anyone I showed you this."

She put the box down in front of the Baron.

"Do you know where these come from?"

"From Le Guen's Cave," he declared.

"How did you guess?"

"It's my job to, Sylvie!"

The archaeologist picked up a piece of flint and showed it to him.

"It's a large blade, a sort of knife which must have been used for cutting up meat . . . When it was found, it was covered with clay and coal dust. I noticed that it had been used, and I'd like to know what for."

"You have no idea?"

"No, not at all."

She picked up a second object.

"Here's another blade. It's nine centimetres long by fifteen millimetres. Do you see how the left-hand blade looks polished. In fact, it's been worn down. In my opinion it was used to chop up meat, cutting through flesh and slicing any resistant tissue."

"But not on men?"

"Maybe! It was a done thing at the time."

Julia Chevallier's leg had been amputated at the knee, the skin tissue had not been cut through with a knife, the epidermis and dermis both bore signs of having been torn open. De Palma looked at the blade Sylvie was holding, and thought about the flint shard found in Julia's skull, and understood that the murderer was not contenting himself with placing negative hands beside his victims. He was using weapons from the depths of time. Sylvie broke his train of thought:

"I'll show you some photos. They're more impressive than a few old stones. Sit down at the computer."

She moved the cursor from window to window before opening a file entitled "Le Guen Photos, MR".

"Here we are."

She clicked a few times, and the hard drive started to hum.

"Here's the most famous hand from the discovery. Its fingers are intact, and part of the forearm is visible. It's the first one Le Guen saw. And its certainly the most beautiful."

From *National Geographic* to *Paris Match*, the picture had been on front pages across the world, as well as in all the scientific journals.

"It looks like a woman's hand."

"That's possible. But we're not really sure . . . Now I'll show you the mutilated hands . . . They're the ones that pose the most problems, and they're the source of huge controversy. Look . . . "

Two hands appeared on the screen, side by side. Both were missing three fingers, the big, ring and little ones.

"These hands were found just above the large flooded shaft, at the far end of the cave."

She pointed to the mutilations.

"There's been a lot of debate on this subject. Some people claim that it's frostbite, others talk of systematic amputations, or else Raynaud's disease, which is caused by stress and the cold and can lead to necrosis of the body's extremities . . . And so on."

"You don't agree, Sylvie?"

"No, I don't. I think these fingers have been bent according to a particular code. A sort of sign language, if you want . . . Some aborigines still use these kinds of signs when hunting, and also during the handing down of initiation stories. They signal to each other to indicate the presence of this or that game animal."

De Palma took his eyes off the photo and turned towards Sylvie. She stared back at him for some time, as though guessing each of his thoughts. Close-up, he noticed the tiny emerald specks which stood out against her dark irises, the fineness of her lashes, her discreet eyeliner and mother-of-pearl eyelids. Something deep inside him had just caught fire and he knew that this tiny flame, born in the darkness of his being, would sooner or later become a blaze to consume his entire body.

He turned back towards the photo.

"I'll show you one more. It's my favourite. It's a black left hand, with its little and ring fingers bent over. It looks really beautiful, like a child's hand."

"True enough," de Palma said. "When does it date from?"

"Twenty-seven thousand years ago," Sylvie replied.

"Twenty-seven thousand years . . . "

"Oh yes . . . when Palestro first dated them, the Parisian set at the Musée de l'Homme dragged him through the mud. They said that it was impossible, and some even claimed that they were fakes . . . "

"I can remember that. In your opinion, why did they think they were fake?"

"They don't like us, that's all there is to it."

Sylvie paused, as though hypnotised by the hand in front of her. After a while, she re-emerged from her daydream and looked at de Palma apologetically.

"I wanted to say sorry for last time. I was rather badly behaved."

"Don't worry about that, Sylvie."

De Palma stood up and went back to the box of flints. He took one in his hand and ran the tip of his thumb across the blade.

"Palestro told me about the theft of some prehistoric objects," he said softly, without taking his eyes off the knife.

Sylvie moved the mouse to one side of the computer and put her hands up to her mouth.

"Goodness, he told you about that?"

"Yes, he told me that some articles were missing. He didn't want to accuse anyone and he didn't mention any names."

"Well, well, well, and I thought Palestro was able to hold his tongue . . . "

"As I said, he hasn't pointed to anyone! But it seemed to be weighing on his conscience."

"And with good reason! He wanted to avoid a scandal."

"That's what he told me. But I didn't really believe him . . . What scandal could there be about two pieces of stone?"

"You're wrong about that. In scientific circles, it's not at all done to lose items which have been found during a dig. Even if they're pieces of secondary importance."

"I suppose not . . . any ideas about the thief?"

"No, not at all."

De Palma approached Sylvie, without taking his eyes off her.

"There was a murder last night, and preliminary evidence suggests that it was committed using flint weapons."

The Baron's voice hit Sylvie hard. She shivered.

"For the moment, I have no proof that the killer was in possession of the flints which were stolen from here. But that's what I think."

De Palma paused to allow her to speak, but she just stared at him in terror.

"I'm going to ask you one thing, Sylvie. Has anyone other than the staff been in here?"

"I . . . I don't think so. Really. We know all the people who come here."

"I'm going to have to question them. All of them."

A malaise drifted like heavy smoke through the laboratory. Outside, the *Danièle-Casanova* blew two siren blasts as it passed through the Sainte-Marie strait.

"Could you show me where those flints were kept?"

Sylvie went to the middle cupboard to remove a box, and placed it on the table. De Palma read the labels and observed that an axe head and a large knife blade were indeed missing. He thanked Sylvie and left the laboratory at Fort Saint-Jean.

To avoid the city centre and to take a break, de Palma drove towards the coast road. The police radio in his Clio started screaming out code words such as "*Pétanque de Solex . . .* ". So he opened the glove compartment and turned it off. The traffic was getting heavier. In Anse des Catalans, the cars were crawling along. "Damn that match," he muttered between clenched teeth.

All of a sudden he placed his siren on the dashboard, switched it on and swerved to his right with his foot hard down on the accelerator. The front wheels spun before gripping the tarmac. One way or another, the tension which had built up during the day was going to have to be worked off. He sped away with clenched jaws, narrowly avoiding the cars which were trying to get out of his way.

He drove like a madman past the tomb of the unknown soldier and skidded to a halt. A rubbish truck was blocking the road outside the Flots Bleus bar. The Baron reversed, his tyres smoking, then drove on to the pavement and continued his journey to nowhere.

A kilometre further on, he slowed as he approached the propeller blade which stood as a monument to repatriated settlers from Algeria. The traffic had thinned out. He forgot about his flat in La Capelette, put away his siren and continued along the coast to the end of Les Goudes, opposite Maire island.

Here was his omphalos, the centre of his world.

It was here, in the lapping waves, that he had kissed Marie for the first time, fifteen years ago now, having trodden on her feet all night in a ballroom run by Ange Naldi, an ex-gangster. They had spent the evening dancing the tango and paso doble amongst a group of hoods. They had been the only young people there. The Baron had gone along to kill time, while she was keeping her cousins company. Ange had placed them side by side, just to see what would happen. It had been the most beautiful day of his life.

On the far side of the bay, Marseille the good-time town was dancing in the lazy reflections of the water, while the lights of a huge cargo ship passed out to sea behind the islands. He would have given anything to be one of the crew, to leave the harbour behind and sail away, nose to the wind, into the evening waves. The lamp of the Planier lighthouse swept the moonlit horizon as though to broaden the destinies of those staring at it.

He went back to the little port of Les Goudes and parked his car like a drifter, between two piles of dustbins and some old fishing nets. The calm, smooth sea was giving off a slight aroma of oil, with a hint of nuoc-mam, scents of dried seaweed, a whiff of varnish and paint, all combined with the dominant fragrance of the still-warm water. A few professional fishing boats, which had been tossed about by the sea breezes further out, were now manoeuvring themselves, sails struck, among the pleasure boats which had been baked in the sun.

Maistre and de Palma had sworn to buy a fishing boat when they retired. They wanted an old one, made of wood, with a navy blue hull and coral rail, a little roof at the back and a real Beaudoin motor which went "tot tot tot tot . . ." without ever getting worked up, just enough to keep its tack while catching the silver bass of the coastline in its dragnet. In fact, retirement was not that far away, and the image of their boat was now becoming fixed in the two officers' minds.

For once, de Palma went home early. When he had closed the door of his flat, images suddenly burst into his mind. He imagined that blood stains were covering his eyes, and that the smell of Julia's corpse had got into his clothes.

He stayed in the shower for a long time.

19.

Vidal parked his car on the pavement of rue Béranger, fifty metres away from the square and the church of Saint-Julien. At 9.00 a.m., the neighbourhood was deserted. He tried to imagine the places that Julia Chevallier would have frequented. He eliminated the bar-cum-tobacconist's in the square – Julia had not smoked – and instead headed towards the bakeries, groceries and other stores where the young woman might have been known. Each time, the answers were vague. Newspaper articles had had their effect: everyone knew Julia, but no-one knew very much about her. She was just one anonymous, bourgeois woman among all the other anonymous bourgeois women in this dormitory suburb.

His enquiries in the neighbourhood led to nothing, but there was still the parish priest, Father Paul Orliac, who had telephoned the day before to say that he had seen Julia on the evening of her murder. De Palma had not wanted to come along, preferring to concentrate on the latest elements of the case in peace.

Vidal had an appointment with the priest at 10.00. He looked at his watch; it was time to head towards the presbytery.

Despite his coarse features, the priest waiting for him at the door was a friendly individual. They crossed a courtyard containing two huge pine trees, with a basketball pitch at the far end.

"I simply can't believe it, Inspecteur. Just imagine, I left her around 11.00 that night . . . it's horrific."

The priest of Saint-Julien settled down in what was presumably the parish's reception room, which was large but half taken up by a huge table covered with an ancient oilcloth. He wore his sixty years lightly, spoke with a heavy Charentes accent and kept rolling his eyes as he looked at Vidal.

"A murder, can you imagine? And such savagery . . . I can tell you I've seen a lot in my lifetime. I've even been a prison chaplain in America. But this leaves me both sad and disgusted."

"Was there anything she told you that evening which surprised you?"

"Surprised? No, nothing. She was the sort of tormented being that we come across, alas, more and more frequently. She was looking for her path . . . She had been to confession and then, that evening, she called me for reassurance. She was a lonely soul. She wanted to take holy orders."

Father Paul massaged his bald scalp with both hands, then raised his large eyes towards the ceiling.

"There's nothing else to tell you. I met her that morning, in the church. She found it difficult to talk about herself. Then, in the evening, she telephoned and asked to see me. I went to her house at around 9.00 p.m., and we spoke for about two hours. When I saw the newspaper, I swear to you I had doubts about my mission in life."

"Why?"

"In this sort of situation, I think everyone blames themselves a little, don't they? I was once a chaplain on death row and, take my word for it, each execution weighs down on you. You say to yourself, my God, couldn't I have done something?"

"Yes, I understand. So she didn't tell you anything that sounded strange?"

"No, she just spoke about her loneliness . . . "

Father Paul stared into Vidal's eyes.

"She was homosexual. I don't know if that will be of any help . . . and I hope I won't see it in the papers tomorrow."

"You can trust me."

Vidal stood up and walked over to the pictures of catechism classes on the wall.

"When you came back to the presbytery, it must have been about 11.00 p.m. You didn't bump into anyone?"

"Absolutely not. Around here, it's deserted in the evening."

"Isn't it rather unusual for a priest to visit a young woman in her home at night?"

"I hardly ever do it."

"Why?"

"Gossip, Inspecteur."

"We say 'Lieutenant' now, Father . . . So why did you go and see her that night?"

"I sensed that she felt lost . . . I was worried she might harm herself."

"That she might commit suicide?"

"Not necessarily, but you never know. I could hear intense anxiety in her voice."

"If I understand you correctly, you arrived at about 9.00 and left at about 11.00, is that right?"

Father Paul stared once more at Vidal.

"Yes, more or less."

"Did she show you out?"

"Yes, of course. She closed the door behind me."

"And then?"

"And then I went home."

"Here?"

"No, I live in Les Caillols."

"What time did you get home?"

"It must have been about 11.30, maybe a little before."

"Does anyone live here?"

"No, not any more. What do you expect? There are fewer and fewer vocations. I look after three parishes at the same time."

A man of about forty pushed open the door of the presbytery, carrying a large cardboard box. He looked coldly at the police officer and then nodded at him.

"This is Luc, a young man who has made himself indispensable. He's here to help me with my three parishes. We're going to let him live here . . . Today, he's bringing us some new missals. We were beginning to run out."

Vidal shook the man's outstretched hand.

"Luc . . . and what's your surname?"

"Chauvy."

Vidal jotted it down on his notepad.

"With a Y?"

"Yes . . . that's right."

"Tell me Luc," Father Paul said, "do you remember what time I arrived home the evening poor Julia was murdered?"

"The exact time, no, but it was at the end of the film on channel three . . . It's awful what happened," he added, turning towards Vidal. "How can one of God's children do such a thing?"

"Listen, we have good reason to believe that the person we're looking for lives in Saint-Julien, or else used to lived here. We think he's a loner, middle-aged, passionate about prehistory and university studies . . . What more can I tell you?"

Father Paul smiled scornfully.

"I don't know if you're aware of it," he said, "but the murderer of the young woman at Cadenet was arrested yesterday. It was in *La Provence* this morning. According to the journalist, he might well be the same man."

Vidal took the news like a bucket of sea water.

*

ARREST OF THE SUSPECTED MURDERER OF HÉLÈNE WEILL

. . . The psychiatrist François Caillol was arrested at eight o'clock in the morning as he was leaving his home, an old house on route de Puyricard, on the way to his practice in Aix-en-Provence. Caillol made no attempt to escape as he was getting into his Mercedes, the same car which apparently took Hélène Weill on what was to be her last journey.

The gendarmes have explained that a certain number of converging details, clues and concrete proof led them to Caillol. During a lightning investigation of six weeks, the gendarmerie questioned a large number of witnesses. Then one testimony in particular, describing how Hélène Weill was seen getting into a grey Mercedes on the night of her murder, pointed towards the psychiatrist. According to sources close to the investigation . . .

De Palma put down *La Provence*. Bitterly he glanced around Le Zanzi. At 10.00 a.m., the bar was empty. Dédé looked weighed down by fatigue. With his elbows on the bar and the telephone receiver stuck between his shoulder and his cheek fat, he was checking the details of an order with one of his suppliers. He hung up angrily.

"Hi, Michel. Do you want a coffee?"

"Sure."

Dédé shakily placed a measure of coffee in the espresso machine, then whistled as he wiped down the bar top.

"Did you read about the gendarmes in Cadenet?" he said in what appeared to be a conversational gambit.

"Yes, apparently they sometimes find out things."

"Don't be jealous, Baron. It takes all sorts to make a world. But that was quick work. They solved it in two months."

"Yes, so it seems . . . "

The coffee arrived.

"Have you heard from Maistre?"

"No, not for two days."

"Yesterday he came in with a journalist friend of his. He was looking ever so pleased with himself. He told me a strange story, I don't know if you know it. Ever heard of the M.L.A.?"

De Palma smiled.

"No, what is it?"

"The Marseille Liberation Army."

"Maistre is a real joke. He pulls that one on everyone . . . I don't know why, but he seems to find it funny."

"It's no joke. He was dead serious. It seems there was a bomb alert yesterday in the town hall of the fifteenth arrondissement. You know, up in the heights . . . "

"Really?"

"Would I lie to you? That's why he was with the journalist."

"So Maistre has taken to talking to journalists. That's bad news."

"You know, he was just explaining the whole thing, was it a bomb or wasn't it . . . and the hack was noting it all down."

"What do you expect him to do? Knit a shawl?"

"Anyway, it's none of my business . . . "

"I'm going to call Maistre."

De Palma dialled Maistre's mobile number.

"Jean-Louis? It's me. I've got some information about the M.L.A. They've kidnapped Dédé . . . that's right, Dédé from Le Zanzi . . . they've said they'll only free him if you agree to retire . . . Really . . . Let's do lunch . . . O.K."

De Palma hung up. He barely had time to ask Dédé for another coffee before his mobile bleated its two strident notes. He had a message. "Good morning, sir. I'm phoning about your message last week. Could you please contact me? I'll be in my office from 10.00 to 11.00. Speak to you soon."

The Baron decoded the message. It was from Gérard Mourain, a.k.a. Tête. It was 10.30. He just had time to dash over to his "office".

The gangster was waiting like a statue outside a phone booth on the corner of rue Roger Salengro and avenue Camille Pelletan, blinking to chase away the dust blown everywhere by the mistral. Pages of newspapers and plastic bags fluttered in the air, rising up the grey façades of the buildings.

When he saw the Baron's car, Tête stepped off the pavement and on to the tarmac. He dived into the unmarked car and put on his seat belt. The Baron held out his hand.

"Good morning, Tête. Are you scared of having an accident, or getting a fine?"

"How are you, Monsieur le Divisionnaire?"

"I've told you a hundred times now that we say Commandant, not Monsieur le Divisionnaire!"

"Yes, I always forget."

"So what can I do for you, Tête? Are you feeling nostalgic about the good old days?"

"I called you because I'm freaking out. I can't keep it all to myself. It's too much."

"Can you be a bit more specific, Tête? What's up?"

Mourain looked down. He did not know where to begin. He knew how ferocious the Baron could be. It was a fact that had often haunted his nights. His fragile brain was becoming increasingly scrambled.

"Come on, Tête, we're not going to beat about the bush for hours on end. Police officers like me have got work to do!"

"O.K., boss. Take the coast road towards L'Estaque. Then we'll have a quiet chat."

De Palma sensed that the gangster had something serious to tell him. Since Mourain had started informing for him, he had never seen him in such a state. He offered him a Gitane.

"Listen up, boss. Last autumn, the Bar des Sportifs gang asked me to trail someone. Just trail them . . . And to keep them informed later. Got me?"

De Palma did not answer. The wind was shaking the car.

"Then, one evening just recently, I was in the bar and I read the papers. See what I mean?"

De Palma stared at the road in silence.

"Well, I saw the photo of the girl they asked me to follow. Understand?"

De Palma indicated and turned left towards the access lane leading to the coast road.

"She lived on boulevard Chave . . . Jesus Christ, I haven't slept a wink since . . . I just can't get it out of my mind."

Without taking his eyes off the road, de Palma spat:

"It's a bit late now."

"I know, boss, I know . . . Put yourself in my shoes!"

"But I'm not in your shoes . . . "

"Jesus, I know that. I've done no end of hold-ups. I've stolen loads of things. But I've never killed anyone. On my mother's soul. Especially not a woman."

"Have you been back to the bar?"

"Of course I have! I don't want to get myself blown away. But Lolo doesn't trust me any more, I can just feel it."

De Palma drummed his fingers on the steering wheel. He took the Saint-André exit.

"Tête, if you know anything else, now's the moment. Who asked you to follow her?"

"Lolo, you know him?"

"Of course I know the little prick. Who else?"

"Someone I hadn't seen for ages. Richard Mattéi. You know, the one they call 'Petits Bras'."

"Why, because his arms are so short that when his arse itches he can't scratch it?"

"This is no laughing matter, boss."

"What date was all this?"

"I can't remember, on my daughter's life, I can't . . . It was in the autumn . . . September, or October . . . "

"Jesus, can't you make an effort to remember the date? What am I supposed to do with all this crap?"

"I know. But being in prison . . . Eight years is a long time. You lose all notion of time."

"When you followed her, what did she do?"

"Nothing much. She went to Aix. To the university there. Then she came back . . . "

"And that's all."

"No, boss . . . there's something else."

"What?"

"Someone else was following her. I'm sure of it. I'm used to this job. But he wasn't. The dickhead never spotted me."

"Oh yes, indeed, trailing people's a real craft."

"Give me a break, boss, I'm bricking it."

"What was this guy like?"

"About one metre eighty tall, forty-something. At the very least. Wearing a cap, like kids do. He had a beard and glasses. I even asked him for a light. He's not from round here. He doesn't speak like us. He doesn't have the accent. He's got blue eyes. I could identify him any time."

On the coast road, de Palma parked on the pavement between two refrigerated trucks, a few metres away from Saumaty fishing port. From his pocket, he removed the official identity photo of François Caillol, which the gendarmerie had sent him. Mourain took a long look at it.

"Negative, boss."

"Tête, is it him or isn't it? Don't screw me around!"

"Definitely not boss. He's not even wearing glasses. No, it's not him."

"Smart, Tête, very smart."

"Don't take the piss, Inspecteur. Everyone can have their doubts, can't they?"

As he spoke, Mourain gesticulated wildly, with stiff little fingers and extended thumbs.

"Listen to me boss, he was wearing specs for his eyesight. Real ones! Almost like magnifying glasses . . . See what I mean? That's why I noticed he had blue eyes. They bulged out, like jelly-fish."

"Wait a second, Gérard."

De Palma called the Cadenet gendarmerie on his mobile. He asked them if the man they had arrested wore glasses or contact lenses, and if his eyes were blue. The answer was no. De Palma hung up.

"Thanks a lot, Tête."

"What's going to happen to me now?"

"You're going to have a nice quiet drink at your friend Lolo's place. Don't worry. He wasn't the one who killed her. Just try to find out why he got you to follow her."

The gangster was now looking more relaxed. Mourain had been working for the Baron for a good ten years now and, as his most faithful informer, gave him the best leads on the market. The one he had just delivered, in the form of a confession, was weighty enough. One name above all worried de Palma: Richard Mattéi, alias Petits Bras, an ex-member of the French Connection and a big player who was making a comeback. The drugs squad suspected him of dealing in Ecstasy and organising raves to flog his gear via his shitty little pushers. As for the vice squad, they suspected him of selling illegal porno cassettes. Meanwhile the serious crime boys thought he was behind a dozen gangland killings. Once again, Petits Bras was becoming quite a number in the mob.

De Palma sketched in another connection: Christine – Lolo and the Bar des Sportifs gang. An intellectual and the mob. And Franck Luccioni. He didn't like the way things were going. And the case was tumbling into a world it would be hard for him to penetrate. A world of silence.

De Palma aimed a friendly smile at his informer. He thought about those glasses. Tête had mentioned lenses like magnifying glasses, so real ones which the wearer cannot do without.

A detail.

A simple detail which complicated everything and upset his thoughts and certitudes. The investigation had gone off the rails. Caillol had not followed Christine Autran. Mourain was a skilled villain; he wouldn't have made a mistake. It was impossible.

"How's your kid?"

"Fine, boss. She'll be leaving school soon. But I think she's seeing someone. Jesus, just let me catch him."

"She's eighteen, Tête."

"If he lays a finger on my daughter, I'll smash his face in!"

"Maybe she loves him."

"Fuck love! At her age, you concentrate on your studies."

"You're right, Tête, watch out for her. By the way, where does she go to school?"

"Lycée Périer."

"A word of advice, don't let her out of your sight."

"What do you mean, boss? Do you reckon . . . "

"I think the guy you ran into on boulevard Chave knows where you live and maybe also knows where your daughter goes to school. It wouldn't be hard. You'll have to do something."

"Like what?"

"Keep your eyes open. If you spot him, call me, O.K.?"

"Right, boss."

De Palma lifted Mourain's jacket. He saw the grip of a police Beretta.

"So you're out in company, Gérard?"

"I'm scared, boss."

"If he gets close to your daughter, stay cool and call me at once. Where shall I drop you off?"

"By Bougainville métro. I'll walk home."

The terrace of Le Robinson provided a spectacular view of Epluchures beach, the only place around Marseille with waves good enough for surfers. Sitting sheltered from the wind, Bérengère Luccioni had been sipping at her mint-flavoured mineral water for the past fifteen minutes as she watched the dickheads parading themselves.

She thought of *Pourriture Beach*, the well-known detective story by Patrick Blaise, which she had just read. A few fluorescent figures were trying to stay upright on the crests of the waves beyond the beach; invariably they flopped down like unstrung puppets and vanished for a few seconds beneath their multi-coloured sails. Submerged in the blue. Three days before, the mistral had changed direction, and the waves were becoming smaller and smaller. The next day, it would fall completely and the sea would be calm.

De Palma was late. From afar, in the sunlight, he stared at Bérengère for a few moments. Her hair flew into her face at each gust of wind, and he was reminded of the little girl he had once known.

Bérengère had recovered her natural hair colour – auburn had replaced that vulgar blonde – and she was no longer wearing an overly short skirt or high boots. Just jeans, a pair of trainers and a cotton top which hugged her hourglass figure. The mobster chick had been transformed into a Madonna by Raphael.

She sensed the policeman's presence and turned round.

"Hello," she said, pushing back her hair.

"Hello, Bérengère."

He sat down beside her. She was not wearing perfume, but the mistral breathed the subtle fragrance of her hair into the atmosphere. De Palma stared at the sea whitened by the crashing of the waves.

"How are things, Bérengère?"

"Fine, Commandant . . . I mean, so to speak . . . "

"What do you mean?"

"I've lost my brother, Commandant. I don't know why, but he's in my thoughts a lot at the moment. He wasn't as bad as all that, you know."

"I know, Bérengère, I know . . . "

The waiter arrived. De Palma ordered a beer, and Bérengère another mint mineral water. She turned to the policeman and looked at him for a long time. De Palma had the impression that she was trying to read his mind.

After he had left Mourain, a detail had disturbed his initial certainties. He remembered that the Luccioni family had for some time lived in the Mazargues quartier, like Christine. It might just be a coincidence, but he wanted to check it out. Franck and Christine had been exactly the same age, so they might have known each other at school, or elsewhere.

He took a photo of Christine Autran out of his pocket.

"Have you ever seen this woman?"

Bérengère frowned as she held the photo. She thought for a while, and something seemed to be rising up from the depths of her memory. Then she put a hand to her mouth, and her chest heaved.

"My God, yes, I do know her! I saw her with my brother a lot. It's Christine, she was a local girl when we lived in Mazargues. She went to school with him."

"Are you sure?"

"Definitely, I'm certain. She's changed, I didn't recognise her at first . . . But it's her alright. They were inseparable when they were young. They were the same age. My brother would be forty-three in . . . "

Bérengère looked down, filled her lungs with sea air and rotated her glass in her hand. She seemed overcome by immense distress.

The murders of Luccioni and Autrane had at last converged. He could no longer believe it was a coincidence. Why hadn't Jo told him about the friendship between Christine and his son? Why hadn't Bérengère told him anything before? Questions like these burned in his mind, but he decided to keep them for later.

"I've got some photos of her at home," Bérengère said. "Do you want me to bring them to you at the station, or do you want to come back with me?"

"Let's go to your place. It'll save time."

They passed by the leprous buildings along the coast and soon entered the quiet streets of Pointe-Rouge and the new suburbs. Newly built houses, as regular as cubes, were set amongst pine trees and alongside a shopping centre with a multiscreen cinema.

Bérengère lived on the top two floors of a stone building in a small complex in Le Roy d'Espagne. The flat's balcony overlooked the Pointe-Rouge quartier and, beyond it, the sea. Planier lighthouse could be seen in the hazy distance. A ferry cruised slowly towards a destination known only to itself, like a tiny, white shoebox on the mother-of-pearl foam. Opposite, lost on the horizon, the solitary lamp of a beacon watched over the comings and goings in the huge bay of Marseille.

"Can I offer you anything?"

"No thanks, Bérengère. Do you live on your own here?"

"Yes, I'm all alone . . . if that's what you mean. How about a drop of whisky?"

"O.K., but no ice."

De Palma looked round the flat of Luccioni's daughter. It was as spick and span as an ideal home exhibition: little knick-knacks, a few holiday souvenirs on the Provençal sideboard, a basalt figurine of the Horus falcon, probably haggled over at a market in Egypt between visits to a temple and a royal tomb. There were three white-washed rooms, containing top-quality Provençal country furniture which must have cost a fortune. The wardrobe had acquired the patina of age and was of a simple beauty, carved with ears of corn and a seashell. Where had she found such a piece? Had she inherited it? Unlikely. Was it her pay as her father's salesgirl? Also unlikely.

"You have some lovely furniture."

"Oh yes, they're my treasures. When I was a little girl, I dreamed of having a beautiful house in the country, with lovely old furniture. I don't have the house, but I do have the furniture. That's something anyway!"

"Where did you find it all?"

"Here and there. In antiques stores . . . My ex-boyfriend was a specialist."

"In antiques?"

A smile flitted over Bérengère's face.

"No, a thief like my brother."

She went into the kitchen and came back with two glasses, then opened the sideboard, produced a bottle of Bushmills Pure Malt and poured out two treble measures.

"Cheers, Michel."

She emphasised his forename, as though to let him know that she wanted to remember.

"I'll go and get the photos. They're in my bedroom."

De Palma knocked back his whisky and went out on to the balcony. Waves as far as the eye could see; the horizon was trembling, moved by an invisible force.

"Look, Michel, here's a photo of my brother, and there she is just beside him, Do you recognise her?"

In the picture, Christine must have been seventeen or eighteen. She already had a wilful, goody-goody look which made her seem a little cold.

"And then in this one they're a bit older. They must be about twenty. Look, that's her there."

"Did they go out together?"

"I don't know. My brother really loved her. But I'm not sure it was mutual."

New line: Autran – Luccioni. Childhood friends, found dead in the same place.

"The last time you came to see me, at the station, you told me about a man on a motorbike. Try to remember. Was he wearing glasses? Did he have blue eyes?"

"I've already told you. He was wearing glasses and his eyes were really blue. That's all I could see because of his helmet."

"No, you didn't tell me."

"Didn't I? Strange, I can really remember the way he looked at me."

"It doesn't matter."

A new character had now entered the scenario: a man with blue eyes. Intuitively, the Baron sensed that this was the murderer of Luccioni and Autran.

"You know what happened to Christine?"

"No," she said, shaking her head. "What do you mean?"

"It's been in all the papers."

"I don't read the papers."

"She was found dead, in the same place as Franck."

Bérengère held her face in her hands.

"But why?" she said with a sob. "WHY?"

"I don't know, Bérengère. I don't know . . ."

A long silence descended. Sounds from the city drifted up from time to time, carried on gusts of wind. Bérengère was no longer crying. Her eyes were vacant, open on to a huge empty space.

"Did your father know Christine?"

"No, he never met her. He was never around. And then he went to prison. No, my father . . . he knows nothing about his children. Nor does my mother, for that matter . . . Christine never came to our house."

"What do you know about their relationship? Was he still seeing her last year?"

"Maybe, but I can't guarantee it. Franck was very secretive. Too secretive even. And I never asked any questions. It wouldn't be right . . . I don't think they saw each other very often, but that's all I can tell you."

She looked at him with her big, green eyes; they told him a secret, a part of her inner self and invited him into a forbidden space in her past.

"Michel, you know, over the years I've often thought about you . . . you can't imagine how often. Even though it was you who arrested my father. No, really! I'll always remember that day, the way you took his handcuffs off so that he could kiss me goodbye, like a father should. You weren't like the others. Please don't laugh. It really isn't funny."

"But I'm not laughing, Bérengère. I'm really touched by what you've just told me . . . I . . . I don't know what to say . . . "

"Then don't say anything."

She took his hand and squeezed it.

De Palma thought about the visiting rooms, the slamming of heavy doors, the bright lights in concrete corridors, the urine-like yellow of the thick walls. The sounds, the metallic clangs. Tannoys. Keys. Clinical colours. Prison car parks, here in the brilliant sunlight, or up north, in a sad drizzle. Fortresses of fury, prefabricated citadels: Baumettes, Luynes, Fresnes, Santé, Clairvaux, Fleury-Mérogis, Douai . . .

A strange pain ran through him, a sword in his guts pushed up to its hilt.

*

A sound: the harsh wood-panelling in the courts of justice. A murmur, too, classroom chatter, the babble of people re-judging what has just been judged.

The magistrates, the vultures, the hacks weighing one another up . . . Luccioni leaves the box. Twelve years.

Soft, white packets, an air pump, acid filling the air in a little mountain chalet . . . Hoods staring at one another in the back rooms of society.

Transfer of inmates at the end of the night. No-one should be disturbed. The elite brigades, armed like Hollywood S.W.A.T.s. Balaclavas. POLICE *written in capital letters. Children, their eyes puffy from sleep, yelling: "Dad, we're here with mum, we love you".*

A LONG SENTENCE

He placed his hand on Bérengère's shoulder and hugged her. Hard. Very hard. Twenty-five years on the force and he still did not know where the borderline lay.

Planier lighthouse vanished into the light.

De Palma went home at the end of the afternoon. On the way, he received a call from Vidal.

"I've been trying to contact you since this morning."

"Sorry, kid, I turned off my mobile. What's new?"

"Nothing at all. I saw the priest in Saint-Julien. He's got a cast-iron alibi, and I looked like a complete idiot."

"Calm down a bit!"

"I am calm, but you could have phoned me this morning to let me know they'd got the psychiatrist."

"Sorry, Maxime."

Vidal then told him how the fingerprints taken from the plastic bag de Palma had handed to Palestro had spoken that afternoon: they were the same as the ones the technicians had lifted in Autran's flat. But those found in Julia Chevallier's house were completely unusable.

"Have you got anything more on the knife and lamp?"

"No, nothing. We decided that was about Luccioni, and so it could wait."

"Not any more. Luccioni and Autran knew each other."

"Really?"

"Yes, I went to see his sister, and she told me."

"But how did you make the connection?"

"It would take too long to explain now . . . It was silly, in fact. I just remembered that Luccioni used to live in Mazargues when he was young."

"So, that means more work for us."

"Indeed it does! And tomorrow we're going to have to start questioning staff at the archaeology lab. So take it easy, you're going to be up to your neck."

"O.K., Michel."

"See you tomorrow, kid."

Three messages were waiting for him on his mobile.

The first was from Maistre:

"Hi there, old fellow. I'll be in your chic neighbourhood to get my car fixed. I'll call by to see you around 7.00 p.m. End of message."

The second was from his mother, who was worried about his silence. He realised that he had not contacted her for days. The third was from Sylvie Maurel, whose voice trembled slightly. She sounded out of breath.

"Michel, I didn't go to work today. I don't know why, but I didn't feel up to it. This morning, when I went out, I didn't feel good. So I went back to bed. I'm in town now. If you're free this evening, I'd like to see you. I've got something to tell you. It's 5.00 p.m. I'll call you back in an hour."

De Palma looked at his watch. It was 5.30. He thought for a moment. He had trouble admitting to himself that he really wanted to see Sylvie. It was a compulsion he could not chase away. He called Maistre and invented an appointment to put him off for the evening. Then he phoned Sylvie and arranged to meet her at 8.00 p.m. in a café on cours d' Estienne d'Orves. That would give him enough time to go home first.

As he entered his flat, he realised that everything about the décor reminded him of his wife: the colours, the odd, dusty knick-knack. She had certainly not left his life yet.

Did he really want her to?

*

Marie has come to his flat for the first time. She immediately notices his collection of books on criminology. Out of curiosity, she goes over to them, reading out the titles: The Criminal Personality, Clinical Criminology, A Criminology Handbook, Crime and Criminals . . .

He simply says: "It's a trade, Marie. Each to his own field of studies, and mine's crime. I'm on the murder squad. And reading is as important as fieldwork. I know everything about murder."

She picks up a door stopper entitled: The Scene of the Crime: the First Elements in an Investigation. *It is illustrated, and de Palma has left a sheaf of notes inside it. In the central section, Marie comes across a series of photographs.*

Horror.

"What's this? It's awful, it looks like . . . "

"A naked nine-year-old child who has been beaten to death, raped, and tied up with electric cable. The case has never been solved. Don't look at it. The human mind couldn't dream up anything more horrific."

"Have you ever seen anything like that?"

"All the time. It's my job."

Marie closes the book and stares at de Palma, distressed.

"Do all policemen read books?"

"No, far from it. Let's just say that I'm a specialist. I try to understand killers."

"And do you?"

"I think so."

Marie puts down the book and gazes around the room. On the sideboard, she notices a chrome frame with a black-and-white photograph which has turned sepia over the years.

"You were a very handsome young man!"

"It's not me. It's my brother," *he replies in a sombre voice.*

"He looks so much like you!"

"We're twins."

"Really, I didn't know you had a twin brother!"

"He died, in an accident . . . I don't want to talk about it."

"I'm sorry. I didn't realise . . . "

She casts her eyes around the room, trying to escape the horrific expression on his face.

"I'll be back," Marie had said. It had been months now. For de Palma, they had flown by . . . He had not heard from her at all for the past fortnight. He did not want to know the reason why. He would phone her parents that weekend, to try to find out more.

Sylvie was waiting for him on the terrace of Le Pythéas. When she saw him coming, she stood up and waved.

"You look tired."

"This job is wearing me out."

"Do you want a drink?"

"I'll have a beer."

Sylvie peered at him. She was more beautiful than ever. He did his best to hide the fact that, just then, he was the least relaxed man in Marseille.

His beer arrived, and he knocked back half of it in one.

"I got some bad news this morning," she announced all of a sudden.

"Nothing serious, I hope?"

"Nothing personal. But I read in *La Provence* that you'd arrested François Caillol."

"We didn't arrest him. It was the gendarmes. And why is that bad news?"

"I know him."

"Personally?"

"No, not really. He's a psychiatrist specialised in neuropsychology . . . And he's interested in prehistory. I've seen him on several occasions at conferences. Apart from his consulting work, he studies hallucinatory phenomena. Christine knew him better than I do. They worked together on shamanism."

"So?" de Palma murmured, pretending not to be falling from another planet.

"They were studying shamanistic practices in various tribes in an attempt to understand certain prehistoric rituals. It's a bit complicated, and to be honest I'm not sure that work of this kind is valid. Anyway, people like that are all half crazy!"

"But not because he's a psychiatrist! The enigma of violence is associated with the uncertainty of our human condition: the greater the uncertainty, the greater the violence. That's what my old criminology teacher used to say, and then he'd add: 'Crime is natural, what's artificial is virtue. It's taken thousands of years, plus a whole bunch of gods and prophets, for humanity to learn this truth.'"

"How true. So do you think Caillol's a murderer?"

"Who knows? A psychiatrist is generally speaking sane. They have fewer doubts about the human condition than we do. But, in the end, you never know . . ."

De Palma stared down at the foam on the amber surface of his beer. He would have preferred Sylvie to talk to him about something other than Christine Autran, even though she had just advanced his investigation significantly.

"Michel . . ."

"I'm the best, Sylvie. I always get my man. Sooner or later, I get them all. I've got the gift!"

"And you're modest with it!"

"I, too, am a great hunter."

"You're off the rails, Michel. He's been arrested."

"I know I'm off the rails. If I wasn't, then you wouldn't be here right now. I can't explain it all to you. This investigation is hard enough as it is. But I have this crazy idea that our psychiatrist isn't the murderer. That's what I think. If you'd seen everything I've seen in my life, you wouldn't even trust yourself."

"But if they've arrested Caillol, they must have evidence!"

"Oh, they always have evidence. So much so that they don't need a confession! An intelligent man, a pervert, and a psychiatrist to boot, who kills then leaves behind a trail of clues that gets him arrested straight away. I mean, really . . ."

De Palma stood up and called to the waiter.

"If this psychiatrist has also studied prehistory, and therefore cave painting, he wouldn't leave a reproduction behind so that he could be identified at once, especially given that the victim was one of his patients. See what I mean?"

"Yes, I suppose so . . . Are you going?" she exclaimed.

"Yes, I . . . I mustn't see you like this! Goodbye, Sylvie."

*

When he got home, he wanted to empty his mind. He went to his CD player, put on the last act of "Tristan" and scanned to the end – the death of Isolde. Birgit Nilsson's sublime voice, smooth and deep, mingled with the obscure depths of the orchestral performance.

> *"How soft and gentle is his smile*
> *how sweetly his eyes open, my friends, can you see?"*

On his balcony, his eyes focused on the dark mass of the Saint-Loup hills, piercing the black sky. He let his memories gently envelop him: long winter walks to the conservatory on place Carli, hand in hand with his twin, his other half; Wednesday visits to the mother superior of the convent of the Sisters of Saint Joseph, who was a distant cousin; the nun's marshmallows, the obligatory prayer in the chapel, bathed in the soft light filtering through the yellow and lazulite stained-glass windows.

> *"These sweet voices which surround me*
> *are they the waves of soft breezes?"*

With his brother, he would kneel before the altar of white marble, which was always decked with freshly cut flowers. A few metres away to the left lay the mummified body of the order's founder, a semi-saint who had lived in the nineteenth century. As he mumbled a 'Hail Mary', Michel would glance at her embalmed corpse. He was so fascinated by her death mask that, one day, he could no longer resist pressing his face against the glass. He had taken a long look at those features, their severity smoothed by death. Her mouth was still crimson, her eyes looked as though they might open again at any moment, and her aquiline nose rose up above her white cowl with her hands crossed on her stomach and a rosary in her fingers, the founder of the order of Saint Joseph of the Apparition seemed to be fast asleep; perhaps she was dreaming of the African savannahs, the ochre stretches of the Sahara, or the deep jungles of Vietnam which she had tried to evangelise during her life as a missionary.

"Are they billows of delicious perfumes?
How they swell, how heady they are,
Shall I breathe, shall I look?"

Death had always fascinated Commandant de Palma. Even though he had lost his faith, it remained the big mystery.

He was fascinated by the death of others, and by his own killer instinct, which surprised him from time to time when he felt unbalanced. He would have flashes of fury, and over-exposed sequences spun in his mind, with images of cold blades cutting into soft flesh, bodies pushed into the void, crushed skulls.

The great darkness.

The big sleep, as they say.

"In the mass of waves, in the thunder of noise,
in the breath of the world, the universe,
I shall drown, be engulfed,
lose consciousness – supreme rapture!"

20.

In the dark corridor on the third floor of the Marseille high court, secretaries were going in and out of the magistrates' offices carrying huge folders. De Palma was waiting beside a plastic fig tree, his bum aching on the hard, varnished bench. He was trying to think of an operatic air to pass the time, but his brain was still half asleep.

That morning, Commissaire Paulin had informed him that the public prosecutor had taken away the investigation into the killing in Saint-Julien from the murder squad. De Palma was there to see his deputy, to try to make him change his mind.

He did not like the high court on Monday mornings. Having failed to find a tune to hum, he had only one solution: to kill time by admiring the legs of the petite brunette, as dry as a stick, who was doing the most toing and froing perched on the high heels of her blue shoes.

The door of office number 4 opened. Christophe Barbieri, deputy public prosecutor, poked out his round head and motioned to the Baron to come in.

One wall of the magistrate's office was taken up by a huge poster for the film *La Femme du Boulanger* and above the desk was the Declaration of Human Rights. Barbieri sat down straight away with an exasperated look on his face.

"So, Michel, where are you at with the Autran case?"

"I'm making slow progress, but I am progressing. Why?"

"As Paulin will have told you, I've spoken to the gendarmerie. They take a very dim view of your insinuations about their work."

Barbieri was all but bald. He was wearing a mauve shirt, from which hung an ageless tie decorated with horses. At times his eyes took on an expression of infinite sadness; at others they were lit by a strange fire. He always worked listening to music, except during hearings, and his favourite composers were Mozart and Debussy. There was a huge laserdisc player on the rickety shelf behind him, between the legal books and his magistrate's hat.

"What did the gendarmes tell you?"

"They found out that your colleague . . . what's his name?"

"Vidal."

"Yes, Vidal; they found out that Vidal paid a little visit to the priest of Saint-Julien."

"So what?"

"And they don't like it."

"I couldn't care less, Christophe."

"You might not, but I do. The gendarmerie has made far more progress than you. So I'm taking the Saint-Julien murder away from you. I don't want to see you meddle again. Is that clear?"

De Palma did not reply. He was afraid of losing his temper, which would not help matters. Barbieri was a tough, but straight, magistrate; everyone respected him, even the roughest villains. He was a hard worker, capable of spending entire days looking for the tiniest details which would scupper even the finest barristers. He did not tolerate police officers who presumed to criticise his working methods. De Palma was one of his few friends on the force; a friendship which had formed around their shared passion for opera.

"I can't drop it now," he said softly.

"Why is that?"

"Because of Christine Autran."

"Why, because of Christine Autran?"

"I have to find out who killed her."

"That's your job! But I want to know more!"

"Before long you will, I should think. The snag is, there's the other one."

"Which other one?"

"The Saint-Julien and Cadenet killer."

"What's that got to do with it?"

"For the past few days, I've been thinking that they're all connected, in one way or another."

"How's that?"

"It's just what I think."

"Just what you *think*? I want certainties and proof. And there, old chap, you have a problem. The Cadenet killer has been put away. The case is as solid as concrete. Before long, he'll confess to it, and the killing in Saint-Julien too."

"It's not him."

"How would you know?"

"I just know. And I'll prove it. For both Cadenet and Saint-Julien."

"Michel, I know you're a great policeman. I've never doubted your abilities, but you're going to drop Saint-Julien. I'm the one who decides, O.K.?"

"O.K., but it's not him."

"Come on now, you're as stubborn as a mule. Out with it!"

"What you don't seem to realise, Christophe, is that a shrink of his abilities would never make those mistakes. What's more, he's got an alibi."

"Some alibi! He was having dinner with friends in a restaurant. I could cook up alibis like that every two seconds. As for Saint-Julien, he has no alibi whatsoever, apart from his claim that he was at home. Highly original. So, Michel, open your eyes. We're sure about him!"

"Has he confessed?"

"No."

"You'll end up looking stupid in court."

Barbieri went purple.

"The court's my problem, NOT YOURS!"

"In fact, you're not sure of anything."

"Watch your step, Michel. I don't appreciate your manners. So, explain yourself, or get out of here!"

"I'll tell you where I'm at with the Christine Autran murder. Firstly, I've found out that Autran and Franck Luccioni – who was found dead in the same place as Autran last July – knew each other. They were childhood friends. They grew up in the same neighbourhood, Mazargues. Luccioni was without doubt murdered in Sugiton. Secondly, someone has been to her flat on boulevard Chave on two occasions. I'm sure of it. I've checked everything out. And I have a suspect: Professor Palestro, a prehistorian like her. Her boss, in fact! We've found his fingerprints all over her flat. But I don't think he killed her, although I can't be sure. In any case, he seems to be the only other person to have the keys to her place. Thirdly, I have a witness, Sylvie Maurel, who worked with Autran and Palestro. It's a small world . . ."

Barbieri interrupted him with a wave of his hand.

"I don't know if you're going crazy, or if you've been drinking this morning, anyway, what can I say? Go on, you're amusing me."

"Really?" the Baron replied edgily. "Well, I have an informer who drinks at the Bar des Sportifs in Endoume. He volunteered the information that Lolo asked him to follow a woman. And guess who this woman was?"

"I give up," Barbieri murmured.

"Christine Autran, Sir. So far, nothing very exciting, but where things get complicated is that he saw a man hovering around Autran's flat: forty-something, about a metre eighty tall, thick spectacles . . . There, you see, things aren't as simple as all that . . . "

"What are you on about? I don't get it. Autran, Luccioni, what's his name . . . What's all this got to do with Caillol?"

De Palma grinned.

"If you hadn't interrupted, you'd already know. Caillol worked with Autran."

"What?"

"I'm not trying to make war between the forces, Christophe, but I learned from Sylvie Maurel that Caillol is a specialist in neuro-psychology and that he used to work with Autran."

"Neuropsychology and prehistory? Can you be a bit clearer? Because I'm having problems taking all this seriously."

"Caillol studied shamanism and hallucinatory phenomena in primitive tribes. And it seems that certain practices haven't evolved since the dawn of time . . . There you are."

"Are you sure about this?"

"Absolutely."

"So, what's your hypothesis?"

"I don't think Caillol is the guilty party, but I think he has a connection."

De Palma drew an imaginary line in front of him.

"Autran, Luccioni, Caillol, the two murders, and the guy who was spotted by two witnesses. And I think we should add the three divers found in the tunnel just before the discovery of Le Guen's Cave was announced. At the time, no-one, least of all me, suspected it was a triple murder. When I think back over it now, we really should have looked into it."

He fell silent for a few seconds and frowned.

"I think we're up against a group of loonies who practised, or still practise, magical rituals."

"Come on, your story is a bit far-fetched."

"I'm telling you, he'll kill again. And the sooner the better, because it will clarify things. But he won't strike yet. He'll wait for the psychiatrist to go on trial, then he'll kill again in a year or two. Unless he goes somewhere else, which would be the worst scenario."

Barbieri leaned back in his chair and sighed. Even if he was not completely convinced, he sensed that he ought to listen to the Baron.

"Put like that, I understand better. Is that all?"

"No. Shortly before Franck's death last July, a man came to Jo Luccioni's bakery. The man with the red motorbike, remember?"

"Yes, vaguely, so what?"

De Palma pointed a finger at Barbieri.

"So I think this investigation is just beginning, and that the gendarmes wanted to pull a fast one. You've made a real balls-up of all this!"

"Calm down, Michel. Don't forget who you're talking to. Another word like that, and I'll take you off the Autran case."

"I haven't forgotten!"

"That's enough, Michel. Control yourself!"

"Sorry, Christophe ... Can I ... Can I ask you for a favour?"

"What?"

"Let me see our psychiatrist friend."

"There are times when I wonder why I don't tell you to piss off, Commandant. Two things. Firstly, I don't want you getting involved in the Saint-Julien case again. Secondly, I will let you see Caillol. But I'm warning you, you've got a fortnight to bring enough evidence to challenge the gendarmes' case. I'm not doing anything without solid evidence. And I mean proof, not just your personal conviction that Caillol is innocent. Clear?"

"Clear."

"You can see Caillol later this week, does that suit? But I'll have to be there with you."

Barbieri looked up at de Palma. This policeman did not want to lose the game of hide-and-seek which had now begun. He would make people talk, whatever the cost, pitilessly. He would devastate everything in his path, without leaving a single initiative to anyone else. Always on the offensive, even if that meant losing everything.

"This week, I'm going to Aix to question Professor Palestro."

"O.K. Are you going to bring him in?"

"Maybe."

21.

The 11.43 bullet which killed Jean-Marc Ferri had entered his left eye and come out through the back of his head. Bits of grey matter and scraps of skull were stuck to the headrest in the Fiat Uno. The blood was still fresh. But the most unusual thing about this gangland killing was that the hit-man had fired just once, from point-blank range.

De Palma walked round the car and examined the body of Véronique Ferri, Jean-Marc's wife. At first glance, he could see three bullet holes, two in her back and one in her right temple. Véronique was lying on the ground, blood still flowing from her nostrils, her hand resting on the running board of the car. The door was open.

"I think she tried to run away, and he finished her off," said Vidal.

"You're right, Maxime."

De Palma walked round the car again, then stood back to get an overview of the scene. A Megane pulled up, its siren blaring. Commissaire Paulin got out, crossed the security tape and strode towards de Palma without even looking at the carnage.

"Well?"

"Jean-Marc and Véronique Ferri, husband and wife. An 11.43 I'd say."

"They've stepped up a gear," Paulin murmured. "It's the first time they've killed a woman."

"And probably not the last . . . " remarked de Palma laconically.

"Any ideas?"

"None, except that for Ferri, it was inevitable. Just a matter of time. Everyone had it in for him. Especially the boys in Aix."

Paulin approached the corpse. He looked at it for a few moments, his right hand on his tie, and then circled the Fiat. Beyond the yellow tape that closed off the scene of the crime, there was a growing crowd of onlookers: the old boys from the Le Globe bar, their racing predictions interrupted by the blasts, had crossed the road to join the schoolchildren on their way home for lunch.

"Have you picked up anything, Maxime?"

"I questioned the manager of the petrol station and his staff. They didn't see anything."

"And the passers-by?"

"I've spoken to four. Nothing doing, they each have their own version . . . "

"Who made the call?"

"The manager."

"We'll talk to him again, he must have seen something."

"What do you reckon?"

"The wife was killed. There can be only two reasons for that: revenge, or else she recognised the guy."

"I thought of that."

"Go and fetch me the manager."

Vidal returned with a short man aged about thirty. He had a dry face and greasy hair and was wearing faded blue overalls with black oil stains on the elbows and knees.

"And you are . . . ?"

"Patrick Fitoussi."

"Well, Monsieur Fitoussi, where were you when you heard the gunshots?"

"I was at the till."

"So, what did you see?"

"Nothing, I've already told your colleague . . . "

"You told my colleague a pack of bullshit," de Palma yelled. "But things are different with me. With me, you're going to talk. Was he alone?"

The mechanic looked at him fearfully.

"Yes."

"On foot?"

"Yes."

"So what did you see?"

"I . . . "

De Palma grabbed him by the overalls and pulled him close.

"DID YOU SEE ANYTHING OR NOT?"

Fitoussi began to shake all over.

"Yes, I did, but it was a way off . . . "

"I can understand why you're scared . . . That's normal. You're coming along with us, Monsieur Fitoussi. We're going to show you some photos. And you're going to tell us if you recognise him, O.K.?"

"O.K., Sir."

"Vidal, go with this gentleman and his employees and see what you can do."

Paulin, who had been observing the scene, walked over to de Palma.

"Well done, de Palma, right in front of the journalists. I don't know what gets into you sometimes."

"If you don't shake them up a bit, they don't tell you anything. That's how it goes in Marseille; people never see anything, hear anything or say anything, just like the three monkeys . . . "

"I don't like that method, and you know it. I totally disapprove."

De Palma almost jumped on him. He knew that Paulin had pulled strings to get him off the Saint-Julien case. He nodded towards the two bodies, which the forensics team had now removed from the Fiat.

"Look, Commissaire, he acted quite openly. They don't even hide any more."

"I know," said Paulin, clenching his teeth.

They were now undressing the victims. Blood was still running from Véronique Ferri's wounds. The smell of death mingled with the odour of benzene. Police officers were holding back journalists and onlookers, who were crowded at the edge of the cordon. The siren of a fire engine could be heard on boulevard des Dames. De Palma went back to the bodies.

"It looks really bad, just a few metres away from the council building," de Palma remarked.

"What do you mean?"

"It's not like in Saint-Julien."

"Watch it, de Palma, you're not untouchable. Just deal with Autran! As for the rest, we'll see what the gendarmes can extract from Caillol."

"I didn't mean to offend you, Commissaire. It's just that there are only two of us working on a highly complicated case."

"O.K., I'll give you Moracchini on a permanent basis."

"She's a very good officer ... excellent even. And what about Ferri?"

"Just see what you can do."

"Thanks a bunch ... "

De Palma had a fleeting vision of the long queue of witnesses at police headquarters, the questions that had to be asked, which were always the same, the reports to be typed out one after another, in other words, the dull side of policing in all its splendour, with nothing proven at the end of it beyond the fact that it was a contract killing carried out by a professional. He turned away and swallowed his anger.

Paulin did not believe in the Baron's theories about the murders of Hélène Weill and Julia Chevallier. He had succeeded in getting him taken off the Saint-Julien case and had now lumbered him with a gangland killing, as part of his great crusade against the mob. This was the only way he would be able to leave Marseille for a comfortable post at headquarters. It was the fast track to Paris.

At the station, Vidal spent an hour with Patrick Fitoussi, showing him dozens of photos. The mechanic shook his podgy cheeks at each one, as if to say "No, I don't recognise him". At 4.00 p.m., a disappointed Vidal took his statement. And that was the end of his Tuesday.

22.

Spring was at its height. Heat enveloped Marseille in a heavy, humid cloak. Everyone waited for thunderstorms, as a deliverance, but the storms failed to materialise. It was incomprehensible.

Hunched up in the police Clio, the Baron cursed the stifling heat. Beside him, Vidal was chain-smoking and fiddling with his mobile. The temperature did not seem to bother him.

It was 10.00 in the morning on Wednesday. Palestro had taken his students to a prehistoric site at Châteauneuf-les-Martigues, just by the motorway between Marseille and Fos.

All of a sudden, Vidal emerged from his torpor.

"Shit, Michel, I forgot my cuffs."

"You always forget something! Don't worry, I've got mine, and we shouldn't need them anyway."

"Really?"

"No, he's a very well brought-up gentleman. Anyway, we're only here to ask him a few questions."

Thirty minutes later, they parked on the dusty track at the foot of the hills of L'Estaque. A wobbly, wooden signpost, its writing half faded, indicated the Vallon de Valtrède.

In the distance they could hear Palestro's voice, coming from somewhere above. The heat weighed down on their shoulders as they followed the path that led up the valley, between pine trees burned in the recent forest fires. A smell of charcoal still hung in the air.

At the far end of the valley, they reached the prehistoric site of Châteauneuf-les-Martigues. From there, despite the tormented shapes of the pines, they had a superb view over the silvery waters of Lake Berre.

Palestro was standing in the middle of his students. "If you wish . . . the Upper Magdalenian, in other words the Magdalenian in its final phase, appears in various sites. For example, a series of cut flints have been found in the remains of the Cornille shelter. It is a very large shelter, which is no longer accessible . . . It has completely collapsed. Note also the sites of Carro, near Martigues, Lamanou, Riaux Cave on the L'Estaque coast, and of course Sainte-Baume. And, if you wish, going further north there is Bernucem and the cavernous shelter of Eden-Roc, in the Vaucluse."

Vidal and de Palma stood back from the group of students. They could still hear the sounds of the motorway, rising up the valley on a slight breeze. At the centre of the site, a corrugated-iron roof protected a wide trench, about two metres deep, that revealed a whole series of strata.

"We note too that Magdalenian culture, so brilliant in other regions – just think of Lascaux – seemed very poor to us in Provence for a long time. Most of the relevant literature was produced before the discovery of Le Guen's Cave, and we've had to rethink our theories ever since . . . Just remember the polemic after the discovery. For example, it was thought that the reindeer, which was still present in Adaouste Cave, no longer existed further south, towards the coast. It was thought that those groups of hunters who had crossed the Rhône were in fact less numerous to the south of the Durance. It just goes to show how difficult research into prehistory can be."

Palestro went over to the trench, followed by his group of students. Vidal caught sight of a pretty brunette who was chewing her pencil and furtively glancing around. When she noticed Vidal watching her, her expression changed and she pulled a nasty face.

"Here we see the Castelnovian industry. This is a very important deposit for the study of the Mesolithic and Neolithic. We are now standing on the bed of a vanished stream, between two strata of Urgonian limestone. There is nothing here that concerns the period we have been studying. I've brought you here so that you might have a better sense of a prehistorian's work and, maybe, before the intermediate exams for this module, gain a better understanding of the transition between the Palaeolithic and the Neolithic.

"To finish with the Magdalenian, in terms of artistic production, it has to be said that we used to have only one engraving. The little Ségriès bison, in Moustiers-Sainte-Marie. And then came the Le Guen bison . . . Remember the fineness of the execution. It was drawn on a curved wall . . . A model of perfection. It's very important to note that it is presented at a three-quarters angle, which is extremely rare. This would have required real artistic mastery. And then, of course, there are the horses . . . which all of you know. Marvellous . . . So that was what upset all our wonderful theories. It was thought that the first man in Provence was crude, and completely stupid . . . But he has turned out to be one of the greatest, our first man. In terms of his lifestyle, I must admit that Le Guen's Cave has not taught us very much. There is talk of hunting, of course. But that's not particularly interesting. He may have gathered plants, buds, berries and shoots. Or else animal produce such as honey, eggs or larvae . . . There is less talk of fishing. It would seem that salmon did not swim up the few streams that flow into the Mediterranean – I mean, there were practically no salmon in the sea . . . This was not the case in Aquitaine. In fact, we think there were a few, highly mobile groups of hunter-gatherers . . . We draw this conclusion from the thinness of the floors in their shelters, their modest living areas, and their distribution . . . There were few or no permanent habitations, which seems to be in contradiction with Le Guen. But that's the way it is."

Vidal stepped down into the trench and ran his hand over the various layers of sediment. From the centre of the excavation protruded a long measuring pole with centimetres marked in white on a yellow background. A colossus of a man, aged about fifty, appeared at the far end of the trench. He looked at Vidal suspiciously.

"Are you one of the students?"

"Not quite. My name's Vidal, from the murder squad."

The man dropped his trowel and brush.

"You're investigating Christine's death?"

"Yes, did you know her?"

"Vaguely. I work on the Castelnovian, and she was only interested in the Magdalenian. To my knowledge, she never came here."

"This looks like really hard labour!"

"We have to do quite a lot of spadework. But most of it was done ages ago," he said, kneeling down. "This is an old site . . . the picks have been put away, now its more about brushes."

"Have you found anything?"

"Less and less. The most important artefacts have already been removed. The last piece we turned up was a very long pebble, with a geometric pattern engraved on it. Very nice."

Palestro had approached along the edge of the trench.

"These Mesolithic Provençals were still hunter-gatherers. They ate rabbits, deer or boar. But in the strata you can see here, there are also sheep bones. This is unique! However, there does not seem to have been any farming. Just remember that this was a moment when mankind's environment changed enormously. There was economic and social evolution. Sheep farming was about to appear, agriculture would then follow and, at the same time, the idea of property. Just think of the huge repercussions this was to have on human behaviour . . . Then read, or reread Proudhon . . . "

Palestro grinned broadly at his students, who tried their best to appreciate this unexpected allusion.

"Any questions?"

A slight wind cooled the air and brought with it a smell of oil from the refinery at Fos. De Palma walked through the site, being careful not to cross the ropes which marked off areas under investigation. He heard a voice behind him:

"So Monsieur de Palma, you have come back to see us?"

"Yes, Professor. You're not easy to find. But your lessons are always so fascinating . . . "

"Thank you, but that's not why you're here!"

"I'm afraid not. Still, I would have preferred it that way. I could listen to you for hours."

"That's what my students do when they don't fall asleep."

"This is a magnificent site. It's a pity about the motorway."

"Yes, but modern man needs to be on the move."

Palestro stood on a little hillock overlooking Lake Berre, and stared into the distance.

"So, Monsieur de Palma, what can I do for you?"

"I have to ask you a few questions; some are routine, others are more serious."

"So let's start with the serious ones."

"I should point out that this is a routine questioning, nothing more. All the same, do not forget that you're talking to two police officers on duty."

"Let's get to the point . . . "

They walked a few metres towards the diggers' shed. Vidal joined them, ostentatiously removing a notepad from his rucksack.

"First question: why did you go into Christine Autran's flat after her death? To be precise, before my first visit to her home, in other words during the month after her murder. And then again, between that visit and the official search we conducted in January."

Palestro was not surprised by the question.

"It's simple. Christine had some papers which belonged to me. That's all . . . I have the keys to her flat . . . "

"You do realise that what you did is extremely serious."

"Not at all. I went to a colleague's flat to reclaim some documents. Full stop. And if that's all, I don't see what you've got on me."

"Let's proceed. Why did you go back a second time?"

"But I didn't."

"Perhaps not. Why did you erase the messages on her answering machine?"

"I didn't erase any messages. I don't see why I would have done that."

"Really?" said Vidal. "On the one hand, you admit to going to Christine's flat, on the other, you deny the facts."

Despite the heat, Palestro seemed to shiver.

"I repeat, I wanted to get back a few papers. I have them in my office in Aix. They're topographical studies of Le Guen's Cave, and they're extremely important because we only have one copy of them. I needed them for an article I'm publishing at the end of May."

"Monsieur Palestro," de Palma said. "Let's say I believe you. But there's something else that bothers me: I don't understand why you went to Christine's flat in early December, after she'd disappeared."

"But I didn't know that she'd disappeared. All I knew was that she'd given no sign of life for a week. She often did that when she had no teaching to do, which was the case at the time. I needed those notes. I tried to telephone several times before going round there. It was about December 7 or 8. I can't remember exactly."

Vidal raised his voice:

"So, she's no longer answering the phone, and all that interests you are your papers!"

The prehistorian scratched his head, and looked condescendingly at the young policeman.

"I've just told you, she would often go quiet for several days. It wasn't the first time I'd been to her flat to fetch some documents."

"What time did you go there?"

"It was in the morning, at about 10.00."

"That's why Yvonne Barbier didn't hear anything," de Palma said to himself. "She must have gone out shopping."

"And is there anything new on the items stolen from the laboratory?"

"No, nothing. I asked around, but didn't find out anything. But haven't you questioned everyone who has access to the lab?"

For two whole days, Vidal had quizzed the scientists and technicians working in the lab. He had even seen the cleaning lady. Nothing. The only lead was a period of two days between the last time Sylvie Maurel had examined the flints and the moment she had noticed they were missing. This was from February 21 to 22 last year, a few days before the disappearance of Agnès Féraud. But nothing in the report on her death provided a connection between these two events. The autopsy had been a mess.

"Monsieur Palestro," said De Palma; "is it possible that Christine took them home with her? Like she did with your documents . . . "

Palestro stopped beside a clump of glasswort, which had grown up in the middle of the dig. He seemed troubled.

"No, no . . . that wouldn't make any sense."

But he was clearly disturbed. He looked round at the lake.

"Did you suspect Christine, Monsieur Palestro?"

"No, I didn't. But it is true that she had changed over the previous few months."

"What do you mean? She'd changed in her behaviour towards you, or in general?"

"She often worked very late at the lab, she hadn't done that before. She wouldn't tell me what she was doing, whereas we used to be . . . One evening, after lessons, I followed her. She went home, then left again a few minutes later."

"How long exactly?"

"Oh, I don't know. Ten minutes perhaps."

Palestro was embarrassed. He started to pace again, but more slowly.

"Did you hide?"

"Not really, I was on the other side of the road."

"Why?"

"Because I wanted to see what she was doing."

"And then?"

"And then I thought she'd take her car, so I'd be able to follow her easily. But instead she got on the first tram, which meant I couldn't. So I went home and thought things over."

Vidal stood in the middle of the path, facing Palestro.

"So you stopped following her?" he asked.

Palestro took a step to one side and paused.

"What struck me was that she didn't take her car, but she was dressed like someone going on an excursion."

"Hang on, you were out to follow her, but you didn't, supposedly because she took a tram! That's a bit hard to swallow."

"But it's the truth. I just thought she must be heading for the creeks. But why at night? I have no idea."

Palestro's eyes clouded over. He breathed deeply and scraped at the small pebbles on the path with his shoe. In the distance they could hear the constant rhythm of huge oil tankers going in and out of the refinery.

"And you never saw her again . . . "

Palestro could not answer him. He was shaking all over. The Baron placed a hand gently on his shoulder and looked round at the dig. The students had gathered near the entrance, waiting for their tutor. Beneath the corrugated-iron roof, the colossus could be heard scraping at the earth with his trowel. From time to time, the noise stopped and a faint whistling emerged from the trench. Always the same tune: Léo Ferré's "Avec le temps".

"There are some things you haven't told me, Professor. You haven't told me why you followed her that night in particular. Why?"

"I can't answer that."

"Listen, Monsieur Palestro," Vidal said, "we're going to be honest with you: we have at least one good reason to take you into custody, and you could end up rotting in prison for a few months. Of course, we could turn a blind eye to what you've just told us, for the moment at least. But you must understand that your statement makes you the ideal suspect. This was a murder, you do understand that?"

"Yes, perfectly."

"So, I'll ask you my colleague's question again. Why did you follow her that evening?"

"I've told you, I have no answer to that. It must have been intuition."

"Perhaps . . . "

They stared at each other for some time, then the scientist set off again. They went as far as the diggers' shed. It was a dilapidated structure, just a few struts nailed to wobbly beams and covered with rusty corrugated iron. Through the window they could see a table covered with trowels of various sizes and a mason's riddle.

"I have one more question to ask you," de Palma said. "The evening in question . . . do you remember the exact date?"

"Of course. It was November 30. I never saw her again."

"November 30," Vidal repeated out loud, "and you never saw her again."

De Palma looked daggers at his colleague.

"Do you know a psychiatrist called François Caillol?" asked Vidal, ignoring the Baron's evil look.

Palestro leaned on the side of the shed.

"In the prehistory world, everyone knows Caillol. He specialises in neuropsychology and he worked with Christine on rituals, trances and hallucinations."

"Do you know him personally?"

"No. Christine knew him well, but I don't. In fact, I don't really believe in all his theories."

"What do you mean?"

"His idea is that, by studying certain ethnic groups, we can get a good understanding of Magdalenian man – Christine agreed with this. Caillol is probably not wrong, fundamentally, but I think we should be extremely prudent about the world of magic and superstition. Otherwise there's a risk of relying solely on inferences, of saying that things are like that among Australian Aborigines, and so they must have been the same in the caves. It's a bit reductive."

"Did you know that he has killed at least two young women over the past few months?" Vidal asked.

"No."

"You obviously don't read the papers . . . Have you ever seen this man?"

Vidal handed him a photo of Franck Luccioni. Palestro looked at it for a moment and replied without the slightest hesitation:

"No, definitely not. She was seeing someone, but it wasn't him."

Vidal and de Palma exchanged glances.

"Can you describe him?"

"O.K., I have to admit that I'm a jealous man. As soon as I noticed that Christine's attitude towards me had changed, I began to observe all kinds of details in her behaviour. I began to follow her, like I said. And that's how I discovered that there was a man in her life!"

"What did he look like?"

"Tall. About one metre eighty-five. Blond hair. What else? He wore glasses. That's all."

"Thick glasses?"

"Yes, that's right."

"Can you describe him in more detail?"

"Listen, the easiest way to describe him would be to say that he looked like Christine. It was striking. He was just like her, but a man."

"Where did you see him?"

"The first time was in Aix. He was waiting in the university car park."

"And the second time?"

"Outside her building, when I followed her. He walked around my car, then he vanished."

The two policemen looked at each other for a long time. Then de Palma held out his hand to the professor.

"She was homosexual, wasn't she?"

Palestro only grimaced.

23.

"Je ne pourrai plus jamais sortir de cette forêt!
Dieu sait jusqu'à où cette bête m'a mené.
Je croyais cependant l'avoir blessé à mort: et voici des traces
    de sang!"

The first thunderstorm broke in the early afternoon. The electricity in the air was disturbing the radio waves of France Musique as it broadcast "Pelléas et Mélisandre"; but Golaud's voice was defiant:

"Mais maintenant, je l'ai perdue de vue;
je crois que je me suis perdu moi-même,
et mes chiens ne me retrouvent plus."

De Palma waited on place La Castellane, behind a McDonald's delivery van. He tried to adjust his radio, and peered outside: heavy drops threw up dust and shook the buds of the plane trees. In seconds, a peppery sauce smelling of hot tarmac began to pour down boulevard Baille, filling the square and beating down on the roof of the policeman's Clio. A couple of pushers who had been hanging around outside the métro exit now dashed inside the station.

"Je vais revenir sur mes pas . . .
j'entends pleurer . . .
Oh! Oh! Qu'y a-t-il au bord de l'eau?"

The storm hammered so hard on the thin metal roof that the din of the city vanished as if by magic, although a few exasperated horns could still be heard through the curtain of dense spring rain. The radio fell silent.

It was 3.00 p.m. He had to be at Les Baumettes prison before 4.00. Barbieri did not like being made to wait, even though he could be dreadfully late himself. He decided to wait another two minutes before turning to the last resort. The rain was now moving down avenue du Prado, blown by gusts of wind which furiously shook the ancient plane trees.

Things were not getting any better. De Palma switched on his siren, drove up on to the pavement and, a few metres further on, dropped back on to the road which took him as far as the Prado roundabout. The traffic was becoming more fluid, but this did not stop him running all the red lights on boulevard Michelet. Golaud's voice re-emerged from the void:

> *"Je n'en sais rien moi-même.*
> *Je chassais dans la forêt. Je poursuivais un sanglier.*
> *Je me suis trompé de chemin.*
> *Vous avez l'air très jeune. Quel âge avez-vous?"*

In the distance, heavy clouds had gathered around the crests of Mont Puget, tinged with pink and black. The cliffs at Luminy were under fire from the sky; huge bolts of lightning came down from the cumuli, hitting the creeks with their jagged shafts.

At Châteauneuf-les-Martigues on Wednesday, Vidal had asked Palestro a great many questions. He was becoming increasingly important, and de Palma did not like it. So later that afternoon, he had given the new boy a bone to chew: a long, routine job concerning the murder of the Ferri couple. The Baron could not help feeling wary of the young officer.

These thoughts deserted him as he parked outside Les Baumettes prison.

There were contorted, hideous statues set in the high outer walls: greed, lust, jealousy . . . The seven deadly sins.

Morality dressed in stone.

The huge, grey door was covered with obscenities and vengeful graffiti. De Palma rang the bell and held his ear to the reinforced intercom.

"Commandant Michel de Palma, murder squad."

When the door opened he walked over to the guard-post, slipped his tricolour card into the drawer and smiled at the warder. The glass which separated them had been starred by the impact of a bullet.

"Monsieur Mariani, the head warder of D wing, is expecting you. Is Judge Barbieri with you?"

"No, he must be late."

"It doesn't matter. Go on, Commandant, you know the way!"

An attractively curvaceous warder in a navy blue uniform was expecting him at the entrance to B wing, her face as dry as a husk. De Palma deposited his Bodyguard and his mobile, then went through some doors, gates and more doors . . .

Thick bars on the grills. Heavy locks.

The warders, positioned at the far ends of the lines of huge wooden doors, communicated from afar by walkie-talkie. A kind of anxiety rose in him. Suddenly, the loudspeakers started bawling: "North courtyard, end of exercise. I repeat: North courtyard, end of exercise."

The warder looked at de Palma with narrowed eyes and gave him a peevish smile. He did not return it.

"North courtyard, end of exercise . . . "

He looked round at the décor, the cream walls, the flaking paint on the bars. He felt the prison's filth envelop him.

"Your prisoner is in solitary, Commandant, D wing. I suppose you know the way?"

"Oh yes, this isn't the first time . . . "

Five minutes later, all the inmates of the north courtyard had returned to their cells. The doors slammed, and only a few murmurs could be heard. De Palma and the warder set off towards D wing.

They passed the sex offenders section and climbed up a first flight of stairs. More bars. The next corridor was in better condition. They went into another wing. More bars. More stairs. One floor. Two floors. Daylight began to filter into the prison. More bars.

The fifth floor. Solitary confinement. The warder took Judge Barbieri's permit and vanished into her guardroom. It was a good minute before he heard the dull sound of a stamp.

"Go to room number 56. I'll fetch him. Judge Barbieri has just called. He'll be here in about half an hour. Do you want to wait?"

"No, I'll start without him."

"O.K. I'll be there in two minutes."

A song rose from the cells. A barbaric rhythm, muffled by the walls. Blows on metal, filling the space with a beat: "Boom, boom . . . Boom, boom . . ." Then, a tiny, muted voice. "Hey boss, come over here . . . boss, I've got something to tell you . . ."

De Palma looked questioningly at the warder, who stared at the floor.

"Hey boss, come over here . . . boss, I've got something to tell you . . ."

He went into the small visiting room, put his backpack on the Formica table and peered out of the window. The storm had passed; the air was now free of humidity. Beyond the prison he could make out the slightest detail in the landscape. Pointe-Rouge bay was a matt, blue patch between the white towers of Le Roy d'Espagne, the green escarpments of the Marseilleveyre hills and the foothills of Notre-Dame de la Garde, scattered with shining villas. Beyond the seawall, the storm had turned the sea white and a cargo ship was wending its way, to Algeria perhaps, or Tunisia, or to the magic of Alexandria . . . Or perhaps even further, beyond the Mediterranean, beyond Suez.

The head warder awoke him from his reverie. He turned round to face François Caillol. He was closely shaved, his eyes were on fire and his face gleamed. The cancer of prison was already at work. Caillol would never be the same again. De Palma could see that the man who stooped before him, his arms dangling, was not a murderer.

"Good afternoon, Monsieur Caillol. I'm Commandant Michel de Palma, from the murder squad."

"Good afternoon."

"Do you want a cigarette? Something to drink?"

"No thanks."

"Take a seat."

De Palma looked at the accused and weighed him up. He was going to have problems making him talk. Neither the interrogation, nor the metallic din of the prison, nor his total isolation had made him malleable. On the contrary.

"How are you, Monsieur Caillol?"

"Fine."

"I'm here unofficially, for personal reasons. But the deputy public prosecutor has given me permission. This never normally happens. Do you understand?"

"Yes."

"I'm here to ask you about Christine Autran. Did you know her?"

"Yes."

"What sort of relationship did you have?"

"We weren't lovers, if that's what you mean. She was just a friend. We used to work on projects together."

"What kinds of projects?"

"We shared the same interests. But for her, it was her profession. To put it simply, let's say that we talked for hours about shamanism."

"Please don't put it simply with me," de Palma said coldly. "I might even advise you to be truthful. Is that clear?"

Caillol nodded.

"We had decided to write a book on the subject. I was to deal with the psychoanalytic and neuropsychological aspects."

De Palma stood up, as though to break the tone of the interview. The psychiatrist would not tell him anything until he had shown that he already knew certain things about him. He took out his exercise book and pretended to look for some information. Caillol observed him discreetly.

"Doctor, why did you go on ethnographic missions with Christine?"

This policeman's ruse went unnoticed. After a few seconds, Caillol answered:

"We made three trips. The first was to Australia in the winter of 1993. The second was to New Guinea in 1994. Then the third was to the highlands of New Guinea in 1997."

"What were you looking for there?"

"Perhaps you know that ethnology can often come to the assistance of prehistorians, in the same way that reconstructions might be used to validate theories. In Australia, we met some Aborigines in North Queensland and in the Wessel Islands. I was able to work on some paintings there . . . A Jingaloo Aborigine explained to me at some length the meaning of certain drawings which evoke the history of his tribe in dreamtime."

"What did Christine do during your stay?"

"More or less the same as me, but her interest was purely ethnographic. She filled up a series of notebooks, especially on their painting techniques."

"Then you went to New Guinea?"

"The first time, we went to the north-west coast, to a huge tropical forest. We wanted to meet the Asmat. It's a strange country, between earth and water, a forest criss-crossed by thousands of streams. The Asmat are headhunters . . . They collect skulls in their homes. The men sleep on them to appease their ancestors' spirits."

"Was it Christine who decided to go and see the . . . I can't remember their name."

"Yes, it was her. She was interested by the fact that the Asmat are cannibals. For them, natural death doesn't exist: you either die in combat or after a magic ritual. This is a basic concept in their civilisation – the creation of a life implies its destruction. In some ways, death becomes the first condition of life. This requires some sort of fertility ritual, such as headhunting or cannibalism, whereby you absorb the vital essence of your victim. The Asmat were the first cannibals I ever met. And I must say that they made a very strange impression on me. I was quite terrified. I thought that such practices no longer existed, that the Protestant missionaries had driven them out, but they hadn't . . . "

"Did you witness any scenes of cannibalism?"

"Yes, but not with the Asmat. It was later, in the highlands, but still in New Guinea, with the Jale. They spend their lives fighting wars between villages . . . The fighting is incredibly violent; they use arrows and lances, if you can picture it. Fortunately, there are taboos limiting the number of deaths . . . The severest form of vengeance is to eat the body of your conquered enemy."

Caillol was breathing heavily. He crossed his hands, squeezing them hard, and in a feeble voice which seemed to come from his core, he slowly added: "And I witnessed that . . . after that, I must admit that I was no longer quite the same."

"What about Christine?"

Caillol gestured vaguely, as though chasing away a painful vision. "I . . . among the Jale, the women bring up the boys; they're totally separated from the adult males. For a psychiatrist, it's interesting to see how the social apprenticeship of these terrible warriors takes place in a female environment. There they have no chiefs. Order comes out of their interminable conflicts."

"Keep to the point. I asked you about Christine."

"One day, she said something which shocked me deeply."

"What was that?"

"I told her how disgusted I was by the practices of the Jale, and she replied: 'There's nothing disgusting about it, I mean, you eat pigs and ducks! But here, they are inferior animals. The Jale eat men because they are the greatest, higher than all other imaginable forms of greatness.' She looked completely hysterical, or possessed. Then she added: 'When you eat an inferior animal, like a chicken, you are debasing yourself.'"

"I don't see why that shocked you. You must have heard similar things in your consulting room! Anyway, why were you so interested in these practices?"

"Like many prehistorians, I believe that activities linked to magic are universal. Shamans enter into a trance, then paint what they see on the other side on to the wall of their cave. I saw that among the Aborigines, and that's why the subject interests me as a psychiatrist. I must also point out that I've studied neuropsychology in some depth. These visions often occur after a drug has been taken. In North America, mescaline is widely used, for example. It comes from a plant, a variety of hallucinogenic cactus. But in the caves, I think the hallucinations came naturally, after the shaman had shut himself inside, and fatigue and total darkness had begun to work on his nervous system. I've tried it, and I can tell you it works. Just try spending three days without eating in a completely dark cave, and you'll see what I mean!"

De Palma lit a cigarette.

"Christine often experimented with these practices. She told me that on several occasions she had succeeded in transforming herself into an animal, while retaining some of her consciousness. In this way, she could explain exactly what she had seen."

"And which animal did she transform herself into?"

"A stag. Strange as it might sound, she transformed into a stag . . . every time."

"Why do you find that strange?"

"Because a stag is more of a masculine representation, an animal dominating a herd of females. It's true that we find many stags in decorated caves; almost all of them have several examples. In that respect, it was not very original."

De Palma walked over to the window. In the south courtyard, some prisoners were playing boules. He recognised the face of the small fat man whose turn it was.

"Everything you've told me is extremely interesting, but I think we're a little bit off the point of my visit."

The small fat man hit the jack.

"Monsieur Caillol, I'm going to show you some photos. Can you tell me if you recognise anyone?"

De Palma produced some photos of Christine Autran, Sylvie and Franck Luccioni. He had also included photos of several women who had nothing to do with the case.

The psychiatrist immediately picked out Sylvie. He smiled. Then an unknown. No reaction. Franck Luccioni. No reaction. He paused for a moment over the two portraits of Christine Autran.

"Try to imagine her with spectacles and short hair," de Palma said. "I mean, a man with Christine's face."

The psychiatrist took a deep breath and leaned back in his chair. He looked troubled.

"Do you know anyone who looks like that?"

"I have seen someone like that. But where? I couldn't tell you."

Caillol's expression had just changed. His eyes were blank. His hands trembled.

"Try to remember. It's extremely important. Both for you, and for me."

"I don't know, I . . . "

"Take time to think. A man of your intelligence must surely remember."

The psychiatrist crossed his hands again and squeezed them even more tightly, as if he were trying to dive into the depths of his psyche, into the faintest traces of his memories, now weakened by solitary confinement. His breathing calmed.

"How stupid can you get! I remember now . . . I saw him with Christine. In Aix. I was coming out of my consultancy and I ran into them."

"Are you sure?"

"Absolutely."

"Do you remember where?"

"They were sitting outside a café, on place de l'Hôtel de Ville. I can't remember the name of it. I never go to bars."

"When was that?"

"Not that long ago. But when? With all this business, my memory isn't what it was."

"Was it before or after Christmas?"

"Before. I'm sure about that."

"At the beginning of December?"

"Let me think."

"Take your time."

Silence descended on the room. Through the wall, they could still hear "Boom, boom . . . Boom, boom . . . " and the same voice: "Hey boss, come over here . . . boss, I've got something to tell you . . . "

"At the beginning of December. Maybe the first or second of the month. I can be sure because I'd just got back from a conference in the U.S.A. In fact, I got back on the second. I must have seen them on the third or the fourth."

De Palma felt Caillol's words run straight through him. Autran had still been alive in early December. He thought about Palestro, who said that he had followed her on November 30, which was possible. It also fitted with what Le Guen had told him. But it did not fit at all with Yvonne Barbier's statement. She must have been alive, but she had not gone home. His entire theory, put together over the past month, had just gone up in flames. He felt exasperated, but at the same time relieved.

"Judge Barbieri will be here soon. This is an opportunity for you."

"Why?"

"I've managed to make him have doubts about your guilt."

"Why did you do that?"

"Because I know you're innocent."

"You're the only one!"

"Why are you interested in the funeral rituals of the first men?"

"Because I'm convinced that the first men were not that different from us. Let's take the example of cannibalism, which I've been accused of ... did you know that it's still being practised? And not just in New Guinea or elsewhere, but right here."

"What do you mean?"

"Churchgoers eat the body of Christ. It's symbolic, of course. Not so long ago, people ate mummies for their therapeutic effect ... It's what Freud called an instinctive desire; the desire which is constantly being forbidden, by education and so on ... There are three instinctive desires: incest, murder and cannibalism. Three things which are absolutely forbidden, of which cannibalism is of course the most monstrous. The taboo placed on these three desires marks the boundary between civilisation – I mean between our civilisation – and the primitive state of barbarism ... what we call barbarism or savagery."

"What about the picture of the hand we found on the scene?"

"It's strange."

"Everything about this case is strange!"

"I know. But it's not logical behaviour. All murderers have a logic to the way they operate. But I suppose I'm not telling you anything new."

The Baron shook his head.

"The particular point about prehistoric hands is that they are found only in decorated caves. In Gargas, there are 231 of them. Just imagine! But the point is , they are found only in caves."

"Why?"

"Because they are not moveable objects. In museums, you can find Venuses, pendants, sculpted reindeer, necklaces, but never hands!"

"So?"

"So they must be connected with what went on in the caves. People went to caves to enter into contact with the spirit world, according to a male or female principle. For a long time, people talked a lot of nonsense about these hands, about disease, or ritual amputations . . . Now people tend to talk about shamanism . . . Are you following me?"

"Perfectly, so tell me about these shamans."

"It would seem that Palaeolithic man practised shamanism. Shamans enter into contact with the supernatural so as to solve the problems of everyday life . . . everyone's routine difficulties . . . For them, going into the spirit world also means acting directly on the real world around us."

Barbieri burst into the room.

"Do excuse me, Commandant. I see you've decided to make the most of the situation."

The judge looked at Caillol.

"Good afternoon, Doctor."

"I showed some photos to Dr Caillol," de Palma said. "When I told him about the man with the spectacles, he remembered having seen him with Autran outside a café in Aix. He knew Christine Autran."

"I see," said Barbieri.

He was silent for a few moments.

"I suppose Commandant de Palma has explained the reason for this interview."

"Yes."

"He's here to ask you about Christine Autran, who was also murdered."

"I haven't killed anyone."

"How did you know her?"

"I've explained that to your colleague."

"He isn't a colleague. He's a police officer. And I'm a magistrate."

"I used to work with her. That's all."

"Very well. I'll read Commandant de Palma's report. Now, tell me about this person you apparently know. The man with the spectacles, as we call him."

"I knew Christine well. Seeing her with a man attracted my attention."

"Did you speak to him?"

"No."

"Why not?"

"Because I didn't want to disturb her."

"That's a feeble excuse."

The psychiatrist repeated word for word the statement he had made to the Baron. Barbieri listened to him calmly, and took a few notes.

"Did you have, so to speak . . . ?"

"Sexual relations with Christine? Is that what interests you?" Caillol asked in a cool voice. "The answer's no. I've been together with the same woman for the past five years. The woman I was at the restaurant with on the night of the murder."

"Franca . . ."

"Bernet."

"Except that there's a problem. You went away for a while during the meal."

"I went out to make a phone call."

"O.K., but for quite a long time. Three quarters of an hour, according to your friends, which is, according to the gendarmes, enough time to have killed Hélène Weill."

"I get lots of phone calls. Some of them are extremely long."

"We checked. There was even one from Hélène Weill. Do you remember?"

"Yes, she said she wanted to see me."

"What's more, we know that you weren't on the phone for three quarters of an hour. Can you confirm that?"

"Yes."

"And you have stated that you bought cigarettes from a tobacconist's on cours Mirabeau, but the tobacconist doesn't remember you, can you confirm that too?"

"Yes, what more do you want me to tell you?"

"Never mind about Hélène Weill's fingerprints in your car . . . As for Saint-Julien . . . Listen, Doctor, I'm not keeping you here for my personal pleasure. As far as I'm concerned, you're still guilty. But if you're innocent, you should help us. This police officer is the best in the region. He needs you. So think about it. Tell him everything that might be used in your defence. Do you understand?"

"Yes."

"Good. We'll leave you now."

Barbieri stood up brusquely. Caillol looked sad. De Palma held out his hand to him, and he shook it hard.

The door opened. At the end of the corridor, there was the same old refrain: "Boom, boom . . . boom, boom . . . Hey boss, listen to me . . . "

Barbieri looked at de Palma.

"I arrived late so that you could do your business. Anything new?"

"Yes, maybe. I'll explain."

"Just give me the main point!"

"I need to analyse all this, but I can tell you right now that our psychiatrist hasn't given us everything. He's definitely innocent, but he's holding something back. It would be no coincidence if he's been framed. He knows far more than he's letting on and he thinks that keeping quiet is his best defence. His lawyer has given him some bad advice. I'll make him talk, but another time, when I have more to go on. We'll leave him to stew for now."

Without another word, they strode down the corridor between D and B wings. When they reached the gate, de Palma turned to Barbieri.

"Did you see 'Faust'?"

"No, did you?"

"Not yet. But I have heard that young William Norton brings the house down. It appears the public haven't heard anything like it since Georges Thill. A divine voice."

"That must be quite something!"

*

"Paulin's offloaded the Ferri couple on me!"

"Romeo and Juliet with an 11.43 . . . What a lovely present!" said Maistre, raising his glass. "So what are you going to do?"

"I'm going to put the kid on the case . . ."

"Poor thing."

"He's in the police force, isn't he?"

Le Zanzi was quiet. Dédé joined their conversation by placing his two large, hairy paws on the bar.

"By the way, have you heard?"

"Heard what?"

"They're talking about releasing Francis Bérard."

"'Le Blond'? Jesus, what a mess!" said Maistre.

"Jean-Louis, do you remember when we collared him?"

"Of course I do! When I took him to the toilet, I went with two armed officers . . . he's a real madman, Dédé. I swear to you, he scared me."

Maistre stood back from the bar and grimaced, baring his teeth.

"Like a wild beast . . . a nasty piece of work."

"Was he the one who killed Judge André?" asked Dédé, creasing his eyebrows, which were as thick as brushes.

"Yup, that was him. Or rather, there were two of them."

"The fuckers . . ."

"That's the way it goes . . . And Judge André respected nothing at all."

"Don't say that, Baron! André was quite a man. What's more, he really liked you, you know that!"

"O.K., but sometimes he went over the top, remember? To make someone talk, Dédé, he had their whole family put away. He was a real crusader. All the same, he was a good man."

"Those were the days, weren't they, Baron?"

"Oh yes, the cases were magnificent."

"Zampa, Hoareau, Le Belge . . . you remember?"

"We copped them all, there was no stopping us."

"Things aren't the same any more," said Dédé, pouring out another two pastis.

"Too right," the Baron replied, throwing away his cigarette butt. "Things aren't the same because they don't want us to catch them any longer. Anyway, organised crime doesn't exist in France . . . So there are no problems. They control the nightclubs, the slot machines, the drugs . . . but without any organisation . . . the Ferri couple died for no real reason. They're going to tell us again that it's all down to gambling syndicates."

"The commissaires aren't what they used to be," said Maistre. "Nor are the magistrates. Nowadays, if you go to a nightclub to suss out what's going down, and you talk to an informer, you get accused of corruption. So what do you do? You get yourself transferred to public safety. Then everything becomes clear!"

"He's right, Jean-Louis. There's nothing else to be done. And the kids couldn't give a damn. They turn up at 9.00 in the morning, they type out their reports and then they go home at 6.00."

"No, it's all over," said Maistre, glancing towards rue de l'Evêché. "Look, the hacks are all on their way out. With this Ferri affair, Paulin and Duriez must have put on quite a show about gangland killings. The TV news should be a laugh this evening."

"Watch out, Michel," said Dédé. "Two of them are coming this way. I reckon they're after you."

"I'm off, then. They can always talk to Jean-Louis."

When he got home, de Palma wandered around the flat.

All four rooms were empty. As empty as the secret drawers of his life. He could not help thinking about Marie, about her departure, and her weariness at spending nights in a bed that was too big for one. To get Marie back, he would have to give up something, an essential part of himself. He would have to abandon the dark alleyways of his character. His bastion. But he couldn't do it.

For a week he had read and reread the letter Marie had left behind: a single page covered with round handwriting which was a little childish, but also rather voluptuous. She had not really said goodbye. Not quite.

My darling,

I'm going to spend the Christmas holidays with my parents, in the Alps. I think we need some time to think. Life with you has become impossible – your fits of anger, your staying out all night, I won't go on . . .

I think you're becoming more and more mad. More and more solitary. You really should see a doctor. Something is wrong and you won't talk to me about it, even though I'm your wife. Think about it while I'm gone. I'll be back. When? I don't know. But I will be back, because you're the only man I love.

Tender kisses. Take care. I love you.

Marie

His knees trembled. It felt as if his legs could no longer support him. He had lost his brother, now he was losing his wife. In matrimonial terms, his destiny was starting to look like that of most of his colleagues. Quite banal. Nothing to talk about, really. He put on some music: "La Bohème", act one, Rodolpho – Marie's favourite aria. He went out on to the balcony.

"Che gelida manina!
Se la lasci riscaldar.
Cercar che giova? Al buio non si trova."

He looked out over his neighbourhood, La Capelette, a scattering of cheap houses arranged according to shady property deals made in the Defferre era, and bordered by Menpenti medical college, avenue Toulon, Le Jarret municipal dump, Saint-Pierre cemetery and the Pont de Vivaux race course. De Palma had grown up in the joyless streets of La Capelette, among factories with jagged roofs and dusty pavements which stank of dried dog turds, where dilapidated lodgings alternated with hastily constructed buildings from the '70s. This industrial quarter had followed the ebb and flow of the port and finally, bit by bit, it had passed away like a little old lady in a nursing home.

"Ma per fortuna è une notte di luna,
e qui la luna l'abbiamo vicina."

When de Palma was a boy, La Capelette had produced sulphur, soap, dates, pith helmets and playing cards. These small industries gave the neighbourhood exotic fragrances, and on hot days in June, in the school on rue Laugier, the teacher would open the windows wide, letting the external odours invade the classroom: sulphur, soda, oil, North African fruits, the sea, fragrances from the entire world mingled with the sweat and acidic breath of children bent over their exercise books.

"Aspetti, signorina,
Le dirò con due parole
Chi son . . . "

Until the end of the '60s, there was still a ghetto where the east motorway presently ran. It was reserved for Arabs.

The streets now bore the names of the neighbourhood's little glories: rue Antoine Del Bello, impasse Palazzo, rue des Luchesi . . .

"Chi son? Sono un poeta.
Che faccio? Scrivo.
E come vivo? Vivo."

24.

When Vidal pushed open the door of the Cadenet gendarmerie, it was as though he had gone back to his native village, south of Aveyron. It smelled clean and neat, authority in uniform. He glanced at the three men waiting on the bench and he could read on their grey faces the uneasiness of the common citizen when confronted with the boys in navy blue.

Capitaine Brauquier received Vidal with military reserve – it was just as well Barbieri had smoothed the way!

"If you want some coffee, help yourself in the break room." Brauquier pointed to an enormous, electric, stainless-steel coffee urn.

"Thanks, but I've already had one."

The gendarme and the police officer sized each other up.

"If we start with the Weill case, there's nothing I can tell you which you don't already know. You'd have to go to the magistrate."

"I read the forensic reports, but I wanted to know if any books about prehistory had been found in her bookcase."

"Look, I know where this is leading . . . But as far as we're concerned, the case has been solved. The gendarmerie have extremely impressive capacities when it comes to leading this sort of investigation. We don't need to check what she reads. In fact, Caillol practically fell into our lap. We get lucky too, sometimes."

"I just wanted to know if you'd seen any books on prehistory."

"They were loads of books, and some of them were about prehistory. Is that good enough for you?"

"Specialist books?"

"Look, we had better things to do than go through her bookcase."

"Commandant de Palma . . ."

"I couldn't care less what Michel thinks. He's a very good policeman, and he's a friend of mine, but here I think he's going completely off the rails. Your Saint-Julien case is connected to ours . . . In fact, I should say your ex-case. Because it was Caillol. There's no doubt about it."

"And yet . . . "

"I've prepared a summary. I've included everything you should find useful."

"Look, Capitaine, I haven't come all this way to be brushed off. I may be young, but I'm a police officer empowered by the deputy public prosecutor, just like you. So either you cooperate, or I'll go and have a word with Barbieri . . . We're not interested in Weill, or Chevallier. We just want to have some details about the victims because we think there's a connection with the Autran case."

Brauquier gave Vidal a venomous smile.

"And what is this connection, Lieutenant?"

"Caillol knew Autran, Weill and Chevallier."

The gendarme coughed.

"There's nothing about this in your reports," Vidal went on. "Have you come across the names Autran or Luccioni?"

"No, never."

"In her correspondence, her phone calls . . . "

Brauquier slapped his palm on the file, which was a good twenty centimetres thick.

"There's enough in here to charge him twenty times over, and these are only the highlights . . . As far as Weill and Chevallier are concerned, don't look any further, you'd be wasting your time. And Autran is none of our business."

"Thanks so much for your cooperation . . . "

"You know, we put a squad of twelve gendarmes on this case, and . . . "

"Goodbye, Capitaine."

Vidal drove through the Aix countryside like a madman. Clutching the steering wheel, he snatched glimpses of the landscape. Young vine leaves, still damp with morning dew, gleamed in the sun, and the white cliff-faces of the Lubéron glittered in the brightness.

Half an hour later, Vidal was walking into the administration department of the Université de Provence. A chubby secretary gave him a pinched smile.

"Are you the policeman who phoned yesterday?"

"Indeed."

"I've already started looking for what you wanted. If you like, we can continue together."

The secretary explained at length how difficult it was to go back ten years into the past. The university kept very few records about the courses of particular students. But the degrees taken by Hélène Weill and Julia Chevallier had enabled her to uncover some valuable information.

"We have a system of units of value, did you know that?"

"Not really, I went to the police academy."

"It's simple – to pass a degree you have to obtain a certain number of units of value, or UV. Some are compulsory, others are extra or optional. You can read English but also pass optional UVs in prehistory. Do you follow?"

"Absolutely. I'm even getting a tan."

The secretary did not appreciate his little joke, but went on to explain that, after delving through the records, she had discovered that Julia Chevallier and Hélène Weill had taken several optional UVs in prehistory at the same time. Julia had read English and Hélène psychology.

"What about Christine Autran?"

"I haven't had time to check yet but, given her age, she must have taken the same courses, except that her UVs were compulsory."

The day before, Vidal had discovered that Weill and Autran had both gone to Lycée Thiers, in the centre of Marseille, while Julia had attended Marcel Pagnol. So these women had all known each other for years.

"Can you give me a list of the other students who took these UVs?"

"That will be difficult. I can only give you the names of people who passed their degrees that year. But many people fail, or else give up during the course of the year."

"That doesn't matter!"

"Do you want the optional and extra UVs too?"

"I want them all, even the compulsory ones."

"It's going to be hard, you do realise that!"

"Listen, lady, I'm investigating a murder and I'm looking for a man who will probably kill again soon. So either you get to work, or I'll ask the magistrate for the right piece of paper and we'll confiscate all your UVs, the extra, the optional *and* the compulsory ones!"

"But I'm the only person who deals with all this!"

"I'm on my own too. I'll be expecting your call."

The sun had just dropped behind the dome of La Major when Vidal burst into the office.

"He isn't working alone."

"Are you O.K., Michel?"

"He's not on his own in all this."

"What do you mean?"

"The psychiatrist saw him with Autran."

"Who?"

"Spectacles." This was the nickname the Baron had given the mysterious man with thick lenses.

"Do you want me to find out more about Christine's private life? We've already seen her friends and professional acquaintances, and I hope we'll get to her university friends soon, but we could extend the net."

"Don't waste your time on that now. There aren't enough of us. In my opinion, if we could find him by going through her acquaintances, he would have done things differently. We'll have to do it some time, but not now."

"Maybe that's why he killed Christine."

"You know, for the past few days, I've had the craziest thought."

"What is it? You never know . . . "

"I think he has an accomplice, a female accomplice."

"What makes you think that?"

"Only two people knew the victims and all the actors in this scenario. The first is Christine Autran, and she's dead. The second is

Sylvie Maurel. Christine and Sylvie went to university together. They worked together and couldn't stand each other. They also studied the same subject: Le Guen's Cave . . . Do you follow me?"

"Yes, vaguely."

"Someone's been leading us astray from the beginning."

"Go on, Baron."

"Someone's been leading us astray, and I'm sure that this someone is a woman. Now, the only woman I know of in this case who's still alive is Sylvie Maurel. She dropped into our little world, just like that! And I wonder if it's a coincidence."

"Wait a moment, what about the Luccioni girl?"

"Impossible. Bérengère's a straightforward lass."

"Maybe she is, but we have to keep her in mind. I'll look into it."

"Leaving no stone unturned?"

"Exactly, Commandant."

"Anything else?"

"I had a lovely time at the gendarmerie. All your 'friend' Captain Brauquier told me was that he'd seen some prehistory books in Weill's shelves. Then I went to Aix. That was more interesting. It turns out the three women really were friends."

"What about yesterday? Any progress?"

"Yes, definitely."

"I'm all ears."

"I got Autran's address in Aix."

"And?"

"Guess."

"Ten to one it was rue Boulegon, where she shared a flat with Hélène Weill."

"Spot on."

De Palma stood up and slapped his hands on the desk.

"We'll go and tell Paulin the good news! Great sleuthing, Maxime."

"That's not all."

"Hang on, I'd better sit down."

"There were three sets of fingerprints at Autran's place: Palestro's, Christine's – obviously – and, more surprisingly, traces of leather gloves. Just like those found in Chevallier's house. And the moral of the story is?"

"It's the same person. I'm sure if the gendarmes had delved a little deeper, they'd have found the same ones at our friend the psychiatrist's place. Very interesting. And then?"

Vidal looked extremely pleased with himself.

"The fingerprints on the photograph, the one you snaffled in Autran's place, are identical in part – and I repeat only in part – to those found on the armrest in Saint-Julien, and an exact match with those in Christine's car. But they've not been found anywhere else, in the flat on boulevard Chave, for example."

"You're quite something! This proves that he was close to Christine. He was close to her, but we don't know who he is, and he never went to her home . . . Even if he wasn't a friend, he did travel in her car."

"Only the edges of the Saint-Julien prints can be used for comparison. The rest have been wiped off . . . Even if they mean something to us, they won't stand up in court. I've been through all the police records. Not a trace. Then there's Franck Luccioni."

"He was no intellectual. Far from it. He's the one that bothers me most. With the women, some kind of rationale is emerging. We can now picture a sex maniac disguised as a shaman who slices up all the lesbians he met at university. It could be that simple. But then there's Luccioni: with him we haven't got a clue."

"No."

"And yet, Luccioni and Autran knew each other. Since primary school."

Anne Moracchini came into the office. She was wearing a miniskirt and de Palma could not help glancing at her legs with a loud sigh.

"Anything wrong, Michel?"

"No, I was admiring you . . . "

"Listen, both of you, I think there's something important in the post-mortem report."

"What?" de Palma asked.

"I don't know, just something that puzzles me . . . "

"Anne, you know I love suspense," de Palma said edgily. "But this really isn't the moment."

"I noticed that her clothes had been taken off, then put back on again later."

Vidal was about to say something, but de Palma cut him off.

"Forensics told me about that. But I must admit I'd completely forgotten. So, what are your conclusions?"

"I don't know, but I feel that the corpse might still teach us something."

"I'm afraid it won't teach us anything any more," de Palma sighed.

"I think she was undressed, then killed. Then her clothes were put back on and she was thrown into the sea. There's no other possible explanation."

"You think so?"

"I'm certain."

De Palma leaped up.

"Jesus, Anne, you've just put me on to something. I'm not sure what exactly, but this could be extremely important."

"Why?"

"If you're right about this, it means that she wasn't killed in the creeks."

"Really?"

"Definitely. There were tracks on the ground at Sugiton . . . Follow me? Two long tracks that led down to the sea, as though someone had been dragged along. But there were no marks suggesting that someone had been undressed. Do you see what I mean?"

"I think so," Vidal said.

"It was all staged. He wanted to make us think that Autran was killed there, but she wasn't."

"How can you be so sure?" Vidal asked.

"Because if you strangle someone and undress them, you're obviously going to disturb the pebbles. Then you cover the traces. That would be normal, yes?"

"I suppose so," Moracchini replied, only half convinced.

"But he then left two huge tracks, which isn't normal at all! He killed Autran somewhere else and then took her to Sugiton, because he knew that she often went there. Because he knew that the police would then put together a scenario which was completely different from the reality. This is our first victory, Anne."

De Palma sat down. He shoved aside the file in front of him and put his head in his hands.

"Anne," he said. "You're going to have to go round everyone who hires out boats. Start at Les Goudes and go as far as Pointe-Rouge. Talk to all of them. They must have hired a boat somewhere in the area."

"You think so?"

"I don't know, but we can't afford to ignore a single thing. Then see if any boats were declared stolen, or anything like that. We shall see!"

"Why do you think there were several people?"

"Because you'd have to be extremely strong to carry a dead body that far. And by land I'd say it would be totally impossible."

"O.K., Michel, I'll look into it. Do you need anything else?"

"Yes, I do. Try to get a list of all the people who went missing at the time. From one month before to, say, a week afterwards. Contact Interpol, Europol, the entire works."

"What are you thinking, Michel?" Moracchini asked.

"I'm not sure yet . . . I don't know . . . I just know that something doesn't add up. That's all."

"O.K., I'll do it, but I don't see why."

"Anne, nothing can be left to chance. We're going to have to close all the doors, one by one."

"And why don't you think there were two killers?" she said. "Why do you think the cases are connected?"

"Because everyone knew each other . . . It's obvious. On the other hand, you're right, there might be two. Or perhaps just one, acting on orders. I'd tend towards the second hypothesis. But don't ask me why. I haven't got a clue!"

"And we've got a gangland killing to deal with," said Vidal.

"Jesus, talking of gangland killings . . . Luccioni! You've just re-minded me, we're going to have to pay a visit to the Bar des Sportifs in Endoume."

"Lolo's place? Shall we tell him the good news?"

"What news?"

"His pal, 'Le Blond', is getting out soon."

"How did you know they knew each other?"

"I'm not as green as you think. When I was a kid, I used to read about the adventures of Commandant de Palma."

"Ah, I see . . . How very impressive."

When Lolo saw the Baron's tall figure walk through the door of the Bar des Sportifs, it was like an old nightmare revisiting him after twenty years: he had thought he would never survive the day he was grilled about Le Blond.

"Hello, Lolo, how are things?"

"Fine, Chief Superintendant."

"It's Commandant these days, Lolo."

The landlord wiped down the zinc bar with a damp cloth and put away two coffee cups which had been left beside the sink.

"What can I do for you, Commandant?"

De Palma placed a photograph of Christine Autran on the bar.

"Lolo, think long and hard before answering. Weigh up everything you'll be risking, and everything you won't. Well?"

Lolo went over to the window and swiftly lowered the iron shutter.

"Never seen her before," he said, going back behind the bar.

"Vidal, when is Le Blond getting out?"

"Should be next week."

"Do you think he knows about our friend here?"

"No, definitely not!"

"You bastards."

The Baron wrapped his right hand around the nape of Lolo's neck and, in a flash, smashed his head down on the bar. Once, twice. The third time, the hood's nose cracked.

"If you don't talk, Lolo, I'll break you in two, you hear me? I'll break you in two! On my mother's life. What's more, I'll tell our friend who's about to come back among us after twenty years inside that you're a supergrass. A supergrass to be mowed down."

"I'm fucking bleeding."

"Bleeding what?"

De Palma smashed him down once again, then hit him with his left hand. On the second blow, his left eyebrow burst.

"We're short of staff on the force. So I have to speed things up a bit."

De Palma released the bloodied barman. His left eye was swollen and his lower lip split.

"Lolo, I'm still waiting for your answer. While I'm waiting, I'll pour myself a whisky. I'll make myself at home. Do you want anything, Vidal?"

The young officer did not reply.

"Aren't you thirsty?"

"No, I'm not," he replied dryly.

"Put it on my slate, Lolo."

"It's the truth, I swear to you."

"Don't swear to me, you piece of shit. You've been swearing all your life, you should have had enough of swearing. What did you want from this woman?"

"Me? . . . Nothing! . . . I've never seen her before, understand?"

"What do you think?"

"I dunno! I mean . . . nothing, that's all."

"No, it isn't all, Lolo."

"I swear it."

De Palma slammed the flat of his hand so hard on the bar that it made Vidal jump.

"Don't swear anything to me!" he yelled.

"Alright. I . . . I . . . I've never seen her . . . I sw . . . It's the truth!"

De Palma stood in front of the photo of the Endoume football club. In the second row, he spotted Gérard Mourain.

"Lolo, for some time now they've been giving you jobs tailing people, you and your little acquaintances. Oh yes! We know a thing or two. We've been watching your team, like your old pal Mourain, for example."

"Who, Tête?"

"Yes, dickhead. We thought he must be reading gas metres. But sometimes chance is on our side. An officer in the serious crime squad tipped me off: 'Mourain has been hanging around boulevard Chave. We've seen him there a dozen times . . . With Petits Bras too'. Do you follow me, Lolo?"

"Ah . . . no."

"Shall we start over?"

"No, no."

"So listen to me then. I want to know why you were having this respectable history lecturer followed. Were you in love with her, or what? Unless you'd rather I ask Tête in person."

The Baron knocked back his whisky, went behind the bar and poured himself a second shot. Vidal glared at him.

"It wasn't me, boss."

"Maybe not," said Vidal. "But I don't see what's stopping us hauling you in."

"It wasn't me. Can you imagine me murdering someone like that?"

"Hang on a second, Lolo, we've got a motive and proof that you had her tailed . . . It doesn't look good. People have gone down for less than that. And given your previous, the magistrate will put you in the cooler for a while, enough time for you to think things through and for us to take stock. Then, if it wasn't you, we'll say sorry. By which time you'll have spent months in the can. But it's nice up there. And there's a lovely view, isn't there?"

Lolo stared at the counter top, his eyes wide open. He appeared to be floating in his own stream of his consciousness.

"I can't go back inside. Never."

"Well, in that case you'll have to change your lifestyle a bit."

Lolo slammed his fist on the zinc.

"I can't . . . Give me a break. The first time, I was sixteen. I spent half my youth behind bars. I couldn't take any more . . . "

"You said it wasn't you."

"Yes."

"So who was it then?"

The mobster clenched his fists. He felt trapped.

"All we're asking is why you were having her tailed. We didn't come here to be told it wasn't you," said Vidal, drawing closer. "I reckon you're not looking like so innocent any more."

Lolo stepped back, beyond the officer's reach. He stared straight into his eyes.

"If I'm supposed to be guilty, then prove it."

Vidal had just lost that round; he had cornered this mobster, who had then hit back at him using his long experience of police questioning. They could not prove a thing.

"O.K., you little fucker," de Palma said. "Everyone knows you're in the mob: you've got your moles, the whores at the Opera, a bit of powder, and a few artworks. We know all about your lousy little business. Who do you guys think you are? Better than the rest of us? You're just shits. Pathetic little shits. You can hardly read or write, your mother was a streetwalker on the Curiol and your father a small-time pimp. You're an arsehole, Lolo. And I reckon you're an arsehole that's been damaged with it. I wouldn't be at all surprised if your sphincter had been stretched wide open."

The Baron winked at Vidal.

"Lolo," said the younger officer. "Have you ever seen a man wearing spectacles who looked just like Christine Autran?"

Lolo thought fast, like a good chess player, anticipating his opponent's next moves, and the questions that his answer might prompt.

"I . . ."

"Be serious, you know what'll happen if you don't tell me what I want to hear . . . The Commandant is beginning to feel a tad wound up."

"Listen," Lolo replied, lisping through his beaten and swollen lips. "He was . . . I . . ."

"Make an effort."

"All I can tell you is that there was this guy there."

"Tell me about him . . . "

"Who is he?"

"Your worst nightmare. If you ever see him again, call me at once. If he gives you enough time, that is."

"I don't get it. I haven't done anything."

"You must have! Let's go back to Autran. Did this guy look like her?"

Lolo took a long look at the photo.

"Yes, boss, he definitely looked like her."

"What's his name?"

"I don't know, boss!"

"His name!"

Lolo glanced round at the Baron.

"You can hit me all you want, but I don't know his name. Once I was with Tête outside her place, and he pointed him out to me."

Vidal stepped back. The Baron produced a photo of Luccioni from the side pocket of his jacket, like a gambler slamming down an ace. He observed Lolo's reaction.

"Jesus, it's poor old Franck. He was a friend. A real buddy."

"Did he talk to you about Christine?"

"No, not at all. He was a good guy. Really he was. There should be more people like him. At least, that's what I think."

The mobster took a handkerchief from his pocket and mopped the blood from his nose as he peered around.

"Was it Jo who called you?"

Silence.

"Did he want to avenge his son's death?"

"His son meant everything to him . . . Jesus, whoever did that . . . ."

"The same man. The one with the glasses."

"The fucker. If he comes here, I'll blow him away. I'll say it before witnesses. On my mother's life. If he comes here, he's a dead man."

Old Luccioni had put out a contract. The mob were after his son's killers, and nothing was going to stop them.

The policeman stared at Lolo, who met his gaze. Like a challenge. That was the last time he'd pin him against the wall like that. Lolo had survived all the mob wars. He was no godfather, just a nasty piece of work, a fighter, a nutter with enough balls to hang out with the killers of a magistrate and make Francis Le Blond carry the can. De Palma knew it: tomorrow, Lolo could well end up nose down in the gutter. And tomorrow Lolo would try to kill Le Blond. It was the law of the jungle.

And this law also meant that the police should hold out a hand to him. A favour for a favour.

"Come over here, Lolo. I've got something to tell you in private."

Vidal looked on in disbelief as the mobster held his ear to the Commandant's mouth. He watched the two men converse but could not hear a word. Then Lolo said out loud:

"Thanks boss. Sorry about just now."

"No, the apologies are all mine. I get wound up sometimes . . . It's because we're short of staff."

Lolo placed both hands on the bar and licked the cut on his lower lip.

"At the beginning of July, Franck came here with a package. It contained a large stone with a hand drawn on it. He told me that it was something prehistoric, and it was worth a fortune. I spoke to someone about it, but they weren't interested. So Franck went off with his package . . . and we never saw him again."

"Did he tell you where the stone came from?"

"No, he didn't."

"Why did you think this had something to do with Autran?"

"I didn't, it was Jo. He knew her, at least I think he did. She was a friend of his. And now she's dead too – but this time we really had nothing to do with it. Then we gave up on it all. Afterwards, when I read the papers, I saw that she worked in prehistory . . . "

Lolo sniffed hard and stared at the football cups and pétanque trophies lined up on a shelf at the back of the café.

"Did you see Autran in December?" Vidal asked.

"No, I didn't."

"What about the guy with the glasses?"

"Tête saw him twice, and I saw him once."

"When?"

"I don't know . . . in the middle of December."

De Palma put away his photographs and headed towards the door.

"Can you go out the back door, boss? I don't want anyone to see you."

"Bye, Lolo," he replied. "Take care of yourself."

When they were back in the car, Vidal could not resist asking the Baron:

"What did you tell him?"

"Nothing much. You'll see for yourself in a few days."

"I'm starting to get fed up with your methods, Michel. You never tell me anything."

"Don't piss me off, kid."

"I'm not a kid, for fuck's sake. You might be a prestigious commandant, but I still have to remind you that this is no longer the way to do police work!"

"So how are we supposed to do it?"

"I don't know you any more, Michel. And don't whisper secrets into a mobster's ear again, otherwise I'll . . . "

"OTHERWISE YOU'LL DO WHAT? . . . Go to Paulin like a good little lapdog and have me sidelined?"

"Exactly."

"What are you going to tell him? That I beat up witnesses? That I do deals with them? When you're up against the mob, that's the way it goes. You punch, you deal, you threaten. PERIOD."

Vidal did not reply. The Baron took refuge behind his sombre expression. Unreachable. Ten minutes later, he said dully:

"Sometimes the hardest thing is to be really mean."

Outside the entrance to Plaisance Plus, a First 32 was suspended in midair, its keel in shreds.

"Don't stand there, lady. Can't you see it's dangerous?"

Anne Moracchini took a step backwards to avoid being hit in the face by the yacht if the crane operator made a false move, or if there was a violent gust of wind. She produced her tricolour card.

"I'm looking for the owner."

"You're from the police! I'm the owner. Step inside."

This was now the fourth boat-hire business she had visited in the port of Pointe-Rouge. She said a prayer and begged to all the gods of creation that it would be the last. At least there were no others in Pointe-Rouge.

They went through a large store full of rigging and lifeboats. Anne stopped for a moment in front of a bronze ship's clock. It was just what she wanted for her living room, with Roman numerals and a white enamel dial.

"Come into my office and take a seat. So, what can I do for you?"

"You are . . . ?"

"François Rina."

"O.K., Monsieur Rina, I want to know if you hired out any boats between November 25 and December 5 last year."

"It's nothing serious, is it?" he asked, running his hand through his greying hair.

"Don't worry, we just need to check out how someone spent their day."

The boss of Plaisance Plus stood up and opened a cupboard. Moracchini examined him from head to toe. He was wearing Docksides which had been eaten into by sea salt, jeans and a sailor's pullover which was baggy enough to hide his pot belly. But despite this, he had a certain charm, like an old seadog or a jovial rascal. He reminded her of de Palma.

"Here we are, these are the logbooks for November and December. It'll only take a couple of seconds – we have very little work in winter."

He flicked though the invoices, turning over the blue, yellow and white pages.

"Do you have a name for me?"

"Autran. Christine Autran. Or else Franck Luccioni."

"O.K. . . . "

François Rina was doing his best, but he clearly did not appreciate the police coming to his shop.

"Here we are. Christine Autran. December 2. At 10.00 a.m. A Zodiac . . . Returned at 10.00 a.m. the next day. In perfect condition."

"How big is the boat?"

"Forty horsepower. A lovely vessel."

"Was she with someone, or alone?"

"Hang on, if I remember correctly, she was with someone."

Moracchini took out a photograph of Christine. Rina recognised her at once.

"She was with a man, but he stayed outside. He was tall. Taller than me . . . "

"Was he wearing glasses?"

"Maybe . . . But all this was ages ago."

"It doesn't matter."

She showed him a photograph of Luccioni.

"No, it wasn't him. He didn't look like us. More like a German or something."

"Whose name was on the licence?"

"Christine Autran's. Do you want a photocopy?"

"If you wouldn't mind."

While Rina busied himself over his photocopier, Moracchini went back to the clock, looked at the price and took a step backwards.

"It's a real ship's clock, not like the ones they sell to tourists in the old port."

"And it's incredibly expensive!"

"I'm afraid so, but it's watertight and it never goes wrong. Here's your photocopy. If you're interested in the clock, I could lower the price."

"Thanks. But I've got another question for you. Were there still two of them when they brought the Zodiac back?"

"No, she was alone. I can be sure because as a joke I asked her if she'd fed her boyfriend to the crabs."

"And?"

"She told me she'd dropped him off in the creeks because he was sea sick, and he'd gone home on foot."

"Did they tell you where they were going when they hired the Zodiac?"

"Of course. Anyway, I always ask. They said they were going to spend the day and a night in Riou."

"Can I see the Zodiac?"

"No problem. But not today. It's out at sea."

"I'll come and see it when it's back. Please don't clean it."

"Since then, we've probably cleaned it five or six times."

"Too bad."

As Moracchini left François Rina she gave the beautiful ship's clock a longing look. Twelve hundred francs was really too expensive. She would have to make do with a fake.

25.

The hand was there in front of him, on a tiny desk of white wood. Like a holy relic on an altar. He could not take his eyes off it. The hand was open, its little and ring fingers were bent.

The bedroom was lit only by two candles which trembled at the slightest movement of the air. The shadows of the wardrobe and iron bedstead mingled and merged as the flames moved. Their monstrous shapes rose to the ceiling in a fluid and disturbing dance.

He had neither eaten nor slept for two days. His stomach had ached all day, but now he no longer felt a thing.

Outside, a dark night had fallen. He was naked. Sitting on his heels on the floor, waiting for the vision.

He stared at the hand for a long time, then began to breathe faster and faster, rocking backwards and forwards. A rhythmic chant came to his lips. Its source and meaning were unknown to him. It was the chant of the ancient shamans.

An hour later, the hand began to shake. An invisible force had possessed it. He had his first vision.

Signs appeared. Long lines at first, then sinuous curves which slithered away like huge snakes. A long tunnel and the light of the afterlife. The spirit world.

He felt the first contractions in his belly. He speeded up his breathing and doubled over. The pain became unbearable. Bitter bile rose to his mouth.

Great Reindeer emerges from the forest and stops. Before him is the great white plain that he must cross. He is old, with long, forked antlers.

The hunters are downwind. Great Reindeer has not smelled them. In the morning, they picked up the tracks of a cave lynx going down towards the cliffs at the edge of the great plain. It augured well.

Great Reindeer raises his nose. The icy cold is making his nostrils steam. The wait will be long. The north wind bites into their faces. Despite their fur gloves, their fingers are going numb around their lances.

A shrill cry. The Eagles hovers above the hunters.

He breathed deeply to ease the pain and closed his eyes. The first convulsion. He opened his eyes. Everything had gone hazy. Forms were now dancing around him. The hand had vanished. The second convulsion.

Great Reindeer has smelled the hunters. Calmly, he goes back into the forest, as though drawing them into a trap. The hunters crawl slowly through the snow and encircle him.

Lying on the floor in the foetus position, he massaged his belly to soothe the stabbing pain.

The hand detached itself from the stone and rose into the room, high, even higher, until it touched the dark sky and the stars. He forced his eyes open and the hand made a sign, with three of its fingers bent over.

The first lance hits Great Reindeer in the side, and the second lands in his neck. The hunters move forwards into the open. Great Reindeer doesn't move. He watches them draw near and grunts. The old man is holding an axe and, in a deep, rhythmic voice, he chants the sacred song.

The fingers of the hand are bent over, leaving just one phalange in view and the thumb extended.

Great Reindeer kneels in the snow. His life slowly flows from his wounds. The old man approaches and with his axe hits him sharply on the nape of his neck, at the root of his antlers. Great Reindeer slumps down.

The convulsions were shaking him more violently. White, acidic saliva was dribbling from between his clenched teeth. He writhed like a wounded animal to expel the pain.

Great Reindeer has vanished, engulfed by the silence. A young woman lies there instead. Her long hair is as dark as a raven's wings and her burning eyes are open, lifeless, looking at the snowy sky.

He screamed. The vision faded.

In the distance, he could hear children playing.

26.

"This case is really getting to me. I thought there was another man in her life, and that it was obviously him who'd strangled her. Now she comes back alone without the guy. So what the hell were they doing in Sugiton at night, in a Zodiac? Making fish soup?"

The Baron was fuming. He had had high hopes for the boat investigation, and now one door had closed while another had opened. Moracchini went to the window and pressed her nose to the glass.

"I've no idea what they were doing there at night," she mumbled wearily.

"And to cap it all we've got Luccioni acting as a fence for Cro-Magnon artworks. I'm completely lost!"

"So are we, Michel," Moracchini sighed.

"Vidal, do you remember what Palestro said?"

"Yes," he said frostily. "He followed her on November 30."

"And he saw Christine set off in hiking clothes, without her car."

"Which means?" Vidal asked.

"It means she was going to Sugiton! Where do you think she was going, to church? But there's one thing which doesn't hang together."

"What's that?" Moracchini asked from the window.

"First, if what Palestro says is true, why didn't he follow her all the way? It's absurd. She's dressed in hiking clothes, she takes a tram – why didn't he guess that she was heading for Le Guen's Cave? By car he could have got there first. Secondly, I'm still wondering what she was doing there at night. See what I mean?"

"We should bring him in."

"You're right, Vidal. But we can't just hold him on suspicion."

"Why not?" Moracchini asked, turning away from the window.

"That's not the way I like to work," de Palma murmured.

"O.K., Michel. But your professor is going to have to tell us everything he knows."

"Go and bring him in. Today, after his afternoon lecture. I think he finishes at about 3.00 p.m. Find him and bring him here, but softly does it. If he puts up any resistance, then press the point. This business has to be clarified. I'll call Barbieri to get his agreement. Have you seen Paulin today?"

"No, not yet," replied Moracchini, as she picked up her jacket.

"Right, while you two go to Aix, I'll try to see Sylvie Maurel. We could use her insight this afternoon."

Sylvie Maurel was tidying away her things and was about to go out to lunch when de Palma burst into the laboratory at Fort Saint-Jean. The bells of Les Accoules chimed twelve, soon followed by the angelus.

She glared at him.

"I have to say, Michel, I didn't at all appreciate being questioned in the police station by that little brat. It was atrocious!"

"He was doing his job, Sylvie."

"That boy is a real pain ... Why weren't you there?"

"I ..."

De Palma did not want to admit that he had intentionally avoided the formal questioning so as to preserve the atmosphere of trust which had been created.

"Are you here to question me?"

"No ... Well, yes."

"So out with it, let's get this over with," said Sylvie, throwing her bag on the table.

"I don't want to question you, but rather to ask your opinion."

Sylvie sat down. She was wearing a miniskirt and black tights. As she crossed her legs, she caught the policeman looking at her.

"I have no idea what Christine went to Sugiton creek for. Is it possible to do research there, or something like that?"

"No, not at all. There's nothing on the surface. Le Guen's Cave is entirely underground ... "

"Well I don't get it . . . It's a mystery. I think they must have managed to open the cave, in one way or another."

"No, it's not that," she said dryly.

"What are you trying to say?"

"Christine must have been looking for a second entrance."

Sylvie picked up a pen and rolled it between her fingers.

"One day, I overheard a conversation between Autran and Palestro in their office at the university. They were talking about the presence of air in the cave – I don't know if you're aware of it, but in most caves sealed by the sea, the air is unbreathable."

She pointed to a cupboard on which had been pinned a cross section of Le Guen's Cave. Sugiton's small pebble beach lay just above the underwater passage.

"In Le Guen's Cave, what strikes specialists is the quality of the air. It's far better than in Lascaux or Niaux! You have the impression that it circulates there. I often spoke to Palestro about it, but he was always rather vague on the subject."

De Palma ran his fingers over the diagram of the cave. He needed time to think. Palestro was the only man who knew the secret of this cave – if there was one.

Sylvie came and stood beside him. With a slender finger she showed him a kind of rocky passageway which led back up to the surface.

"You shouldn't go by this diagram. It's extremely imperfect. Even I noticed that there's a black hole in the ceiling."

With a varnished nail, she tapped on the glossy paper at the place marked "Large mural of hands".

"No-one has ever been inside this black hole. It's complicated, because it's about ten metres from the ground. Beneath it, you're in water up to your belt."

"And do you think . . . ?"

"I have no idea. All I can tell you is that Christine was looking for something, and Palestro didn't like it. He wouldn't tell her anything."

De Palma tried to piece everything together in his mind. But it seemed that each time anything became clearer, another problem arose in its place. Everything remained a muddle. Sylvie went back to the table and picked up her bag.

"That's all I know, Commandant. Can I go now?"

All of a sudden her cold beauty made her inaccessible.

"Sylvie, I don't want there to be any misunderstandings between us! I . . ."

"You suspected me, didn't you?"

"Yes."

He was expecting a scornful look, but all he saw in her eyes was extreme disappointment. She shook her long, black hair.

"I'm sure all these murders are linked to Le Guen's Cave," he said, trying to soften his voice.

"Do you still suspect me?"

"No."

Sylvie showed him the way out.

"Can you forgive me . . . I . . ."

She stared at him with her dark eyes.

"Watch out, Monsieur le Policier, you're becoming painfully clumsy."

Palestro's gaze was empty and sad. De Palma shook his hand for a long time, staring straight into his eyes. Then he drew his two colleagues to one side and gave them a rapid, whispered summary of his chat with Sylvie. He also asked them not to reveal what Lolo had said about the hand.

"About this man who was with Christine, when did you see him last?"

"I've already told you: the day I went to get my papers from Christine's flat. When I came out, he was lurking around my car."

"And then?"

"And then nothing. That's what worries me the most. A tram passed by, and he vanished. How can I put it? It was like in a film!"

Palestro was silent for some time.

"That's all I know," he added in a low voice.

Moracchini walked over and sized him up for a moment. The prehistorian blushed. It looked as if his breath was sticking in his chest.

"I think the best thing," she said softly, "would be for you to tell us the truth. And I mean the whole truth. Why didn't you tell us that you followed Christine all the way to Sugiton?"

The professor started, and then stared at them mistrustfully.

"Shall I repeat my question?"

"No, there's no need . . . I admit that I did follow her."

"And you got to the creek before her?"

"That's right."

The professor fell silent and peered anxiously at the three officers who were scrutinising him.

"So?" Moracchini asked.

"When I saw her dressed for hiking, I guessed immediately that she was going to Le Guen's Cave. So I drove out to Luminy, parked my car and – as I walk fast – I got to the creek some time before she did."

"And then?"

"Then about an hour later, she arrived. I watched her. She took a folding spade from her bag and started digging. At the base of the cliff . . . That's when I approached her."

"What did you say?"

"I can't really remember."

Palestro waved his left hand vaguely, as though to chase away his embarrassment.

"Professor, I'm no fool, you know . . . Why did you say 'going to Le Guen's Cave'?"

"Why, what do you call it?"

"I just want to know why you didn't say 'going to Sugiton'?"

Palestro was at a loss; his defences were no longer intact.

"It's the same thing!" he exclaimed shrilly.

"No it isn't, and I think you're hiding something. So now you have a choice between leaving this station a free man and spending the night downstairs. Do you know what it's like downstairs?"

Palestro looked up at Vidal and de Palma. He stuck his right hand in his jacket pocket and started fiddling with his keys.

"There's a second entrance," he stammered.

"And where is this second entrance?"

"Beneath the fallen rocks, to the left of the beach. I'm the only person who knows about it. You have to crawl to get to it. If you want, I'll draw you a map, I can even . . . "

"We'll see about that later," Moracchini interrupted. "How did you find it?"

"It was simple. What strikes you when you arrive inside Le Guen's Cave is the quality of the air. I suspected immediately that there must be ventilation. I mentioned this fact in my first research report, but what I didn't say is that if the air is that good, the ventilation has to be considerable."

"And so you concluded that there must be a large air hole, at least big enough for a man to pass through."

"Exactly."

De Palma got up and stood behind Palestro, leaving the professor facing a bare wall.

"So you went back inside via the air hole?" he said.

"Yes."

"O.K. Let's go on. What happened when you saw Christine in the creek?"

"Christine was furious. She insulted me. She accused me of keeping things to myself. Of not loving her . . . That kind of thing."

Moracchini took Vidal's chair and sat down beside the professor.

"I see," she said slowly. "Christine was angry with you for not trusting her. She was quite right, when you think about it. You find a second entrance, and you keep it to yourself because you know that you're the only researcher who's capable of getting to the cave via the sea entrance. Christine couldn't, and nor could all the idiots who attacked you after its discovery. By saying nothing about this access by land, you were able to control all the research into Le Guen's Cave. It was the pinnacle of your career."

"I . . ."

"It was pride, Professor Palestro . . . pride!"

Palestro's face crumpled. His complexion was like clay.

"So," Moracchini said, waving her hands in the air. "Tell us everything! You bawl her out, she insults you . . . then what did you do?"

"We spoke a little longer, then I left her to her search. Strange as it may seem, I went home. No-one could have dissuaded her from doing what she wanted to do. She was extremely stubborn. And I was in despair."

"Your story is a bit hard to believe when you consider that it's at least a two-hour walk to the car park in Luminy. Especially at night."

"But it's the truth."

"Why?"

"Because what she said to me really hurt. I mean, I was the one who *made* Christine, do you understand?"

Palestro looked at his hands. They were trembling. He had lost his orator's confidence, despite his years of experience.

"Yes, I understand," Moracchini said softly.

"When she started to insult me, I left in disgust. You know, I may be a university professor, but I'm still a bit, how can I put it?"

"Naïve?"

"Yes, perhaps. I thought that my presence would be enough to win her over. And all I got were insults. Among other things, she told me that she had used me. That was hard to bear. She didn't give a damn about my feelings for her."

"And then?"

"The following Sunday, I went down into the cave. I spent the night there. I checked everything. Nothing had been touched. Nothing at all!"

"Have you seen her since then?"

"No, never."

"So, at the moment you're the last person who saw her alive, and in a situation which was rather . . . unusual."

"You could say that . . . "

De Palma produced a file of photographs which he had taken from Autran's flat. He spread them out in front of Palestro.

"How odd," he said, clearly surprised. "These are pictures of the large hand mural. They're . . . "

"Hands from Le Guen's Cave. That is to say, photographs of hands which we found in Autran's flat. How can you explain that?"

"But . . . I've never seen these before. Never. I'm certain of it."

"But they're real!"

"I suppose they are. But it's extremely strange. Only Le Guen and the photographer from the D.R.A.S.M. took pictures. And they're all of far better quality. Incomparable."

"They could have been taken by another member of the team?"

"That's impossible."

"So Christine, or someone else, managed to get inside the cave."

Palestro did not try to hide his bitterness. He now understood that Christine had indeed got inside Le Guen's Cave. De Palma showed him another photograph, which had meant nothing to him. It showed long lines carved on a wall of the cave, without any apparent form.

"It's the Slain Man," Palestro said.

Moracchini picked up the picture, turned it this way and that, then handed it to Vidal.

"Can you see a man here?" Vidal asked, giving the photograph back to the prehistorian.

"Look . . ."

The three police officers leaned over Palestro's shoulders like schoolchildren.

"Here's the head, there's the torso and here are the legs, crudely represented. The two long lines you see here are arrows, or lances."

"He wasn't much good at drawing!" said Vidal, sneering at the carving.

"One last question," said de Palma. "Your answer will not be held against you, whatever it is. When was the last time you went inside Le Guen's Cave?"

"Um . . . a fortnight ago."

"And everything was intact?"

"Yes, absolutely everything."

Palestro could not take his eyes off the photos. He shook his head, trying to deny their existence.

"Professor, you can go now," de Palma said. "But you must make yourself available to the police and magistrates should we need any further information. You're a free man, but we might have to call you in later."

The professor got up slowly. He glanced around the room once more, as if to convince himself that he would never be back.

De Palma motioned to Vidal, who understood at once that he was to follow Palestro to his destination, then call him.

When the professor and Vidal had gone, Moracchini stared intently at the Baron.

"Congratulations on your session with Lolo!"

"Drop it, O.K.?"

"No, we don't do things like that in the police. I spoke with Vidal. What did you promise that shit?"

De Palma picked up his jacket and turned on his heel.

"Leave the kid out of this."

"He's not a kid, Michel, and you disappoint me. See you tomorrow."

De Palma walked down rue de l'Evêché. It was almost dark. He opened the door of Le Zanzi and headed straight for the bar.

"Good evening, Michel. You've been making yourself scarce."

"Too much work, Dédé."

"What are you having, the usual?"

And a pastis arrived on the bar in a flash.

Dédé had had Le Zanzi repainted off-white. Above the bar, his artistic brother-in-law had produced a variation on Marcel Pagnol's card players from his Marseille trilogy. And he had done a decent job, especially in his depiction of the actor Raimu, with his cap cocked, his hands full of cards resting on a pot belly, and his rascally look. Raimu as César was the patron saint of Marseille's bar owners, the inventor of the Mandarine-Picon cocktail, and here he was, splitting his sides in the fug of Le Zanzi. The painter had made a mess of Monsieur Brun. But then Monsieur Brun came from Lyon.

"The new décor's not bad!"

"You haven't seen it yet?"

"Well, it was about time . . . "

"True, we hadn't done it in ages."

Jean-Louis Maistre strolled in.

"Hi Baron, have you been in hiding?"

"I've been working, unlike someone else I know!"

Maistre looked round the smoky room.

"All the fascists are in this evening," he whispered. "It's nostalgia night. They're all here! Completely pissed. Pour old Dédé. How does he put up with them? There's even an ex-member of the Luftwaffe."

"And that old bastard Antoine."

"Who's that?"

"An old Corsican, an ex-bandit. He often comes to Le Zanzi. You've never seen him?"

"Sure, but I've never spoken to him."

"He must be about eighty. He's half paranoid, and an old member of Sabiani's team. But you know all that, it's hardly news."

"Wasn't Sabiani the Maire of Marseille?"

"No, he was a town councillor before the war. He was a bit communist, a bit socialist and extremely fascist. He was with Doriot, collaborating with the Nazis at the time of Carbone and Spirito."

"It's funny that you know all this ancient history!"

"If you want to understand the mob, you have to. And in that respect, Antoine is quite a reference book."

"Oh really!"

"Just think about it. He was Sabiani's henchman, condemned to death after the Liberation . . . then mysteriously freed by Defferre and Guérini and their network. He's the real thing!"

"You say he was condemned to death?"

"Absolutely! He worked for the Gestapo, in the Mangiavaca gang . . . "

"What a bastard! And he got away with it?"

"Oh yes, when you know the right people, you always get away with it. And he knew them all. He was a mobster who rubbed shoulders with everyone – the police, crooks, and a few bigwigs in the town hall. In the old days, when one of the Le Panier kids got into trouble, Antoine would go and see a commissionaire he knew, and they'd hush the whole thing up."

"Where are you at with the Sugiton girl?"

"I'm making progress, but I'm falling out with just about everyone."

"With Anne and the kid?"

"The kid's got teeth! Right now, he's like a moray eel."

"Calm down, Michel. Working with you isn't easy! You always have your little secrets."

Without a word, Dédé placed a pastis in front of Maistre. The Baron's mobile rang.

"It's Vidal."

"Where are you?"

"I followed our professor to rue Paradis. The bugger walked all the way. He rang at number 28, and the person who lives there shares his name. Do you want me to stick around?"

"No, go home. We'll meet up tomorrow for a situation report."

Maistre took an olive from the bowl on the bar.

"You're starting to get seriously depressed, Michel."

"I'm overworked."

"Come round to mine this evening."

"I can't. I have to go and see someone."

"So drop by on the weekend. We'll go fishing. It's the best time for gilt-heads and sea bream."

"O.K., but let's not use sugared mussels!"

The vast hall ended in a corridor lit with bright striplights. Anne Moracchini stopped for a moment and laid her hand on the cast-iron banister which led to the upper floors. She looked up and saw how the spiral staircase vanished into the dark night. The walls were the decrepit reminder of a splendid past; paint was coming away in large flakes, puffed up by the swollen saltpetre plaster. She could just make out the fine remains of *trompe l'oeil* marble columns which framed a rustic landscape half washed away by the dampness. The strong smell of a hookah, a combination of charcoal and tobacco, floated through the air.

At the end of the corridor, a sign on the wall read: *The Friends of Constantine* in French and Arabic. Moracchini rang the bell. A man of indeterminate age, as dry as a root, opened the door and held out his arms.

"Anne, my child, how are you?"

She took his hands.

"I'm fine, Saïd."

Saïd squeezed her hands hard and drew her inside.

"It's not wise for you to come here at night."

"Don't worry," she said, patting her side. "I'm not alone."

"You were brave even when you were a child. You weren't afraid of anyone. Even though you had every reason to be!"

Moracchini had first met Saïd when she was a small girl, in her native town of Constantine. In the '50s, Saïd had been an important figure, a moderate lawyer in the Algerian independence movement, in the tradition of Ferhat Abbas. Anne's father had begun his legal career in Saïd's practice, which had meant that he was later put on the Organisation de L'Armée Secrète's blacklist as a "Communist traitor".

After 1962, Saïd stayed in Algeria, but the Front de Libération Nationale confiscated all his property and caused him so many problems that he ended up coming to Marseille.

"Is there building work at the moment in rue Thubaneau?"

"They're renovating the entire neighbourhood. In other words, they're bulldozing everything. Except for the façades to keep an old-time look. But all the interiors are going. They haven't got to rue Thubaneau yet, but they will before long. They've demolished the Alcazar and everything that was behind it. Anyway, that's the way it goes. What can we do about it?"

"It's a shame," Moracchini said.

"No it isn't, my child. A city needs renovation! What does worry me though is that they're throwing everyone out. What will become of all of these people?"

"They'll be moved to the north of the city."

"You think so?"

"I'm sure of it."

"The problem is there's too much criminality around here. Too much violence. But then there are also a lot of people like me. What can I say? It's the end of a world. Immigrants have always lived in the centre of Marseille, but now they want to put them on the outskirts. They want to empty out Le Panier as well. Marseille will never be the same again. Never."

In the main room of the association's premises, a few pensioners were sucking on their shishas and conversing in low voices. Others were staring at the television, which showed the Algerian national station. It was time for the football league results.

"Come into my office," said Saïd.

"Are you still the association's president?"

"I am. But I'm going to have to step down. I'll be eighty-three next month."

"You're still a young man!"

"Don't talk nonsense. Would you like some tea?"

Saïd went out for a moment, then came back with a brass tray on which he had placed a large teapot, two glasses and a dish of cakes.

"Ah! Zolabias, my favourite!"

"I know, my child. I still have a good memory."

Moracchini gobbled down a cake and watched as Saïd poured the tea. She noticed with sadness that his old, brown hands trembled slightly.

"First we drink the tea, then we talk."

He raised the glass to his lips, blew gently on the surface of his tea and took a sip.

"Tell me, Saïd, have you ever heard of a market for prehistoric artefacts?"

"You know I collect only Algerian antiquities, especially Roman ones, and two or three pieces from Carthage, nothing else. Prehistory is a little too distant for me . . . "

"I'm working on a case concerning fences selling prehistoric art. Do you have any ideas?"

"It's very difficult to find prehistoric art. Practically impossible, in fact. There are very few pieces, and the experts know every one of them."

Saïd produced a packet of Gauloises from the pocket of his waistcoat. He lit a cigarette and left it dangling from his dry lips as his gaze evaporated in the blue smoke.

"There were some thefts and fencing going on in the '80s. It rather struck me at the time. I mean, how can people sell pieces like that? They're part and parcel of mankind's heritage . . . There was a Venus and some stone necklaces, but I can't remember where they came from. What I can tell you is that prices are extremely high."

"But you haven't heard about any deals going on in Marseille at the moment?"

There was a knock at the door. Saïd got up and opened it. He exchanged a few words in Arabic with another man who had come to say that he was the last person to leave.

Saïd sat down again and drew heavily on his cigarette.

"I've heard there have been requests from an association of enthusiasts in America. They've got plenty of money. I seem to remember they're in New York State and they never argue about the price. Americans are very interested in prehistory."

"Do you know the name of the association?"

"No . . . there are so many lunatics in that country. An antiques dealer told me about it – an Egyptian art specialist. He has some amazing pieces."

"He didn't mention any names?"

"No, of course not. These people are very discreet. Antiques dealers are a bit like crooks," Saïd laughed.

"He didn't say anything else?"

"No, just what I told you."

"Have you ever heard of a Professor Autran?"

"Of course I have, my child. You know I read every newspaper. I'd already worked out that she's the reason you've been asking me all these questions."

Saïd stood up to his full height. In a flash, Moracchini saw once again the man who had lifted her up so often in his arms, after Sunday lunch, in the cosy salon of his house in Constantine.

"Thank you, Saïd."

"It's nothing, my child . . . "

The old lawyer's expression grew sad and he took out another cigarette.

"You know, recently I have been thinking about your father a lot. I shall be going to join him soon."

"So have I. I often think about him."

"Go on, run along home. It's late. And come and see me a little more often, not just to ask for information."

Moracchini placed a kiss on her old friend's forehead and left.

27.

When de Palma got up after a short sleep, the hills of Saint-Loup were crowned with a heavy black beret, a sign that another series of thunderstorms was going to rip open the sky and bring the temperature down by a few degrees.

He had slept badly. The growing tension in his relationships with his two team mates was starting to create difficulties. That night, he had woken up in a sweat. An old memory which had been haunting him for years had just resurfaced.

September 27, 1982. For over a year, Sylvain Ferracci, or "The Dustman" as he was called by a leading journalist on Le Méridional, *had been taunting a dozen inspectors and Commissaire Parodi, who had been given the job of putting him behind bars. His victims were always alike: secretaries in strict suits who were strangled and raped before being sliced into three parts: the head, the torso and the legs. The killer put each part of the body into a dustbin liner, which he then left in a particular place, like an infernal paper trail in which the police were forced to participate; at the end lay unadulterated horror and a feeling of powerlessness that set their nerves on edge.*

It was during the debate about the death penalty, and the case had taken on an unprecedented importance. The right wing was bellowing, the left complaining about political exploitation. Gaston Defferre made it a personal issue during the lead-up to the election. This sadist, now splashed across all the front pages, was still methodically slicing up secretaries in strict suits with a circular saw.

De Palma had spent entire nights trying to understand the killer, entire nights exhausting his eyes over the huge pile of notes and documents which had built up on his desk and that of his team mate,

Seitboun. Nothing doing. Then, on September 26, a witness formally identified Sylvain Ferracci from an identikit picture which had been widely published in the press. He had seen the murderer coolly walking up rue de Rome, in the town centre, with his wife at his side. Ferracci had been pinpointed.

September 27, 6.10 a.m. Things were moving quickly. The head of the murder squad arrived at his home address, accompanied by a dozen plain-clothes inspectors and an escort from the city brigade in crisp suits, with their MAC 50s and their kepis down over their eyes. But Ferracci had not come home that night. They had to raise the siege and wait, discreetly.

De Palma, stationed at the top of rue Dragon, spotted him first and went after him alone. As he ran, Ferracci dropped his P.38, the preferred weapon of O.A.S. veterans. De Palma picked it up. Finally, at the end of a chase which had seemed interminable, the policeman had found himself alone and completely out of breath in the basement of a detached house on rue Breteuil, face to face with the Dustman, who was frenetically rubbing his arms and erect penis and repeating in a high-pitched, scarcely audible voice: "Not that, not that . . . " as though he was quietly invoking the clemency of the gods of murder.

De Palma slowly went over to the sadist, who was looking at him like a guilty dog. He put the bronze-coloured steel barrel over his mouth, as if to say "Hush". Oddly enough, the Dustman looked relieved; his face relaxed, wrinkle after wrinkle, until it was as smooth as marble. His eyes seemed to be saying a prayer. Then, suddenly, his sphincter and bladder let go. A smell of piss and shit filled the dusty air. De Palma could think of nothing but the monstrous images which had been haunting him for months: the flickering striplights in the autopsy theatre; the bodies of dismembered women, sliced methodically; their puffy faces, violated vaginas, gaping bellies, pubis half eaten through. The image of his brother, a close-up of his soft, fine eyes, then replaced all the others.

De Palma rammed the barrel into the Dustman's mouth, closed his eyes and pulled the trigger once. The report of the P.38 filled the cellar with its dull thunder, blood exploded like a splash of ink into the middle of the room, propelled by the final contractions of the sadist's ventricles.

Life had gone.

It was now just a thin, dark stream vanishing into the ground, absorbed by the earth floor.

De Palma did not understand. Another person had killed, not him. Another person had committed the irreparable.

He pulled himself together. He carefully took out his handkerchief to wipe the fingerprints off the gun, then placed it in the still-quavering hand of the corpse, closed its fingers around the grip and stuffed it into the Dustman's mouth. He went back up to street level. In a haze. He had just opened the door on to the stinking corridors of his soul.

The head of the brigade considered his state of mind worrying, and incompatible with the responsibilities of a police officer on the murder squad. He requested a physical and mental check-up.

The conclusion of the specialist's four-page report read:

```
. . . . Michel De Palma is in good general
health. However, he is showing symptoms of
depression, quite common among the police.
This may be temporary. He switches between
periods of anxiety and nervous attacks.
In addition he has an occasionally violent
personality. This violence can sometimes
be of an obsessive nature, especially when
heightened by feelings of guilt.

However, Inspector de Palma has a great deal
of control over his impulses. This officer
is extremely sensitive, highly intuitive,
and very intelligent. While his condition
requires treatment, it is not incompatible
with his responsibilities on the murder
squad . . .
```

After Ferracci's death, instead of confessing, he had looked for absolution in his job as a policeman, in the combat against what he had been taught to look upon as evil. It was light versus darkness. He had sold himself a pack of lies about the justice of his mission, even though he knew deep down that all he wanted was to enjoy the fruits of darkness. His favourite plants in the shadowy jungle of the human psyche were carnivorous, devouring dreams and innocence.

By screwing his conscience, he had managed to convince himself that he wanted to fight against those who destroyed innocence. And yet the truth lay at the opposite extreme, in the dubious adventures he courted at the margins of society, in his quest for heroism.

But the police force does not produce heroes, and he knew it.

He slipped on some jeans and a T-shirt, gulped down a coffee and joined the morning traffic; an invisible force seemed to be drawing him towards headquarters.

When he emerged from the lift on the second floor, a dozen men from the serious crime squad were rushing around in the corridor. From their excitement, de Palma could see that an important page in Marseille's history of organised crime was being written. Captain Zuccarelli came over to him, looking like an old wrestler. De Palma saw that he could barely contain his emotions.

"There was an armoured car in the north of the city. Just beside the old shipyards . . . Richard and Jean-Pierre were on the case . . . They tried to intervene, and . . . "

De Palma said nothing. He met Zuccarelli's gaze.

"Richard is in a coma. The quacks won't tell us anything. Jean-Pierre's in hospital too, but he should pull through. It's terrible, Michel."

"What about the fuckers who did it?"

"They've been tracked down to a villa in La Viste. The special branch and the flying squad are on to them. We're on our way. See you later, Michel."

"Take care of yourself."

He watched Big Zuccarelli vanish into the lift, then opened the door of his office and slumped into his chair. He did not even notice Moracchini and Vidal standing by the window. When he sensed their presence, he said:

"I want him before the end of the summer . . . "

"Do you want a sitrep now, or shall we wait?" Moracchini asked.

"Why wait? We'll have some coffee and start at once."

There was a strained atmosphere in the room. Vidal attempted to catch his boss's eye, but de Palma was trying to conceal his anger and look calm by rifling through some files. Moracchini broke the silence.

"We're in shock, Michel. I don't think we're going to do much useful work today."

"Whether you're in shock or not, we need to keep going," remarked the Baron simply.

"I can't understand you sometimes, Michel. We might have lost a colleague, and another is fighting for his life, and you talk to us as if . . . "

"AS IF WHAT?" he yelled, slamming his hand on his desk. "I knew Richard when you were still at school. He was a friend, and he isn't dead yet as far as I know. I'll cry about him this evening, but right now I'm doing what society wants me to do. There are only three of us looking for this guy, and there should be twenty. And what's more, they've offloaded the Ferri couple on us! Duriez prefers gangland killings – the Maire must have told him that they need cleaning up; that it's bad for the city's image. After the next elections, our Maire may be a minister; he's already hustling for the Intérieur. So Duriez, our big boss, is shitting himself. There are three of us, and three we'll remain. So, get that into your heads, because we're on our own until the end. O.K.?"

"Loud and clear. Maistre has phoned several times," Vidal said. "Maybe your mobile doesn't work."

"I'll call him later. Right now, I don't want anyone to disturb us. So, I'm all ears, Maxime. What's new?"

"Nothing."

"And you, Anne?"

"Yes, I do have one thing."

"Go on."

"Yesterday evening, I went to see someone who knows the art market well, and he told me that he'd heard about an association of American fanatics who were buying prehistoric art works. Apparently, they're rolling in it. They're based in New York State . . . it's a kind of cult."

"Nice work, Anne. Really nice. I see you work like I do. Doing little investigations on the side . . . Personally, that doesn't bother me."

De Palma waited for her reaction. It didn't come.

"Look both of you, we can't keep scrapping like this. I treated you badly, and I'm sorry."

"Oh, that's a bit too easy," Moracchini said. "You treat us like dogs, then apologise!"

"I mean it, sincerely."

"Apology accepted, team mate, you're as stubborn as a mule, but I still like you."

Vidal went out to the coffee machine. De Palma strode after him.

"I couldn't care less about your apologies, Michel."

De Palma poked his index finger into Vidal's shoulder.

"Listen kiddo, just don't forget one thing: I'm in charge of this case. You stab me in the back, and I'll make your life hell."

"O.K., I've got the message," said Vidal, drawing away.

"You're going to call up Ron Hoskins, the F.B.I. agent in Lyon. He covers the whole of France. Tell him that you're calling on my behalf. He's an old friend. Ask him what they know about an association in New York State interested in prehistoric art. If he's uncooperative, tell him it's urgent and hint that I'm going to put him on to a market of ancient artefacts being exported to the U.S.A. Is that clear, Maxime?"

"Crystal."

"Do it now."

De Palma returned to his office and went over towards Moracchini, who could not help recoiling slightly as he neared her.

"If we leave aside Agnès Féraud, the murders start with Luccioni's. The deaths of Autran, Weill and Chevallier followed on from that one."

"True," Moracchini said, tapping her right cheek with a pencil. "There's just one thing that surprises me . . ."

"What?" asked the Baron, glancing at her.

"Yesterday, when I was thinking back over the reports, I remembered that Autran was taller than her corpse. According to her identity papers at least. There's a difference of three centimetres, to be exact. Forensics told me that the cold water must have made her shrink, that her scalp had been eaten away, and so on . . . But three centimetres is a lot."

"I see what you mean," said de Palma bitterly. "But on identity papers, people's height is often a bit approximate."

The phone rang. Moracchini answered it.

"It's for you, Michel."

It was Maistre. They exchanged a few words.

"I'll see you at 6.00 p.m., at your place," the Baron said, before hanging up.

He looked at his teammate for a long time.

"You've just given me an idea. But before I tell you about it, I need to sort something out this afternoon."

"There you go again."

De Palma decided to come clean.

"I'm going to see the Luccioni girl."

"And may I ask why?"

He noticed a hint of anger in her voice.

"Because I've got a vague idea which I need to check out. That's all."

"And what is this vague idea?"

"I think she might be able to tell me who Autran used to see."

"Is that all?"

"That's all. If I'm wrong we'll have to go through everyone Autran, Luccioni, Féraud, Weill and Chevallier knew, which will do our heads in. We just don't have enough staff, my lovely. My intuition might spare us all that work. So let's be friends. Don't try to screw me up, just trust me," he said bluntly to put an end to his teammate's awkward questions.

At 2.00 that afternoon, de Palma rang Bérengère Luccioni's doorbell.

"Sorry to disturb you. Aren't you working today?"

Bérengère welcomed him with a sunny smile tinged with a wicked gleam. She took his hand gently. As her long, soft fingers touched his, he felt as if a wave of heat had lifted him off the floor. He walked into the salon, then turned towards her. She was barefoot, dressed in a simple dress of crimson shirting.

"I know I shouldn't be telling you this, but I think you're extremely beautiful."

She blushed and tidied away an electricity bill which was lying on the table, to hide her embarrassment.

"I wanted to see you because I need to ask a few questions."

"Are these the last ones?"

"I hope so . . . "

He went out on to the balcony. A storm had just blown by, leaving behind a shattered sky. Beyond the islands, blue patches pierced the grey, while a white light sank into the tin surface of the sea.

"I wanted to talk to you about your brother's private life . . . Apart from Christine, who did he hang around with?"

"People I didn't know. He had friends, but I couldn't name any."

"What kind of people were they?"

"What do you expect? Crooks, like him!"

"And did you see Christine often?"

"No, not often. She didn't live in our neighbourhood any more. But I think they still saw each other regularly."

"Even just before he died?"

"Yes, I think so. If he'd fallen out with her, I think he would have told me. When it came to that, Franck and I told each other everything."

Franck's violent death was still a gaping wound. Bérengère's eyes were full of tears. She offered the Baron a drink, which he refused.

"And do you know anything about the Autran family?"

"Not much. Except that her mother was completely mad. And I mean completely."

"That's what I heard. Apparently she abused her son."

"Not half! Anyway, they're all dead now . . . "

All of a sudden, de Palma had an odd feeling, deep down, an idea which was starting to shift around in the jungle of his brain.

"Did you know her brother?"

"A bit . . . But Franck knew him well. They were the same age, and they often used to play together. Christine's brother – his name was Thomas – was totally crazy. I mean really, an utter loony. When I was little, he used to scare me. We didn't see him very often. After their mother's death, he was sent to a psychiatric hospital, the Edouard Toulouse . . . I remember because Franck went to see him several times."

"You wouldn't have a photo of him, would you?"

"Sorry, no."

"Never mind."

De Palma sensed that the pieces of a complex edifice were now coming together, one after the other, like in a child's game. But he could not master the rules while the overall structure remained imperfect. Many scraps of truth were still missing.

"Did her brother have blue eyes?"

"Yes, really blue. Like his sister."

The man on the motorbike. Luccioni's bakery. De Palma felt his guts tighten.

"Do you remember the date of Thomas' death?"

"No, I don't . . . My brother told me about it . . . It was so long ago."

"Was it before or after their mother died?"

"After, I think . . . At the time, Franck was . . . "

Bérengère could no longer hold back her tears.

" . . . was in prison. So . . . it must have been after their mother's death . . . "

De Palma looked away to hide his emotion. Bérengère was right next to him. She put her hand on his shoulder. He quivered.

"Why did you become a policeman?"

Her question took him unawares. He would have liked to reply that, as a boy, he had wanted to be a great conductor, a lead violinist or a seafaring captain. He heard himself describing how he pictured the ideal man.

"I thought it was the perfect job for a man. I wanted to be useful to society. I wanted to have a purpose."

"And do you still think that?"

"I dunno."

"I think you do."

Her words were reassuring. Something in the way her lips trembled showed that she understood his inner truth. They spent the rest of the afternoon deep in conversation. She told him about her childhood, her hardships and occasional moments of joy, despite everything . . . She laid out her painful past, her dislocated life, heavy as a limp body.

They went their separate ways at about 5.00 p.m.

De Palma drove aimlessly for a while, plagued by contradictory thoughts. Then he picked up his mobile and called the office.

"Anne, has Maxime got in touch with Hoskins? Good. Leave that aside for moment and head straight to the Edouard Toulouse to see if they treated a certain Thomas Autran in the '80s . . . Sometime after 1982. Do it quick, then call me."

Moracchini placed her tricolour card on the reception counter in the psychiatric department of the Edouard Toulouse hospital and clacked her signet ring on the Formica. It was one way of showing her claws, and it made the receptionist contact the head of the department. She was so unpleasant that Dr Bentolila turned up within five minutes.

"Good evening, Madame. How can I help you?"

"Anne Moracchini, murder squad. I want to know if you treated a certain Thomas Autran in the early '80s."

The psychiatrist rolled his eyes and whistled, then stared long and hard at his watch. It was nearly 6.30. He frowned behind his tiny spectacles.

"I'd like to help you, but this would mean going through the registers. I didn't work here at the time. Can I ask why you need to know?"

"It's part of a murder investigation . . . several murders in fact," Anne stressed. "Your former patient might be able to give us some vital information."

Given Bentolila's reluctance, Anne laid it on with a trowel. She spoke of investigating magistrates, legal procedures and even threatened to spend the night going through the archives herself.

"O.K., O.K. . . . I'll see what can be done. Come with me."

He led her down a corridor which ran alongside the drug addicts' unit. It was cluttered with chrome-plated trolleys and three muscular nurses – one male, two female – were loading them with nocturnal medication; multi-coloured horse pills to knock out head-cases.

Dr Bentolila shoved open a heavy door and they entered a room lined with files from floor to ceiling.

"Here we are. It was 1980, was it?"

"No, a bit later. Let's start with 1982. A-U-T-R-A-N, Autran."

The doctor grabbed a ladder and clambered up to the middle of the left-hand wall.

"You must be surprised that a departmental manager also works in records?"

"Well, yes, a bit."

"We're short of staff. It's a pity, but that's the way it is. Quite apart from our problems with care nurses . . . it's an utter catastrophe."

A few moments later, Bentolila came down with a huge folder.

"This is for 1982."

Moracchini reached for the file, but the doctor drew back.

"Some of this information is confidential. I'll have to check first."

He sat down at a white wooden table in the middle of the room and flicked through the folder, his glasses perched on the end of his nose. A few minutes later, he came across a plastic slip file and stopped.

"I think I've found what you want. Thomas Autran, arrival September 21, 1982 . . . Departure January 6, 1985. Dr Caillol's department. He no longer works here."

Moracchini had been expecting anything and everything from the records at Edouard Toulouse hospital except that name. Caillol.

"And was it Caillol himself who treated him?"

"Yes. He signed his release form in 1985."

"Can you tell me why Thomas Autran was interned here?"

Dr Bentolila shook his head in disapproval. Moracchini realised that pressing the point would be a waste of time. This was something she could sort out later. She asked if the file mentioned an address for Thomas Autran after his release.

"Let's see. He went on to a Catholic institution here in Marseille for some kind of convalescence, the Saint-François institute in Château Gombert. It's just round the corner."

The doctor explained how to go there. It was five minutes away. She thanked him before driving straight to the institute. On the way, she tried calling de Palma on his mobile, but all she got was his answerphone.

*

The Saint-François institute was hidden behind high stone walls. Only an absurdly small door and a gleaming brass plaque indicated that this was indeed the right place. Moracchini parked her car a few metres away from the entrance and rang the doorbell.

A shrill female voice emerged from the intercom.

"Anne Moracchini. I'm a police officer."

The door opened to reveal a gravel driveway which ran between lawns dotted with exotically scented trees, before finishing several hundred metres away at an austere nineteenth-century manor.

Father Bouvier was waiting for her at the end of the avenue, between two ancient olive trees.

"Good afternoon, Madame," he said in a baritone voice with an unidentifiable, slightly harsh accent. "So you're from the police?"

"Yes, Father. My name is Anne Moracchini, from the murder squad." She showed him her card.

Father Bouvier was about sixty and completely bald, with little sparkling eyes behind national health glasses.

"And how can I help you?"

"We're looking for a man who was here between 1985 and a date which is at present unknown to us. Does the name Thomas Autran mean anything to you?"

"Thomas Autran? Yes indeed. He was here until 1988."

"I'd like to ask you a few questions about him."

"Go ahead. I'll be pleased to help. But I must ask you to remain discreet."

"Don't worry, Father. I just want to know how he behaved when he was here."

With a wave of his hand, the friar invited her to stroll with him through the olive trees, yews and cypresses in the institute's garden. Some way off, residents were playing football in the ochre light. Two men were leaning against the wall of the manor, staring into space and chain-smoking.

"Thomas behaved extremely well. He was a tormented soul when he arrived."

"Did he tell you about his past?"

"No, never. All I know is that there had been some sort of a family tragedy, but he never really spoke about it. He almost lost his sanity after his mother's death, but that's all I know. And he loved his father more than anything. They were very close."

"You never noticed anything abnormal in his behaviour?"

"'Abnormal' is a fairly meaningless term here. We take in people who are convalescing after hospital treatment, and often it's extremely severe. Thomas was a case in point. He came to us from the Edouard Toulouse, if I remember correctly, where he'd spent three years on particularly strong medication. In the beginning he was very edgy, sometimes even violent. Then, with time, he recovered his sanity. At first he refused to communicate, rather like someone with autism. But gradually he recovered his speech."

"So you think he was cured when he left here?"

"Yes, I think so. But with that kind of illness, you can never be sure."

"What was he suffering from?"

"I'd rather not say."

"He was schizophrenic, wasn't he?"

"Yes."

Father Bouvier stopped next to a bed of rose bushes in bud. He put out a hand and gently stroked the tips.

"Why are you asking about Thomas?"

"His sister has been murdered."

"Oh, so that's why!" he said, glancing at her furtively. "I read about it in the papers. Poor Christine, I prayed for her several times."

"Did you know his sister?"

"Christine? Of course I did. She used to visit him two or three times a week. She was his twin. They seemed inseparable."

Father Bouvier set off again.

"They used to spend hours in the gardens here. In the beginning, Thomas got into a terrible mood every time she went home. It was as though he had shut himself in. But this got better over time. He even managed to accept the separation. I should also tell you that, little by little, he came to know Jesus. He found his vocation."

"What do you mean?"

"Well, after he left, he came back to tell me that he wanted to leave France to help those people who were suffering the most."

"You mean, in poor countries?"

"That's right . . . though not only in poor countries, rather in places where people suffer the most. He'd contacted various Catholic institutions like ours, and I think the Church accepted his request, because a year later I got a postcard from Australia. It said that he was in a programme to help Aborigines."

"And then?"

"And then, nothing. I must admit that's a little surprising, when I think about it. It is rather odd that he hasn't been in touch again after all this time. Especially now that his sister is dead. He should have come to see me."

"Yes, that is odd. Do you remember where he went exactly?"

"No, not exactly. I'll have to look for the postcard."

"It doesn't matter, Father. Just try to remember. Any inkling?"

"No, really, I have no idea. But I'll call you if I remember anything, or if I find the postcard."

"Thank you, Father."

The sun had just disappeared behind a hedge of cypresses, and a cold shadow fell across the Saint-François institute. The football match had finished.

"You seem to remember Thomas extremely well. Is it the same for all your residents?"

"No, I'm afraid not! If only it were so. But I'm like everyone else. I only remember people who are out of the ordinary."

"And Thomas was out of the ordinary?"

"He was an extraordinary person. With exceptional intelligence. I singled him out at once when he arrived here."

"Why?"

"It's hard to explain . . . For example, he devoured every book in our library. Whenever I ran into him, he'd ask me questions about all sorts of subjects, such as the scriptures, or history. I didn't always have the answer, in fact, because his questions were so precise."

"Did he talk to you about prehistory?"

"A great deal. It must be in the family. He asked me about Teilhard de Chardin, Leroi-Gourhan . . . and also a lot about Lévy-Strauss. His sister brought him lots of books."

"When you read about his sister's death in the press, did you try to contact him?"

"Yes, I did. I contacted the institute he'd been with, and they told me they would do what they could. But I haven't heard from them since."

"Try to find out everything you can, Father, and call me as soon as possible."

Moracchini gave him her card and left.

It was nearly 7.00 p.m. For the past two days, Sylvie Maurel had been phoning the Baron, asking to meet up. He had not responded because he did not want to give her any false hopes. But the previous evening, he had agreed to see her. His mobile rang just as he was parking on rue Caisserie, about a hundred metres from the marine archaeology laboratory.

"Michel? It's Anne. I've just been to the Edouard Toulouse."

"And?"

"They definitely treated a Thomas Autran between 1982 and – hold on to your hat – 1985!"

"So?"

"1985! Wake up Michel, 1985!"

"Jesus Christ!"

"They wouldn't tell me exactly what was wrong with him. But they reckoned he'd been cured, because they let him go. Then there's a second piece of news."

"I'm all ears!"

"It was Dr Caillol who treated him."

"WHAT?"

"You heard me: Caillol."

"Have you got anything else?"

"Yes. I went to a Catholic institute for convalescents. He stayed there after leaving the Edouard Toulouse. Until 1988."

"1988!"

"That's right . . . Anyway, I'll explain it all tomorrow. But tell me, was it the Luccioni girl who gave you this lead?"

"Yes."

"I must admit, you've got incredible intuition."

"It was just luck, Anne."

"It's odd we didn't think of it earlier!"

"That's probably my fault . . . What can I say? There are only three of us on the case . . . Anyway, it would have come out sooner or later. Now we have to find him. They didn't tell you anything else at the Edouard Toulouse or at the institute?"

"Yes, they did. But the rest is less important. I'll tell you tomorrow."

"Nice work, Anne. I'm lucky to have you with me."

"Keep your compliments to yourself, Michel."

He hung up.

When he got to the tower at Fort Saint-Jean, he could hear Sylvie calling to him from the quayside. He turned and saw her on the deck of the *L'Archéonaute*, a thirty-footer used for marine exploration.

"Do you want a guided tour?"

She smiled at him broadly and he stammered something incomprehensible.

"Come on board."

When he was on deck, Sylvie held out her hand and looked at him shyly. A man came out of the boat's bridge.

"May I introduce Lieutenant Laffitte?"

The man looked at him and gave a nod before disappearing back into the bridge.

"This is the boat we used when we investigated Le Guen's Cave in 1992. I remember how choppy the sea was; it was awful staying on board all day. We'd set up a video link which meant we could follow the work in the cave as it happened."

The lieutenant was sitting in front of a radar screen in the bridge, turning knobs this way and that. He didn't bother to look up when they came in, so they continued on down to the mess.

"This is one of the areas we use as a laboratory and meeting room when we're out on a mission. We keep all our equipment here: microscopes, measuring instruments, and so on . . . everything we need."

"Do you often go out on missions?"

"For me it's quite rare, because I'm a prehistorian. You don't find something like Le Guen's Cave every day! But the boat's used a lot for Greco-Roman archaeology."

They could hear Laffitte calling from the bridge.

"Sylvie, it's time to go."

"O.K., Sylvain . . . it's a shame you didn't get here earlier. You could have seen the whole boat. Maybe some other time!"

"If you want."

Laffitte's voice grew more insistent.

"Sylvie, I'm locking up!"

It was busy on the quay: there were pensioners soaking up the last rays of the sun, and executives walking home briskly having taken the ferry across the water. A group of tourists were photographing one another in front of *La Bonne Mère*, and kids on bikes were chasing each other, weaving between the passers-by.

They strolled towards the town hall in silence. As they passed the Fishermen's Association, de Palma lingered in front of a stripped-down Marseille fishing boat on blocks. A man was busy sanding the hull.

"I'd like one just like that, if they weren't so expensive!"

"They're lovely boats," Sylvie said.

"They're the loveliest."

They walked on for another twenty metres, with Sylvie glancing at him timidly, like a teenager. He just managed to avoid a kid on rollerskates who was wiggling his hips and swerving between the walkers. When they got to the old riggers by the town hall, de Palma went over to a forty-ton schooner.

"This one's my favourite, *Le Caprice des Vents*."

"What a nice name for a boat."

De Palma touched the hull of *Le Marseillois*, a three-master, then stepped back as though estimating its tonnage. The rigging and yards stood out against the hill of Notre-Dame de la Garde.

He gazed at Sylvie, and she looked back at him tenderly. After a long silence, he said:

"You know, I've just found out that Christine had a brother."

"How odd."

"Why is that odd?"

"She never mentioned him. I always supposed that she was an only child. She was so temperamental and bossy, it seemed obvious."

The day was coming to an end. Headlights and restaurant signs shimmered blue and red on the gentle lapping of the heavy waters of Lacydon. A dark and humid night was settling in across Marseille.

Sylvie lived at 35, esplanade de la Tourette, on the eleventh and top floors. As de Palma came through the door, she hastened to raise the shutter in the living room. The balcony overlooked the entire port of Marseille. In the foreground was the ferry terminal, then the seawall and, beyond that, the Frioul archipelago.

"Would you like something to drink?"

"Whatever you're having, Sylvie. I'm easy."

"Whisky, then. I don't have any pastis."

"A whisky would be fine."

While she was in the kitchen, de Palma took the opportunity to go out on to the balcony.

In the distance to his right, the cranes and scaffolding down in the port glittered in the night, like motionless, steel sentinels bent over the cargo boats. From Arenc to L'Estaque via the Bassins National, Pinède and Président Wilson, the huge port was sending out its fireworks.

Sylvie came and stood so close to him that they were almost touching, and gave him his whisky.

"It's so beautiful," she said.

"It's magnificent. It's the Marseille I love. My father worked down there, and his father and grandfather before him. They were all sailors. Except me – I became a lousy policeman instead."

"But that's also a wonderful profession!"

"Don't talk nonsense, Sylvie . . . "

A horn sounded and the *El Djézaïr* sailed into Grande Joliette dock, heading for Sainte-Marie strait and the open sea, with a pilot ship in its wake. The cargo ship with its Algerian flag slowly cruised past the ruins of huge hangars on the Joliette quayside. These temples of Marseille's fortune, were marked with a capital J followed by a number. J1, J2 and J3 were no more, now reduced to dust, bulldozed into the depths of the dry docks.

There had been plans for a new harbour, with marinas and the renovation of the Le Panier neighbourhood, in the hope that this would rid the "boulevard of crime" of its tawdry inhabitants, thus finishing the work begun by the Germans when they razed the city centre in 1943. Bombed and wrecked, could eternal Marseille now rise again, like the demi-gods of Greece who bit the dust but never wanted to die? The Greece of the Republic, the *demos*, poets and brilliant thinkers; Phocaea and her daughter Marseille, the swarthy-skinned rebel who talked with her hands and enveloped herself in nonsense when she got the blues.

Sylvie touched his shoulder.

"A penny for your thoughts."

"Nothing special. Do you like opera?"

"I've never been."

"I'll take you, one day."

Sylvie stroked the rim of her glass with her index finger.

"I'll put on some music. It's a kind of jazz-rock. I don't know what you like."

De Palma immediately recognised the '70s sound of a Telecaster guitar.

"Is that Mike Stern's latest album?"

"Yes, it is. Do you know his stuff?"

"He used to be in Blood, Sweat and Tears, and he played with Miles Davis once or twice . . . a really good guitarist, though his style's a bit conventional."

"I thought opera lovers only listened to opera!"

"Only fools and sectarians. Music is a whole universe. I've got all of the Stones' albums, real rarities which I bought in London in the good old days . . . But don't talk to me about The Beatles or Georges Brassens!"

"A bit sectarian all the same . . . "

A surging saxophone-and-guitar duet immersed Sylvie's flat in a soothing atmosphere. They listened to it for a while, without looking

266

at each other. When the second track started, she went over to the hi-fi and turned down the volume.

"I wanted to see you because there's something I forgot to tell you last time."

"What's that?" he asked darkly, worried that she was about to break the charm of the evening.

"I was the one who first told her about Le Guen's Cave. I knew about the discovery before it was announced in the papers. In fact, I know Le Guen well. We spoke about it a few months before. I was the one who told him that he would have to reveal his discovery. And then . . ."

The charm had been broken. The Telecaster sounded as though it was light years away.

"Who are you talking about?"

"About Christine . . . And then there were those divers found dead in the tunnel. Do you remember?"

"Of course. Why?"

"Because something struck me at the time. One day, after their deaths, she was with me at the lab and she said: 'You see, the first man has got his revenge'."

"Anything else?"

"No, nothing."

"It's rather a silly thing to say."

"I'm not so sure. Anyway, it struck me. And for several days I haven't been able to get it out of my mind. Why did she say it?"

"I've no idea. But people say strange things sometimes."

"Of course, but what struck me was the expression on her face. I can still see it, there was something lugubrious in the way she said it."

He thought over what Sylvie had just told him. Without knowing why, he felt certain that it was important.

"I'd like you to tell me about shamans. I've been told that Le Guen's Cave was used for shamanistic rituals, is that true?"

"Nothing is a hundred per cent sure in prehistory, but it is a serious hypothesis . . . We've long tried to understand why Palaeolithic man always went into the darkest depths of his caves to paint his frescoes. A great deal of nonsense has been written on the subject, which we'll ignore . . . But then ethnology came to our rescue. In Australia, the Aborigines produce wall paintings too, and then draw the same hands as those you saw in the lab and elsewhere . . . The same goes for South America, in places where initiation rituals are held. You see?"

Sylvie drew away from de Palma and paused for a moment.

"The significant point about our caves is what is depicted, and what is not."

"What do you mean?"

"I mean that there are animals, but never any representations of man's environment. No huts, or landscapes, or the sun and moon . . . Drawings of men are extremely rare too, which makes us think that there is magic at work in Palaeolithic art. Personally I think these hands are signs for entering into contact with the spirits that lie behind the walls. Hence those ideas about shamanistic rituals. They went into the caves and invoked spirits, to treat a sick child for example, or to make the hunt as favourable as possible . . . "

She sipped at her whisky.

"It's a little like all religions. God is put to use to soothe the great and small ills of daily life. Shamans are mediators between the real world and the supernatural world. There are many of them still in Siberia, in Africa of course, and in America . . . And they all have one thing in common: they seek out trance states, hallucinations and visions. Trances allow them to see mythical beings, animals and spectres which are invoked to favour the hunt, or to make it rain. We think that it was the shamans who painted the pictures in the caves. And that they also used chants and healing rituals. I saw these kinds of practices among the Bochimans in the Kalahari."

"Have you heard of the Slain Man?"

"I see that you know more than you're letting on!" she said, adopting an elegant pose. "Slain men are quite common. But the most interesting examples are in Pech-Merle, Cougnac and Le Guen's Cave, of course. They seem to be intentionally poor drawings, just line sketches and nothing else. In Pech-Merle and Cougnac, they apparently show lines of vital energy flowing through individuals. In Le Guen's Cave, on the other hand, there can be no doubt that the Slain Man is a murder victim. Was it a ritual killing? An early form of crucifixion? Or else a bewitchment, like sticking pins in dolls or figurines? Nobody knows. In any case, Le Guen's Slain Man is unique."

Another connection formed in the Baron's mind.

"So you think that these prehistoric shamans might have performed ritual murders?"

Sylvie shook her long, brown hair.

"Yes, I think so. But it's just one hypothesis among others. In any case, murder is there as a possibility. Those people who think that murder only started during the Neolithic period, along with the concept of property, have got it wrong."

"Did Christine share your opinions?"

"Completely. We didn't like each other, but we were in the same school. The Palestro school," she added, laughing.

"Did she ever talk to you about the Slain Man?"

"The one in Le Guen's Cave? Of course she did. She thought it was a human sacrifice."

"And what do you think?"

"I think she was wrong to be so categorical – after all it's only a drawing. It might be a sacrifice, yes, but perhaps merely a symbolic one in a carving. As you're beginning to realise, we can't be sure about anything."

He went into the living room and took off his jacket. She noticed the gun he was wearing on his hip.

"Do you always have that on you?"

"Almost always. Except when I sleep. Though sometimes I do keep it under my pillow."

"What a strange existence."

"What an awful one, you mean! I live with violence and anxiety. They're my two best friends. We could have had a lovely evening together, but here we are talking about Christine Autran. Death, always death."

"I'm sorry I spoke to you about her."

"No, it's my fault."

"But I broached the subject. I've been clumsy . . . I wanted to see you in fact."

"I've learned some interesting things."

Sylvie stood up and poured more whisky into their glasses. She was wearing a simple blouse and a skirt with tiny flowers, as light as a silk veil. His body trembled and he felt disconnected from reality. He breathed deeply. His ideal was there before him. She was beautiful; like those images from his childhood that he had torn up so long ago.

He felt lonely, exhausted by life. He had not touched a woman's body for ages now. It had been months since Marie had left.

He made love to her slowly. Until the lava trapped in his guts erupted from all the extremities of his being.

In the middle of the night, she stroked the livid, badly stitched scar that crossed his shoulder.

"What is this, a zip fastener?"

"A souvenir from 'Le Blond'. A .357 Magnum. It's an old story. An old story which, in a few days' time, might be coming out of prison, where my friend Jean-Louis and I sent him."

"What had he done?"

"Violation of drug laws, to put it technically. Plus the murder of a magistrate."

"And the one on your thigh?"

"Are you giving me a full examination?"

"No, I already have."

"I can't tell you about that one."

28.

"Today or tomorrow, Sylvie will talk. She knows things."

He kept repeating this to himself, and it was making him nervous. Everything had been going as planned, or almost. The goddess had not been wrong. The goddess was never wrong.

Yet he was disturbed by what he had seen the night before. It was a policeman, he was sure of it. He had followed them all evening, all the way to her building. When he examined the Clio, he could tell straight away that it was a police car.

He cursed the heavens. Why had this little creep crossed his path? It didn't really worry him, but this unexpected factor had upset his carefully laid plans.

He had a method, which he kept to. He could not bear it being faulted.

He thought about the risks, but he could not see any. Objectively, there were none. But his instinct told him that he should be wary of this policeman; he seemed to be made of different stuff from the others. He was never wrong about things like that.

In any case, his plans had been carried out according to his characteristic method. And without the slightest slip-up. This policeman would never be able to identify him. He hammered out this truth so as to imprint it on his mind.

Yet the last time, with Julia, he had taken extraordinary risks. Just a few metres from home! But his instincts had again been proved right. He was right to be bold. He had become the best, fed by the strength of his victims. Like the great hunters of prehistory.

François Caillol would try to defend himself. But how? The hunter had no idea. He knew that the doctor would be unable to find an explanation; none of his alibis would stand up to such a huge amount of evidence. No way.

But there was the policeman. He had to be eliminated. He had to be prevented from hanging around Sylvie Maurel and talking to her. His blood began to beat like mad in his temples. His throat swelled. He felt drops of sweat running down his spinal cord.

The goddess had said: "Today or tomorrow, Sylvie will talk. She knows things." The idea of this devastated him. He sat down on a bench and laid out his thoughts like a pack of cards, trying to devise a strategy with what he had. Sylvie was the only bad card in the hand, like an imperceptible wind that conveys the hunter's scent and alerts his prey. She had to be eliminated. She had to fall.

He banished the thought for a moment.

But the method would have to come first. And he knew it. Time was short. The goddess had said: "Sylvie has met this policeman. She'll tell him sooner or later. There is no other answer. Eliminate Sylvie or disappear."

It was impossible right now.

He took a deep breath. His instincts had gone silent. He felt life biting him, gashing his flesh. Lacerated body tissue. A wound slowly bleeding the meaning of existence.

His mother's face appeared, cruel and tense with that mocking grin which had so often terrified him. Drops of cold sweat now dotted his forehead. He wiped them away with a sleeve and felt weak. Images suddenly came from nowhere and smacked him in the face: his father's body stretched out, people crying, a hospital bed, his mother kicking him, his sister's sweet belly. He could no longer hear children yelling in the distance. The sun had gobbled them up.

The warrior has been hit by an arrow in his belly. He can hardly breathe, his vision is hazy. Beside him lies his lifeless uncle, pierced by a dozen bolts.

The shaman approaches as though in slow motion. He is wearing a rattan breastplate and protective netting hangs from his neck. His nose is pierced with a wooden stick. He pushes aside the other warriors and, moaning softly, bends over the wounded man. Slowly he paces round the body, blowing on each part of it, then he stands and invokes the spirits.

For a long time the shaman fights death. He makes small incisions to let the "black blood" flow out and invokes the spirits once more. But the spirits do not come; the warrior's stare has frozen.

He rubbed his arms hard and looked at the ground. In the gutter, a thin rivulet of water was slowly pushing on a ball of dried chewing gum. It got stuck in a tiny hole and formed a damn. The rivulet swerved round the obstacle and continued on its way. Sylvie's name hammered in his head, bouncing like a rubber ball against each bone of his skull. Then it infiltrated the painful pathways of his brain.

The shaman takes out a fetish of multi-coloured feathers stuck in a cane rod and shakes it over the warrior's motionless body.

Arrows and lances are brandished with a cry of fury. A band has captured an enemy. The chief approaches him, his axe gleaming in his hand. He strikes once, then twice.

An inner voice rose up from the depths of his being.

"She must be eliminated."

He looked up and stared at the street full of everyday people.

"She must be eliminated. But first, use her to eliminate the policeman," the goddess told him.

He would use his method, as ever. He would take his time. The time he needed to find his righteous anger. To lay a fatal trap as only a great hunter can.

29.

To: Commandant Michel de Palma. Murder squad.
From: Ron Hoskins, F.B.I., Lyon.

Michel,

Here's some of the information you wanted:

There are many amateur prehistory societies
in the U.S.A. Most of them have websites.
There are many in Arizona and Utah and they
are interested in the first settlements of
Pueblos. I don't think that they concern you.
There are others in Texas who focus on the
Clovis (the first inhabitants of the American
continent) . . . But I won't make a list of
all of them.

Regarding the lead you asked me to follow
up, i.e. a "sect-like" society based in New
York State, I haven't found anything. There
is a prehistory club called "The American
Prehistory Society", several of whose members
have been charged with the (alleged) homicide
of another member. Its headquarters is in
Albany, N.Y.

These events occurred in the summer of 1996,

and the case has never been solved.

The victim was Anna McCabe, aged 40, born in Oakland, California. She was a researcher in the ethnology department of the University of San Diego. She was found dead on July 21, 1996 in Lake Otapah, Colorado. Her death occurred before July 8, 1996, from a heart attack caused by an overdose of unidentified hallucinogens (presumably from plants from the mescal family). The body, which was partly decomposed, bore several quite deep wounds made by an unidentified sharp object – these wounds were not the cause of death. (I can find out more, if you want, but I'll need time.)

With a little effort, I unearthed the names of the people who were questioned by our units. They include both men and women. All but five are U.S. citizens. They are:

– Paco Rivaldo, an Argentinian, aged 40 at the time. Professor *honoris causa* at the University of Buenos Aires, Argentina. A specialist in the prehistoric inhabitants of Patagonia. He was not charged.

– François Caillol, a French citizen, aged 40 at the time. A psychiatrist from Aix-en-Provence, France. Member of the A.P.S. He had come to deliver a series of lectures on shamanism and prehistory. The F.B.I. file states that he was not charged. He was in fact no longer in the U.S.A. at the time of the murder, so he was considered innocent.

- Julia Chevallier, a French citizen, aged
38 at the time. A teacher in Marseille,
France.

- Hélène Weill, a French citizen, aged 39
at the time. Profession unknown (?).

- Christine Autran, a French citizen, aged
39 at the time. A lecturer in Aix at the
University of Provence. A specialist in
prehistory. She had come to deliver a series
of lectures on shamanism and prehistory.
Member of the A.P.S.

When I read these names, I saw the connection
with the case you're investigating. I think
that this Caillol and the three women will be
of interest to you.

The addresses of the A.P.S. are 26, Monroe
Drive, Albany, New York State and 1236,
Falcon Boulevard, Denver, Colorado.
There are other addresses which I'll send you
if you want.

The American Prehistory Society couldn't
really be described as a sect. They are
enthusiasts interested in a particular
subject. Like the "Indianists", they organise
weekends where they adopt the lifestyle of
early humanity. They shut themselves up in
caves, hunt big game with rudimentary weapons
and practice survival techniques. Most of
its members are wealthy, some extremely so.

```
Their ideology is rather vague, except that
they defend nature and perform shamanistic
rituals, a little like the medicine men
in the American Native Church. They also
organise and finance serious expeditions to
investigate primitive peoples. So it's not
really a sect, but more of a society, like
many others in the U.S.A., which helps to
promote research, even if some of their
activities are not very conventional.

That's all I can tell you for now. I'd like
to carry out more detailed research, but
under American legislation I am not allowed
to. That's the way it is. Let's talk soon
about your market of stolen artefacts.

See you soon, your friend,

Ron.
```

The Baron put down the piece of paper without saying a word. Moracchini and Vidal were silent too, waiting for their teammate's reaction. First he picked up the phone and called Barbieri.

"Good morning, Christophe, I want to ask permission to see Caillol again ..."

"I suppose you've got something new?"

"Yes, something quite incredible. A real bit of luck. I've just been told that he was questioned by the F.B.I. about a homicide carried out by a bunch of prehistory loonies in the U.S.A. I have to see him. It's really urgent."

"O.K., how about this afternoon?"

"Perfect! About 2.00?"

"O.K. But this time we'll go together. Pick me up at court at 1.00 p.m."

De Palma headed for the coffee machine, followed by Moracchini.

"Richard came out of his coma an hour ago," she said as she slipped a coin into the slot.

"I knew it!" de Palma almost shouted, waving his arms. "Can we visit him?"

"No, not yet. The doctors aren't even letting his family see him. They want to avoid any emotional shocks."

"And so?"

"He should be alright, but they don't know if there will be any after-effects. If there are, they shouldn't be very serious."

"And where are they all at?" the Baron asked, pointing at the closed doors of the serious crime and murder squads.

"They're seeing the prefect. They're lodging a demand to organise a demonstration. We wanted to go along too, but we waited for you. And now it's too late. Plus Maistre's been looking for you."

"I know, my mobile battery is flat. Jesus, that's good news about Richard! So what's the demo all about?"

"We've had enough of being shot at!" snapped Vidal, scathingly. "Three dead and two seriously wounded in less than a month. Enough is enough."

"So you think a demo will change anything?" de Palma replied coldly, dropping his coin into the slot. "It's our entire society which needs changing . . . "

"Cut the crap, Michel!" Vidal interrupted. "They should provide us with what we need."

"That's right, more money and Kevlar body armour, and like that we'll be rich and well protected! But definitely DO NOT slap mobsters around."

"You really do lose it sometimes, Michel," said Moracchini.

"Tell me why young kids shoot at us like they're plugging farm pheasants! Tell me why in this damned city there's a crazy guy obsessed with eating people! Tell me why there are only three of us on this case!"

"Well . . . "

"Then what do you want to do with all your dosh and Kevlar jackets? Create good little children, good little killers, healthy in body and mind?"

"So, what do you suggest?"

"I don't have anything to suggest. I'm just a poor dickhead of a policeman who's seen the prisons fill up over his twenty-five-year career. It's not my fault if society is falling apart. Half the restaurants in this city feed the mob's bank accounts. All the nightclubs belong to those guys and imagine what you'd find if you looked into the politicians' finances. Not to mention our bent colleagues . . . So don't ask me what I suggest! I can remember a time when crooks didn't shoot police officers."

"So, can we count on you for the demo?"

"As long as those fascist trade unions aren't there! Do I not look like someone who'd go to a peace and love rally?"

"O.K., don't get so wound up."

"I'm not getting wound up. I just don't know where I stand any more. The whole world is turning into a nightmare. We used to arrest a maniac every five years. Now it's every week. When will we get the next one? Tomorrow? Maybe today?"

De Palma swallowed a mouthful of coffee which burned his lips. He grimaced.

"And we're not even up against a classic maniac . . . this guy refuses to accept our civilisation or morals. He thinks he's a Cro-Magnon man. Just imagine it! The Middle Ages and antiquity are already too civilised for him. Let's go back to animal skins and a good old lump of flint! Talk about a profile – he's a sociopath who soothes his impulses by imitating prehistoric hunters. Or, at least, the image he has of them. But I reckon those hunters weren't as savage as some people think."

Another mouthful. Another grimace.

"In any case, they're no more savage than hoods who blow each other away for no reason – they don't think any more, they just shoot. Just look at the Ferri couple!"

"You're right, Michel," Moracchini answered. "I also get the impression that everything's speeding up."

"So, shall we have a sitrep?"

"O.K., let's go."

Commissaire Paulin burst into the office.

"You didn't go with the others?"

"No," said Vidal. "Except in spirit."

"Very good . . . De Palma, where are you at with the Ferris?"

"They've been buried."

"You mean they're no longer in the morgue?"

"No."

"Why not?"

"Because a Ferri bloats."

Paulin stared at him, then burst out laughing, showing his horse's teeth stained with nicotine.

"I prefer it when you talk about opera, de Palma."

Vidal felt ill at ease.

"What is it, Maxime? Anything wrong?" the Baron asked sarcastically.

"I don't agree with you, Michel. If we don't do something, who will? That's all I want to say."

"Apart from that, are you still pleased to know me?"

"I can see that today is getting off to a good start," Moracchini mumbled.

"Commandant de Palma and I wanted to see you again in order to obtain further information. I should say that I've not yet made a decision about your possible transfer out of solitary confinement. But I shall during the course of this week . . . Everything depends on your cooperation."

François Caillol looked uncomfortable in his chair. He had laid his fingers on the Formica table and was now tapping out the Andante movement of an imaginary concerto. Barbieri and de Palma sat in front of him and stared. Caillol arrogantly met their gaze. The prison world was already at work.

"I think I've told you everything I know."

Barbieri turned towards the Baron. With a nod, he invited him to step in.

"Dr Caillol," he said, standing up, "I've had enough of being taken for a fool. From now on, we're going to put all our cards on the table. All of them, you hear me? Does July 1996, Albany, New York State – and Denver, Colorado – ring any bells?"

Caillol looked like he'd been punched in the stomach.

"Yes," he said, swallowing his saliva.

"I want proper answers, not just yeses and nos. I want to know what you were doing in Denver with Hélène Weill and Julia Chevallier, just a few days before the murder of Anna McCabe."

The doctor squirmed in his chair and leaned forwards to avoid their eyes.

"I was taking part in a series of lectures about . . . about shamans in prehistory. I left the U.S.A. on July 1, that's all. I explained all of this to the American police."

"So you knew Julia and Hélène?"

"Yes."

He spoke in a loud voice to conceal his panic.

"Dr Caillol," said Barbieri, on the verge of losing his temper, "I can't help wondering why you didn't tell me about all this before."

"Why should I? Since my arrest, no-one's believed a single word I've said!"

"Fine . . . But there's still something that intrigues me about your trip: you are no scientific authority. Experts such as Christine Autran, or Professor Palestro were better placed than you to lecture on the subject. So why were you chosen? Why you, and not someone else?"

"Because I was a member of the American Prehistory Society."

"And you are no longer?"

"No, I left the A.P.S. in 1996, after the death of Anna McCabe."

"Can you explain your reasons in more detail?"

Caillol concentrated, as though trying to dispel his confusion.

"I left the American Prehistory Society when I realised that, beneath its scientific veneer, it was in fact some kind of cult with dubious practices. That became clear to me when I heard about Anna's death."

De Palma noticed that he had just referred to the victim by her forename. He decided to try his luck.

"Did you first meet Anna in Denver?"

"No, in Aix. During a symposium under the direction of Professor Palestro."

De Palma and Barbieri were flabbergasted.

"Dr Caillol," said the magistrate. "The time has come for you to tell us everything. The police officer sitting in front of you will work out the truth sooner or later. Talking to us will alleviate your suffering. I know that solitary confinement is not easy. So, I beg of you, please give me a reason to transfer you to another wing."

The psychiatrist laid his hands on his knees. He lowered his head, thought for a few seconds, then spoke to the Baron directly.

"The first time you came to see me, I didn't tell you everything because I wanted to get out of here. That was my lawyer's advice . . . Just don't forget that I never lied to you."

"I didn't say that," murmered de Palma.

"Christine Autran proposed me when I joined the A.P.S. She'd been a member since 1990. The first time I visited the U.S.A., in the summer of 1991, I went with her. We met various members of the society, and Christine delivered a series of lectures about prehistory. That's all."

"And did you take part in any of their weekends?"

"Twice. We went into the mountains and lived like prehistoric men. Christine was extremely knowledgeable. She knew all the plants and fishing techniques. It was really fascinating. I suppose that must sound strange to you! But you have to realise that some of the most serious prehistorians take part in this kind of reconstruction. For example, my friend John Davoli from the University of Austin, cuts flints. He's a real expert. I can even . . . "

"What about the second time you went to Denver?"

"It was in 1993. Once again, Christine gave a few lectures. But this time on a different subject."

"What was it?"

"The seminar was about the first inhabitants of the continent of America. Christine's contribution was to show that the first men in America didn't come from Asia, as is generally thought, but from Europe. She based this idea on the fact that flints have been found over there which were cut in the same way as those discovered here during the Solutrean period. She interpreted these similar industries as a sign that migration came from the east, not the west. In other words, she didn't believe that the Mongol-like Indian was America's first man . . . "

"Is that all?"

Caillol's face suddenly began to twitch.

"No. During one weekend, Christine and one of the organisers conducted some shamanistic rituals."

"What do you mean?"

"They arranged to meet in a Palaeolithic hunter's shelter, not far from Denver, where they invoked the spirits. Rather like Indian medicine men."

Despite his anxiety, Caillol was controlled, still able to negotiate with himself and keep his emotions in hand.

"Were you there too?"

"Yes."

"What happened?"

"Christine went into a sort of trance. She really shocked me that day. Afterwards, I decided to keep my distance from her."

"Tell me how a psychiatrist of your standing can be shocked by someone in a trance."

Caillol remained silent for some time, his chest rising a little higher each time he breathed.

"Christine wasn't one of my patients . . . When she started foaming at the mouth, with her eyes popping out of her face, and then convulsing, I panicked. How can I explain? I was the one who'd encouraged her to conduct the experiment. I . . . I had no idea of the sort of state she'd get into."

"Did she become violent?"

"Yes, extremely violent . . . It took several of us to control her."

As he finished, his voice broke slightly, and he suppressed a sob.

Barbieri placed his hands over his mouth. He let the doctor pause for a moment. Under the table, one of his legs was jiggling up and down.

"Let's sum things up, Doctor," he said. "You became a member of the A.P.S. in 1991, and made your first visit in the summer of that year. So far, so good. Then you go for a second time, to Denver in 1993, and you realise that something is wrong, that Christine is not completely normal. And you decide to keep your distance from her."

"Yes, that's right."

"So why did you go back in 1996 to give a series of lectures?"

Caillol all of a sudden looked pained.

"They asked me to . . . I . . . I had no reason to refuse. I suppose it was pride really. As you said, I am not a scientific authority, so I can't lecture here. The A.P.S. gave me an opportunity and I accepted it."

"Was Christine there?"

"Yes, of course."

"And did she perform magic rituals again?"

"I don't know. I wasn't invited to the weekends. It was as if they didn't trust me any more. I was excluded from their activities outside the seminar itself."

"Had you seen Christine between these two trips to Denver?"

"Yes."

"In what circumstances?"

"We weren't lovers, if that's what you mean. I told you that the last time we spoke. She was just a friend. And we worked together on various projects."

The psychiatrist had regained control of his emotions. They were going to have to trap him, but not too hastily. De Palma once again took the lead in the questioning.

"In your opinion, could Christine's death have been the outcome of a shamanistic ritual?"

"Yes, I think that's quite possible. It's no coincidence that she died just by Le Guen's Cave. There must be a connection, as I'm sure you've already worked out."

"Did you know Franck Luccioni?"

"Not personally, but she did mention him to me. Apparently he was an excellent diver, a treasure hunter. I suppose she used him for underwater investigations."

"Does the A.P.S. own any prehistoric artefacts?"

"Yes, of course. I had the opportunity to see some of them. They have an incredible private collection, which can only be seen by invitation. They own a large number of flints from the Solutrean and Magdalenian periods, a Venus and quite a few necklaces . . . Some sculpted bones, too. A fine collection . . . they use them in their 'ceremonies.'"

"Are these objects stolen?"

"Yes, for example they have a negative hand, which came from some mysterious source."

"I see," said Barbieri. "But we're going round in circles. So, doctor, tell me: who could have it in for you to the extent that they've framed you like this? Someone who hates you enough to want you condemned to a particularly long prison sentence. Who detests you, Caillol? Who?"

"I have no idea . . . really I don't."

Caillol's eyes clouded, and the smell of fear filled the room. De Palma went to sit beside him, so that their faces were only a few centimetres apart. The trap was now ready.

"Did you know that she had a brother?"

"No, I didn't."

"I don't believe you, François," de Palma said, drawing back. "I think you've known for quite some time. I've been looking into your career. You worked for many years at the Edouard Toulouse hospital, and among your patients you treated a ferocious spirit, a natural born killer, a certain Thomas Autran. True or false?"

Caillol did not answer. He went pale and his lips trembled.

"In fact, you knew everything about Christine. EVERYTHING, do you hear me?"

His head drooped. He was beaten.

"Look, François, this is the first time you've had anything to do with the police. But as far as I'm concerned, you're just the most recent in a long list, a very long list, and tomorrow it will be even longer . . . hundreds of names, faces, social deviants, barbaric acts . . . You might think you know about people's psychology, but so do I! I learned on the job, twenty-five years on the murder squad dealing with beasts and the craziest of predators. If you knew what I've seen in my life, you'd shit yourself."

Caillol remained perfectly still. Barbieri slowly went over to him.

"Now, François, we're going to change gears, because we're about to attack the mountain road. You know, the one that leads to a lovely panoramic viewpoint. I need a clear vision of things. In my humble opinion, it's her brother who's put you in this mess. Have you any idea how, or why?"

"I don't know. I honestly don't know."

"Having it in for someone that much," the magistrate said, "means that there must be a solid motive. Don't forget, he could just as easily have killed you."

"Did he break into my house . . . ? I don't understand."

"Try to concentrate! Try to remember something!"

"I think he used me to cover up his crimes."

"What crimes?"

"The murders at Cadenet and Saint-Julien!"

"Why do you think it was him?"

"I'm sure of it, absolutely sure. You found a hand beside the corpses, didn't you?"

"Yes . . . so?"

"It's his signature."

"How do you know that?"

"He used to draw hands in hospital."

"Wait a minute, Caillol," Barbieri said, barely containing his anger. "You knew it was him and you said nothing to the gendarmerie! And nothing to me. Do you realise that this is extremely serious?"

"I know, but . . . "

"But what?"

"I couldn't."

"And may I ask why?"

"A whole series of reasons . . . I was arrested soon after the murder. At the time, I didn't know about the hands. I realised when the gendarmes showed me one."

"So why didn't you explain everything?"

"I did tell the gendarmes, but they wouldn't listen to me. Do you know what it's like being held in custody, Judge?"

"YES I DO," Barbieri yelled. "And you should know that, in the eyes of the law, you're at the very least an accomplice, if not guilty of aiding and abetting a murderer."

Discreetly, de Palma gave the judge a slight tap on the shoulder, then sat down beside the psychiatrist.

"François, you're not being very coherent, as I'm sure you realise. And this incoherence is making things even worse for you. So pull yourself together! Let go of the fear that's paralysing you and crushing your guts. I still think you're completely innocent. So nothing you tell us now will make you look any more or less guilty."

Caillol trembled slightly as his defences weakened, one after the other. Soon, he would be incapable of keeping his mental ramparts from collapsing under the blows of the policeman and the judge.

"When did you last speak to Thomas?"

"Just before he was released from hospital."

"In 1985, is that right?"

"Yes, in 1985."

"What was wrong with him?"

"Behavioural problems which were ... deep-rooted. Incredibly violent impulses which, oddly enough, he was able to control. He was suffering from paranoid schizophrenia. He lost all touch with reality and became alienated from the outside world. He lived in ... in an imaginary chaos and had auditory hallucinations. He had the impression that his thoughts were being imposed on him."

"And I would add that he had a fascination for magic, and that his craziness had a mystic, almost religious side. He thought he'd been given a divine mission."

"That's right."

"And did his sister come to see him?"

"Often, extremely often."

"And what did you do?"

"Nothing."

"No, François, don't say that! I'm going to tell you what you did: you freed her brother from a place he should never have left."

Caillol collapsed into his chair.

"Yes."

After a long silence, de Palma stood up.

"It was Christine who stole the negative hand from the A.P.S. collection. Yes or no?"

"I don't know."

"She would have stolen it to give it to her brother. Yes or no?"

"I ... I don't know."

"Christine Autran, Hélène Weill and Julia Chevallier killed Anna

McCabe during a shamanistic séance. Yes or no?"

"I think you're wrong."

"Why do you think so?"

"From what the F.B.I. told me, she died of a heart attack caused by taking hallucinogenic drugs. So the cause of her death was not criminal, if you see what I mean . . . "

"It wasn't the F.B.I. who told you that, it was Christine when she got back from America. And Christine also told you that Anna had been cut up with flints, hence the police investigation and the involvement of the F.B.I."

Caillol did not deny this. De Palma looked at him with unconcealed scorn and then let the judge have his turn.

"You see, we're now starting to have a clearer view," Barbieri said. "Let's proceed. It's 1985, and Thomas Autran is released from the asylum. You're guilty of that at the very least."

Caillol did not respond.

"And you knew that he was a killer. A real killer who murders for pleasure, to calm his impulses. In other words, a serial killer."

"He . . . he'd never killed anyone. He controlled his instincts, as I've told you."

"And you said nothing to the gendarmerie, not only because they would be able to track down your 'release form', but also because you felt guilty. Guilty about freeing such a dangerous person."

"I didn't think he'd do anything like that, I promise you. When I heard about Chevallier's death, you can't imagine how bad I felt. And how bad I still feel."

"That's the least of it," cried Barbieri.

"Let's get back to our motive," said de Palma. "Thomas broke into your home and set about framing you well and truly . . . Isn't there anything that bugs you about all this?"

"No, I mean . . . I don't know."

"Well, I do. It's not typical behaviour for this kind of killer. Setting you up like that wasn't about obeying his impulses; instead it required cold, methodical and patient planning. What's your opinion?"

"You seem to know more about all this than I do. I don't have any answers."

"I don't think he's alone. I think he's obeying someone."

"The only person who had any real authority over him was his sister. She could make him do whatever she wanted. As long as his sister was with him, he would never go off the rails."

"And do you think someone else could have taken his sister's place?"

"I've no idea. But it is possible."

"You can't imagine who it might be?"

"No, really I can't."

"I'll tell you something, Caillol. You took part in these superstitious practices not out of scientific curiosity, but in an attempt to live in the primitive state of humanity – or the first state, to use your jargon, before the Neolithic revolution and the notion of property set brother against brother . . . I read about all this in your books. Your first folly was Anna McCabe, and the second was Thomas Autran . . . which was far more serious. Today, Thomas is destroying your entire group of lunatics. As he's more intelligent than you, he used you. And you saw him with his sister long after the date of his supposed death. Did you speak to him?"

"No."

"Or to Christine?"

"Nor to her."

"I hope you're not lying. If you are it might cost you dear. Very dear."

"This morning, I finally understood your strategy," Barbieri said. "Your lawyer called me and asked for D.N.A. tests to be run on the sample of ochre paint found in your house. These tests proved your innocence . . . And, above all, this would have meant not having to talk about the darker side of your activities. What if it all leaked out to the press! That wouldn't look very good for someone who bears the name of one of Aix's finest families, and who is a highly reputed psychiatrist, would it? A psychiatrist who knows everything, but refuses to collaborate with the justice system."

Caillol understood the judge's barely veiled threat, but he chose to ignore it. De Palma cast his eyes round the walls of the visiting room.

"I've got no more questions," he said, turning towards the judge.

"Nor have I," said Barbieri as he stood up. "Now we're going to have to sort this all out."

Ignoring Caillol, the judge walked out with heavy steps, as though dragging a burden behind him. De Palma gave the detainee a long, hard handshake. When he saw that Caillol was on the verge of tears, he left him to his solitude.

30.

For three days the mistral had been shaking the city by its mighty shoulders. Up in Saint-Julien, the wind doubled in violence before plunging towards the Huveaune valley and invading, gust by gust, the large, white estates of the southern quartiers.

He had not slept all night. He had smelled the dusty air which was blowing around the presbytery like a ravenous beast, banging on the shutters before leaving and coming back again in a further fit of rage. In the early hours, he went out into the yard to unwind a little. He sat down on the small, green, metal bench between the large pine trees with their silver trunks, and stared into the infinity of that weary night.

For a long time he watched the bristly crowns of the trees brushing the great void of the sky with each blast of wind. The last scraps of cloud had finally disappeared behind the limestone bastions of Saint-Loup. The immaculate blue swelled, without a single mark, as virgin as in the dawn of time. In three days, it would be full moon. The mistral would probably last until then. Then the weather would change. Summer would arrive, and reign supreme until the autumn. After consulting the spirits, the goddess would claim another victim.

In the middle of the village, they have set up the fetish with its multi-coloured feathers. The enemy ghosts now know that the warrior's soul is being protected.

All day, the men and women of the clan have wept. Now, on the funerary fire, they are burning the warrior's body. His spirit is free and has gone to the enemy territory to cause the most terrible tortures. In the next season, the spirit will return to its own. It will wander around the water gourd which its brother has left under a tree, near the border that separates the two territories.

He breathed in the air. It was heavy with the smells of the city, and he stared at the sharp gravel on the ground in front of him. His thoughts focused on the policeman he had tailed.

Time was running out. It would not take the detective long to track him down. In this respect, he had not underestimated him. And sooner or later the young officer who had come to the parish might make the connection too.

Full moon was approaching. He had to strike. His trap was ready. Sylvie Maurel began her day's work at the marine archaeology laboratory at 9.00 a.m. She was never late. He would do nothing until she had breakfast. Then, at about 2.00 p.m., he would carry out the first part of his plan. Methodically.

He went back into the presbytery and down to the cellar. He switched on an ancient light, and a yellow gleam shone from a bulb fixed to the vaulted ceiling by two old wires wrapped in mouldy cloth. At the end of the corridor, he opened a door and went into a tiny room, with plain stone walls. It was piled high with all sorts of objects: old Christmas cribs which were no longer used; large notices made by children for the spring fair; a stack of cardboard boxes containing knick-knacks collected by previous priests. He deftly slipped a hand under one of the boxes and removed a long packet wrapped in cloth and secured by two pieces of string. He undid the knots and laid out its contents on the floor.

He breathed deeply, looking with delight at each of the objects in front of him: an axe and two pieces of sharpened flint. Nothing more.

He picked up the axe and made two large, circular movements in the air, as though testing its solidity, then he inspected the strips of gut which attached its stone head to the ash-wood handle. It was all in perfect condition. He picked up the two blades and inspected the edges. The flint had not been damaged during his previous hunts. All was well.

He opened another cardboard box, removed a plain sheet of paper and laid it on the floor. From the same box, he took out a bottle containing a yellow liquid, with an ochre deposit in the lower third. He shook it vigorously until the mixture was perfect. He poured some of the liquid into his mouth, placed his left hand on the paper and sprayed it with the ochre earth and water. After a moment, he removed his hand and examined the print of his palm and fingers. The little and ring fingers were cut in half. Perfect. The first man could not have done it better.

He stood up, closed his eyes and performed the ritual.

"*Spirit of the hunt*
Goddess of life
Here is the hunter's sign
Take her life to fortify mine
May her death be swift
May I not make her suffer
May your spirit guide me in the shadows
May the force of her blood enter into my blood
May her flesh fortify the first man"

He remained motionless for a while with his eyes closed. Then he suddenly came to life, picked up the sheet of paper, the axe and the two blades, and went back up to the ground floor.

Fifteen minutes later he was walking rapidly along avenue Saint-Julien towards the vast city. He was wearing faded jeans, a baggy T-shirt and a baseball cap which barely concealed his large bifocals. These glasses deformed his face so much that no-one would recognise him. He had to wear them on the end of his nose when he was walking because, in fact, his vision was perfect.

When he got to avenue Saint-Barnabé it was almost deserted, and the sun was already high in the sky. Violent blasts from the mistral were blowing bin-liners about and he had to lean forwards. He looked at his watch. It was now 8.00 a.m. If he walked at this speed, he would be at Fort Saint-Jean in an hour.

His plan was simple: kill Sylvie then draw the policeman into his trap. Then he would sacrifice him on the altar to appease the goddess's anger.

A few days earlier, the goddess had appeared to him in a dream. She had spoken to him from the spirit world and reproached him for not having been careful enough about the girl in Saint-Julien. It could turn out to be a fatal mistake if he did not eliminate the only man capable of tracking him down. He would have to trap him and then vanish. For ever.

Beside the clan's flat, green, sacred stone, the valiant band have come together around the enemy's body. They will devour it. In supreme vengeance.

At 7.00 a.m., police headquarters resounded with a din that de Palma knew well. Hulks from special branch were on their way in through the courtyard, followed by two journalists from the local telly. The serious crime squad were hauling in three people responsible for the bloody hold-up in La Viste: two adults and a minor.

There was hatred in the corridors, crawling like a rattlesnake, ready to bite anyone unwise enough to tread on its tail. De Palma leaned out the window. He saw Big Zuccarelli and an officer he did not recognise, presumably a new recruit, accompanying a figure covered by a jacket. This was the first gunman; the second and the third would soon follow.

When he heard footsteps, de Palma went out into the corridor. Zuccarelli was pushing the figure ahead of him. He stopped in front of the Baron and took the jacket off the man's head to reveal a brown face with matt skin and a childish grin. He was wearing trainers which looked too big for him, and a tracksuit left open to reveal a huge crucifix. His small eyes sent off sparks in all directions, without ever coming to rest on the police officers. He was hunched, aware that he was going into the ring for the final combat. After the last round there would be prison, with a minimum sentence of twenty-five years. No problem.

"This is the motherfucker who shot Richard," Zuccarelli said. "The little shit."

The Baron's slap went off on its own, like an extraordinarily powerful mechanism. A sharp, cold clack echoed down the corridor. Moracchini and Vidal, who had just arrived, recoiled. The gunman began to shake all over. Zuccarelli shoved him into his office. Duriez, the departmental head, arrived completely out of breath.

"Go and get some rest, Zuccarelli. Your men, too," he said. "Let the pressure drop. We've nailed them, and now I'll take over. Come back this afternoon. We've got the press downstairs . . . "

The Baron turned on his heel and disappeared into his office.

"O.K.," he said, without looking at Moracchini and Vidal. "We've learned a few things. After the hospital, he convalesced with priests. Then he worked in one of their institutions. So far so good. He went to Australia and then, nothing. In my opinion, it was there that he started making up his little scenario about prehistory."

When he had returned from Les Baumettes the previous day, de Palma had spent a couple of hours telling his teammates about the interrogation he had conducted with Barbieri. Moracchini had made several objections, all of which came back to the same question: why would a killer like that frame Caillol? De Palma's explanations had failed to convince his two colleagues. Something did not gel.

De Palma had spent all night turning the shaman story this way and that. His first step had been to convince himself that the most widespread ritual, apart from those associated with hunting or mastering the elements, was healing. A second step had led him towards Christine and her brother. By combining all these elements, he had reached the conclusion that Christine had practised healing rituals on Thomas to save him from insanity. Christine's death, for as yet unknown reasons, had liberated her brother's instincts because she was no longer there to control him. The scenario was now starting to stand up, despite a few grey areas. It was clear that everything depended on the relationship between the twins but, before he talked to his teammates, he wanted the fog to lift a little more.

The phone rang. Vidal answered it.

"Yes, Father. You're an early riser! I'll hand you over to Capitaine Moracchini."

"What a day of grace!" said de Palma, turning on the loudspeaker.

"Good morning to you, Madame. I've found the postcard . . . It came from the Queensland Catholic Mission, in the Gulf of Carpentaria. The town's called Kajabbi. I think you'll be able to find it easily enough. That's all. I can't do anything more for you."

"But that's already plenty! Thanks again, Father, and don't hesitate to call me if even the slightest detail occurs to you."

Moracchini hung up.

"Well, well, new leads are springing up all over! Maxime, do you know what time it is in Australia?"

"No, early evening I should think. Hang on, I'll look in my dairy. Here . . . If it's 9.00 a.m. here, then in Australia it's about 8.00 p.m. But it depends on the region."

"Good, we'll have to call them up. Can you do it Maxime? After all, you do speak English."

De Palma called Sylvie's mobile and got her answerphone. He called her landline and got her answerphone there too. Each time, he left a message. He then tried the laboratory at Fort Saint-Jean. A researcher by the name of Pierre Craven told him that she had just gone out to buy croissants from the bakery on rue Caisserie, and that she would be back soon, because she had to finish preparing a meeting scheduled for 11.00 a.m.

The Baron frowned.

"Our man is convinced that he reasons like a Palaeolithic hunter," he said. "From what I know, cannibals obey a ritual, or a code if you like. They eat their enemies' flesh to absorb their strength. That's all. There's no pleasure in it. In this respect, his behaviour is consistent."

"If I follow you," Moracchini said, "he's eating these women because he thinks they're his enemies, but at the same time he's trying to capture their strength. Is that it?"

"Yes, that's what I think. And I also think that he's obeying some kind of shaman, who might be either real or virtual. This being tells him that these sacrifices have to be made if the community is going to recover its harmony. That's where the hands come in. It's a ritual!"

"Yes, why ever not?"

"Anne, this is just a feeling I have. You don't know what twins are like . . . We now know that his sister was into shamanistic rituals and that she also experimented with them. It could be that, after her death, her brother decided that he had to re-establish some sort of harmony. Let's imagine that he's been unable to accept her death, and that he thinks his sister is talking to him from the spirit world. Do you see what I mean?"

"Of course. But these are just hypotheses."

"Yes, they're hypotheses . . . but we need a scenario if we want to be able to anticipate his actions. And time is running out!"

"There's a big piece missing from your scenario."

"What's that?"

"Who killed Christine? It can't be him, because according to you he loved her more than anything."

"I'm beginning to have a few ideas about that."

"Are you thinking of Caillol or Palestro?"

"Neither."

"Could you tell us a little more?"

"No, not right now. You'll think I'm completely crazy."

"Sometimes you really get on my nerves, Michel!"

"We'll have to run D.N.A. tests on the negative hands and ask the gendarmes to send us the sample of ochre paint found in Caillol's place. Then test that for D.N.A. too . . . then we'll compare them."

De Palma rang the number of the archaeology lab. Pierre Craven answered and seemed nervous: Sylvie had not come back and he was worried. It was nearly time for the meeting.

When he hung up, the Baron sensed that something terrible had just happened. Moracchini noticed.

"She's still not back?"

"No, I'm going to check. Can you try to contact the missionaries in Australia?"

On the way, de Palma called the laboratory once again. Still no Sylvie. He went to the bakery on rue Caisserie. A middle-aged woman behind the counter confirmed that Sylvie had called by at around 9.15. She also said that she had seen a man in the street who had then quickly vanished. When the Baron asked for a description, all she could remember was that he had been wearing a cap. He immediately made the connection with the man Tête had described running into on boulevard Chave.

A shiver ran through him, despite the overpowering heat. Sylvie had been missing for over an hour. Given this sort of killer, he knew that she would not be long for this world. She might be already dead. Images of Hélène's and Julia's sliced-up bodies flashed through his mind. He sat down on a doorstep and tried to think fast. But an awful pain in his guts stopped him from concentrating. Ideas spun in his head. He tried to cry, to release his anger, but his anger wanted to stay within and dominate him.

All he could do was phone Moracchini.

"I'll come at once," she said.

Five minutes later, she arrived at the bottom of rue Caisserie in an unmarked car.

"What are we going to do, Anne? Shall we put out an A.P.B.?"

"I don't think so. The press will be on to it within minutes."

"So what the fuck shall we do?" de Palma yelled.

"Pull yourself together, Michel. Keep calm and cool, just like you taught me."

"I'd like to see you in my place!"

"But I *am* here, Michel!"

"And?"

"And, how do you know she's been kidnapped?"

"The woman in the baker's saw someone out on the pavement. Exactly his description . . . "

"Did they leave together?"

"No, but he followed her."

"How do you know that?"

"I just know, that's all. She didn't go back to the lab. Where do you think she is? At the hairdresser's?"

"It isn't funny, Michel. I'm just trying to understand."

De Palma raised his hands towards the sky.

"That's right," he said. "Let's try to understand. Meanwhile, that fucker will be . . . "

"I don't think so."

The Baron wheeled round to face Moracchini.

"No, Michel, I don't think he's abducted her. That's not the way he works. You would have expected him to break into her place, or else draw her into a trap. Like he did with Hélène and Julia. That's what I think."

"So you think he kidnapped her to ask for a ransom?"

"Don't be silly, Michel. If you ask me we still have some time in hand. First, we'll put out a call, but without explaining exactly why.

Then we'll go to the lab while Maxime is dealing with the Australians. So, teammate, let's get going," she ordered.

Two minutes later they were knocking at the door of the marine archaeology laboratory. The man who opened it was clearly put out by their visit, but he calmed down when Moracchini showed him her tricolour card.

"Can I speak to Pierre Craven, please?" de Palma asked over his colleague's shoulder.

"That's me."

"Has Sylvie come back yet?"

"No."

"And you still have no idea where she could be?"

The only answer he gave was to look up towards the heavens and whistle in exasperation. De Palma moved in front of Moracchini.

"What's up with this guy. Doesn't he want to answer our questions?"

Anne tried to push her teammate to one side. Too late. The Baron had already pinned Craven to the stone wall.

"Listen, you fucking pathetic little student, your friend might already be dead. Got me? So please be good enough to tell us everything you know, or I promise you'll soon have a good conversation piece about police violence for your zit-head parties."

Moracchini's mobile rang. She stood to one side to take the call.

"I've got nothing to tell you," Craven replied, trembling from head to foot.

"No unusual phone calls this morning?"

"No."

"How many people came here this morning, between 9.00 and 9.30?"

"Just Sylvie and me."

"Did she seem nervous?"

"No."

"When you arrived, was there anyone waiting by the door? Anything odd?"

"No."

"What about the past few days? Any strange phone calls?"

"No, nothing."

"Who's here now?"

"Only the lab team, that's all."

"O.K."

"Has she been . . . ?"

"I don't know. But she certainly seems to have disappeared. Maybe she'll resurface again any moment. We're a bit tense right now."

"Is it to do with all those murders?"

"No, it's because of the thirty-five-hour working week, what do you think?"

"I don't know!"

"O.K., here's my card. If anything unusual happens, call me."

"I will," said Craven.

De Palma turned and went to join Moracchini, who had just finished her call.

"That was Maxime. He's managed to get in touch with the Australians."

"Anything new?"

"Yes. Thomas Autran was indeed in Australia from 1992 until last year, when he returned to France."

De Palma did not listen to her answer. He was already thinking about something else. The worst thing of all.

"Right, I'm going to Sylvie's flat. Are you coming?"

"Do you want me to call for reinforcements?"

"We haven't got enough time, Anne."

As he emerged from the lift, de Palma drew his Bodyguard. The corridor was twelve metres long, ending in a broad window that looked out over the sea. He nodded towards the door of Sylvie's flat. It did not have a spyhole.

They crept towards it. De Palma stood to its right. With the tip of her finger, Moracchini rang the bell and leaned against the wall to the left. Once, twice . . . No answer.

The last time he was there, de Palma had noticed that the door was reinforced. It was impossible to break in. He rapidly tried to think of a plan. Calling a locksmith from headquarters would take too long.

But they had to get inside Sylvie's flat. Even if the worst scenario was waiting for them. He rang her neighbour's bell. No-one. Another neighbour. Again no-one. He was beginning to feel desperate when he caught sight of the window in the corridor. It opened on to the front of the building and Sylvie's balcony might well connect with it.

He walked down the corridor, opened the window and looked to see if he could reach Sylvie's balcony. By stepping on to a fifty-centimetre-deep cement ledge, he could make it easily.

Moracchini did not have time to stop him. De Palma clambered out the window, put one foot on the ledge and grabbed the guardrail of Sylvie's balcony, while still holding on to the corridor window with his left hand.

He closed his eyes. The void attracted him inexorably. His legs quivered. He made a superhuman effort not to climb back into the corridor. The noises of the city reached his ears, though they sounded distant, wrapped in cotton. He opened his eyes and saw the steeple of La Major in a blur – drops of sweat were obscuring his vision. He gathered all his strength in a crouch, like a wild cat. In one bound he landed on the balcony, completely out of breath and trembling all over.

Sylvie had not closed the shutters. He burst into the living room, gun in hand. The room looked just as it had the last time: cosy and tidy. Nothing had been disturbed.

In the hallway, he found a rack with a spare set of keys. He opened the front door and Moracchini stepped inside.

Gingerly, he walked towards the bedroom and pushed open the door with his foot, expecting the worst. The bed was still unmade. He breathed in deeply and smelled the body lotion Sylvie used. The sight of this empty bedroom both reassured and terrified him.

"I've checked out the other rooms," Moracchini said. "Nothing and no-one. No clues. Do you want us to call in forensics?"

"No. I think she was picked up between the bakery and the lab."

Moracchini put away her revolver.

"If you say so," she said. "But . . . when she was just walking in the street?"

"Let's see if we can find her car."

They went down to the ground floor and wandered around for a while looking for the concierge.

"I was delivering the mail and, as there was a parcel, I went up the eighth floor. What can I do for you?"

"We're from the police, Monsieur," Moracchini said. "We'd like to know if you saw Sylvie Maurel leave in her car this morning."

The concierge was a short man aged about fifty, with slicked-down hair and a small moustache which made him look like a tango dancer attempting a comeback. He eyed the two officers warily.

"The police? So what's going on?"

"We asked you a question," de Palma said angrily.

"In her car . . . ? I've no idea."

"Do you know which is her car?"

"Yes."

"Can we take a look?"

"O.K., we'll go down to the car park."

Space 138 was empty.

"She doesn't often use her car on weekdays," said the concierge.

"Did you see her come back this morning at about 9.00?" Moracchini asked.

"No."

"Can you get into the car park without going past your lodge?"

"Yes, you just have to come through the door from the street . . . At the back there, you see? It takes you straight out on to esplanade de la Tourette. Assuming you have the key . . . "

"Can you tell me the make of her car?"

"I don't know," the concierge said, apologetically. "I think it's an Audi. A big car, but I don't know which model it is. There are more than 150 cars in this building."

For the past fifteen minutes, Vidal had been pacing up and down in front of the coffee machine. He was relieved to see his two teammates arrive.

"I've spoken to the mission in Queensland!"

"And?" asked de Palma, throwing his jacket on to a chair.

"Two things. First, they had a sort of handyman who came from France and who answers our description. But according to them, he never showed the slightest sign of madness . . . He behaved more like a holy man."

"What else?"

"The man in question didn't have the same name."

"Not the same name?"

"That's right. When I mentioned Thomas Autran, they told me they'd never heard of anyone by that name. Their man was called Luc Chauvy."

"So?"

Vidal started paced up and down.

"So I described Autran to them in detail – I even emailed the photo of his sister – and they positively identified him as Luc Chauvy. Which means that our man has changed identities."

"That's not possible," Moracchini said. "You can't change your identity just like that. It takes time . . . The Church isn't the Foreign Legion!"

De Palma leaped up, and as he did so, he knocked over a cup of cold coffee.

"Maxime, think fast. You too, Anne. Let's drop our wonderful logical scenarios and get our brains in order. When you think about these three murders, is there anything that strikes you?"

"I don't think so," Vidal said.

"What about you, Anne?"

"Nothing."

"There must be a detail we've overlooked. A detail which could take on real significance, given what we now know. There must be something that opens up the whole case."

Moracchini and Vidal were silent.

"He's holding Sylvie. In my opinion, we've only got a few hours. I just have to nail this fucker."

De Palma sat down again in exasperation.

"He's got her, but you're right, Anne. He won't do anything until there's a full moon. All the murders took place on nights when the moon was full. He has to be performing a ritual, and let's suppose he consults the spirits. That's why his sister wanted to find the other entrance to the cave."

"Hang on, Michel," said Moracchini. "Try to be coherent."

"I'm being perfectly coherent. She wanted to find the entrance so she could contact the spirit world. She thought she was a shaman too."

"What about her brother?"

"He's taken her place. Maybe he's even found the entrance."

"That's quite possible, isn't it?" Vidal said, with a hint of irony. "But to commune with the spirits, she could have gone to Lascaux, or any old cave."

"The Slain Man . . . " the Baron murmured.

"What's that?"

"It's a picture which occurs in only three caves . . . I can't remember the other two, but the only one the specialists are certain shows the victim of a ritual killing is in Le Guen's Cave."

Vidal and Moracchini stared doubtfully at the Baron and said nothing.

"I can't see any connection to the Church." Moracchini asked. "Let's go back over it. Maxime, what about the first murder?"

"Hélène Weill. She lived alone. He followed her and managed to frame Caillol. I can't see any connection to the Church."

"What about in his *modus operandi*?"

"No, nothing."

"O.K.! On to the second murder."

"Julia Chevallier. Let's skip her age and so on. The *modus operandi* doesn't teach us anything new. And here, too, he framed Caillol."

"Hang on," said de Palma. "He got into her house, just like that. He knew her. He killed her and then left. We followed his tracks and they ended up in the cemetery."

"That's something which has always puzzled me," Moracchini suddenly said. "I can't imagine how he knew there was a door at the bottom of the garden."

"That's my point," said de Palma. "He got into her house via the garden, then left the same way."

"Before Barbieri took us off the case, I checked out everything," said Vidal. "No-one I questioned in Saint-Julien knew about that pathway. No-one. Not even the old guys. You'd have to live next to the canal to know about it. So I think he must live, or have lived, in Saint-Julien"

"Yes, that's always bugged me," said Moracchini.

"And the path ends up in the cemetery," said Vidal.

"And at the far end of the cemetery, there's the church. And Father Paul was the last person to see her alive. But we can't accuse the poor man, not at his age."

De Palma leaned his elbows on the table and rubbed his eyes. He was beginning to have doubts about himself. The worst of it was he was beginning to question his intuition. When he opened his eyes, Vidal was staring at him with a strange expression.

"If only we had the model of her car," said de Palma, "we could put out a call to every unit in this fucking city."

"Let's try anyway," said Moracchini. "I'll deal with it."

She was on her way out of the office when Maxime started hammering madly on the edge of the desk. Then all at once he spat out the tension which he had been building up over the past few months:

"LUC CHAUVY!" he yelled.

"What's the matter, Maxime?"

Vidal frantically searched for his notepad in his jacket pockets.

"Luc Chauvy, for fuck's sake. He was the man there with Father Paul when I went to the presbytery. Shit."

There was a long silence as Vidal flicked through the pages of his notepad.

"Now that I think about it, he fitted the description pretty well: tall, blond . . . but he wasn't wearing glasses."

He slapped his notepad with the back of his hand.

"Luc Chauvy . . . IT'S HIM!"

The Baron stared straight at Vidal. For a few seconds, they confronted each other.

"I couldn't have known, Michel, I . . . "

"It's nothing, kid. It happens to the best of us."

If the man he had seen at Saint-Julien was their killer, then they would have to go together. Arresting him was not going to be easy, and the young officer might have to use his weapon. A baptism of fire. However ambitious he was, he still needed the old guard.

"Let's go, Maxime. Anne, stake out the cemetery. If he tries to jump you . . ."

"Don't worry, teammate. I was the best shot in the academy."

When the two officers parked their unmarked Megane in front of the church, the only people on the square were two old timers talking in whispers, like sextons.

Moracchini arrived two minutes later in a Golf and parked twenty metres away from the cemetery entrance. She felt nervous; if things went wrong, the killer might well come her way. Then she would shoot, as she had already done once. She opened her jacket, placed her hand on her revolver and tried to calm down.

She went into the cemetery, without taking her eyes off the church, and spotted a door in the presbytery which led directly out to the graves. She proceeded slowly and took up position beside a burial vault at the end of the graveyard, where a low wall ran alongside the canal. She pretended to be in silent prayer.

De Palma walked towards the church and leaned on the heavy, cast-iron door handle. It was locked. He went round the right-hand side of the building, followed by the censorious eyes of the two old boys, and rang the presbytery bell with his other hand on his Bodyguard. As he waited for an answer, he read the cellophane-wrapped sign which had been pinned up beneath the bell:

THE PARISH PRIEST IS AVAILABLE ON
THURSDAYS AND FRIDAYS FROM 10.00 TO 16.00.
IN CASE OF AN EMERGENCY, PLEASE CALL 04 91 93 00 56.

Lower down were the times of masses written in a neat, regular hand.

"Locked?" Vidal asked.

"Yes."

"So what do we do now?"

"What do you think? We're going inside."

"Just like that!"

"Too right!"

"Hang on, Michel. That's not legal . . . "

"Get out of my face. This isn't the moment."

Vidal drew back as the Baron took a piece of twisted thick metal wire from his pocket. He shoved his improvised tool into the lock, which gave way after a few clumsy twists.

The officers entered the vast, gravel courtyard with its two large pine trees.

"Michel, I'm going to head for that half-open window over there, the second one along . . . can you see it? Cover me."

"No, Maxime, I'll go. He hasn't been armed before now. So you cover me."

Vidal quietly drew his gun and held it against his thigh. De Palma headed straight towards the window, and managed to clamber inside without having to break it.

The room smelled of stale cooking. He looked for the switch, which was to the left of the sink, half hanging off the door frame. Vidal joined him.

They were in fact in the presbytery's dining room. In its centre stood a table covered with an oilcloth which was so worn that its bright-red cherry pattern could only be seen on the edges that hung over the sides. On the wall were several yellowed photos showing catechism classes. De Palma glanced at the faces and captions: *J4 Skiing Group, Orcières Merlette, 1988; Confirmation class, Cotignac 1990* . . . In each of the photos stood the parish priest, a slight man with a piercing stare, despite his ruddy, peasant-like features. He was clearly not the person they were after. In the penultimate photo, labelled *J2 Class in Paris, 2000 Jubilee*, there was another man standing beside the priest. De Palma took it down from the wall and laid it on the table.

"There's no-one upstairs. Have you found anything?" Vidal asked.

"I don't know. Come and see. Your eyes are better than mine."

Vidal bent over the picture and almost yelled:

"I think it's him, Michel!"

"So he looks like Christine Autran, and like the man you saw?"

"Absolutely. It's him."

"Let's give the place a thorough search. Go and see if there's a cellar."

"I've already been all round. There's the cellar door, under the stairs."

De Palma drew his Bodyguard and headed towards the door. It was ajar.

"Stay here for the moment," he told Vidal. "You never know."

He slowly went down the staircase to the basement and paused at the bottom. A vision of the Dustman came into his mind like a cannonball. Icy sweat poured down his back. He found a switch and turned on the light.

A corridor about eight metres long led to four little rooms, two on each side. The first was empty. He pushed open the door of the second but all he could see were ancient prayer books lined up on rusty metal shelves. The third contained stacks of boxes. Their contents were marked with a red felt-tip pen: 'candles', 'old missals', and so on.

He went into the last room. It was far smaller than the others and had not been tidied. The remains of an old crib balanced on top of some rickety chairs. On the left-hand wall were two large notices for the parish fair. One read 'Aunt Sally', the other said 'Raffle'. There was a wobbly pile of cardboard boxes in the middle of the room.

De Palma noticed that the room had a clay floor. He crouched down and made out a print of a bare foot. When he examined the ground and the boxes, he noticed that someone had been rummaging around in the centre of the pile: the clay had been scuffed up, cobwebs had been pushed aside, and a fine black dust covered all of the boxes except the two in the middle. He moved over to them, careful not to disturb the footprint, and opened one. It was empty. He opened the second. It contained a half-litre bottle of strange-coloured liquid with a thick layer of deposit on the bottom. He put the bottle in his pocket and went back upstairs.

Vidal had searched the ground floor thoroughly and had found nothing, apart from a number of fingerprints.

"Found anything, Michel?"

"I'm not sure."

De Palma removed the bottle from his pocket and raised it to eye level.

"What's that?"

"I don't think it's altar wine. I'd guess it's a mixture of water and powdered earth . . . making a . . . what's it called?"

"A pigment."

"Yes, that's it. An ochre pigment."

"What shall we do now?"

"Behave like serious police officers. We take this to forensics for the fingerprints. We'll get the result this afternoon."

"I wanted to tell you . . . "

"It's O.K., Maxime, don't bother. Just call Anne and tell her to move off without drawing any attention to herself."

"I wanted to tell you that I've thought things over, and I've been unfair on you."

"It doesn't matter, kid. Simply leave the force at once, or else give up on the idea of staying normal. Call Anne."

The little old men were still sitting there when they left the presbytery.

"Just look at those two," the Baron said as they pulled away. "They see two suspicious-looking characters break into a presbytery and they don't even call the police. And then they start complaining . . . Fuck them."

The first results from forensics arrived at the end of the afternoon. All of the fingerprints taken from the presbytery matched those found in Chevallier's house and Autran's car.

Commissioner Paulin came into the office without knocking.

"Where are you at, de Palma?"

"We've located him. I mean, we've put a name to a face."

"Moracchini has already told me. Do you think . . . ?"

"I don't think," de Palma butted in. "The only thing we're sure about is that the fog we've been walking through is less dense. We can now see shadows. The outlines are less hazy, but they're still only shadows. With a third of a fingerprint, we've got nothing. He can always say that he paid a visit to a member of the congregation. There's the bottle, but that's not enough. We'll have to run D.N.A. tests and compare them with the samples we got from Caillol's place – the gendarmes omitted to do that as well. The fact that he's Christine's brother doesn't make him guilty. We need more: a confession, or else the kind of solid evidence that they like in Aix."

"I'll put as many men at your disposal as you want."

"Thanks, but we still have to find out where he's hiding."

"How are you going to proceed?"

"First, we'll have to watch the presbytery and Saint-Julien church. You never know. Second, we'll have to stop him from leaving the city. In other words, distribute his description and an identikit photo to all units, the airport, railway stations and so on. For once, the anti-terrorism law might serve another purpose than pissing off Blacks and Arabs."

"And then?" asked Paulin, frowning.

"Then, I reckon we've been lucky once and won't be lucky a second time. We'll have to think things through. Rack our brains. Figure out the sort of place where he could be hiding, and where he could have taken Sylvie Maurel. Anne, take care of the description, please. But don't spend too much time on it. We need your brains. That's all for now."

"I have to congratulate you, de Palma, and your teammates too. I was beginning to lose hope."

"The fact that we know what he looks like doesn't mean we're going to be able to catch him like a goby. Far from it."

"Allow me to trust you! I'm sure you've got a good idea."

"I'm afraid not. Nothing at all. Not the slightest hint of a lead."

"I'll let you get on with it," said Paulin on his way out. "See you later."

Just as he was closing the door, he added:

"By the way, de Palma, an old acquaintance of yours died in an occupational accident this morning."

"Who's that?"

"Francis Le Blond. Two charges of buckshot and six bullets from an 11.43. Yet another settling of old scores. But done in real Sicilian mafia style. Not a clumsy local job."

"At least this time you can't say it's the gambling syndicates."

"Who knows?" said Paulin, closing the door.

De Palma stretched in his chair. He sensed that Vidal was thinking back over their meeting with Lolo and analysing it. He did not dare look at him, and tried to take refuge in Moracchini's eyes, but she was staring at her trainers.

"I think he's using Sylvie Maurel as bait," she said, "as something which will lead us to him. He must have realised that it's all up. He's just too intelligent not to know that. I think he wants to get this business over with."

"Logically speaking," de Palma said, "he'll probably go to Le Guen's Cave. It's his sanctuary."

"But how would he take her there?" Moracchini asked.

"I've got no idea. He kidnapped her outside the lab and forced her to use her car. But to get to Sugiton creek is another matter altogether! You have to go by foot, and he couldn't take that risk."

"You're right, Michel," she replied. "But you never know what people like that are capable of. He might have found a solution which you could never imagine."

"There aren't that many ways to get to Sugiton creek," Vidal said. "Either you go on foot or by boat. Unless you fly there. Anyway, it would be practically impossible to take someone along against their will."

"Unless you're not alone," observed de Palma suddenly.

"What do you mean?" asked Moracchini.

"I mean that I've always suspected that he's not working on his own. For a time, I even thought Sylvie was with him."

"And who do you imagine this second loony might be?"

"I have absolutely no idea."

"Let me tell you something," Moracchini said. "To work with someone like that, you'd have to share his madness . . . just think about it! There aren't that many people around who eat their victims. It's the first time it's ever happened in Marseille."

"Still, I don't think he's alone."

"O.K., but I reckon you're on to a false lead."

"Whatever," said the Baron, shoving his computer keyboard away. "Logically he would have gone to Sugiton. That would be the most obvious thing for him to do."

"But he can't have gone there . . . At least not if he were taking Sylvie Maurel."

"What do you mean by that?" de Palma snapped, more aggressive than ever.

"I mean that he would either have gone there without her, or . . . "

"WITH SOMEONE ELSE!" yelled the Baron.

"Calm down, Michel," shouted Anne. "Calm down for Christ's sake! It's a point we can't neglect. Maxime's right."

The Baron got up. For the first time, he really imagined that Sylvie might be dead and sliced up, like Hélène and Julia. He had been haunted by the idea since 11.00 that morning, but had refused to admit it. He felt bile rise in his throat.

"Maxime, look at your diary and tell me when the next full moon is."

"I've already checked. It's tomorrow!"

"Right, in that case, if this loony raises his head, it will be then."

"What do you suggest?" Vidal asked.

"Tomorrow, we'll go to Sugiton. Just a small group, four or five at most. Too bad if we've got it wrong."

"What should we do in the meantime?"

"What do you expect me to say? We'll try to force the hand of chance again. If a patrol happens to spot him . . . "

De Palma slumped in his chair. He felt all in. Moracchini had never seen him in such a state, looking so beaten.

"Professor Palestro told me he was the only person who knew where the second entrance was – even Christine Autran didn't know," he added. "So, in theory, she can't have told her brother. In that case, he might think that Sylvie is one of the few people who knows, and try to force her to speak."

"Does Sylvie know where it is?"

"She told me she didn't. But I'm not so sure."

"So, supposing that he wants to find the entrance, why take her and not Palestro?"

"You're right, I'd start with him. You're quite right . . . but that's why I'm sure that he's going to try to get into Le Guen's Cave – I reckon that he thinks that his sister's talking to him from there. He's going to invoke her spirit . . . "

De Palma paused for a moment before adding softly:

"And, obviously, the spirit will tell him to kill Sylvie."

He withdrew momentarily, faced with his own powerlessness. No terrible visions had haunted him over the past few days; it was as though his ghosts had taken a break. He just felt powerless; and it tormented him.

"Your idea of trapping him in Sugiton creek sounds like a good one to me," said Moracchini. "Our only good one!"

"What about Sylvie? What shall we do?"

"I can't answer that, Michel. We're up against a wall. We've got no choice. All we can do is hope that everything turns out well."

"If I've understood correctly, you're going to catch our man tomorrow."

"I hope so, Commissaire, I hope so . . . " de Palma said.

Paulin enjoyed these briefing sessions before an arrest. They made him feel important, and he liked them to be marked by a certain solemnity. He paced up and down behind his desk, glancing occasionally at his three bloodhounds.

"What's the plan?"

"We're going to catch him in Sugiton creek," said de Palma.

"That won't be easy! I don't know the creeks well, but I do know that the terrain is difficult."

"We'll have to be discreet. I don't want anyone else to be there. We'll go at night, just the three of us."

"O.K., just the three of you. But what if he slips through your fingers?"

"Sugiton is a dead end. It's impossible to escape, except by sea."

"That's one way already!"

"Of course, if you put it like that . . . "

Paulin tried to look important.

"I can give you as many men as you want. And boats, a helicopter, anything . . . anything you want."

"I don't think all that will be necessary."

"Listen, de Palma, I don't want him to elude you. Don't try anything if you're not sure of the result. What do you think, Moracchini?"

"I think we'll need about ten men, in case . . . "

"And you, Vidal?"

"I think so too. But Michel's right. We'll have to be more or less invisible. We're dealing with someone who knows this place from old. If he hears the slightest suspicious noise, he'll find a way to vanish before we can catch him."

"As a matter of interest, de Palma, why Sugiton?"

"That's where his sister died . . . I think each time he commits a murder, he goes there to invoke the spirits."

"His brains really are messed up," Paulin said, shrugging his shoulders to push up his jacket collar. "So, you need a dozen men."

"O.K.," de Palma conceded, realising that this would not be the right time to fall out with his superior. "We'll set off from the Luminy car park at dusk. Or at nightfall, to be exact. We'll need five men: two to stay in the car park until he arrives – they'll let him go then follow him twenty minutes later; the other three will be stationed on the path. We'll have to check out the scene tomorrow morning. Anne, you'll position yourself around Sugiton pass with another five men, in case he decides to backtrack. I'll go down into the creek with Maxime."

"Good, de Palma."

The commissaire clapped his hands.

"Tomorrow morning," he said, sitting down, "at 9.00, we'll go and take a look with the boys from the flying squad. Then be back here at noon. O.K.?"

"Fine, boss."

"Go and get some rest. It feels like I've got three ghost officers here."

*

"*They struck you in your bath, your blood
ran over your eyes,
and the bath steamed with your blood...*"

It was hot. De Palma sat exhausted on his balcony and let Elektra's sad voice take hold of him. Through the open windows, the low and middle register notes of Birgit Nilsson mingled with the subdued symphony made up of the sounds of his neighbourhood at night. He had come home late, thinking that he would be able to sleep for a few hours.

> " ... *So, he took you*
> *by your shoulders, the coward, and dragged*
> *you out of the room, head first,*
> *your legs trailing behind, your eyes open*
> *staring at the interior of the house* ... "

The siren of a distant patrol car broke the atmosphere. It was probably coming from one of the Pont-de-Vivaux estates. A madman in the asylum opposite began to moan dully. De Palma knew this faceless voice; he had known it for years.

That week – he had forgotten which day – he had got a letter from Marie. In it, she told him she had found work in the suburbs of Grenoble. There was a new man in her life, he could tell by reading between the lines. He had felt neither sad nor angry.

Sleep would not come. As the night progressed, he felt his body grow colder; his joints cracked like old beams. This investigation was coming to an end. Never in his long career had an attempt to understand a killer, and himself, given him so much pause for thought.

Tomorrow he would find himself face-to-face with the sickest murderer he had encountered since the Dustman. What would he do? Kill him? He could telephone Jo Luccioni. He had been thinking about that since the day before. Jo had the necessary fury, that hatred of the human species which must haunt his mind. This thought chilled him even more, so he cast it aside.

> "*And so you come back, putting one foot in front of the other,*
> *and suddenly you appear,*
> *a purple crown on your head,*
> *fed by the gaping wound in your forehead.*"

He thought of Sylvie and tried to imagine the situation she must be in, but he failed to build a mental image of it. His inability to visualise the horror made him shudder. This was something new to him; usually, he managed to picture the darker side of his investigations. His ability to imagine a perfectly precise scenario was the secret of his legendary intuition. But that night he did not have a storyboard, or any images. Sylvie had become an element, a cog in the mechanism which was grinding his consciousness. Each time he conjured up Sylvie's face, his brain rejected it as though trying to impose the cold reality of the facts.

"Facts, nothing but facts," as Barbieri would say. "Proof, and only proof," he said aloud. "But you might not have any proof," he went on in a whisper. Justice suddenly seemed too rapid to him. Barbieri would tie the whole thing up. The jury, "good little French people like you and me", would have no doubts when confronted by such pure horror. His lawyer would probably appeal. Recent legislation meant that he would be able to. After a quarter of a century on the crime squad, issues like this no longer bothered him.

He remembered his early cases. At the time, the men and women he put on trial were literally risking their necks. And these necks were being gambled on a dice throw. He thought of Robert Ferrandi; his last death penalty. An ordinary man he had hunted for several years. A shabby fifty-year-old who crucified the women he loved. De Palma had got to know him over a period of forty-eight hours and despite his barbaric crimes had ended up liking this sincere, solid, little man with the round face, who had left his lawyer speechless by asking the judge for the death sentence himself. To put a stop to his madness.

Possessed, insane Ferrandi. The death penalty had been announced that evening, and this had disgusted de Palma. He felt responsible, guilty about not having been able to prove that Ferrandi acted under another person's authority. In this case, his brother's.

He remembered the words of his old mentor at headquarters in Paris: "It doesn't matter if the law is just or not, the law is valid not because it's just, but because it's the law. As a matter of fact, this isn't your problem. Your problem is putting the guilty on trial and trying not to make mistakes."

The next day, if the grim gods presiding over police affairs had not been mistaken, he would arrest a man and hand him over to be tried.

And the justice system would not fail him. His long years on the force had worn him down so much that he no longer gave a damn. All that interested him was catching his man. And finding Sylvie alive. That at least made sense.

He stood up, stiff from the chill that had gripped him, and poured himself a whisky which he knocked back in one. He poured another and went back on to the balcony. The night was receding into stardust. The hills of Saint-Loup were beginning to lighten as the day dawned, somewhere far away, in the mysteries of the Levant. He thought to himself that the man he had been tracking for months must be looking up at the same sky.

Perhaps at that precise moment this redoubtable killer was doubting his own powers?

Perhaps reason and madness were struggling with each other in his poor head, as on a battlefield where the enemy has taken the initiative.

He would be invoking the spirits of prehistory.

Leaning on the grey metal rail that had been corroded by the sun and sea air, de Palma realised that his legs could barely support him. Fatigue and whisky had overwhelmed his being and his thoughts.

Society baffled him. First, there had been little Samir's murder in a block of flats to the north of the city. And now a man was asserting his barbarity. Never had de Palma been confronted by such a killer, and a voice whispered to him that he would not be the last, but rather the first in a new wave of criminals. It occurred to him that a society ultimately has the murderers it deserves. Even the mobsters had evolved towards heightened barbarity. Gangland killings had speeded up to a regularity never known before. Each time, the law of the mob broke down slightly and gangster society became more corrupt.

What new killer would arise at the night's end? Only yesterday, an eight-year-old child had gone missing from an estate in Aix, the seventh since the start of the year. It seemed to him that the thick layer of morality covering the surface of society was cracking more and more, and was now coming away in pieces. He did not like morality, but that was another story.

A vision obscured the darkness of the city: Ferrandi's round face, his small, dry eyes and the terror which had filled them every time he spoke about his brother.

Then he saw the face of his twin, Julien de Palma. Julien was staring at him, and his eyes were showing him the way.

A thought which had plagued him for days now returned. "He's not alone," he said to the night.

This thought became a certainty and he took it to bed with him.

Everything was clear now.

> "As time goes on running from the stars,
> so the blood of a hundred throats will burst up from the tomb!
> It will spread as though from spilt amphoras,
> the blood of enchained killers,
> like a stream in spate, in floods, it will spring from their lives."

31.

For some time, a diffuse glow had been spreading from Mont Puget to the east as far as the Sugiton pass. To the left, through a gash in the cliffs, they could see mighty Marseille, shifting slowly, turning its heavy body this way and that in its stone sheets, trying to sleep in this long night. A few, barely audible sounds reached the creeks. In its dream, Marseille was gasping, as though tormented by illusions of grandeur.

To the right, the sea was silent, magnificent in its ancient, silver robe. Not even the slight motion of the waves could be heard. Two days without a breath of wind had been enough for *mare nostrum* to fall asleep, as melancholic and languorous as a beautiful lady clad in a rare, silk lamé dress.

De Palma looked at his watch. It was 12.40 a.m. From the corner of his eye, he looked at Vidal, who seemed to be shivering slightly in the milky night.

"We'll wait for the moon. Then we'll go down to the bottom. O.K., Maxime?"

"I just hope he'll turn up."

"In theory, he's got to. As long as he didn't spot us this morning. But I reckon he'll come."

A barely perceptible breeze arrived with the moon. De Palma stood like a basalt statue in the middle of the path.

A discreet crackling broke the silence.

"Green on Green to All Powerful. A car's just parked. Someone's getting out . . . I think it's Spectacles. Over."

"All Powerful here. O.K., Christian, take it easy now. Follow him on foot after twenty minutes. But before you set off, puncture his tyres.

That way he won't be able to get away. O.K.? Over."

"Message received. What if he turns back? Over."

"You cry for help. Over."

"What? Over."

"Don't worry, Christian. He won't turn back. Just follow him after twenty minutes, like I told you. Over and out."

"O.K."

"Time to go, Maxime. We're at least an hour ahead of him."

They went down the slope. Forty minutes later, they were facing the limestone blocks that filled Sugiton creek. They gave themselves a moment's rest before clambering across the fallen stones until they were just above the pebble beach.

De Palma's guts were in knots. He had eaten nothing since that morning, and all the coffee he had drunk throughout the day was making him jumpy. He picked up his walkie-talkie.

"Red on Red from All Powerful."

Moracchini's voice echoed slightly in the creek.

"Red on Red. I receive you loud and clear. Over."

"He left the car park forty minutes ago. He'll pass at ten o'clock from you in ten or fifteen minutes. Over."

"Message received. Over."

"Over and out."

"O.K."

"Hey, Michel, what's all this about green and red and being all powerful?"

"A hangover from the army. I'll explain later . . . "

De Palma leaped down on to the beach and set off towards the cliff-face. He produced a torch from his bag and pointed it at the base of the large rocks.

"Let's see now. Palestro said up towards the left . . . You have to go beneath the rock. You might have to dig a little in the pebbles if the sea's been strong . . . Then you have to crawl for a few metres. The entrance is to the right, beneath a barrier of stone. So, Maxime, station yourself where we agreed. And quickly. I'm going down. Don't forget: when he arrives, give him fifteen minutes, then follow him."

"For Christ's sake, be careful Michel."

"Don't worry."

Pebbles were not blocking the access beneath the slab of stone. The Baron went head first through a hole which was about eighty centimetres wide. He crawled for two metres before finding the barrier of stones and the entry to the passage.

A cool odour rose from the earth's intestines. Without pausing for breath, he put a miner's lamp on his head and slipped into the gap feet first. He slithered down for about three metres, slowing himself with his knees and elbows until his feet came to rest on a flat surface.

He was in an approximately oval cavity measuring about twenty square metres. At the far end, to the right, he saw a narrow opening which led to the second chamber: Le Guen's Cave. Without wasting any time, he crossed the oval antechamber and, on reaching the entrance, put down his bag and took out a climbing rope coiled in two loops. He knotted it around a rocky spike and checked that it slid correctly. With his back to the opening, he passed the two loops of rope between his legs and over his left shoulder. He then abseiled down through the gap, allowing his feet to slide along the rock face which ran down towards the murky depths.

A few metres further down, he found himself waist-deep in water. He looked up and saw the rope rise above him. He pulled on one coil, gathered in the entire length, rolled it up carefully, then emerged from the water and sat down on a red rock which had been smoothed by the sea. He put his damp rope back into his bag and took out a second torch which was more powerful than his miner's lamp.

In front of him was a huge, cold, damp gap which opened like a slit into absolute darkness. He advanced gingerly between the limestone stalactites and stalagmites. Drops of water were falling rhythmically on the floor or into puddles, filling the cave with a mournful pitter-patter. He stopped when he saw in front of him a gleaming slab of rock which sloped gently towards the inky sea.

He remembered what Le Guen had told him years earlier, and his heart started beating madly. In vain, he tried to calm it and pointed his torch to the left, running its beam over the rugged limestone until he saw what he had been waiting months for: a negative hand on an outcrop of rock.

This little hand seemed to be waving in friendship at everyone who entered the dark salon. On a limestone slab there was another larger one, presumably of an adult, making a gesture of peace. Further on, positive hands decorated a rocky shelf a metre off the floor.

He played his torch to the right and, in the distance, almost beyond the beam's range, he picked out horses swimming calmly in a line. One of them was observing him cheekily, acknowledging his discovery. De Palma breathed deeply and tears of emotion filled his eyes. A gust of cold air penetrated his bones and made him shiver. He stood up, his legs wobbling.

He walked towards the far end of the cave and stopped when the ceiling, hacked away by the first men, became too low for him to stand. He aimed his torch at the far wall and saw a series of positive hands decorating a huge column of rust-coloured rock. Awakened by the electric light, the spirits of prehistory had begun to converse in the secret language of hands, some with their little fingers bent, others showing only their thumbs and index fingers. The first man was watching him from beyond time. Further on, other hands responded from shafts of reddish stone. De Palma felt a kind of vertigo. The shadows of the great hunters enveloped him.

It was then that he heard breathing. He withdrew into the darkness, turned off his torch and put all his senses on alert. Initially he thought it was the gentle motion of the sea as it lapped at the rocks. But then he noticed that the sound was coming from somewhere only a few metres in front of him. The breathing was human, and it was quickening. He drew his Bodyguard.

De Palma tried to reconstruct the last thing he had seen before turning off the torch. Ahead of him there was a relatively long, flat surface. Without switching on his light, he crawled forward for a few metres until his arm hit an obstacle. He paused. The sound was clearer than ever. Someone was there, in the darkness, just beside him.

De Palma rapidly flashed his torch. Two metres away sat a human form, leaning against a stalagmite. He crawled on for another metre and flashed his torch again. Sylvie Maurel had been gagged and tied to a column of stone. A terrible fear radiated from her shattered features. Her eyes were wide open, her pupils dilated fully. She had been positioned between two negative hands, to the left of a bison and an ibex. On the ceiling, crude lines were carved into the limestone. In the beam of his torch he could make out the shape of a head, then a torso and legs. With a few blows from a flint, a prehistoric sculptor had engraved the figure of a man. His body was criss-crossed by several lines that ran from one side to the other.

THE SLAIN MAN.

The first depiction of a murder.

De Palma was about to rush towards Sylvie when he realised that a trap had been laid for him. All of a sudden, the paintings seemed to free themselves from the walls and dash towards him. A hand brushed against him. The great bison raised its head and hammered the floor with its hoof. The ibex leaped into the void of the night. The spirit of the hunt was sounding the alert. De Palma quickly drew back and turned off his torch.

He heard a short whistle and the sound of a small object falling into the water, followed by more whistling and a slapping sound which reverberated in this cathedral of stone. De Palma made the most of the disturbance by moving as far as he could away from his present position. When he hit an obstacle, he lay down on the cold, damp floor.

A tinkling of metal objects rose from the main chamber. Suddenly, light from a flame, presumably a burning torch, made the rippling rocks dance in a ballet of dark shadows. De Palma was now in a kind of vestibule two metres above the chamber. Trying not to make the slightest noise, he moved over to the edge of his hiding place.

In the dim light, he made out a motionless figure crouched in front of Sylvie. A few moments later, the figure picked up the torch and played it around the walls. Then it stood up and placed a hand in one of the negative prints. A strange, raucous voice, the voice of a wild beast, echoed around the walls of the cave.

"*Great hunter*
Here is the sign
May it make you strong
The spirits are troubled . . . "

In a flash, de Palma leaped into the main chamber, gun in hand, and pointed his Maglite at the figure.

"Turn round," he yelled.

The figure did not move.

"Turn round, or you're dead. Understand?"

The figure slowly turned round. In the flickering light a face appeared, zigzagged with shadows. It was a closed, strangely rigid face which seemed possessed by an incredible force.

"Christine Autran," murmured de Palma.

He was paralysed by the sight of this woman who stared at him without the slightest expression on her frozen features. She had cut her hair extremely short, and now looked more like a man than the rather reserved prehistory lecturer he had seen in photos. A faint sound nearby chilled his blood. He spun round and fired twice. In the flashes of gunfire, a fleeting apparition emerged from the darkness: Thomas Autran's ghastly face was just a few metres away from him. He shot again and heard a piercing cry.

At that instant a violent pain seized his shoulder and he felt his flesh being torn apart.

Everything went red. A powerful hand struck him in the face and pinned him to the ground. The walls of the cave melted like liquid metal.

Then there was a voice. Far away:

"I am the hunter

May the spirits guide me through the darkness

May my enemy's strength enter my blood . . . "

32.

Commissaire Paulin raced like a bullet through Accident and Emergency at Timone hospital. He shoved aside a nurse who was pushing a trolley out of lift B, and grunted at the boys from special branch and the flying squad who greeted him with silent nods. Maxime Vidal and Anne Moracchini sat at the end of the corridor looking exhausted. Paulin sidestepped them and pushed open the door of the last room.

It was 5.00 a.m. Thomas Autran was lying on a metal bed, handcuffed at both wrists and both ankles. Paulin adopted his toughest expression and inspected him for a few seconds.

"When can we take him away?" he barked at the doctor who was finishing off a dressing.

"In about a quarter of an hour, after I've signed the necessary papers. The wound is superficial. The bullet didn't touch his kneecap, it just went through the muscles."

"Very good, I'll arrange the necessary transport."

Paulin went out into the corridor.

"Don't you want to get some rest, Vidal? You look awful . . . "

"No thanks, Commissaire. I'd rather stay."

"What about you, Moracchini?"

"I'll stay with Maxime."

Paulin leaned on the wall facing them and stuck his hands into his jacket pockets. Moracchini's eyes were red with fatigue and her forehead was creased. Her shoes were stained with the red soil of the creeks. Vidal's face was deathly pale.

"I've just come back from La Conception hospital. He's been in theatre for a hour now. That's all I know."

Anne Moracchini stood up and walked towards the lift to calm herself down. Vidal kept staring at the corridor's gleaming floor tiles.

"Sylvie is in the psychiatric department," he stammered. "No-one can see her for the moment."

"I . . . It would be better if . . . I'd rather you waited at headquarters," muttered Paulin. "There's nothing more you can do here . . . "

Vidal was lost in the darkest stretches of his conscience. He was playing back over and again the film of that night.

He bursts into the main section of Le Guen's Cave. Thomas Autran raises his tomahawk above the Baron's bloody head. From the end of his rope, Maxime draws and fires once, twice, three times . . . He aims at the head and torso. The thunder of shots echoes from one vault to the next, making the entire cave quake. He no longer knows how many times he has fired. Thomas Autran bends over and collapses. Two men from special branch rush across and overcome him. There are kicks to his stomach, a boot in his face . . . Then the clicking of handcuffs.

De Palma is unrecognisable. He is covered with blood. His forehead has been cut open and his shoulder torn apart. Disfigured. His breathing is weak, almost non-existent, a long rasping sound emerges from his paralysed throat. His life is wavering between here and the great void beyond. His heart beats irregularly, his chest rises suddenly, then falls again. His body is stiffening, trembling all over, tormented by death which seeks its prey.

"Luc Chauvy," Maxime repeated. "Why didn't it occur to me before? Why didn't I say anything to Michel?" He felt nauseous.

"Are you listening to me, Maxime?"

Vidal jumped.

"Yes, Commissaire . . . "

"I was saying that you should go back to headquarters and get some rest, if you can."

Moracchini took him by the arm.

"Come on, Maxime. There's nothing more we can do here."

Before going to headquarters, Moracchini and Vidal spent some time at La Conception. Since 6.00 a.m., Jean-Louis Maistre had been prowling like a wild cat in the waiting room of the Accident and Emergency Department.

"Still nothing," he yelled, clenching his teeth. "NOTHING AT ALL, for fuck's sake!"

A doctor emerged from the operating theatre and took off her mask. She seemed exhausted. The three police officers surrounded her at once.

"I can't tell you anything yet," she said, raising her hands. "We brought him back from the edge . . . twice. We've now stabilised his condition and put him in an artificial coma. This means that the surgeons will be able to operate in the best possible circumstances. But the operation could be a long one. A very long one."

Maistre took the doctor by her arm.

"You're going to save him, aren't you?"

"Are you a member of the family?"

"No, but we'll have to tell his parents. They're old now . . . "

Maistre squeezed the doctor's arm.

"Please stay calm, sir . . . I can reassure you that there's now a good chance he'll pull through."

"Will there be . . . "

"Any after-effects? Maybe, but I really can't say. That's not my speciality. Anyway, we don't yet know what they might be."

"What do you mean?"

"I mean that . . . that we just don't know."

8.00 a.m. Vidal and Moracchini dashed through the courtyard of headquarters, where swarms of journalists had started to gather. On the murder squad floor, by the planning board, officers were talking in hushed tones. When they caught sight of Vidal, his features twisted in anger, they silently stepped aside. Anne Moracchini passed through the group like a shadow.

The door opened on Paulin and Didier Salerno, a murder squad veteran who knew nothing about the case.

Paulin stood up at once and dragged de Palma's teammates into the corridor.

"I told you to get some rest. I'm looking at the situation with Salerno. The two of them are in their cells, and I'm not going to let you question them in the state you're in now."

"With all due respect, sir," Vidal replied coldly. "This is our case, and we'll see it through to the end."

Paulin's eyes glittered with anger.

"Maxime means we're the only ones who know the case and . . . "

"I gave you an order," he said.

Vidal clenched his fists. He swallowed back his rage and stared at Paulin.

"Commissaire, I don't know what you have in mind . . ." he retorted in a calm voice which disarmed Paulin. "But let me tell you something. We worked hard on this case, our teammate is now fighting for his life, and you have no right to take this away from us. NO RIGHT AT ALL."

Paulin cracked his finger joints. Moracchini felt on the verge of oblivion. She observed her superior and barely managed to conceal her scorn.

"O.K., calm down. I'll give you two hours to ask your questions," Paulin murmured, pointing his index finger at Vidal. "But if there's the slightest irregularity, I'll . . . I'll take over again. Two hours, and then we'll discuss the situation. Understood? Barbieri will be here at 11.00."

They brought Thomas and Christine Autran to the offices of the murder squad. The hunter was drained; his lips were drooping slightly and two long wrinkles ran the length of his temples. Moracchini and Vidal decided to separate the twins, and Moracchini led Thomas into her office.

Vidal was left alone with the prehistorian. Since her arrest in the cave, he had not had time to look at her properly. Contrary to what he had feared, he felt nothing for her her, neither hatred nor pity. He sat down opposite her.

"You have been placed in custody on suspicion of murder, aiding and abetting murder and sequestration. I suppose you realise that you risk life imprisonment. Do you have anything to say before we begin?"

Christine remained silent. Vidal had not handcuffed her to the radiator. She was sitting on the edge of her chair, completely self-absorbed, with her knees together and her hands clenched around the chain of her cuffs.

The morning sun shone through the window. Vidal stood up and drew the curtains. He then opened the communicating door between the two offices so that Christine could hear her brother being questioned.

"O.K.," Moracchini said. "Let's begin at the beginning. I'll go through some of the things you are accused of, as Commandant de Palma, Lieutenant Vidal and I see them. Agreed?"

A long silence, which was unbearable after the tension of the previous night. Moracchini started to prowl around Thomas Autran.

"First point. When Le Guen discovered the cave, your sister soon heard about it . . . In my opinion, it was Luccioni, who knew the diving community well, who told her what had become an open secret in that small world. But she also told you that Le Guen was going to announce his discovery, and she asked you to be on guard day and night. We've checked, and you were in France at the time. You were supposed to be just passing through . . . We think that when you saw a group of divers going into the entrance tunnel, you drowned them by stirring up the mud on the seabed – that would have been enough. No-one can see anything through such a murky deposit. That was nine years ago."

Thomas Autran did not respond. Vidal watched his sister. Her eyes were glazed, and she did not seem to hear what was being said in the next room.

"But," Moracchini went on, "Le Guen was not one of those in the tunnel, so you failed to stop the existence of the cave being revealed. You left again on your travels, to Australia I believe. During your absence, your sister decided to look for a second entrance. She searched for a long time, but only found it quite recently, just before . . . her death. Agreed?"

Autran was not looking at her. An image of de Palma on his stretcher flickered across her mind and struck her like a sword. She had to draw on her last reserves to stop herself from exploding.

"Sometime last year, you came back to France. Agnès Féraud, one of your sister's friends, was killed . . . we think by you . . . Then everything speeded up. There were the murders of Luccioni, Hélène Weill and Julia Chevallier. Right or wrong?"

Autran remained locked in silence. Moracchini stopped pacing and approached him.

"But by killing Luccioni, you made a terrible mistake, because straight afterwards his father, Jo Luccioni, put a contract on your heads . . . You were being followed and you knew it. Things were getting out of hand. So you both had to disappear, and fast! You then cooked up Christine's fake murder."

Autran straightened up. His expression softened slightly; the long wrinkles melted into his skin and his lips trembled.

"Thomas," Moracchini said in a more gentle voice. "I think you're sister's been using you right from the start. She's been manipulating you. She knows all about your fits of madness and how to exploit them."

With his eyes, Thomas Autran made it clear that he did not want to talk about his sister. Nor his father. Nor his mother. He did not want to talk, and he would not talk.

She did not press the point. The face of the man sitting in front of her was loquacious enough about the sufferings he must have endured all his life.

In the other office, Vidal stared long and hard at Christine. "Christine, you've heard what my colleague has said. What do you think about her version of events?"

She did not react. Her entire body was frozen. For a moment, Vidal wondered if she could hear what he was saying.

"I think it would be better for you if you spoke. In any case, you'll be formally charged, by tomorrow at the latest."

This dialogue with the deaf continued until 10.00 a.m. Vidal sensed that he had failed to exploit the interrogation. He went to see Moracchini and took her to one side.

"I don't think we're going to get anything out of Christine. I reckon we ought to send for a quack. She's dead on her feet. Come and see."

"No thanks, she terrifies me. Anyway, we're going to put them up before the judge this afternoon. Just lock her back in her cell and forget it. Jesus Christ. If only Michel was here . . . "

"We'll have to do our best, for his sake . . . She's got to speak! Because . . . apart from the fact that she vanished and is an accomplice, we haven't got much on her."

"O.K., do you feel up to going on with him?"

"Yes, I'm ready."

"Perfect. But first, we'll go and see Paulin. We'll give an initial report then start again this afternoon. I need to eat and get some rest."

At 11.00 a.m., Maistre's mobile rang.

"Jean-Louis, it's Marie . . . what's happened? My parents were incapable of telling me . . . "

Marie was in a complete panic, her voice was shaking.

"They're operating on Michel . . . He's been . . . Jesus Christ, Marie."

There was a long silence. Maistre flopped on to the sofa in reception and, for the first time in ages, started to cry.

"I'm in Paris at the moment, I'll take the first train . . . or the first plane . . . I don't know . . . I don't know any more."

"I told him to slow down a bit, to watch out for himself, but he always had to push things even further . . . "

"Is he . . . ?"

"The medics have no idea, they haven't told me anything . . . "

"I'll be there by mid afternoon."

In theatre, the surgical team had just added a final stitch to De Palma's shoulder; there were twenty-one of them in all. His trapezoid and deltoid had been cut almost in half, and two pins had been inserted into his clavicle. The operation had taken longer than expected. During the first hour, they had had to revive him twice.

On the other side of the operating table, Dr Semler, a brain surgeon, was waiting for Dr Janssen, head of the casualty department, to remove one by one the last pieces of the miner's lamp from his naval cavity.

Semler felt tense. Which nerves had been touched? The frontal nerve, for sure – Janssen had just confirmed that fact – but what worried him most were the optic nerves. The lamp and its battery had turned the flint axe away from the skull towards the space between the eyes.

Semler glanced at the skull X-rays. The weapon had hit the frontal bone, but without reaching the dura mater or the brain. The nasal bones and cartilage had been completely shattered, and the pyramidal and triangular muscles severed. It was difficult to form a precise and complete diagnosis. Professor Riaux, the ophthalmologist, would be there around noon.

3.00 p.m. Moracchini had fought with Barbieri and Paulin to keep control of the questioning. She now knew that she had to contain her anger and change tactics. She sat down next to Christine Autran and held her hand.

"In your articles, I've read your theories about the rising sea level . . . Well before Le Guen's discovery confirmed your work! You were ahead of your time and the laughing stock of your colleagues. Even Palestro didn't really believe in you."

Christine coughed. She looked less tense.

"But you couldn't bear it that a man like Le Guen stole this discovery right from under your nose."

Christine's hand trembled a little. Moracchini gripped it tighter, and they stayed like that for some time. Then Christine slowly raised her head.

"Le Guen . . . is a wonderful man," she mumbled. "He gave us our . . . our Provençal Lascaux."

Her head drooped again. She breathed in deeply.

"I . . . I never asked my brother to kill him. That was his own idea . . . he wanted to please me."

Christine gulped. Moracchini stroked the back of her hand with her thumb.

"Can you explain how all this happened?"

"There's . . . there's nothing to explain . . . My brother became a killer long ago . . . When our mother died . . . If you can call her a mother . . ."

She stared at Moracchini, as though she could see her tormented existence mirrored there.

"Thomas acts only in relationship with me. He . . . he interprets everything I say or do in his own way . . ."

She squirmed in her chair and took a deep breath. Two beams of light glittered across her face.

"He knew I was working on anthropophagy . . . One day last year, he brought me a woman's leg."

The police photos ran through Moracchini's mind like a sordid slide show. A half-naked woman on a blood-soaked mattress, her guts hanging out, her leg severed. A woman lying on leaves in a wood, wearing a mauve suit and high heels. A mash of brains and bone. A vision of de Palma lying on the stretcher. She was almost suffocating. She closed her eyes and concentrated.

"What about Franck Luccioni?"

"Thomas couldn't bear it when someone grew close to me. When he came back from his trip to Australia last year, I thought he'd been cured, but . . . "

"He wasn't . . . The contact he'd had with shamans he'd met during his travels had in fact exacerbated his insanity."

"He couldn't stand me having friends, or anyone touching or hurting me."

Christine let go of Moracchini's hand and started rocking on her chair.

"The only male friend I ever had was Franck . . . Poor Franck . . . If our father had lived, Thomas would never have turned out this way. If our father had lived, we'd all still be together."

"Why?"

"When our father died, Thomas was struck dumb. He was incapable of saying anything . . . "

For the first time since the start of the questioning, Christine's knees relaxed.

"Then what happened?"

"He became so self-absorbed that he stopped going out . . . At certain times, he communicated only with signs."

"What about your mother?"

"The only thing she could think of doing was to send him to a home. It was hell . . . Violence became his only defence . . . "

Moracchini stood up and gently laid her hand on Christine's shoulder.

"Then you and your brother killed your mother . . . "

She felt Christine's entire body quake. It was enough of an answer.

"It was then that he began to become interested in prehistory and everything to do with the first men. He saw it as the ideal state of humanity. Before our morality, before all the evils of our civilised society . . . In fact it was he who led me to start studying the subject . . . It was a passion we shared."

"What strange concepts!"

"Strange to you . . . but if you knew these men and women, you wouldn't think like that!"

"I suppose not, but all this doesn't explain such horribly violent murders!"

"It may not excuse them, but it does explain them . . . When you've been humiliated all your life, you end up losing your reason . . . "

"So it was you who enabled Thomas to meet primitive tribes?"

"Yes, it was me. He came with me on several occasions, and I pulled strings with the Kajabbi mission to get him odd jobs. At the beginning, he did rather well . . . "

"Why do you say 'at the beginning'?"

"Because after about a year, he started to miss me. He was beginning to lose the ability to speak again."

Christine twisted her fingers nervously.

Vidal got nothing out of Thomas Autran. For an hour it felt as if he were questioning a slab of granite. On several occasions he had to stop himself from hitting the man in front of him. Yet he never let his hatred show, nor raised his voice. As time went by, he became more and more surprised that he was not succumbing to fatigue or anger. He was still in control of himself.

After an hour, he showed Thomas irrefutable proof of his guilt: the results of the D.N.A. tests on samples taken from Caillol's house and the negative hands. It was a perfect piece of evidence, but it did not draw a single word from Thomas Autran's lips.

At 4.30 p.m., Vidal handed him the transcript of his interrogation. He signed it without hesitating, without even reading it. The text accused him of murdering Franck Luccioni, Hélène Weill and Julia Chevallier, of kidnapping Sylvie Maurel and of the attempted murder of a police officer. Autran accepted the whole package without even trying to defend himself. At 5.00 p.m., he was taken back to his cell.

Moracchini opened the window to let in the sea air.

"Why did you ask Caillol to let Thomas out of hospital? You knew what would happen – you did just the opposite of what you should have."

"No, at the time, I had no idea."

Christine explained that Thomas had been interned a month after their mother's death, and it was then that his unhealthy affection for her had intensified. Caillol had done a lot for him.

"There's still something I don't understand: why did your brother try to frame Caillol?"

"Thomas is extremely intelligent, far more so than you or I. Despite his madness, he realised that the police would track him down, so he used Caillol as a scapegoat."

"O.K., now let's go back to when he left France for the second time . . ."

"I asked him to go."

"After the deaths of the divers?"

Christine's eyes clouded over. She went pale.

"Did you hear my question, Christine?"

She nodded her head nervously.

"And what's your answer?"

"I . . ."

"You didn't know it was him?"

"No."

A gust of fresh air spread through the office, carrying with it the din of the city. Moracchini sat down and stretched in her chair.

"Why did you decide to disappear?"

"After Franck's death, I noticed a man following me. I knew about his father's past, and I soon realised that I was going to have to vanish for ever."

"How did Luccioni find out?"

"I have no idea . . ."

"What about the corpse we found in Sugiton creek?"

"My brother set up the entire thing."

"And you did nothing to stop him!"

"My brother's ill. He doesn't reason like you or me. He presented me with a fait accompli . . . But you're right, I didn't say anything."

"It's odd that you're not trying to defend him."

"I did that for years. I tried everything, but I've had enough. Anyway, sooner or later, all this was bound to happen."

Anne was not sure if Christine's answers were a simple strategy to make herself look innocent, or if they reflected the truth. Fatigue suddenly swamped her; she had not slept for two days. But her brain was still working overtime.

"If you had so much power over him, why didn't you try to stop him from turning into a monster?"

"I did . . . by entering into his madness. By making him believe that I could communicate with spirits . . ."

Moracchini went over to her and spoke almost directly into her ear.

"Christine, I really can't swallow all this. In fact, I don't believe you. So why don't you tell me everything? There's a gaping wound, an awful trauma in your life. You love your brother more than anything, even more than you love yourself. You loved that little boy who was so gentle and happy, and you hated your mother who beat him like the crazy woman she was. That boy who was your other half, your flesh and blood . . . And that terrible mother who let you get away with everything because you were her daughter, and who tortured him because he was unwanted, who mistreated him so badly that the neighbours thought he was ill. It should be Martine Autran sitting here today. Whether it was an accident or not, she was behind your father's death, and your brother avenged him. After that, he lost his sanity and started killing anyone who threatened to separate you. And you let him get on with it."

"I . . ."

"I think that's the explanation for Luccioni's death . . . He must have known many of your secrets . . . he knew about the hand you brought back from the U.S.A., which he tried to sell to a fence because you'd asked him to . . . The same hand we found in your brother's bedroom. You needed the money to start a new life."

"You're right."

Moracchini drew back suddenly.

"I know what you did during your first hours in custody. You had a long think and you said to yourself: 'the only way to be with him again is to get as short a sentence as possible'. Because, as you must realise, prison is going to separate you for decades. Perhaps for ever. So you thought: 'I'll make them think that he's the murderer, then at most I'll be accused of aiding and abetting him . . . ' It was a good idea, Christine, but men and women have lost their lives, and this evening I'm sending you in front of the judge. What will you say to him?"

"My only crime is to have loved my father and my brother more than anything."

"Your crime is to have followed your brother, and perhaps even encouraged or manipulated him. That's what Commandant de Palma thinks. Your crime is to have taken part in the kidnapping of a woman and helped to draw our fellow officer into a fatal trap. These are the facts."

Moracchini could no longer control herself. She felt like slapping Christine Autran, but then she pulled herself together at the last moment.

"Your CRIME IS TO HAVE TRIED TO MURDER OUR TEAM-MATE! DO YOU HEAR ME?"

Vidal was on his way back from the cells when he heard her outburst. He rushed into the office. Paulin and Salerno were already there, separating the Capitaine from Christine. Moracchini was at the end of her tether; fury and hatred twisted her features.

Paulin had already decided to send the twins in front of the judge, and then examine the rest of the case file the following week. Given de Palma's absence, it would be pointless for his teammates to go through his papers; they would find nothing of any use. De Palma was totally inscrutable. It was his main failing. Only he could take this questioning any further.

The Commissaire took Moracchini by the arm and led her into the corridor. Despite his exhaustion, Vidal wanted to ask Christine a whole series of questions about her trips to the U.S.A. and the death of Anna McCabe. But he settled for asking her why she had so wanted to go inside Le Guen's Cave.

"For the past ten years, I've been working on shamanism. It might sound odd to you, but I thought I had acquired certain powers. I thought that the animal-spirits could heal my brother. So, I needed a gateway to the other world. My brother is utterly obsessed by Le Guen's Cave. My only hope was to get him inside the sanctuary so that the spirits could do their work . . . I knew there was a second entrance, but I didn't find it until the beginning of December. The first thing I did was to take my brother inside. And, for the first time for . . . "

Christine was holding back her tears. Her chest rose and fell violently.

"He was really mad with joy . . . "

She was prostrate for a moment. After a long period of silence, she added:

"But I'd forgotten about the Slain Man."

That was all she said.

At 6.00 p.m., the police van took the twins to see the magistrate.

On the floor of Le Guen's Cave, the police found two diving suits and some oxygen cylinders. If Thomas and Christine Autran had managed to kill de Palma and Sylvie Maurel, they would have got away via the underwater entrance. The next day, divers were sent down to explore. They discovered that the gateway had been opened and one of the concrete blocks moved aside.

33.

"I have had to give up everything that I was.
I have sacrificed my modesty, which was sweeter than anything,
Modesty which, like the milky
Silvery mist of the moon
Envelops each woman and guards her soul
From the horror of life. Do you understand, my brother?"

Elektra's voice rose from nowhere, a dark melody from the catacombs of his soul. De Palma tried to open his eyes, to move one hand, then the other, but an unknown force was pinning him to his bed, inert.

"I had to sacrifice these sweet frissons for my father.
When I experienced bodily pleasure
Do you think that its sighs and groans
Did not echo even unto my bed?"

In the distance, a dark sun was rising, mounting rapidly in a red sky. Stone drawings of two Slain Men quivered on the horizon. Geometric shapes were taking on a human appearance: a man and a woman. De Palma recognised them at once: Thomas and Christine Autran, feeling their way towards the unknown meaningless of their madness.

"The dead
are jealous: and as a fiancé
he has sent me hatred with hollow eyes . . . "

He felt a sharp pain in his belly. Cold steel. Barely audible voices were all around. He did not recognise the one closest to him.

"We brought him out of his coma yesterday morning. You can speak to him, but don't be surprised if he doesn't answer. It's a little early for long speeches."

The needle emerged from his guts.

"He'll be able to go home soon . . ."

"Thanks, Doctor . . ."

It was Marie's voice. He made a superhuman effort to open his eyes. His wife was there in front of him, leaning against a white wall. Beside her were his old father, his mother and Jean-Louis Maistre.

"He's opening his eyes!"

"Are you O.K., Michel?"

An intense pain dug into his forehead. His mouth was leaden and his tongue as hard as wood. The ward consultant came in and asked the visitors to leave.

"Can you hear me, Monsieur de Palma?"

The Baron tried to answer, but not the slightest sound came.

"You have wounds to your shoulder and head. It's been three days now. We've given you sedatives to help you cope with the pain, but you're much better now. I'll give you another jab tonight, then tomorrow I think you'll be alright . . . You're going to sleep now, O.K.?"

The ceiling of the room started spinning and the medic's face vanished into a blur. In the distance, a wood fire crackled in the darkness of the night. The trembling voice of an old man hammered out metallic sounds, in an unknown, rhythmic chant.

At about the same time, Sylvie emerged from police headquarters after an interview lasting more than two hours. She had refused Vidal's offer to drive her home. The sleeping pills and psychotropic medication which she had been given in large doses had left her in an altered state. She walked slowly across esplanade de la Tourette, thinking about the police officer who destiny had put in her path.

That morning, she had seen a women his age and two old people outside de Palma's hospital room. She had felt ridiculous with her bouquet of roses and turned on her heel.

Near police headquarters, several sirens wailed in the humid evening air, and a police van set off for Les Baumettes prison. Sylvie listened to their din until they were swallowed by the Vieux-Port tunnel.

She stopped on the square in front of Saint-Laurent church and gazed at vibrant Marseille laid out at her feet, curled up around the Lacydon. To her left was the Greek amphitheatre and further on place de Lenche with its dilapidated houses, the ancient agora of the Phocaeans. One world above another.

The blood-red and gold sun sank into the sea beyond the islands, beyond the vast plain of the great hunters, now submerged for ever.

ACKNOWLEDGEMENTS

My greatest thanks and admiration go to Henri Cosquer, who discovered the extraordinary painted cave which now bears his name and which, after a few changes, acted as the focus of this novel.

Thanks also to Jérôme Harlay, my unpitying editor, and to François Thomazeau who gave me my title.

Thanks to my wife, Eliane, for putting up with me.